THE
LAUGHING
FALCON

BOOKS BY WILLIAM DEVERELL

FICTION

Needles
High Crimes
Mecca
The Dance of Shiva
Platinum Blues
Mindfield
Kill All the Lawyers
Street Legal: The Betrayal
Trial of Passion
Slander
The Laughing Falcon

NON-FICTION

Fatal Cruise

THE
LAUGHING
FALCON

WILLIAM DEVERELL

National Library of Canada Cataloguing in Publication Data

Deverell, William, 1937–
        The laughing falcon

ISBN 0-7710-2704-4

        I. Title.

PS8557.E8775L38 2001   C813'.54   C2001-901148-2
PR9199.3.D49L38 2001

We acknowledge the financial support of the Government of Canada through the Book Publishing Industry Development Program for our publishing activities. We further acknowledge the support of the Canada Council for the Arts and the Ontario Arts Council for our publishing program.

Text design by Blaine Herrmann
Typeset in Bembo and Optima by Sharon Foster
Printed and bound in Canada

McClelland & Stewart Ltd.
The Canadian Publishers
481 University Avenue
Toronto, Ontario
M5G 2E9
www.mcclelland.com

1 2 3 4 5   05 04 03 02 01

For the Sierra Legal Defence Fund

Dear Jacques,

Midtown Manhattan looks like a painted whore in December, the weather would freeze a polar bear's nuts, and the Rangers just lost their fourth straight. What depresses me more is the thought of you lolling around in the tropical sunshine while I break my ass up here.

But I'm doing too well to kill myself. It turns out getting disbarred was the best thing that could have happened, career-wise. I just signed up this big horse for the Bruins, the agency flourishes, and life is fat – and now suddenly your whining letter lands on my desk. No, Jacques, I do not intend to advance you a "small tiding of faith" until your latest poems get published. Your mooching has inspired me with a more breathtaking idea, which doesn't require you to suffer the mortifying shame of indebtedness to your oldest, dearest friend. When you sent me that last batch of verses, asking me to try to flog them, I started thinking – why not a literary sideline? So I have decided that instead of you having to grovel, I will personally advance you a couple of grand against royalties for the smash best-seller you are about to write.

I'm *not* talking poetry, which doesn't sell even if you're Shakespeare and you've been dead for five hundred years. This may hurt, Jacques, but I never thought you were much of a poet anyway. In fact I found the shit you mailed me too depressing to read. *Hymns to a Dying Planet?* But you can turn out a phrase, and my idea is to have you rip off an old-fashioned thriller that I'll flog to publishers as the work of a triple agent hiding in the tropics. Put the right ingredients in and the big houses will be flocking to the doorstep of the R. B. Rubinstein Agency, waving fistfuls of dead presidents.

One of those ingredients is blood. I want a body count. I want a two-fisted hero, not some whining patsy crippled with sorrow and woe like the schnockered poet who's right now reading this letter. I'm thinking more James Bondish – maybe he's hiding out in the tropics, only he can foil Dr. Zork's plan to take over the world, and Zork is trying to blip him off.

I looked up the rules. You throw in a big red herring near the start. You invent a twist that comes at you like a slapshot. You create a kick-ass hero and a ravishing heroine with whom you ultimately engage in explicit sex. And you pay me my standard commission, no reduction for failed poets.

Are the girls still going topless at the far end of the beach? Someone better put a stop to that, some poor schlemiel could get a heart attack.

Give me an outline, a chapter.

Rocky.

THE TORRID ZONE

— I —

Maggie Schneider stirred from a dream of balmy breezes on a tropical shore. She fought for the dream and lost it as she squinted out her window at the brittle crust on roofs and frozen front lawns. The sky was a murky mat, spewing snow that the wind whirled into white cyclones, setting them dancing on the street below.

Beyond, across the river, smoke was pumping from the chunky buildings of downtown Saskatoon: a pleasant-enough city were it not twenty degrees below zero and fifty-two degrees above the equator (much closer to the Arctic Circle).

As full wakefulness came, Maggie remembered with a jolt she would be serving just one more day and night under the tyrannical reign of this Saskatchewan winter, and then . . .

Costa Rica! Two weeks she would spend in a lush land where tires do not freeze square, where the tears brought on by the biting winds don't freeze on your face.

An agent at Hub City Travel ("Escape from those winter blahs with our ticket to paradise") had shown her a brochure: a mist-thick waterfall, a hummingbird in a poinciana, a breast-shaped boat-filled bay and its sweeping crescent of sandy beach. Seduced by these promises, she had signed on for four days and three nights in an exotic jungle retreat: the Eco-Rico Lodge. "A wilderness experience you'll never forget," though you are not likely to forget the thousand-dollar price tag, either.

She had found the tiny country in her atlas — squeezed between Panama and Nicaragua along a mountainous isthmus connecting the two American continents, with the Pacific Ocean and the Caribbean Sea lapping lovingly at its shores. Central America! Tropical jungle! Non-stop hot days and warm nights: two glorious weeks to inspire a novel of romance.

There, in the sticky heat of the tangled rain forest, Fiona (sassy, bright, and self-reliant) will find romance with Jacques (suave, cosmopolitan) in a seething epic to be called *The Torrid Zone*.

She powered herself to her feet, trotted to the shower, stood under it for several luxurious minutes. Maybe she would find a grass shack in Costa Rica; maybe she would never come back. She had paid her penance, surviving twenty-nine Saskatchewan winters. Her needs were simple: a pen and a pad and a pina colada. Maybe throw in Jacques.

In the meantime, Maggie must gird herself for the office Christmas party at CSKN–TV ("Voice of the Wheatlands, Your Channel Ten Eye to the Universe"). Her job as copywriter was the career equivalent of a temporary filling; she had not spent six years in university and authored an applauded thesis on the satirical constructs of Jane Austen to rhapsodize about sports equipment and bargains at the Bay.

Maggie had faith she could make a full-time living from her writing — if she broke out of the mould, those assembly-line paperbacks from which Primrose Books makes its millions. Maggie Schneider (alias Nancy Ward, her WASPish pen name) would give Primrose Books a full-lipped goodbye kiss when *The Torrid Zone* was published in hardcover by the highest bidder. She had a track record: her first three Primrose romances under its Ecstasy imprint had sold well enough, and she had actually found her way onto supermarket shelves on her fourth try, mastering all the euphemisms for body parts conjoining in the act of love.

With her latest, best-selling author Nancy Ward breaks new ground . . . Yes, it must be a different book: a sweeping adventure, sinuous in style, resonating with danger and desire, plumbing the elusive essence of love (though, never having been gripped by that apparently indispensable life experience, Maggie was not sure if she would recognize it if it landed on her head).

Creative Writing 403: The serious writer is intrigued by the unknown, and is driven to explore it. But where? Down what misty byway? Does it take one gently by the hand, or do its pitiless arrows wound the heart? Do stars glow fiercely and violins soar as they do for Fiona?

Towelling off before the mirror, Maggie sought to reassure herself she would not be the object of pitying stares on the beach with her broomstick figure. At almost six feet, with her hair clipped short, she looked vaguely androgynous. As a girl, Maggie had endured much schoolyard humour: the Giraffe, Maggie Flamingo – or often Maggie Klutz, because she was awkward at times.

Her mother kept insisting she had a poor self-image, that she had no idea how "ravaging" she looked, just like one of those swan-necked supermodels. She meant ravishing: Mrs. Malaprop.

From the stairs to her office, Maggie could survey the main studio, where Connie Veregin was fussing with a clove-spiked ham: spiffy food ideas for the holidays on *The Happy Homemaker Show.* She made her way past the cages where they kept the artists to a large glassed-in cubicle where sat her desk, her computer, and Brod Kipling, a friendly gasbag who bought twenty minutes a week. "AutoWorld on Eighth Street East: we have the wheels, you make the deals."

Brod wanted a different image for the Christmas push. "Instead of my ugly mug, I was thinking about using a hockey star. Saskatchewan boy, like Hit Man Hogan on the Ducks."

"That would cost scads. You'd be better off spending it on more air time. You've no idea how telegenic you are." She bit her tongue.

"You think so? I've been getting some feedback from my wife. She says I can't do the soft sell; it just don't sound like the real me."

"Ever thought a more sincere approach might work better?"

"Yeah, like what?"

"Hi, folks, my name is Brod Kipling, and I'm a used car dealer. Now, I know most of you have heard the fancy expression 'pre-owned vehicles,' but I talk straight, and I give the straight goods – there, you come across as honest; that's what you have to overcome: the common belief car salesmen are a little shady."

"Okay, write me up something sincere like that."

Maggie hated this job.

⁊

Just before seven, Maggie joined the CSKN staff in the main studio, where everyone was waiting for the news to wrap and the party to get underway. "And that does it for Friday, December eleventh," said Roland Davidson, the agonizingly handsome news anchor. His gaffe seemed to go unnoticed: right day, wrong date. It was the twelfth.

He turned to Frieda Lisieux for some hour-ending happy talk. "Going to any Christmas parties this weekend, Frieda?"

She hesitated, as if unsure how to answer. The weatherperson, if she held to previous form, would party with gusto as soon as the news-sports-and-weather team uttered its final banality to the wasteland.

"I think I'll just curl up with a good book," Frieda chirruped. Maggie almost gagged: first, you have to learn to read.

"Good way to stay out of trouble." Roland turned to Art Wolsely, whose wavy toupee seemed unusually lopsided this evening. "Big game for the Blades tonight. Going to be there?"

"Yep, I sure am –"

Roland, glancing at the clock, sliced Art off. "Have a good week-end and, folks, *please* drive safely." His words flowed like warm corn syrup down a stack of pancakes.

Credits roll, voices off, a wide shot of the *Eye on the City* team smiling fondly at each other, their lips moving soundlessly, Roland tidying his stack of news copy. An arm chops the air, the harsh lights dim, and Frieda explodes. "What do you mean, good way to stay out of trouble? You make it sound like I have a reputation."

"At least you didn't get a fucking cork stuffed down your throat halfway through a sentence." Art Wolsely snapped off his clip-on tie and made his way to *The Happy Homemaker* set and its self-help bar.

6

Roland was engaged now with the station manager, who was saying something about him "screwing up again" – obviously over the date miscue. Maggie wondered if his career was littered with a history of similar fox paws (as her mother would put it), offences for which he had been sentenced to Saskatoon.

He caught her eye: a wan smile. Maggie felt . . . what? *Fiona felt a curiously erotic tingling.* Not quite; more a sensation of prickles. She smiled back, remembered not to slouch. He had not spoken more than ten words to her in the three weeks since he transferred from the network's Montreal station. He was said to be married, but no one had seen his wife; maybe she had remained behind.

Frieda Lisieux, like a nectar-laden flower, had gathered several hummingbirds about her while drifting casually toward the sprig of mistletoe above the control room door. What lucky fellow would deposit his pollen on the stigma of her poinciana tonight? The personnel director, maybe, or the comptroller or one of the lusty camera operators?

Maggie sensed liaisons were subtly being made, and felt lonely. She fled to a haven behind the Christmas tree, lit with strands of chili lights, red and green, tiny flaccid penises.

"We've never been formally introduced. Roland Davidson."

Startled, she whirled in a half-circle, losing her balance and nearly knocking the drink from his hand. *I'm Maggie Klutz, such a pleasure to meet you.* Recovering, determined not to appear shy, she offered a firm, unwavering grip.

"Margaret Schneider. Maggie."

He held her hand for slightly longer than etiquette required. An unruly lock of hair had come unstuck, curling down his forehead and spoiling his perfectly-in-place image; she wanted to brush it back.

She erupted in mindless chatter, like Frieda filling the space between news and commercials. Yes, she was in advertising, she had been with the station three years but writing fiction was her passion, she had published four paperbacks, though they were maybe not his cup of tea, and she was taking holidays starting tomorrow, off to

Costa Rica on some horrible late-arriving flight. An amiable discussion about her fear of flying was followed by this:

"Would you be interested in getting together, Maggie, if you have some time later?"

"You mean tonight?"Why was he seeking this social engagement?

To that unasked question came an improbable answer: "When our eyes met, I . . . I don't know, I felt a kind of connection."

That seemed to come from the outer limits of corniness; she wondered if he was joking. "I can't stay up late."

They met at a dark downtown lounge. A "quick one," Maggie had stressed, blushing then, concerned he might read an improper innuendo in the phrase. The quick one had turned into two; his were doubles.

She tried to persuade herself she was not playing the role of Christmas party pickup. *I felt a kind of connection.* Well, sometimes it happened: one suddenly, mysteriously, clicked with another person. She had written often enough about the blinding flash that mesmerizes her heroines but had felt nothing remotely so profound with Roland.

What were the rules of engagement here? No affairs with married men, she told herself. He had mentioned, with a weary shrug, some "personal problems." Was he separated? Did not that bring a liaison within permissible bounds?

"So tell me about these problems."

"I think my wife and I are splitting up."

"You think."

"I . . . I'm not ready to talk about it. Too crowded here." He looked searchingly through the lenses of her spectacles. "Do you have a place where we could talk?"

"Yes, but . . . I'm not sure about this."

"Why don't you take those glasses off for a second?"

She took them from her face, and he blurred around the edges.

"Your eyes are very attractive."

"I can't use contacts. If you're not five feet in front of me, I can hardly make you out."

"We could always get closer than that."

She put her glasses back on. "Is your wife at home?"

"She's not expecting me till late."

"Kids?"

He hesitated. "Two boys."

"Did you do this a lot in Montreal?"

"What?"

"Fool around on your wife."

"Is that what you think this is?"

"That's what I know this is."

— 2 —

Maggie braved the wind tunnel between her mother's house and the neighbour's, entering by the back door. Beverley was in the kitchen rolling dough for cinnamon buns; she was still shapely at fifty-six, though tending to a thickness of hip. Maggie inherited her skinny genes from her father.

"Well, here's Maggie now." The cordless phone was crooked between Beverley's shoulder and ear: the walkie-talkie, she called it. "She's off to some little dictatorship in Central America that is probably owned by the drug lords and full of thieves and addicts. I don't know why she can't go to Hawaii." She put her hand over the mouthpiece. "You're not going to make it for Christmas at the farm?"

"Tell her, sorry, I get back on Boxing Day."

Beverley was talking to Aunt Ruthilda, long-distance to the family farm near Lake Lenore. The name of Maggie's hometown hinted of pastoral charm, but Lenore was a typical prairie town. The Schneiders and the Tsarchikoffs – one set of grandparents German, the other Doukhobor – had farmed there for three generations; mostly wheat, a quarter-section of canola, some milk cows and chickens.

Maggie rolled up her sleeves, washed her hands, and took over the rolling pin as Beverley wandered about the kitchen armed with phone, cigarette, and cup of coffee.

"No, I'll come as long as Woodrow isn't there. And how is Woody and his mid-term crisis?"

"Mid-life, Mother."

"Mid-life. Whatever."

Maggie watched Beverley's expression cloud, as it did whenever the topic of Maggie's father arose. Two years ago, Beverley had won an order ousting him from the farm, then had moved to the city herself, leaving Maggie's three older brothers to work the two and a half sections with Aunt Ruthilda and Uncle Ralph. Woody was staying on in Lenore, managing the lumberyard and living with the waitress who caused the breakup, a brainless frowzy, to use her mother's term. She meant floozy.

"Uh-huh. I'm not surprised." Beverley's face lightened. "Well, it's poetic licence." She hung up with a flourish of satisfaction.

"Poetic justice, Mom." In her compositional struggles, Maggie tried studiously to avoid malapropisms and mixed metaphors, concerned that they were traits subject to inheritance; her proneness to misplaced modifiers was burden enough. "So it didn't last."

"No, dear, it didn't. His little cupcake up and left him after he tried to make out with the manager of the Co-op's wife. I wouldn't take him back if he came crawling on his behind."

"I had a truly syrupy come-on last night from a married man, the news announcer; you've probably seen him on the tube. It was flattering in a way – he's very handsome."

"You didn't go to bed with him or anything?"

"Are you kidding? He was so transparent it was like talking through a pane of glass." Why did only married men come on to her? She must be giving off a scent to these hunters – of desperation and weakened resistance, a willingness to surrender after the niceties of protest were mouthed.

She was saving herself for Jacques. She would meet him, bronzed and flat-bellied, on a wave-battered beach. A Frenchman of culture, soldierly, tortured with the pain of forsaken love. Then she realized how trite that sounded: M. Jacques Cliché.

"Darling?"

"Sorry?" Maggie took a moment to flutter back to reality.

"I asked, are you all packed?"

"My gear's in the car." She had no intention of loading herself down with more than a flight bag, backpack, and camera case – her telescopic lens had set her back two weeks' wages. "By the way, Mom, Costa Rica is not a dictatorship. It's one of the oldest democracies in the hemisphere. They abolished their army five decades ago. They call it the Switzerland of the Americas."

"Tell me about it when you come home with malaria."

Maggie cut a grapefruit in half. "They have good health care. They spend on medicare and education instead of guns and soldiers." She had garnered these facts from a guidebook, *Key to Costa Rica*.

"I suppose that's all you're going to eat."

"I'll be lucky to hold that down." Rooted to the prairie gumbo by her flying phobia, Maggie had never travelled south of Yellowstone Park.

"So do you think you'll find any vegetarian restaurants in this tropical paradise that you think is so perfect even though you don't know anyone who's ever been there?"

"The staple is rice and beans, all the nutrition you need. And while we're on the topic of health, do you have to smoke that thing right down to the filter?"

Beverley butted out. "I hope you brought another set of specs. Or you'll be stumbling around the jungle blind as an ostrich."

"I brought extra glasses and ostriches aren't blind. I want you to get me to the airport in plenty of time, Mom, so I can compose myself." Outside, the birch trees were bending helplessly to the wind. Obviously the airline would cancel if the weather did not improve.

From a pay phone in the departure lounge, Maggie called Woodrow at Lenore Lumber and Feed; he sounded depressed.

"The whole family's against me, even the boys. When I go out to the farm, Ruthilda looks at me like I just tramped manure in the house. Felt like sleeping in the barn with the stock."

"Darn it, Dad, you're the scandal of Lake Lenore."

"Oh, I suppose Beverley's just clicking her heels in glee. She was right, I lasted exactly two years with Codette. Okay, I was stupid. I deserve not to go to Ruthilda's Christmas dinner, though everyone and his dog is going, including Beverley." After a long, morose sigh, he said, "I don't suppose she wants to talk to me."

"Not if you come crawling on your behind, she said, for which you'd have to be a contortionist."

"Look, this is the thing, Maggie, I . . ." He grappled for words.

"What is the thing, Dad?"

"I've decided I . . . I miss our life together."

"Maybe you should explain that to her."

She told him to start off with a heartfelt apology; if he promised to do that she would attempt some romance-writer patching when she returned.

Her flight was being called, to Minneapolis and Miami, connecting there with an airline called LACSA. "Got to go, Dad. Love you."

Maggie steeled herself and marched forward to seat 11F, right above the maw of one of those jet engines that have been known to explode in flames. Outside, a buffeting wind was sending whirlwinds of snow across the tarmac. Dr. Vicky Rajwani had given her a catalogue of helpful hints: relax and sit calmly, engage your seatmate if possible, but most important, think positive. Repeat after me: Flying is a wonderful way to travel . . .

Dr. Rajwani, who had taught Maggie self-hypnosis, had described her phobia as "unusual in its context." Maggie was not claustrophobic, not afraid of heights. If anything, she was abnormally well adjusted, upbeat, adventurous, an outdoors person. Positive thinking was in her very nature, said Dr. Rajwani. (Maggie Poppins: that is what her mother used to call her.)

The aircraft was not moving. Were they having second thoughts? A voice of doom crackled from the speakers. "Ah, this is Captain

Webb. Sorry for the delay. Just a little glitch with the panel lights here. Should be off in about two minutes."

She cinched her seat belt tighter, then blanched as the blast furnace outside ignited, and shut her eyes tightly as the aircraft rolled toward the runway. She felt it roar and shudder, race ahead, lift off. She delved into her bag for her notepad: writing was release; she would find deliverance in *The Torrid Zone*.

"Okay, folks, we'll have a bumpy few minutes until we get on top of all this rough stuff, so I'd ask you to be comfortable but keep buckled up."

The captain's utterly bored tone brought some reassurance. The plane jounced a few more times, then suddenly she was aware of a southern sun pouring through her window. She peeked out; the plane was soaring sedately above the clouds, on top of all the rough stuff.

A smiling flight attendant was cruising down the aisle with a cart; a man across the aisle was frowning over a crossword puzzle. No one else seemed in distress or even curious as to why Maggie was clenched like a crab.

✺

Fiona Wardell gazed pensively at the wind-tossed clouds below her window. She had hastened to the airport from her father's funeral in a turmoil of sorrow, vowing she would triumph in the challenge of Professor Wardell's last great ambition: to find the wintering home of the Buff-Breasted Blue Warbler, and save this forsaken songbird from extinction.

That task might only be accomplished, however, with the aid of the man her father had mentored: Jacques Martin, who knew the upper reaches of the Río Perdido. But it was said this brilliant scholar had lost all ambition, become a recluse, and had sworn never to return to the valley of the Perdido, to the grave of the woman he had never stopped loving.

She had met Jacques once, and remembered him as lithe and handsome in a way that turned women's heads. He was thought still to be in Costa Rica; perhaps Fiona would discover this vanishing member of her own species there — but she had long given up her fool's fancy that she might one day find love. She was not interested in pandering to the weak egos of shallow men who

feared strong women, which was why her intimate encounters had been few.
Nor had many such experiences been satisfying; no man had ever . . .
Knocked her socks off? Found the keys to her heart?
. . . found the wintering home of her distant lonely heart.

Losing herself in composition, Maggie no longer felt so unsettled.
Fiona was not afraid to soar above the clouds, why should her author
not be equally at ease? Fiona must face even graver menaces, both
physical and of the heart, in her quest for the Buff-Breasted Blue
Warbler. But what did the fates – or at least the muses of creativity –
have in store for her?

She realized she did not have much of a plot in mind yet. Nor
any real sense of M. Jacques Cliché. *As they listened to the warbler's sweet
evening song, he slipped off her glasses and looked into her buff-breasted blue
eyes as if for the first time.* And you, Mr. Warbler, do you have the wings
to stay aloft? Or has Fiona been saddled with too arcane a mission?
An idea with more pizzazz ought to be devised . . .

I have already flown thousands of miles. I have landed safely at two
airports. This is a wonderful way to travel. Maggie silently chanted
these mantras as her aircraft grunted into the sky and levelled off for
the final section of her journey: Miami to Costa Rica. Outside, the
sun was going down like a rocket, setting the horizon briefly on fire.

In a few hours, God willing, she would be in San José, capital of
the Republic of Costa Rica. She pictured the town – colonial churches
and winding cobbled streets, the rippling notes of a guitar floating
through the jasmine-scented air, women in colourful skirts, gallant
Latin men, couples walking hand in hand around a square.

Maggie relaxed enough to take note of the person next to her: not
a mad bomber but a stout gentleman in a bright tropical shirt working
on a double rum-and-Coke. He was craning his head toward her, as if
trying to peer down her shirt. To every rule – including Rajwani's
number three, engage your seatmate – there was an exception.

Maggie flicked a look in his direction; he was staring not at her bosom but her notepad. She covered it as he met her glance.

"You a writer?"

"Yes. I'm making some notes for a book."

"Yeah? What sort of book?"

"I write novels."

"Like what? Maybe I know some of them."

"I would be flattered and surprised if you do."

When Love Triumphs. No Time for Sorrow. Return to the House of Heartbreak. Strange Passion. Unlikely to be his literary preference. She noticed the embossed promotional type on the cover of the paperback on his lap. *What they don't want you to know about the lost civilizations!* She could ignore him or change the subject.

"Is this your first time in Costa Rica?" she asked.

The question served as a launching pad. Hell, no, he had been down there a dozen times. Owned a couple of lots at Flamingo Beach and a hundred shares in a teak plantation. Hadn't made a profit yet, but wait. World's wood supply was getting scarce, so his time would come. Nelson Weekes, from Fort Lauderdale, owns a mattress outlet.

"How about you — first time?"

"Yes."

"Hey, you'll like San José, it's a swinging town. Where you staying?"

"I haven't decided yet." She had compiled a list of modestly priced hotels; she was going where the tourists did not.

"I could show you around."

"I'm meeting someone."

She felt bad not about her lie but her abruptness; it produced a brief pall of silence. "I'm sorry if I seem unfriendly. I'm a little afraid of flying."

"Well, it'll be a thrill a minute coming down into that little airport in the valley. We go real close to the mountains."

☙❧

Though exhausted by the tension of landing during a thunderstorm and jittery with too much coffee, Maggie was feeling quite exuberant as she made her way up the aisle to the aircraft door. A whole new country awaited her.

Within minutes, she was proudly examining her first passport stamp. An energetic young woman at the Instituto de Turismo counter helped her change money and make a room reservation – at an inn half-heartedly recommended by her guidebook: "fair value for a short stay."

Outside, it was like a night in July at home on this high plateau of the Central Valley. But Maggie was disappointed by what she saw during her long taxi ride into the city. San José, even at night, seemed bedraggled, bereft of interesting style or architecture. Where were the strolling musicians, the red-tile roofs, the colonial arcades?

Pensión Paraíso was an unassuming three-storey hostelry above a noisy bar. Upstairs, no one was at the desk to check her in, so she made her way into a sitting room, where five older men were watching television, their eyes glazed with boredom.

"If you're looking for Louie," one of them said, "he's down getting beer."

Louie finally came huffing up the stairs, laden with several cases of beer; Maggie followed him to a refrigerator down the hall. "You wanted one with a bath? Number twelve, it's in the back. Beer's a buck or three hundred colones, you gotta keep track of what you owe."

"May I see the room?"

He turned to study her. "Oh, you're a lady."

"Sorry to disappoint you." It was the short hair.

The room was dreary, but it offered a small table at which she could scribble notes after her intended walk. A quick look revealed no cockroaches, and the linen was fresh. She could hear the thrum of music from below: the Lone Star Bar.

Eleven o'clock did not seem too late for a walkabout; San José was open for business on a Saturday night, and so were the women she had seen patrolling the street below. Maggie had not thought prostitution would be so overt. She threw her bags on the bed, and washed and touched her face up.

Once on the street, she paused to look in at the Western-style bar, full of middle-aged men exercising their elbows. These gringos did not seem typical tourists. Maybe there was a convention in town: the American Association of Mattress Vendors.

Next to the Lone Star was a noisy, smoky bistro also filled with men, but locals: Latins, rather short. The women, she assumed, were home with the children. She'd read they were called Ticos and Ticas, which made them sound like munchkins.

"Change dollars?" She avoided the sharp-eyed man who was riffling a fistful of notes at her.

Ungainly at the best of times, Maggie found the sidewalk an obstacle course, its unevenness camouflaged by litter. A diesel bus grunted past, spewing a toxic cloud. So this was Costa Rica, the fabled eco-tourist paradise – maybe her mother was right, maybe coming here was a mistake.

A soft rain had begun to fall. She returned to her hotel, and tried to write but felt stalled; Fiona's quest seemed petty in comparison to . . . *What they don't want you to know about the lost civilizations* . . . The vanished city of the Mayans? Dr. Fiona Wardell, the noted archaeologist, has come upon an ancient map of an unexplored vastness. There, bedecked in tangles of lianas, lay the lost pyramids of Itzmixtouan.

She mulled over the concept, but was distracted by grunts and squeaking bedsprings coming from the next room.

— 3 —

In the morning, Maggie found her way to the Eco-Rico offices. Taped to a locked glass door was a typed notice: "The orientation talk for Sunday, December 14, at two p.m., has been cancelled. Costa Rica Eco-Rico Tours S.A. regrets any inconvenience."

"Oh, fart," she said under her breath. If they had closed for the weekend, how was she to find her way to their wilderness camp tomorrow? She had vouchers; she had paid a thousand dollars for them.

She saw someone moving within, a secretary. She rapped on the door, and the woman, a young Tica, unlocked it.

"Excuse me, but I have a reservation for your lodge tomorrow."

"I am so sorry, we have to cancel."

"But you can't. I paid for four days and three nights."

The young woman beckoned Maggie inside and fetched her boss, a scrawny scraggly-haired American in his fifties, rings in both ears, possibly a late-blooming hippie. He introduced himself as Elmer Jericho. "This is a real hassle. How about we slot you in a week over Christmas for the same price?"

"I'll be gone then. I'm afraid you'll have to honour my reservation."

"See, this here's the problem. We had to cancel nine others. We had to make way for some heavies, VIPs."

"I intend to report you to the tourist bureau."

"You better take it up with the American Embassy, lady, because it's the ambassador who's coming, with his wife and a bunch of suits from Washington. And Senator Chuck Walker and his wife."

Maggie recognized the name of the junior senator from South Dakota from CSKN newscasts: a conservative ex-marine colonel who had his eyes on the White House. But she wasn't about to be bumped by these Washington grandees. She needed this wilderness experience for her book.

Fiona Wardell wouldn't be put aside so easily. "The *Geographic* is going to be very unhappy. Well . . . I guess there are other wilderness tours. Who would you recommend?"

Elmer Jericho retrieved a reservation slip from a file on the desk. There she was: "Margaret Schneider, Saskatoon, Sask., occupation, writer."

He looked at the camera case slung over her shoulder. "That what you do — travel writing?"

"Everything. Freelance, travel." She had in fact written a couple of pieces for a naturalist magazine: "Seeking the Burrowing Owl," "Birds of the Drylands." "Mostly novels, though. Here, I have one." From her bag she produced a copy of *When Love Triumphs* — on the theory that anyone can blithely claim one's a writer, she usually carried with her a selection of her paperbacks, along with written proof Nancy Ward was her pen name.

Jericho studied the cover copy: "A heart-searing tale of forbidden passion by the author of *No Time for Sorrow*." Her feats of creativity seemed to impress him. "Hey, man, I'm gonna write a book some day. Interstellar travel." His hand glided through the air, a swooping spaceship. "You got a letter from the *National Geographic*? They got to give us advance notice, don't they?"

"I never thought to bring my contract. Phone them." She was flirting with exposure; would he be able to reach their offices on a Sunday?

"Jeez . . . just a minute."

He disappeared into his office, and Maggie could hear him on the phone. Her mask would soon be stripped away.

When he came out, he said, "Hey, lady, far out, the senator wants to know if you'll include him in the article."

"Sure, that would make an unusual sidebar."

"With pictures and all."

"Absolutely."

"Okay, I'll have a driver pick you up for the airport."

"The airport?"

"Yeah, to Quepos. Staging area, man."

"I'd rather go by bus to see the countryside."

"See it on the way back; it'll still be there."

"I'm not keen on flying."

"How did you get down here from Saskatoon, by dog-sled? A travel writer who don't fly?"

"No, I . . . I get tired of all the flying I have to do. Never mind, I'll take the plane."

"There'll be a ticket waiting at the SANSA counter. The rest of the way is by four-wheel taxi, and here's a map so your driver don't get lost. The others are going in by Mixmaster."

"By what?"

"A beater, a chopper. There'll be Secret Service, too; hey, man, the colonel's running for president. The lodge has got twenty staff up there with a combined forty left feet, it's gonna be like a Mexican fire drill. I used to run tours for these guys; now they got me down here doing the orientation sessions, clicking slides, man." Jericho had the rambling ways of a stoner. "Where you staying?"

He frowned when she mentioned the Pensión Paraíso. His driver, he said, would pick her up at seven the following morning.

❧

Back at the hotel, Maggie showered away the almost disastrous beginning to the day. She had brazened her way past Mr. Jericho, the interstellar traveller, but what were the ramifications if the U.S. Embassy started asking questions? If her ruse went undiscovered, though, she might find literary fodder in holidaying with a controversial senator.

She laced up her expensive new walkers, then studied her San José map. The University of Costa Rica: that is where Fiona Wardell could bone up on pre-Colombian history.

Outside, sunlight was filtering through a hazy smog; the city seemed creaky and slow, hungover on a Sunday, a tacky tropical America – Ronald McDonald and Colonel Sanders looked misplaced here. After a half-hour traipse east, she came to the San Pedro district, the university area, where she found a vegetarian restaurant. She bought a bran muffin and a bundle of carrot sticks, and munched these while strolling through the campus, a clutter of low buildings. Students were lounging outside the library; a few were studying within.

In the deserted history section, she found several shelves of pre-Colombian Americana, many of the texts in English. As she was carrying a few books to a long table, a dark-skinned Latino strolled in, withdrew some maps from a drawer, and sat down to study them. He looked up at her, caught her eye and smiled, then returned to his maps.

She glanced furtively at the man. Tan slacks and a short-sleeved white shirt, skin the colour of milk chocolate – she presumed he had Indian blood. With his thin waist and broad shoulders, he could have been a flamenco dancer. He was tall for a Tico, almost her height, jet-black hair curling over his shoulders, dark eyes, and a long savage moustache. His smile had been unforced and dazzling.

She could sense him still staring at her as she flipped through the books. He said something in Spanish, a polite mellifluous voice.

"I'm sorry," she said, "I don't understand."

He rose and walked to her side. Looking at her texts, he said, "Ah, you are interested in the history of my country." His accent charmed her: *heestory, contry.* Not quite forty, she guessed; no sign of grey. Although laugh wrinkles webbed from his eyes, his lined face reflected a world-weariness.

"I'm a writer. From Canada. I was thinking of setting a book here. A novel."

"It is what I teach. Our history. And what do you seek to know?"

"I'm searching for, um, a lost Mayan city. My heroine is, I mean; she's an archaeologist. I need something with intrigue as backdrop to a . . . well, it's a romance novel. That's what I write."

She strove to curb her babbling, and scrambled in her bag for a copy of *No Time for Sorrow.* He studied the cover for a moment: the heroine, eyes ablaze with desire, giving token resistance to a shirtless male.

"So. You are rich and famous."

"Not yet, but I'm working at it."

His expression hinted at disbelief. "A lost city . . . We had the Choretegas, who were linked to the Mayan people. But they had not so much advanced. They did not lose any cities, I am sorry."

"Well . . . it will be fiction."

"But it is best to base on truth, no?"

He extended his hand. "Pablo Esquivel."

"Margaret Schneider. Maggie."

"And for your romance you seek some unusual mystery."

"Mm-hmm." She cleared her throat. "Yes."

"Then you must write about the buried treasure in the valley of Río Savegre – the Savage River. It is a story of desperate men and desperate times. But may I be permitted to tell you over lunch?"

☙

He insisted on paying for the taxi, which let them off at a plaza where vendors hawked hammocks, pottery, and assorted gewgaws. The restaurant was on the terrace of one of San José's grander, older hotels. This was the heart of San José, Professor Esquivel told her: the Plaza de la Cultura and, across from it, the National Theatre, a down-sized copy of the Paris Opera House.

That graceful building, the plaza extending to it, the hum of activity – buskers, a juggler, a guitar duo, children clutching cones, their faces slathered with ice cream – persuaded Maggie she was finally discovering the San José that had been waiting for her.

As he spoke, Pablo Esquivel gestured a great deal, and she found herself mesmerized by his hands, so sinewy and slender. Flattered beyond measure, she wondered at the attention being showered on her. Did he find her attractive? Maybe it was the cachet of being a novelist; the well-read were often curious about writers. Professor Esquivel himself had authored a text, a history of Mesoamerica, he said.

Maggie nibbled at a fruit salad, listening intently to his colourful though gory tale of the sack of Panama in 1671 by a mob of buccaneers led by Henry Morgan. Before the fall of that wealthy colonial city – "ah, Panama, she was the most prized jewel of the Spanish crown" – three galleons escaped, laden with gold, silver, and jewels. Two ships found their way to Ecuador.

"The third was galleon La Naval; she disappeared. There is a local myth that she put into a faraway island called Cocos, that the crew buried the treasure and were later lost at sea."

Pablo was a masterful storyteller; his words cast spells – Maggie could visualize the swashbuckling Morgan and the desperate men of La Naval. That vessel, newly unburied journals revealed, had sailed up the coast of Central America, the crew seeking refuge at a mission in Costa Rica – the only Spanish habitation for a thousand miles.

It was in Costa Rica, in "thees, my contry," in a river valley high above the Pacific coast, that the treasure was most likely buried. "The Savegre, I believe, but there are other rivers near, the Parrita, the Naranjo. Sadly, the mission was destroyed not by arms but by the scourge of plague, and its site has never been found."

Finding a lost Spanish mission by the Savage River, buried gold and silver and emeralds – this could be Fiona's quest. Buffy the warbler would stay vanished.

Where had she heard of this river before? It came to her: a brochure. *Beautifully situated in an isolated valley near the Savegre River, the Eco-Rico Lodge affords all the comforts of home.* "What an odd coincidence, I am going to the Savegre." She described her wrangle at the Eco-Rico office, how she had cajoled Elmer Jericho.

He found her story droll, and chuckled. "Then you, Maggie Schneider, who are so delightfully conniving, you could be the one to find the treasure." He shrugged. "The whole business, it is maybe a myth. But I have given you some truth to work into your fiction, no?"

"No. I mean, yes."

"But tell me about yourself."

She struggled for anecdotes that might entertain him, but her humdrum life in Saskatchewan seemed pale and uninspiring. She talked about her girlhood on a farm, the thrill of her first publication, her love of birding and bicycling, any inane matter that came to mind. The Christmas party at the Voice of the Wheatlands, the people she worked with. He began smiling, and finally broke into laughter.

"What can possibly be so funny?"

"You are most engaging, unlike some of the empty-headed women I have been forced to know."

They parried for the cheque, but Maggie insisted, dipping into her fanny pack for her colones.

"You are alone here in San José?"

"Yes."

"I am alone, too. Maybe you will do me the pleasure of returning the favour this evening. There is a delightful restaurant I know in the hills above Escazú."

"Actually, that sounds enjoyable. Yes, I'd like to."

The restaurant at which they would meet, La Linda Vista, was in the hills west of the city. Pablo had been apologetic about being unable to escort her there, but, alas, his car was in the garage. She told him she was happy to take a taxi.

All afternoon, Maggie was in a turmoil of anticipation. Strolling through the streets, she suddenly found San José much more appealing. The stores were crammed with Christmas knick-knacks: a Santa Claus or a Rudolph in almost every window, cheek by jowl with a crèche, three wise men beneath a star.

From a tourist shop she bought a postcard, and wrote a note to her mother, hinting of developments to come with "the world's most gorgeous man – he could charm the nose off your face." She posted it, then walked past the public market to the wide commercial artery of Paseo Colón, and tramped many blocks west, into Sabana Park, where children played boisterously and young couples strolled hand in hand.

I am alone, too. Those four little words had been tinged with melancholy, making her wonder if he had recently emerged from some deep, wounding affair. Though she had seen no wedding ring, she could not quell the fear that he was another in the long list of the unfaithful, and that she would learn the wife and children were off on a beach holiday.

How could such an attractive man escape matrimony? Was he divorced? She could not bear the thought he was a married hypocrite and resolved to put him through some verbal tests. Decisions must be made now, in the cold light of day, before reason becomes corrupted in the night. She must not present herself as either loose or tightly laced. She would set limits on this first date. Later, perhaps, after her week in the jungle, a return engagement . . . But these were such implausible plots.

Yet she had felt a genuine interest emanating from Professor Esquivel; perhaps he was seeking beauty beneath the surface. It was her mind that drew him, her sense of humour. He was tired of empty-headed women – though she could not remember, in her nervousness, having said anything so clever as to entirely remove herself from that category.

She was no longer slouching, but walking tall, and, sensing eyes on her, she glanced around to see two young men gazing at her. Maybe she did look ravaging: the remarkable bustless Maggie. Thank goodness the supermodel had packed the hugging green low-cut sheath that she occasionally dared to wear braless; not tonight, though: that would be too bold.

She whirled, performed a dance step, almost stumbled over a wayward soccer ball with which some boys were playing, then gaily kicked it back.

— 4 —

Clambering from her small taxi, Maggie saw Pablo Esquivel in a crisp grey suit, no tie, seated at a table for two on an upper terrace of La Linda Vista. As he rose to greet her, he plucked a hibiscus from a vase, and with a bow presented it to her, then smiled and brushed back the strands of long hair that had fallen over his eyes.

She pantomimed surprise at his generosity. As he laughed, she noticed he undertook a quick tour of her body. She hoped the effect of the tight sheath was not too much marred by the fanny pack; she must not slouch.

He held her chair as she sat. "You are in time for the sunset. Later, you would not see the view."

The restaurant afforded a grand panorama of the Central Valley: rolling fertile plains encircled by cloud-draped volcanoes, the lights of the city below blinking on at dusk.

Their conversation was tentative at first, literary, a shared success-ful search for authors they respected: Márquez, Allende, Neruda. These bookish intimacies were interrupted by a loud, raucous bird call from a shrubby glade: "Haw, haw." It sounded of derisive laughter.

"That has to be the Laughing Falcon," she said. *Exceptionally vocal raptor*, said her bird guide, *feeds almost entirely on snakes, including venomous ones.*"

"Ah, you are a bird fancier. The *guaco*, we call this *halcón*; it is the masked bandit of the skies. Maybe we will hear the full *guaco*."

"What is that?"

"Allow me to try. The bird goes 'wah-wah-wah,' ever faster and louder. Then it breaks into 'Guah-co! Guah-co!'"

His mimicry caused her to smile. The full *guaco* – that strident voice might even cause the hairs of intrepid Fiona Wardell to stand on end. *Alone in the jungle, the sun dying, she sought to close her ears to its jeering call . . .*

"May I suggest a pina colada?"

"Let me at least pay for the drinks."

"I would not dream of it."

She ordered a pina colada, he a vodka. She did not want to burden Pablo with a costly bill, so when the waiter returned, she asked for the local cuisine: refried beans, baked plantains, a salad with papaya and palm hearts. Pablo chose a steak.

After the menus were removed she barraged him with questions about Costa Rican food, customs, politics, history, but was unsure how to direct their conversation toward the crucial subject. Should she be blunt or subtle? *I'm always getting propositioned by married men – isn't that ridiculous?* She would not be able to digest her *plato típico* if he delivered the usual worn-out line: "We've been unhappy for years."

The pina colada disappeared all too quickly, and soon there was another in front of her. In the meantime, she was learning that Costa Ricans loved salsa music, were obsessed with politics no less than *fútbol*, and that the custom at bullfights in this warm-hearted nation was not to injure the bull but tease it.

There was no subject, with the possible exception of himself, with which Pablo did not seem at ease. Maggie's male protagonists tended to be academics like her imaginary Jacques, and Pablo, too, was a professor – but with a Latin beat. He was even courtlier than Jacques, whose portrait seemed to blur in the presence of this urbane reality.

Pablo waited until the dinner plates were taken before lighting a cigarette. ("Forgive my minor addiction.") Maggie had become tipsy: three pina coladas, and now liqueurs, Café Ricas, heavy and sweet.

As the blush faded from the western clouds and the Laughing Falcon stilled its voice, crickets made cheerful night music; the air was fragrant with citrus blossom. This was the Costa Rica she had imagined.

Pablo still seemed reticent to talk about himself; preferring to carry on proudly about his *contry*.

"When people think of Central America they think of revolution, of armed guerrillas and bandits, but we have escaped that. There are paramilitary groups; however, these are merely a nuisance. But unhappily, with tourism has come street crime. It is not so safe for a woman alone; you must be careful."

Caressed by a warm breeze, dazzled by the sparkling panoply of stars, Maggie drifted off again. *"The city, too, is a jungle; stay close to me." Fiona feared only what was in her heart.*

"I think you have disappeared on me."

She returned to find Pablo looking at her quizzically. "I'm sorry?"

"I was saying that maybe you will find room in your book for a lonely history professor."

She had been granted the right to make inquiries. "Why is he lonely?"

"I will not sadden you with the story, but two years ago my wife died of cancer. Let us go on to something else. I think for a moment you were in another world?"

"I was wandering." Lonely, he said — not just alone, but lonely. She felt guilty relief at his loss.

"To wander. This is what I had in mind: a wander through the grounds. There is a pretty waterfall."

As he held her chair, the toe of one of her sandals struck a table leg, and she rose awkwardly. "Sorry, I seem to be all feet."

Leading her down tiled stairs to the gardens, Pablo continued to talk about Costa Rica. "It is a little republic with a little history, but interesting to know nonetheless. Tomorrow, after my classes, I will take you to the National Museum."

"Tomorrow . . . No, I can't. I'm expected at that jungle lodge for four days." Quickly, she added, "But I'll be back by Friday. I'd love to go to the museum with you then."

He did not respond. They had arrived at the waterfall, where a rivulet splashed over rocks into a pool ringed with flowering bushes. He leaned on a railing, staring into the water, and seemed deep in thought, his silence making Maggie tense. I am free for a whole week afterwards, she wanted to stay. She need not spend it on the beach; her plan could change.

Instead, she asked, "What are these flowers?" The bushes were mantled with delicate purple and white blossoms.

"We call them Yesterday, Today, and Tomorrow. This is because so quickly they shed their petals. Yesterday they were violet, today they are white, and tomorrow they are gone."

His gentle words and the tinkling water sounded as a melody. She felt light-headed; she wanted to touch him, to let go, to be daring and even foolhardy.

"Friday is too long," he said in a soft voice.

"Excuse me?"

"Too long to wait."

She looked into his grave dark eyes, her chest thumping. She started involuntarily as he closed distance between them, and now felt unable to move. He held back at the last moment, as if waiting for her to bridge the remaining few inches.

She closed her eyes and took the jump, landing awkwardly, their lips misaligned; her initial sensation was of smoky sweet breath and bristly moustache. She was overcome by the gentle power of his kiss, and she put her arms around him and pressed herself to his body and opened her mouth to him: overbold, abandoning reserve. When she drew back to catch her breath, his lips traced paths down her cheeks and the long curve of her neck and the hollows beneath her ears.

"Forgive me," he murmured, "I cannot hold inside what I feel."

Again he kissed her on the mouth, and she was caught up in a rapture she could not resist. His hands were clasped behind her hips, and his tongue was moving in her mouth. The feel of his phallus engorging against her groin was sending electric messages down her spine to her toes, messages answered by a sudden cramp in her right foot. She pulled away from him, hopped several times on her left leg, a performance that recalled to her mind a one-legged barnyard chicken at Lake Lenore.

He took her elbow, expressing concern, and she said she was fine. "Just a cramp."

When her foot muscles finally unwound, she started babbling about her narrow size-ten feet, of all things. What a disaster.

Pablo, however, seemed to find the episode funny, and she began to relax enough to share in his laughter. He offered his arm, and after escorting her to their table, he bowed, excused himself for "the untimely demands of nature," then made his way to the washroom.

She sat down heavily on her chair and gulped back her Café Rica, her heart pounding, her hands unsteady, her mind a snarl of anxiety, hope, and desire.

Never on a first date: the ancient rule existed for a reason. And he would probably think her of easy virtue if she disobeyed it. Pablo possessed Latin sensibilities and would respect her for declining such an early invitation. She would hint that the subject could be reopened when she returned from the Eco-Rico Lodge.

Several minutes passed as she romped in the playhouse of her mind. "*One must grab thees moment in life. The flowers of tomorrow will soon be gone, but tonight they bloom for us.*" Dare she speculate that this might be that explosion of stars she had long dreamed of? Can love truly come at first sight? Surely, it grew slowly, survived longer than the flowers of Yesterday, Today, and Tomorrow.

The waiter asked if she cared for anything else; when she shook her head, he joined the maitre-d', and they began staring at her and whispering. Was Pablo ill – what was taking him so long? Suddenly, she was feeling needles of anxiety.

From a distant copse came the full *guaco* of the Laughing Falcon. "Guah-co! Guah-co! Guah-co!"

"Oh, God," she said aloud. Quickly, she unstrapped her fanny pack and zipped open the money compartment. It was empty except for a few coins: eight hundred U.S. dollars had vanished.

She opened the compartment with her traveller's cheques. Relief allayed some of her outrage; they were still here, but she had cashed in all but three hundred dollars. He had not taken her Visa card, but she was near her limit.

Never had she felt so betrayed, so damaged, so emotionally defiled. She felt dizzy, sick to the stomach. The waiter laid the cheque before her; she paid with her card, then asked him to order a taxi, and she waited for it outside on the steps, feeling so empty within she could not find tears to shed.

HYMNS TO A DYING PLANET

— I —

As Slack pulled up to his gate, the curtain of night was about to ring down, the sun diving toward the mangled hills, the virgin forest raped last year, squatters swarming, slashing, burning. Where guapinoles and cedros once stately stood, where cassias had showered the jungle with coral flowers, now were clapboard shacks. What God gives, man fucks.

There had been lusty birdsong here, sublime voices that perfumed the air with sound. Now instead, brassy rasping radios bellowed syrupy *rancheras*. At night, no longer came the haunting moans of the pootoo, lamentations to the moon. Slack should have heeded this bird's gloomy warnings, fled into the jungles before the conquistadors came with their noise and squalor, their clutter of offal, discarded wrappers and plastic Coke bottles littering the road, fouling his driveway.

The fifty acres across the road had been a forest reserve, nature's lush living factory, pumping out oxygen for man and his evil machines. When the squatters came, government officials stood by shrugging, shuffling their feet, at a loss. The forest is gone, señor. *Se fué.*

Slack felt a back spasm as he closed his gate. To add to his distemper, he had slipped a disc on the river today while fishing a Prussian housefrau from a foaming back eddy of the Naranjo River. She had clung to him like an octopus as he strained to boost her into her inflatable kayak – a vaudevillian interlude for the others in the package group, mingy Germans who thought a tip was a piece of advice.

His elderly Land Rover toiled up the parallel strips of cement toward the house he had painstakingly built in a grove of mangoes and flame trees and wild forest, eight acres of solitude. Defiled now by the barrio across the road, its *precaristas* casting him furtive guilty looks. They were not landless poor, not campesinos, but shop owners from town, friends of the *jefe* of the municipality, a man on the pad.

The owners of the former reserve were seeking an eviction order; the Costa Rican courts moving with their characteristic blinding speed, the case might get to court in a decade.

It wasn't until the diesel engine coughed and rattled to a stillness that Slack looked at his house and saw its gaping wound – window shutters had been forced open, the grill bent. A car jack, that's how the pissers do it. He rent the air with expletives.

His back twinged as he stepped from the vehicle and climbed the steps, bending to ease the pain as he checked the boat shed – still secure, his kayaks safe. He unlocked the front door. Had they got into the bodega? No, but they'd tried, he saw the pry marks by the lock. A pair of birding binoculars, his cell phone, and his short-wave radio were gone, he had forgotten to put them away. Some clothing, too. T-shirts. His best hiking boots. *Se fué.*

He could drop by the Rural Guard office. He was a generous tipper, he could offer a reward – if the cops nabbed the thieves might they agree not to fence his goods at their usual outlet in San José?

The home invaders were uncouth, lacked culture – they had not taken any of his poetry collections or his Dickens, Molière, or Conrad. Even more miraculously, still gracing his shelves was a third of a bottle of Ron Rico. He tilted it to his lips and felt its burn, its pain.

The hole boarded up, the bottle emptied, Slack returned to his vehicle, morose, pondering the machinations of vindictive God. Why was He persecuting Slack Cardinal? Why, when there were so many more qualified assholes?

These were the days of his despair, futile, lonely, his muse barren – no lines had he penned for months, not since Esperanza left with a thief of love for the glitter of McDisneyland, conveyed there on a sixty-foot sloop, bought like a beautiful slave with promises of diamonds and Cadillacs. Lady Esperanza, how vain behind the mask of Tica innocence.

No other woman had tempted him since, though many had offered, budding flowers from Oshkosh or Oshawa, down here for the tropical romance: de rigeur, can't go home without it, a tale to tell their pals in the office, almost made it with this big gangling beach bum with a kayak business. Claims he's sort of a poet or something.

Slack was intimidated by women, though he wasn't sure why. Women were different now, direct, determined, ballsy. They had left Slack behind. He was forty-eight, old-fashioned, a child of the sixties, that conservative age: he fell for the unliberated ones like Esperanza, splashy and narcissistic, flirty and false. He had not been able to keep up with her, she had taunted him: *qué hombre más macho*, what a man.

Now there was no one to endure his black moods, no one to massage his aching back. Maybe he would return to the Bronx, that borough of his wasted youth, and marry a chiropractor. Though he would be better off pairing with a shrink, he had been becoming more neurotic over the years, excessively eco-anxious, blocked creatively. Illness was in his genes, his mother had suffered a paranoid disorder.

His shockless Rover jounced over potholes past rolling farmland, fields of rice and sorghum, pastures where flop-eared Zebu cattle browsed, abandoned now by their camp followers, egrets toiling for home, white slingshots in the darkening sky. Now the vast holdings of the *compañía*, its palm plantations, their clusters of orange fruit. Above, grumpy clouds were blotting the sun's dying rays, still rainy season in the Pacific wet zone, and only two weeks to Christmas with its annual swarm of locusts in their bikinis and Birkenstocks.

Ah, yes, the eco-warrior Cardinal: how haughty and patronizing you are to the vacationing bourgeoisie upon whom you depend not to starve. How Janus-faced is this protector of the wilderness, complicit in its betrayal, a card-carrying member of our doomed destructive species. Environmental angst, that's what it was called, helplessness in the face of this planet's coming Armageddon.

He could see the lights of Puerto Quepos, the old banana port, ramshackle and impoverished when Slack first came here, now fattening on tourism, cashing in on the golden beaches that lay three miles beyond the hills. The town had folded up early this Sunday evening, no cars beside the brothel, businesses shuttered, streets abandoned to a few strolling tourists and the fallen drunks they were cautiously stepping around.

He rolled through the silent town, toiled up Cardiac Hill to the ridge, the ancient spew of a volcano, a thousand feet above the ocean. The new hotels blinked past, freshly painted vacancy signs beckoning guileless guests: this was Manuel Antonio, instant resort, buy a chunk of land, put up a piece of crap and call it paradise.

There had been almost nobody here twelve years ago, when Slack first beheld these exotic shores and declared himself at the end of life's sweaty journey. Manuel Antonio was forever to have been his hideaway, his final safe house. Now it had been discovered, desecrated, carved up by roads and power lines.

Turning off the main road, he descended to Bar Balboa, where there would be friends and sympathy. His back still aching, he hobbled painfully from his vehicle as a ribbon of lightning slithered through the western sky, starkly sketching the jungle below, the national park, its beaches and islets, the infinite sweep of the Pacific. A long surly grumble, then Zeus's angry bark. The gods were displeased with Slack Cardinal; he was a snivelling complainer. Did they know how quickly his self-pity could turn to rage?

He paused near the entrance and, out of old habit, clocked the area. Never enter a place suddenly, observe what's around you, evidence of the enemy's presence, escape routes. The drill: burned into memory, recast as instinct. He spotted two top-of-the-line Land Cruisers, both with American diplomatic plates. A man lounging in the shadows nearby, a quiet watcher. What occasions this visit from the agents of the imperialist raj?

The restaurant was small, eight tables, six bar stools, the rich essences of garlic wafting from the kitchen. The food had much improved since Billy Balboa hired a Spanish chef. Slack eased his aching body onto a stool at the burnished bar and asked Billy for a double Ron Centenario with orange juice. Billy handed him a pile of old tabs instead, his bar bill unpaid since July.

"*Pura vida*. With sorrow I bring up a matter of two hundred thousand colones." Billy was pot-bellied and pale, his skin never touched by the tropical sun. Slack had once seen him sober, a few years ago, during national elections, when they padlock the bars.

"Billy, I've just had a day like the Battle of Stalingrad. I got robbed, my back is fucked, and I'm suicidal."

His voice had raised dangerously. Billy held up a hand in warning.

"So shoot yourself. I have big customers tonight, *personas de clase alta.*"

He brought out the bottle, topped up his drink, splashed some in a glass for Slack, and nodded along to the tale of his Falstaffian labours on the river, the pillaging of his house, an unbroken torrent of gloom.

The rain had begun to pummel the tile roof, drowning conversation. Slack looked around: a few familiar faces here, gringos, permanents, some illegal, hiding from *Migración*. Slack no longer had that problem, he was a citizen now, a legal, a Tico.

At a corner table, eating jumbo shrimp, those must be the big customers, diplomats, three men and two women. More careful scrutiny, however, revealed one of them to be a local blackguard, Juan Camacho, the mayor of Quepos. El Chorizo, they called him, he even looked like a sausage, mottled and soft and meaty.

"With Camacho, that is the U.S. ambassador and Senator Walker from Washington with their wives." Billy had to shout over the rain. "They are paying cash. They are not running a tab since five months."

Senator Chester Walker? Here? Chuck, he liked to be called, thicker of waist than he appeared on the tube, but a tall, ruggedly handsome man, you could mistake him for Charlton Heston. Soldier's haircut, metal grey, he'd be about sixty. Next to him in melting makeup, poured flawlessly into a tight dress, his wife, Gloria-May Walker, the former Vegas dancer.

What the hell were these banana Republicans doing in this far-flung outpost of their empire? Then he remembered – there'd been a conference in San José, something about Pan-American security, terrorism, he'd heard about it on the short-wave he no longer owned. A day off for sun and surf, Mayor Juan Camacho their guide to the hot spots of Manuel Antonio, looking for some way to shuck them.

Ex-Colonel Chuck Walker: Vietnam war hero, U.S. army secret ops, a dubious history of piloting America's undeclared war in Nicaragua. He was probably here to enhance his international image, he was about to make a run at the primaries, all the right noises, God, unborn babies, and the freedom to bear Uzis. A political lightweight, a dark horse, sitting on the far right rim of the Republican party.

The other man would be Ambassador Gerald Higgins, a presidential crony from the deep South, rewarded with a pleasant little trough in Latin America. Older, avuncular, good listener. Polite, tightly wrapped wife. The Secret Service agents were easy to spot, two at an adjoining table, one at the far end of the bar with a mug of coffee.

Slack was so absorbed by this sighting of a rare species that he paid little attention to a voice behind him, something in Spanish to Billy about a radio for sale. He slowly swivelled in his seat and saw a Sony twelve-band short-wave in the clutches of a skinny hand. The young man holding this radio was brazenly wearing one of Slack's T-shirts, "Mono Titi Tours, River and Ocean Kayaking." Slack had seen him hanging around the squat, Flaco, they called him, his nickname, thin enough to squeeze between bent bars. A crackhead like most of the local thieves, it showed in his eyes, his spastic movements.

"I am interested in that radio," he said.

Flaco paled, recognizing Slack, and he began to back-pedal as Slack slid off his stool. "I found it on the road! By the Boca Vieja bridge!" As Slack took one long step forward, Flaco peeled open the blade of a knife: it was Slack's, his Swiss Army knife, the *raton* had ripped that off, too.

Slack feinted, bobbed, caught Flaco by the wrist and twisted it, driving him to the floor with a scream of pain. He kicked the knife loose, then lifted him by the ankles and shook him like a salt dispenser until the birding binoculars and the cell phone fell from his pockets.

Slack retrieved them, along with the knife, and bent to Flaco and sliced through his belt. "Now I'm going to cut your *pinga* off." It would be a noble gesture in support of population control.

But Slack contented himself with jerking down Flaco's pants, shaming him, revealing the shrivelled apparatus of his sex. Still screaming, grabbing his crotch, the skinny thief scrambled out into the rain. The Secret Service guys stopped looking distressed, removed their hands from their jackets, humourless, not joining in the general laughter.

Billy Balboa put on a sour face, letting him know matters could have been handled more delicately, Slack wasn't good for business. But friends who'd enjoyed the show bought him drinks, and even the senator was smiling at him, maybe he liked the way Slack handled the natives. His wife kept staring at him, a contemplative smile as if she was sizing him up.

Slack treated his comrades in turn, generous, his credit was good here. Boisterous with drink, he launched into one of his harangues: this was a land where thievery was a respected way of life, the beaches unsafe, the cops crooked, mobs from Spain and Italy moving in, taking what that asshole Camacho over there wasn't keeping for himself, look at him truckling to the rich and powerful. The mayor was glancing at him, nervous. Slack realized he was fairly *borracho*, told himself to slow down, maintain some vestige of aplomb.

"I gotta see an ol' friend," he said, and pointed himself in the direction of the men's room, a route which took him near the senator and his group, he had to squeeze past Gloria-May Walker's chair.

"Looked like you had some training," Walker said. "Military?"

"Yeah, something like that."

"Well, keep it up, soldier." A resonant deep voice, it carried well and with authority.

"Damn rights," said Gloria-May Walker, "y'all keep it up now." Throaty, melodic, the sound of southern bells.

Juan Camacho tore his eyes off her tits and nodded curtly at Slack, a reluctant token of recognition. Sponging as usual, wolfing down U.S.

taxpayer jumbo shrimp, the mayor was behind the squatters, getting them electricity, water, padding himself with a prime cut of the land.

At the urinal, he felt unsteady, and he had to brace himself with a hand against the wall. He had better reduce his intake. Ocean tour tomorrow, bunch of aging jocks from Philadelphia, sports fishermen, they'd be bringing girls from San José. Two groups this week, he could pay down some of his debt.

He stood in front of the mirror, crouching to see the top of his head, the tousled red hair streaked with the rust of age, the four days' growth of beard. Looked like a scarecrow. *Le grand slaque*, the French had called him, gangly, loose-limbed, but now with the threat of a paunch.

Gloria-May Walker gave him a look as he squeezed by again, a skeptical raise of a lacquered eyebrow. The senator was carrying on in his bull-moose voice about how you can't give in to terrorists. "Once you start doing that, you're playing by their rules." The ambassador and his wife were nodding, machine-like, no disagreement there. Camacho forced himself to smile at Slack, who pantomimed a sloppy kiss in return. Slack leaned to Gloria-May Walker's ear. "You might want to warn the senator that guy owns the local whorehouse." She smelled good, he liked the way she laughed, a lusty chuckle.

He returned to his stool and to a refilled glass and watched as she whispered to her husband, repeating the calumny, he hoped. A few minutes later, she rose from the table and joined him at the bar. "I hear tell you're one of the local characters."

She was thirty-five, though looked younger: flawless tawny skin, sly wide eyes, golden hair. Her lips were large and fruity. Eager breasts thrust out above an hourglass waist, though the sands of recent time had trickled around her hips and rump.

"I've been around long enough to qualify."

She swung gracefully onto the next stool and told him everyone called her Glo. She and her husband had just come from a conference in San José that had bored her to her toes. Chuck was going to take her up to the Eco-Rico Lodge for their wedding anniversary — had he heard of it?

A luxury joint in which tenderfeet played at roughing it. "You'll like it. Lots of wildlife."

She slowly stretched a leg out for Slack to examine, then crossed it over her knee. "I feel so white next to you. Where do y'all buy a tan like that?"

Slack should have showered, he felt grungy. She seemed a little drunk, too; he guessed all this flirting was a game she played.

"So I hear y'all have some sort of river guiding enterprise."

He ordered himself to be sober. Might be able to sell a tour here, a senator and a diplomat, it could be lucrative.

"Ocean, too. Kayaks." Try not to slur.

"Sounds like a right nice way to pass a little time."

He was a sucker for a Southern accent. *Riot nass way to pass tahm.* "Nothing to it. Like riding in a big rubber ducky."

"Well, now, I think I might just get off taking a ride on your big rubber ducky."

Slack regained his balance after nearly slipping off his stool. He looked at Senator Walker, and their eyes locked briefly: a steely look like a warning. But the senator continued his monologue. Terrorists. He's an expert.

Slack held a match to Glo Walker's cigarette, and when his hand wavered, she cupped it in warm slender fingers. Again he smelled her, something expensive, something a honeybee would like. Slack wasn't going to get into anything here, this also smelled of peril.

"Chester's staying at this eco-joint only a couple of days, he has to get back to Washington for a vote. Then I'll be coming back here by myself."

She was about as subtle as a nail through the head. Chuck Walker was rising now, approaching them, his smile taut. A cuckold, obviously, an undesired quality in a politician, hinting of impotence, inability to deliver.

"Can I stand you another one, soldier?"

It wasn't until Slack was well into his latest double rum that he felt everything fall out of focus. He was vaguely aware the others had joined them, Ambassador Higgins and wife, Juan Camacho, wiping shrimp dip from his lips. Senator Walker had claimed his wife, his arm around her waist, and was continuing his oration, a jumble of words, a man obsessed: communism wasn't defeated by a policy of spineless pacifism, terrorists are the new world enemy, America wasn't going to stand for it, time to draw the line, can't neutralize the enemy without adopting a policy of acceptable loss.

It was the Pentagon bafflegab that finally got to Slack. "Terrorism has piss all to do with warfare," he heard himself saying, a slurred growl met by an abrupt heavy silence. "It's theatre. It's not aimed at the victims, it's aimed at the people watching, at the fucking CNN cameras." He was unable to brake his tongue, but suddenly he realized he didn't care, so he added, "Anyway, who's the terrorist when some damn schmuck in Baghdad or Belgrade gets his ass blown off by an air-launched missile?"

The discomfort at the bar was palpable. Eyes shifted away from him, a mistake had been made here, these solid pillars of America had engaged the wrong person, an ugly customer, some kind of agitator. A Secret Service agent was heaving into sight.

"He's just a drunk, señor, a beach bum." It was Camacho.

The last thing Slack remembered was rising to advance on Camacho, but in doing so falling off his stool. The rest wasn't clear . . .

— 2 —

At half past five, a defeated moon was turning pale and stars were dimming. The clouds had fled to the horizon, packing up like sandbags, a dam the sun would breach, already sending heralds of its coming, gentle daubs of peach and rose. Hermit crabs scuttled away and hid until the lumbering creature passed on, running barefoot on the silky sands of ebb tide.

Playa Espadilla, a mile from park entrance to Punta Quepos, thrice each way today, penance for the sins of the night – when, presumably, grave felonious acts had occurred. Slack tried to piece together the ugly scene. He had bruises on arms and shoulders, so more than words had been exchanged. The Secret Service agents had obviously got into it. He had an uncertain picture of one of them intervening when he'd made a grab for Camacho, whom he'd sent sprawling to the floor with a bloody nose. He remembered staring at a spinning ceiling fan. He had somehow got home. He had not been arrested. He wondered why.

A few bumps, some minor aches. A head-crunching hangover was the worst damage he had suffered, a self-inflicted wound, acceptable loss of brain cells. This morning he had found two hundred-dollar bills in his jeans pocket, how did they get there?

He moved onto the soft dry sand near the forest better to hear the songbirds awakening in the almond trees and mangroves, and turned to see the sun bulling above the massed cloud, slapping it with colour. Now Slack reached the western end of the beach, El Final, it was called, barred by a wall of rock and jungle, and here he turned to the ocean, he would swim the final mile.

"Let him go." Slack remembered Senator Walker giving that order. Why?

Slack stood panting at the water's edge, possessing this ephemeral moment, the canvas of ocean and sky, the jungle canopy kissed by sunlight, the whisper of the waves, a pair of sanderlings dipping at the surf's leavings.

He ducked a crashing wave and plunged into the water.

Three hours later, leading a herd of Philadelphia kayakers around the gentle rolling waters surrounding Punta Quepos, Slack was still pondering why he had not been arrested or had his face kicked in last night. Colonel Walker had commanded his troops: "Don't touch that soldier." Why?

It was hard work remembering, especially since his partner in the inflatable K-2 kept interrupting with the dozen questions most commonly asked. Where you from, anyway? How did you end up here? What's it cost to buy a chunk of this neck of the woods?

The talkative red-faced stout preferred to piddle with his paddle while Slack did all the work. Harry Wilder, that's his handle, pet food sales is his game, specializes in a line called Bow Wow Chow. Harry likes it down here. The girls are cheap, it beats Philadelphia.

"I wouldn't advise buying around here, it's going downhill. Full of thieves and squatters."

It was a dilemma. Do you try to earn enough *plata* to pay your bar bill, or save some wilderness by turning off the tourists? Costa Rica – everyone wants a piece.

"Now, out there by the park entrance, that's where you don't want to swim, it's an outlet, some of the hotels open their septic tanks in rainy season."

"They said it was safe to swim."

"What do you expect them to say?"

That shut Harry Wilder up.

Maybe he'd been saved from injury and arrest last night because the senator hadn't wanted to cause an even bigger scene.

No. Now he remembered.

"I'll tell you about fucking terrorists," he'd said. He had taken off his shirt, showed them the scars.

Dear Rocky,

How's that for an opening grabber? It's on its way, sucked bleeding from my soul, a shocker starring a neurotic beach bum and unsung poet. But the author's identity must be masked from Dr. Zork if he is to foil his evil plan to conquer the world – the nom de plume should be simple, jaunty, but hinting at a life lived dangerously. Harry . . . everyone loves a Harry. Harry Wilder, how about that? Zap, there he is, crawling from the pages with his bloodshot eyes and foul breath and twisted back.

I can hardly believe I have been so cheaply bought, selling out my art, pulping some fiction for your mingy two-K advance. I ask but one extra emolument: find me a goddamn publisher for *Hymns to a Dying Planet* – I don't care if it's a back-alley office – and get those poems into print before they rot of the sweat and tears that stain them.

Most of the ingredients for a convoluted page-turner are available locally, but your recipe also calls for blood, and I'm not sure if I can kill any more, Rock; I can't even step on a blade of grass without feeling guilt. If not blood, there's enough shit going on around here to feed the pigs of inspiration: clandestine airfields, roving bands of former Contras, Sicilian capos seeking to expand their empire, cops running the coke pipeline north. Throw in a few coral snakes, poisonous frogs, and rampaging peccaries, shake, stir, bake, and (if personal experience holds) the good guy gets to eat it in the end.

Or does he die at the beginning, crushed by an enormous writer's block? I finally figured out why I'm a slow starter, Rocky. I suffer the poet's curse, the obsessive need for the perfect phrase, flawless, pure, and I get stuck on the opening line. It doesn't sound right. "Recumbent on the floor, staring at a spinning ceiling fan, Harry Wilder tried to figure out when he'd first become an alcoholic." Recumbent, as a word, does not sing.

Other reasons for this long delay in faxing you: my back is killing me, I'm still recovering from a bruised heart, and I'm becoming a raving maniac. But I finally managed to haul out my old Underwood. Despair inspires.

As you read through my rough initial pages you will observe there has been some early action drawn from a blurred eyewitness account. (The last man standing was not our hero, who, lacking his usual grace, slipped from a stool and banged his head against the bar en route to neutralizing the enemy with new warfare options.)

But do we not have possibilities? A high-ranking politician, his sultry wife, the brooding Harry Wilder. A hero for the ages! Enough angst to fill a septic tank. The final essential ingredient, the ravishing heroine, is more troublesome. What are we looking for here? – a shy hidden flower plucked from danger and pressed to brave Harry's lips? Or should she be a bold, hot copy of Gloria-May Walker? Frankly, what Harry needs is good old home cooking – give him someone who can make cabbage rolls, give him someone to love, unadorned, unaffected.

Look over this initial offering, fax me at the post office, Apartado 92, and tell me if it can suck enough air to stay afloat.

Happy Hanukkah,

Jacques.

— 3 —

It was four-thirty when Slack rose from his siesta, awakened by the *precaria* dogs, a bitch in heat, a posse of suitors in braying pursuit. He groaned, stretched, looked out at the neighbouring slum. A television set was on full volume over there, booming out an afternoon soap. Mayor Camacho had bribed installers from ICE, the power company, to bring electricity to his subdivision. Though Slack ran his kitchen on propane, the rest of the house was solar, he'd be damned if he'd hook up to the line, hydro power spews tons of carbon dioxide into the atmosphere.

He wanted to eat out, but he was broke again. A month ago he'd had two grand sitting in his account, but he'd drained it today, dropped off a cheque to Billy Balboa, a gesture of penance for last night. He couldn't even afford a helper's wages, he had no one to haul his boats. Then he remembered the two hundred dollars that had mysteriously appeared in his pocket . . . Where had it come from?

He made ready to go out, paused, thought of celebrating his good fortune with a small tot, but then remembered his resolution. He was not going to become one of those *norteamericanos* who come down here and rot from the inside out. Jungle fever, they call it. Not for Slack Cardinal.

As he was about to lock up, his cell phone rang.

"You standing me up, honey?"

Gloria-May Walker. The shock he felt was like touching a hot wire.

"What happened to our sunset cruise?"

Two hundred dollars – she'd paid triple, and in advance. "Where are you?"

"All by my lonely old lonesome outside your empty office."

∾

Slack had told her to meet him at the park end of the beach, and he raced there, his inflatable roped to the top of his Land Rover. He had no memory of it, but he must have given her his card.

He parked behind a Mitsubishi four-wheel rental, her car, he guessed. No official vehicles around. Had she slipped the watchers? It's the cocktail hour, the senator would be wondering why she wasn't beside him with her gin fizz.

There she was on the wet sand, barefoot, a bikini under something gauzy that fluttered in the wind, showing off her Vegas legs. She turned to watch him as he dragged the kayak down to the sand, her hands on her hips, a kind of sexy smirk. This was the kind of woman he feared, aggressive, high expectations.

"So what do I get for my dough?"

"A two-hundred-dollar sunset and an hour and a half of hard paddling."

"And you guarantee the sunset?"

"Yeah. But it goes down fast here."

"And then what? Comes up just as quick in the morning?"

Innuendo was flying thick and heavy, she'd somehow decided he was for sale, a gigolo, a whore.

She removed her wrap, tucked it in the kayak's sealed hatch. She looked good in just two bits of cloth. He strapped on her life jacket, his hand recoiling when it brushed one of her breasts. He helped her into the front seat and shoved off, the K-2 rising on a swell as he clambered in behind her.

"I've only got time for a fast sunset, anyway, sweetie. Dinner at seven." The Walkers were at the Si Como No, southern California elegant.

Gloria-May seemed fit, she wielded a mean paddle, he assumed she did aerobics, something like that. He would take her around Punta Catedral, maybe dip between the islets. He wanted to ask if Senator Walker knew that she had contracted him for this sporting event.

The sun began to send shafts of colour far across to the high cirrus in the east, the puffballs above the horizon pinking around the edges. The grumble of the surf grew dimmer, and the sounds now were just the splosh of the paddles and Gloria-May humming old show tunes. A line of pelicans wove above the swells, one dive-bombed into the water, rose again, thrashing from the sea, water pouring from its beak, a fish tail waggling.

They stopped to watch, then Glo turned to him, a large, full-lipped smile. "You're hiding out here, aren't you?"

Slack felt a twinge in his back as he resumed paddling. "Without apparent success." Where had she heard this?

"What's your real name?"

"Harry Wilder."

"I surely don't think so. Chester had his security geek look you up on the computer. Leftist shit-disturbing poet, busted for sedition or some damn thing, went underground, settled in Cuba, and got yourself kicked out of there because you wouldn't toe the party line."

She had the whole book, Slack was shocked. Chester must have friends high in the CIA, getting his information that fast. Then in the course of pillow talk he pours it all out to his indiscreet wife.

"You did a political turnaround, or at least that's what the CIA thought when they recruited you."

Blackmailed into the job, press-ganged, threatened with twenty years in the brig on that false sedition rap. Walker's geek obviously had top-level clearance, he'd been allowed into the secure files, searched the alias. *Cardinal, see Sawchuk. Warning, restricted access.*

"Infiltrated terrorist squads in Paris and the Middle East, I hear tell. Chester says after a dozen years you got so confused you couldn't figure out which side you were on." She laughed. The woman was full-throttle blunt, telling tales from the bedroom, critiquing his sterling record of service.

"Yeah, I couldn't find my way in from the cold. This is just a kayak tour, it doesn't come complete with the story of my life."

She was paddling again, silent for a moment as she gazed at the sky dancing with the blushing hues of sunset.

"Who are you hiding from?"

"The Saudis, Iraqis, the Red Brigades, the CIA, and Harry Wilder." They'd given him new ID, fifty thousand Ben Franklins, and a one-way ticket to Costa Rica.

"Who's Harry Wilder?"

"You mean he's not on the computer, too? His cover is pet food sales, he specializes in Bow Wow Chow."

"Well, aren't you just so full of bullshit."

She went silent momentarily, picked up her stroke as the sun flattened blimp-like beyond the ends of the earth. A green spark as it sank.

"The green flash," she said. "Heard somewhere only lovers see it."

Slack said nothing.

She was relentless: "Chester says y'all got into some kind of screw-up with the French government, that's why you got pensioned off."

"Let me ask you something. Does Chester talk in his sleep, or does he just have a loose tongue?"

"He doesn't think it's a big deal. It's history, honey, the cold war's over." Again she turned, a big smile. "Anyway, my lips are sealed." But they were slightly parted, plump, inviting. "I'll keep your secret, you keep mine."

"Which is?"

"I'm not here. They're in a meeting. They haven't missed me, so don't worry."

"Do I look like I'm worrying?"

"All the time."

"It's getting dark, I think we should head back." He swung the kayak around. She didn't argue, and they headed toward shore.

As they neared the breakers, she said, "Well, now, I surely did enjoy this kayaking experience, so how about the river next time? Or that lagoon thing y'all advertise. Can we do that when I get back from the Eco-Rico Lodge? Think you can pencil me in, secret agent?"

Slack began to wonder if she was just teasing him, enjoying his discomfort. He had to admit she was entertaining, quick on the uptake.

When they slowed to surf the first breaker, she dove into the water and began swimming to the beach. He tried to follow her in the boat, but she grabbed his arm, spilling him. Kayak, Slack, and Senator Chuck Walker's wife were swept onto the foaming beach, and when the waters ebbed he found her sprawled on top of him. She was laughing, tugging at her wayward bikini top.

As Slack helped her up, he spotted, on the road, one of the Land Cruisers the Americans were using, a black guy leaning against it, glaring at him, one of the steely-eyed watchers from the bar. Slack escorted Gloria-May to the road, where she blew him an imprudent kiss and got into her Mitsubishi.

Slack wondered if the Secret Service also kept secrets. Probably not from Senator Walker. Maybe he should close up shop for a week, hide out in San José until she winged her way home. He could still smell her scent, her salty sweaty skin.

On his way home he bought a fifth of Ron Rico, something for his pain. Tomorrow, he promised, tomorrow he would quit this nasty habit.

THE TREASURE OF SAVAGE RIVER

— I —

Maggie, in a foul temper, glared at the two-propeller aircraft on the tarmac outside the SANSA building – it was to have departed an hour ago, at eight a.m., and Maggie's fellow passengers were grumbling. In a better mood she might have considered this lack of punctuality a quaint national trait, but there was little today that she found endearing about Costa Rica. That oily fanny-pack picker . . . The plunge from rapture to wretchedness was total; never in her life had she felt so degraded and betrayed.

The university switchboard ought to be open by now. After seeking instructions for the pay phone, she dialled, finally connecting with a history lecturer who confirmed that no Professor Pablo Esquivel was on faculty. Why had this crook been in the library? – a place of learning seemed an odd location to seek out his victims. How could she have been so naïve? Had she not heard stories about ingenuous tourists being fleeced by Latin swindlers? Frieda Lisieux, the CSKN weather reporter, had fallen prey to such a one in Mexico, her misadventure a source of callous humour at the station.

Now, eight hundred dollars out of pocket, Maggie would have to scrimp like a miser – but at least the next four days were paid for, including overnight lodging in a beach town called Quepos and the two-hour taxi ride to the Eco-Rico Lodge. Her remaining consolation was that she would enjoy literary revenge, recasting Pablo Esquivel as a fictional villain. Sleepless for hours with anger last night,

Maggie had written furiously, recording every word of every sentence spoken, their entire interaction, even her fumbling missteps and the sensations she had felt during those two deep kisses.

A lost Spanish mission with its buried treasure: bullshit. She should have realized his tale was too tall to be true. She was stunned at how silky he had been, how adept with his hands. Why would a classy operator waste time with such small change as she? Or maybe he *had* believed she was rich and famous.

"Quepos, Quepos, Quepos." A man was calling out like a train conductor and collecting boarding passes. Maggie and another dozen passengers scurried outside, where a heavy rain had begun to fall. Her destination, pronounced Kay-pos, lay beyond those cloud-sheathed mountains ringing the Central Valley. She knew any effort to summon Dr. Rajwani's rules would be wasted, her ire and sense of desolation swamped every other concern. Last evening, she had dared believe she was attractive to that man . . .

As the plane groaned into the skies, Maggie sat stiffly in her seat, her eyes closed, but she couldn't blot out Pablo Esquivel, his black, calculating eyes. When she looked out, the aircraft was sailing through a mountain pass, straight into a cloud. A few seconds later, she gasped as they suddenly burst into sunlight. Below her she could see a coastal plain beyond which the blue waters of the ocean stretched to an endless horizon. The aircraft curled toward a narrow asphalt strip and touched down gently.

Maggie stepped off the plane into a wall of wet heat. By the time she reached the bus sitting by the small terminal building, she felt damp with it, heavy with the weight of this thick, hot, aromatic climate. She was about to encounter her first tropical beach – she should brace up, banish this dark mood. She tried to persuade herself that now the true holiday would begin; she should not permit one awful night to plunge her in gloom for two entire weeks.

The rickety tourist bus jounced her down a twisting road between groves of trees and fields where spindly horses grazed. Quepos arrived suddenly, unexpected, a crosshatch of streets behind an earth dike. She got off the bus by a soccer field, hoisted her backpack, and set off to find the Kamuk Hotel, walking past wooden-framed buildings offering food, drink, gifts, and window arrangements of pots, shoes, sunglasses, floor wax, and plastic Christmas decorations. Every third or fourth door seemed to lead to a dingy saloon filled with sad-eyed men.

Her hotel sat across from the dike and offered a pool, a pair of restaurants, and a small casino. She was shown to an air-conditioned third-floor room that looked onto a well-treed boulevard and, beyond it, the dike and an estuary, where gaily coloured fishing boats bobbed: a pretty picture that allayed her gloom for a moment.

How could Pablo have been attracted to her? A handsome character like that . . . He had seen her exactly for what she was: a lonely rube from the boondocks of the frozen north seeking a little Latin excitement.

She was determined to snap out of her foul mood. Yes, she was going to have fun, fun, fun. It would be an adventure, living simply and stretching those colones. She would start with a dip in the Pacific Ocean. And why taxi to the beach when she could mingle with the locals on the bus? Anyway, she should be flattered that such an attractive man would even bother to steal from her. *Think positively.*

She showered, then slathered sunblock; she was as white as the Canadian snows. After slipping shorts and T-shirt over her bathing suit, she belted on her fanny pack and abandoned the shelter of her cool room.

The sight of an absurdly long lineup in a bank dissuaded her from cashing a traveller's cheque; she had enough colones for the day. Downtown Quepos extended for only a few blocks, and she quickly spotted the bus station at the centre; the beaches of Manuel Antonio were twenty minutes away.

But the heat made her thirsty, and the prospect of a cold beer tempted her into an open-air bar. From her outer table, she watched the passing parade: a street seller wheeling a cart loaded with bags of fresh shrimp; the town drunk, staggering and accosting strangers; a local law enforcer with a billy club on his belt, scratching his groin and looking none too sober himself.

The waiter spoke to her in Spanish. She indicated one of the bottles on the table next to her, where two men and a woman were in loud conversation. A chilled Pilsen quickly arrived; it tasted agreeably like Canadian beer. She tuned into the threesome at the next table: expatriates, she guessed, running local businesses.

"He's got rocks for balls."

"Slack's a tank."

"Yeah, a pisstank, man. A walking fucking disaster when he gets juiced up."

"I heard he laid El Chorizo out on the ambassador's lap."

The laughter seemed malicious. Slack Cardinal was a name they kept mentioning, apparently a drunken brawler.

"Saw him taking out a group this morning; he looked like a head-on collision. How come Slack never got busted over that?"

"Beats me."

A few minutes later, as Maggie was window-shopping while waiting for her bus, her eye was caught by a display of snapshots of tourists in inflatable kayaks. In one picture, the white-water rafters looked scared; it seemed like poor advertising.

"Mono Titi Tours, River and Ocean Kayaking," said the sign. She doubted she could afford it. "Jacques (Slack) Cardinal, gerante, manager," read a smaller sign. Good Lord, here was her Jacques, not at all like the man she'd imagined: the flesh-and-blood Jacques, alias Slack, was the infamous local tank. She would definitely take a pass on any kayak trip. Now she saw the scrawled note behind the door window: "Closed until creativity restored."

The message was too enigmatic for her.

The grunting bus was crowded. Maggie gave up her seat for a pregnant woman and caught only glimpses of the ocean until the bus stopped near the beach. She got off and made her way between stalls of vendors offering fruit and juices. She bore straight for the water and did not pause until a tongue of an expiring wave licked her foot, then she removed her sandals and felt her toes sink into the wet, golden sand.

The visual banquet spread before her was so beyond her experience that she could not take it all in. She removed her glasses, fogged them, cleaned them, then slowly surveyed the long curve of beach at low tide, the canopied jungle promontory abutting it, the rocky islets in the distance, their sheer walls topped with green brush cuts, waves crashing, birds calling, a rich humid salty smell suffusing the air. The bleak prairies had not prepared her for such sensory extravagance.

She strolled along, her feet splashing through waves as they petered out by the tide line. Sandpipers scattered before her, regrouped, and flew off again on stiff, beating wings. She studied the tall, cresting waves, which had attracted several surfboarders. Though Maggie was a strong swimmer she decided to seek out the quieter beaches of the nearby national park; she had never swum in an ocean before and worried about currents.

At a wooden booth, she paid an entrance fee and was handed a brochure, then made her way to a placid stretch of beach – a scimitar of soft sand cupping a bay of blue-green water and fringed with leafy trees twisting toward the shore. Behind her rose the virgin jungle of Manuel Antonio Park.

Her new-found bliss shattered when, out of nowhere, like an unexpected burp, came Pablo Esquivel's sugary words. *You are unlike some of the empty-headed women I have been forced to know.* She felt seared; no one's head had been emptier than hers. Here, however, was medicine for her soul: the sweet healing waters of the ocean. She laid out a towel, shucked her shorts and T-shirt, tucked her glasses in her pack, and ran, arms flailing, into the tropical sea. The warmth of the water felt almost sinful.

After several minutes of a leisurely swim, and a longer time letting the surf toss her aimlessly like clothes in a washer, she began to chide herself for her glumness. What an idiot she had been: the stereotypical naïve tourist; Pablo must have seen her coming a mile down Rural Route Two.

But adversity was not without its rewards; Pablo had inspired an admirably villainous foil for her heroine's affections. Even if spurious, his story of a lost mission was a plot that might even be worth eight hundred dollars, plus the bill for the meal and the tip. She would steal from the thief: he held no copyright on his tale of buried Spanish treasure. Several weekends of toil at the University of Saskatchewan library would bring Captain Morgan and the sack of Panama into bold relief.

As she bobbed in the waves, she felt her spirits rising on the wings of inspiration. She would refashion her novel – every second of last evening would be recreated for *The Torrid Zone*. (Will the worldly Dr. Fiona Wardell be seduced into the rascal's bed? Will he slip away with the treasure map?)

For this conceit to succeed, however, the heroine must become more Maggie-like; Fiona, once so graceful and lithe, will find herself slightly uncoordinated: if not an endearing trait, this will add verisimilitude. The early chapters will reek of authenticity; the characters will jump from the pages. Her bad encounter could well have been a lucky turn of fate: a career-enhancing soft collision between woman and man.

After playing in the waves for half an hour, Maggie crawled onto her towel and brought out her notepad, feeling perkier, more like Maggie Poppins. She was intrigued by the concept of reshaping Fiona in her own image. *Creative Writing 403: Seek character in yourself.* Perhaps, in doing so, she will find a pathway to the meaning of love, discover the elusive glue that binds woman and man. (Surely that overpowering rush she felt last night was a false symptom, brought on by deceit, a fleeting thing, almost forgotten now.)

She must create a role for her hero. *Only one other person knew the upper reaches of the Savage River.* Just as Fiona had begun to metamorphose, so would Jacques; someone of a different mould was now required. Discard these: intellectual, debonair, suave – those were the qualities of the scoundrel Esquivel. Jacques must be roughly hewed, a seemingly hopeless cause, turned dissolute by dejection. She wrote down the name, "Jacques Cardinal."

Closed until creativity restored. Decoded, that probably meant he was too sick to work today. A tank who looked like a head-on collision seemed an unlikely choice for male lead, but if she was to confound the sniggering critics of her genre, why should he not be cut of the roughest cloth? She hoped the real Cardinal would not sue her for libel; though from what she had heard of his reputation, he could not claim much of a case.

☙

Discouraged almost to the point of abandoning her explorations, Fiona summoned the fortitude to enter one last tavern, as usual smelling of must and stale spirits and urine, where she found him leaning against the bar, his only companion a bottle of gin.

"You're Jacques Cardinal, aren't you?"

"Slack," he said, slurring the name. "That's what they call me around here."

He did not turn to her, but continued to gaze motionless into his glass. Her impression was of a man defeated by life's challenges. He was wiry and nearly as tall as she, a mat of dark curls atop his head and a rough scrape of beard darkening his jaw; and he was in a high state of intoxication.

"I am told you know the Savegre River."

"Only too well."

"You have been up to the headwaters. To the mission site."

He finally raised his eyes, and regarded her reflection in the mirror behind the bar. "I was with your father ten years ago. Yes, we looked for it."

"You know who I am, then."

"He showed me your picture a thousand times. Proud of you. Must feel good to have pride in something." A thick, sardonic laugh, and he saluted her in the mirror with his raised glass, then drained it.

"Dad used to say there aren't many geniuses left in the field. He also said you're one of them."

"Forget the Savegre. There's no point. No point in anything."

She slid the bottle from his reaching hand. "How about a walk in the fresh air, Dr. Cardinal?"

He finally turned toward Fiona, and with one eye closed, because otherwise he seemed unable to focus, he undertook a long examination of her, his

*declining gaze finally settling upon the long toes protruding from her sandals.
As his eye commenced an equally slow return journey he grunted in what
Fiona took to be approval. "But I'm still not taking you up the Savegre."*

*"We'll talk about it." As she tugged his arm, one of her feet became entan-
gled in a stool; she lost her balance and fell against him in ungainly fashion.
He laughed. "Where'd you take your ballet lessons?"*

*Close up, he smelled rancid. "I'm putting you under a shower," she said.
"Only if you'll join me."*

— 2 —

The barest blush of dawn was in the east, and outside Maggie's hotel
one of the streetlights sputtered, flashing orange, then yellow, on an
old dog slumbering on the sidewalk. This was Quepos in the warm,
empty hours of night: lag-behind and weary, grumbling in its sleep.

Maggie looked up the street impatiently. Where was her driver?
Ticos may rebel against the governance of time, but the *National
Geographic* expects a certain degree of promptness. Maybe the Eco-
Rico Lodge had discovered her ruse and cancelled the taxi.

She gazed up at the reverse-angle Big Dipper, and the eyes of
Pablo Esquivel seemed to twinkle at her; but with a pleasant day
behind her and an adventure ahead, she found his image easier to
bear. Such an engaging man . . . Had the night been extended, she
would have gone to bed with him; she knew that absolutely. In a way,
she wished it had happened: for the novel, of course . . . *She looked up
from her book-signing table and again, after so many years, felt herself drawn
into those coal-black eyes. "Now you are rich and famous, señorita. See what
I have done for you."*

Finally, a boxy red four-wheel taxi pulled up. The driver, stout
and short and seeming still half-asleep, asked, "You the lady for the
Eco-Rico Lodge?"

Maggie agreed that she was, hoisted her pack in, then climbed
aboard. The driver introduced himself as Guillermo Brenes and asked,
"You know where is this place?"

"You've never been there?"

"No problem. We find it."

As they pulled out of town, a rosy light began to permeate the eastern sky, enough to illuminate Maggie's map: the route to the fabled Savegre, then up into the mountains. She would be navigator. They drove between seemingly endless plantations of African palms, the road unerringly straight but poorly gravelled and scarred with bumps and ruts. Maggie made her first sighting of a king vulture, striking in white and black, which barely raised its harlequin head from its roadkill feast as the taxi lumbered past. Small villages drifted by, neatly laid out: company towns, said Brenes, whom she was trying to keep alert with questions.

But at one point, after a lull in conversation, he almost swerved off the road, and Maggie had to grab the steering wheel and shake him awake.

He apologized. "You got five kids at home you no sleep too good."

To keep Brenes awake, she prodded him into talking about his home life. It was a litany of grief: he was supporting not only his five children with his current partner, but four from a failed marriage and two from other relationships. He hammered nails all day and drove cab all night to make ends meet. She supposed he was trying to fatten the tip.

Maggie feared that the four days ahead promised to be more nerve-racking than entertaining unless she quickly confessed her deceit. But what could she say to Senator Walker, who wanted his picture in the *Geographic*? "I told Mr. Jericho I would *try* to sell an article. Between you and me, I think he was on drugs." No, she would be honest; they would not have the heart to send her back.

They came to a long, narrow concrete bridge spanning a river. This was the Savegre: swollen from the rains and rushing turbulently to the sea, a much smaller river than the wide meandering South Saskatchewan. How far into the mountains would Spanish missionaries have built their settlement? The padres would have wished to distance themselves from marauding pirates. *The Treasure of Rio Savegre* would be her title, it had more punch than *The Torrid Zone*.

Where a smaller road turned off beside the river, Maggie saw an Eco-Rico sign. "Why they have hotel up here?" Brenes said. "No beach. Is crazy." They ascended past plantations of papayas and bananas and spindly yucca to an almost deserted village with the apt name of Silencio. The narrow, humped road seemed to disappear at the eastern bank of the river, but it was wide and shallow here, and Brenes gunned his car across, sending spumes of waves. Then they toiled up into the hills high above the churning river, the road now just two dirt tracks.

For the next hour, Maggie frequently held her breath as their route took them up a red-clay track that clung to the side of a mountain, the views both dazzling and terrifying. At one point she could see directly down the rubble of an old landslide above the Savegre River. She cast a look at Brenes to ensure her exhausted driver was still fully awake. "*Temblor,*" he said. "Earthquake."

The country grew wilder — there were no farms up here, or even signs of habitation, just forest, an undulating canopy below them, trees and lianas flowering yellow and violet, the valley a vast bouquet. Maggie felt disoriented; she was used to flat lines, uninterrupted horizons, a monochrome palette.

The track grew steadily worse and finally became just a foot path where a fence of living tree posts and barbed wire met a gate bearing another Eco-Rico sign. Standing by this outpost of civilization, incongruously, were two men in crisply pressed shorts, a third man who was older and unshaven, and a young woman, about twenty-five.

After Maggie retrieved her backpack, the woman shook her hand. "Hi, we've been waiting for you; these folks want the cab. You're the writer, aren't you? My name's Celeste Nieuwendoork; my husband's the manager." She was nearly a foot shorter than Maggie, pretty in a cherubic way, with a nervous smile.

The three men tossed their bags into the trunk and climbed in the taxi; the older one was carrying a laptop. "You won't find a story here," he told Maggie. "Wake me up when it's all over."

"It's the driver you want to keep awake," Maggie said. A yawning

Guillermo Brenes had to reverse a few times to make his U-turn, but was soon on his way.

The man with the computer was a reporter for the *Miami Herald*, Celeste explained; the other two were Secret Service agents. "Senator Walker told them, 'I'm giving you boys an order – go have fun at the beach.' He's such a super guy."

Maggie hoped so; she should simply apologize to Mr. Walker for her chicanery and appeal to his apparent good humour.

Beyond the gate, a few metres up the path, stood a Ford tractor to which was hitched a cart with wooden seats. "It's not much of a luxury bus, I'm afraid," Celeste said. She had insisted on carrying Maggie's pack, but just as she was about to lift it onto the cart, she paled and leaned against its wooden slats; Maggie thought the woman was about to be ill.

"A little morning sickness. I'm okay."

Maggie steadied her. "Take slow deep breaths. Congratulations."

"It's scary when there are no doctors around. This is scary, too." Celeste gestured helplessly toward the tractor. "Going down wasn't so bad, but . . . I can barely drive a car. We're so busy; I had to be pressed into service."

"Want me to drive?"

Celeste smiled wanly, apparently assuming Maggie was joking. "If you're nervous, we could walk. Though it's a thousand metres up, and you have to be careful. There are snakes." She made a face. "Jan says there are hardly any and they keep to themselves, but I've seen a few."

"I was driving a tractor when I was ten." Maggie climbed up, got behind the wheel, turned on the ignition, and the engine rumbled loudly into life. "Ran a combine at twelve." She pulled Celeste up beside her onto the big roomy seat.

"What's a combine?"

"Where are you from, Celeste?"

A brownstone in Boston, she said. A year ago, as a graduation gift, her generous father arranged an Eco-Rico holiday for Celeste and an Ivy League girlfriend. Celeste found romance with the manager, Jan Nieuwendoork. He proposed; they married.

She was an open woman, an eager talker who seemed impressed by Maggie's tractor expertise; it was needed – this was a narrow path with many hills and turns. It was not as if she was pulling a disc harrow, but on the inclines, Maggie felt the engine straining.

The Eco-Rico camp, Celeste said, accommodated sixteen guests, but it would be half empty after today. The ambassador and his staff were flying out that morning, and most of the senator's aides would leave after lunch. Two Secret Service men would remain with Senator Walker and his wife, along with his campaign manager, his media officer, and a reporter for Associated Press.

"We have only seven plus you, so there's plenty of room. Oh, dear."

A deluge! – a wall of rain that soaked them to the skin. Just as suddenly, a few minutes later, the tap was turned off and the sun emerged, sucking up mists from the foliage. Maggie was not used to such fast shifts; it seemed a paranormal weather experience.

From the lush, coloured woods came a loud turmoil of insects and birds. At home, even in spring, she might be lucky to hear a meadowlark; here countless voices were raised. The gap between the mountains gradually widened, and when they crested a rise, a valley was spread luxuriantly before her. It was shaped like a pair of butterfly wings; at its indentation, a long spindly waterfall splashed down a wall of almost sheer rock, reformed itself as a small river, and raced toward a far outlet of the valley. A rainbow wove through the mist wreathing a mountain.

Almost out of breath with exhilaration, Maggie stopped the tractor. "That's so beautiful."

"You get used to it."

How could she be so blasé?

They drove downhill toward a cluster of handsome guest cottages set in ornamental gardens: sturdy post and beam, wide thatch-roofed porches, tall screened windows, and solar panels on every roof. Behind them was a barn-like utility shed from which Maggie could hear the putt-putt of a generator. The buildings were distributed within an oval clearing where workers were chopping at the grass with machetes. Two helicopters were parked there.

"We'll put you up in what we call the Jungle House. Make sure you close all the doors at night to keep out the . . . you know, animals. Lunch at twelve – the dining hall's in the lodge." Celeste indicated a central building with a high-peaked metal roof supported by thick varnished tree trunks and enclosed by a wide balcony.

Beyond the lodge, where the valley tapered to a bottleneck, Maggie could see a narrow suspension bridge strung between the trees. "That takes you right over the canopy to the other side and a lovely hike up to a hot springs. There are so many trails, but you always need a guide. Jan will be doing a slide show this afternoon."

As Maggie pulled in by the side of the lodge, she saw several people boarding one of the helicopters – the ambassador and his retinue.

A man of stringy build and stringier hair came quickly toward them, looking none too pleased that a guest had been allowed to operate the heavy machinery. Jan Nieuwendoork shook Maggie's hand while Celeste gushed an explanation – she had felt ill; Ms. Schneider was raised on a farm in Canada and knew all about tractors.

Nieuwendoork looked relieved, though he seemed preoccupied. "And you have come to write a story about us?" The accent was Dutch, but barely noticeable.

Their exchange was interrupted by the clatter of propellers. They watched as the helicopter lifted off, then Maggie followed her hosts up a winding path through dense foliage to the Jungle House, a narrow wooden structure with a thatch roof. Celeste showed her to the bedroom loft above the living area and left her alone to unpack. While hanging her clothes Maggie was entertained by two small lizards bobbing at each other, their air bags expanded: male territorial display, no doubt. What other creatures were sharing this luxurious hideaway? She was glad of the mosquito net suspended above the bed.

She started when she heard a creak from her front balcony. Outside her screen door, looking in, was a square-jawed black man with intense eyes that were examining her as if collating data. He introduced himself as Ralph Johnson, U.S. Secret Service.

"Well, you're a little too secretive."

"We have to check out everyone. Mind if I look through your things?"

"Sure, go ahead." She was in trouble: an untrustworthy character with no proof she was here to write an article.

But he was not looking for papers. He shuffled through her backpack and flight bag with quick expert hands, examining the camera carefully, as if for hidden incendiary devices.

"No pictures of the copter, please, nor of anyone in the senator's party without prior arrangement. I'm not going to make an issue of it, but we know you're not with the *Geographic*. The TV station you work for says you're a highly unlikely terrorist, and the senator doesn't want to raise an embarrassing ruckus over your cancelled reservation."

It came to her that Senator Walker probably had little choice but to be seen as magnanimous, of presidential timber – there was an AP correspondent at the lodge.

"I'm sorry, but I paid a lot of money to come here. I just got my fanny pack picked for eight hundred dollars more."

Though he listened with sympathy to her plight, he seemed more interested in the cover art on one of her Nancy Ward romances: a beguiling enchantress not-quite fending off a shirtless man.

"These some of your books, Miss Schneider?"

"Take that one with you if you like. It's about a photojournalist who aimed her camera at all the wrong men – but one – and the camera couldn't see the unbearable secret he harboured within." Her mimicry of the dustjacket blurb brought a smile, but he declined the book. "Please thank Senator Walker. Oh, and tell him his gesture will be mentioned when I sell this story to a travel magazine with a circulation of millions."

Johnson was studying her with new-found respect. "Actually, ma'am, the senator's press aide may have some ideas along those lines. Mr. Walker doesn't seem too happy about the poor coverage this vacation is getting."

The walkway to the lodge was bordered with hibiscus; bougainvillea was in riotous bloom by the entrance. Barn swallows glided gracefully above the eaves, swooped about the open area. Several inviting hammocks were strung between porch beams, and in one of them, a middle-aged man in a baseball cap was making notes and filling an ashtray with butts. She guessed he was the AP reporter.

The central area of the lodge was open, offering shelves of books, reading chairs, tables for pool and ping-pong, and maps and enlarged nature photographs on the walls. Ralph Johnson was seated by the partially open door of an adjoining room, from which issued a murmur of conversation. Soft squawks were sounding from a CB radio on a shelf.

Johnson pointed her to the dining hall, where, standing by a massive hand-hewed banquet table, a waiter was tending to its lone patron. A red hibiscus was in this woman's hair, a cigarette in one hand, a half-full glass in the other, a bottle of tonic by it. She beckoned Maggie with a brisk, insistent wave. Maggie recognized her from the glossies: Gloria-May Walker.

"You come right over here, sweetie." *Riot ovah heah.* "You are the sly one, you are, Maggie Schneider from Saskatoon." Obviously, she knew about Maggie's subterfuge. "I'm Glo Walker from the equally odd-named town of Tuscaloosa." She clasped Maggie's hand firmly, and drew her into a chair beside her. "Miguel, don't just stand there, fetch the lady a damn drink."

Skinny Miguel looked nervous and confused. She addressed him loudly in pidgin Spanish: "Por favor, una gin and tonic for la señorita."

"I get."

Maggie would have preferred a coffee, but Mrs. Walker seemed not the kind of person with whom one argues.

"When I saw you pull in on the tractor, I just knew you were the kind of spunky gal I'd be able to team up with, Maggie. I am head-sore with boredom dealing with all the inflated male egos around here. It's all dicks and jocks, except for that sweet little college girl – what's her name, Celeste? – and I am not comfortable with pregnant women. I don't know why – maybe it's the unending palaver about the joy of being with child. The whole concept gives me the willies."

Maggie was not prepared for a personality so forthright, so genially bumptious. She knew that Gloria-May had been raised on an impoverished farm, but it was a farm nonetheless, so she lacked city pretension. She had ambition and intelligence, too: she had earned a college degree after her marriage.

When Miguel brought Maggie's drink, Gloria-May ordered another for herself. All Maggie could do was sip silently, barely able to breach the torrent of words. "Chester told me everything, about how they were fucking rude to y'all, a famous writer, cancelling your reservation. And how you cleverly outsmarted them."

"I'm about as famous as a lump of cheese, Mrs. Walker."

"Glo does fine. And please don't be modest – that sounds so Canadian, honey. I truly admire what you do, writing romance novels. Serves a fundamental need, the way I look at it. Dick Do-nothing is glued to the couch watching the Rams and Bulls, so you either take a good book to bed or a vibrator."

"For what it's worth, *Romance Journal* said my last one started off too hot and went limp."

"Been there, honey."

"Can I ask what you and your husband are doing here? Or is that a state secret?"

"We're *supposed* to be celebrating our seventh anniversary. I told Chester, bring in that writer, someone who works with her head, I'm surrounded by brainless political hacks. Thank the Lord, he's sending most everyone away. Ever since he announced for president it's been like a football team following us around. No wonder Chester can barely hoist the flag up the pole."

Maggie was shocked that she could speak so blithely of her husband's performance in the conjugal bed. She had always assumed a politician's spouse would be coyly close-mouthed, but salty-tongued Gloria-May had once been a show dancer in freewheeling, fast-talking

Las Vegas. Maggie had trouble envisioning her as the First Lady of the U.S.A.

Gloria-May's flow of words continued unabated, and Maggie began to enjoy her candour. It was all gals and pals with her, winking and nudging, a continual touching of hands. According to Glo, this sudden budding friendship was predestined: "I know it's bullshit, but the charts said I'd meet a wonderful new friend this week, and I've decided you're it, so you don't have a choice."

"Okay, that's a good deal; I need someone I can unload a bad night on. You're going to laugh, and it's okay."

Over a lunch of fruit salad and fresh-baked bread, Maggie described her encounter with Pablo Esquivel. Gloria-May at first reacted with sympathy, then, having guessed the end, with a cynical, knowing smile. Warming to her account, Maggie began smiling, too, and played to Glo's obvious bent for comedy with her imitations of Esquivel. She mimicked a husky male voice: "Friday is too long – too long to wait."

Glo was inhaling from a cigarette as she started to laugh, and had to cough and wave the smoke away. With this telling, Maggie felt a lifting, a freeing; venting was curative.

"There's a saying where I come from: When a good girl gets bad luck, good luck finds her. Give me that again, sweetie, when you asked to pay for the drinks."

"He said, 'I would not dream of it.'"

Glo laughed even more heartily. "'It's not safe for a woman alone' – you have to like a guy with a sense of humour. Honey, I'll tell you what would have most riled me – not getting laid for my eight hundred bucks."

Maggie laughed – it felt good – but fell silent when a squad of mostly overweight men filed in, flanked by Ralph Johnson and the other Secret Service agent, a burly fellow applying a handkerchief to a runny nose. In the lead, and looking born to the position, was Senator Chester Walker. In his early sixties – older than his spouse by about thirty years – he had a face carved from the granite hills and a camera-ready smile. For one who had trouble hoisting up the flag, he looked virile enough to Maggie.

He gave Glo a gentle shoulder squeeze. "Having a good time, I like that."

"I'm glad you approve, Chester."

When Glo introduced Maggie, he said, "Canadian, eh?" Maggie laughed with him, dutifully. "A fine country, America's best friend in a dangerous world. Been up your way several times – don't want the folks of South Dakota to know, but you Canucks have some fantastic duck hunting. Well, you two gals seem to be getting on like a house on fire."

He bent to Gloria-May's cheek, kissed it, and whispered in her ear. Glo seemed not to care if anyone heard her response. "I'm *not* going to get sloshed."

Walker's face seemed to set in cement for a moment; then he turned to Maggie with a forced chuckle. "The bride and I have a few plans tonight to celebrate our anniversary. I want her on her toes." He winked. "So to speak." He led his team to the bar, ordering refreshments from Miguel in excellent Spanish.

Just as the orientation slide show was about to begin, Maggie was drawn aside by a thickset, almost neckless man gripping a video camera, who introduced himself as Clayton Boyer, media relations: another Southerner. He was genially forgiving about Maggie having intruded upon this gathering.

"That's what I call grit. Now, if the truth be known, Maggie, we're more than happy to have you here. In fact, I have an offer I want you to ponder. I understand you've done some magazine writing, and I think we can arrange something with one of the better women's magazines. A light piece, human interest. How a romance writer stumbled onto Chuck and Gloria-May's seventh anniversary."

There was no question: they were having a problem earning mileage from Walker's Costa Rican pilgrimage. He had been keynote speaker at a conference on terrorism, after which most of the media deserted him. But there could be a hitch to this offer: they would want Walker's buckles and badges to shine on the page.

"And when did the inspiration for this idea strike?"

"Your fortuitous – and may I say attractive – presence among us today brought it to mind."

She was sure they had given the matter more thought than that. "I'm not going to write a three-thousand-word commercial – I'd expect a free hand." Would they wish her to tone down his wife?

"Absolute integrity, that's our aim, nothing censored. Not asking you to glamourize him, Chuck doesn't work that way, he believes in telling it like it is – that's the thrust of his whole damn campaign. Could net you six or seven thousand for a week's work. Circulation five million."

Across the room, Senator Walker was glancing at her while talking with his campaign manager, Orvil Schumenbacker. They seemed to be awaiting her reaction. Walker smiled at her, she smiled back; he gave her a snappy salute.

Boyer seemed insistent on writing the article for her. "You're down here searching for a plot for your next romantic novel and stumble onto the Walkers' romantic escape to paradise. Here's a soldier going off to war for the presidency but thoughtful enough to first reward his wife with a tropical holiday."

"You must have connections with this magazine."

"Let's say the publisher is not entirely in the camp of the enemy."

Maggie found his war-like metaphors grating, but the magazine he named was in every supermarket. "Okay, it could be a good story; I'll do it."

"Excellent. We'll have a chance to sit down together and work some ideas out."

Despite Boyer's keenness to orchestrate the desired spin, she was elated; she would actually turn a profit from her expensive holiday. When a good girl gets bad luck, good luck finds her.

The sound of rotor blades drowned further conversation. From the window, she watched the second helicopter lift off, bearing away more of the senator's entourage. Only two Secret Service agents remained and two aides: Boyer and Schumenbacker, the walrus-sized campaign manager.

Suddenly, the entire building seemed to move; the roof was rattling – and then just as abruptly all was still. "Just a little *temblor*, folks," said Jan Nieuwendoork. "Nothing to worry about."

❧

Jan's orientation lecture previewed their midday hike to the waterfall – "I advise you to wear your bathing suits." Maggie was looking forward to it, already in her walking shoes, her camera and bird guide in hand, but Boyer and Schumenbacker seemed exhausted merely from watching the slides and begged off going.

The trail was well-kept but gruelling, three switchback kilometres up the Savegre valley; Maggie had readied herself for wilderness hiking – by bicycling until first snowfall and taking long Sunday treks with her fellow birders. Surprisingly, Gloria-May had little difficulty keeping pace despite having consumed four gins with her lunch. Chuck Walker was in excellent condition, too, though he seemed distracted, observing little around him and moving as if on a forced march to a new jungle base. His two Secret Service men were at his heels. An assistant tour guide was far behind with the AP reporter, Ed Creeley, a slow-walking heavy smoker.

With Jan's help, Maggie was able to make several entries in the margins of her bird book, a Kiskadee, an Antshrike; she photographed a Long-Tailed Motmot from only three metres away. *Not timid, enjoys showing off its clothes.* She saw mammals, too: a pair of spider monkeys resting in a tree, a family of coatis – or *pizotes*, as they were called locally – scampering through the undergrowth. Jan pointed to several small pies on the road that looked like pigs' droppings.

"White-collared peccaries," Jan said. "But if they were near, we would smell them and we would be looking for trees to climb – they have sharp teeth, but can't raise their heads very high." Jan's information was often not reassuring.

The trail ended at the waterfall, a scene that might have been lifted from a Disney cartoon: sun sparkling on a pool hollowed out by a twenty-metre cascade roaring down a sheer rock wall, Rough-Winged Swallows chasing white and yellow butterflies that spiralled and swooped above the mist.

"Isn't this beautiful, Glo," Walker said, his hand on her shoulder. She squeezed it, then stripped off her sweaty shirt. Not much was hidden behind a string bikini top; the senator looked almost shocked at her choice of swimwear. "Pretty as a picture, and so are you, darling."

"You sweet-talker, you." She kissed him lingeringly on the lips. Maggie caught the moment with her camera: the magazine might pay a handsome bonus for such a cover shot. A discriminating reader would gag at the dialogue, however: Walker's words had sounded forced, stagey. Now he was on his knees, helping Gloria-May untie a knot in her laces.

Maggie heard a whisper at her ear. "What a couple of ham actors." It was Ed Creeley, the AP reporter, who had finally straggled in, puffing, his bristly face sheened with sweat. Maggie had gathered from earlier cynical comments that he disliked the Walkers.

All she desired right now was a swim in that natural pool. She was the first to jump in – with a flailing splash – and the first to the waterfall. She held on to a rock, exhilarated by the cold pour upon her head, and watched the colonel and his consort toe the water, then slip hand in hand into the pool.

After they had all emerged dripping to dry in the sun, Glo joined Maggie: "Look at the zucchini in that guy's front pocket," referring to a protrusion in a pair of Secret Service swimming trunks. Everyone else was striving not to stare at the former showgirl in her daring bikini. Maggie felt almost invisible beside her.

— 3 —

After dinner, Maggie was smearing aloe on her legs when Glo barged into the Jungle House with a bottle of tequila and a bag of sliced lemons. "It's gals' night out. I didn't quite make it onto Chester's busy agenda. He's with his fellow athletes, huddling or scrimmaging or whatever they do at their circle jerks. Anyway, I'm so worn out I could fall asleep having an orgasm."

Maggie accepted Glo's kiss, then slipped her night dress on over her bra and briefs – growing up with three older brothers had instilled in her a lifelong modesty. "I could use something for the pain." The backs of her thighs were so pink she could sit on them only delicately, and her knees were sore from the climbs.

They poured drinks; Maggie raised her glass. "To your seventh anniversary."

"Its highlight was a rumble in a restaurant. I have a funny story, but don't tell that poor critter working for Associated Press. It's bad media for Chester."

This was the episode Maggie had heard about in Quepos. She winced as Glo described a ridiculous set-to in which the strength of three Secret Service men had been called upon to subdue Jacques Cardinal.

Maggie was embarrassed slightly – but unsure why – to admit that the gossip she had overheard had inspired her to use the same Slack Cardinal in her next novel, but Glo thought the idea amusing. "Have you got a part for a shy southern belle? 'Ah do declare, suh, you do say the most wicked thangs.'"

Glo offered a physical description of Cardinal for the novel: "Late forties, cute but shy, doesn't own a comb, six-five and built like a work truck; bay window with love handles, and great glaring green eyes, full of suspicion. Someone has to teach him how to smile."

Glo perched beside her on the bed, took her hand, and looked at her meaningfully. "I hired him for a private cruise – out of sheer boredom, understand? – to escape the cigar smoke and beer farts. But I didn't tell Chester, and I had to threaten the agent who tracked me down. If this shows up in your book, know that I still have friends in Las Vegas who break arms."

Maggie looked at her skeptically. What could anyone do in a kayak? Sex would seem impossible even in one built for two.

"Light flirting was the most I had in mind, just a little frolic." She hesitated, as if unsure what more to divulge.

Maggie, who was more titillated than shocked, hoped Glo was not censoring. *He drew her trembling body onto the wet sand, his glaring green eyes hot with desire.* "Well? What happened?"

"Shit all, honey; he was as nervous as a turkey on Thanksgiving eve. Reacted like I was trying to bust his balls."

Maggie felt let down; the story lacked an appropriately erotic punchline.

"Chester says he has a record of screwing up. Delete – I'm not supposed to say that. Classified shit. Anyway, Cardinal has a right curious background. Change of subject. You look good in this joint; it's Jane of the Jungle in her tree house. Let me see one of your wet reads."

Maggie rummaged in her bag for one of her Nancy Wards. She hoped it wouldn't be too difficult to draw details about Slack Cardinal from the loose lips of her confidant. A state secret, a nervous screw-up of a spy with a dark history: that did not tally with her other meagre information. ·

The sign on his shop had said, "Closed until creativity restored." What mysteries were concealed behind the bay window of the brooding kayak man?

— 4 —

Maggie was woken by the trilling of nature's early risers. She threw back her mosquito net, breathed in the pungent tropical air, picked up pen and pad – she enjoyed writing during the early morning while the world was stretching awake. It was a time of inspiration. This was her second day at Eco-Rico Lodge: her idyll was passing too quickly. Tomorrow evening she would return to the beaches of Manuel Antonio for a week of tropical tanning before retreating north. She shivered at the thought of cold winds whipping across the stubble.

Here she could lie under light cover all night, with the windows open, and awake not to the cruel jangling of an alarm clock but to serenades of birds. She could not count the number of melodies in their repertoires. Her *Birds of Central America* recited light-hearted names: Black-Capped Pygmy-Tyrants, Scaly-Throated Leafscrapers.

There were bugs, naturally: Bare-Necked Umbrellabirds must eat. Some tropical species were delightful: fairylike fireflies that danced through the dark of the forest, priggish praying mantises, plodding rhinoceros beetles.

She had seen three species of monkeys: the grumpy, slow-moving ones were howlers, and their harrowing *whoofs* were resounding outside her window at this moment, though they could be a mile away. She had been shown a glass frog, almost transparent, and a gaudy poison-dart frog; she had seen tracks of a jacaranda.

Yesterday, Maggie had stared in awe at the green living sea of the canopy before being lowered on harness and zip line to a catwalk in the treetops. She'd found she was not much in fear of the heights despite her phobia about flying. Later, a steep hike had taken them up a trail to the hot springs, where they had luxuriated in a rock-lined bathing pool, steam billowing into the cool mountain air.

Enraptured by all that she beheld, her holiday gloriously recovered from its disastrous start, she was already plotting her return next winter. Maybe she would bump into Pablo Esquivel. Maybe she would thank him. Maybe she should stop thinking about him – why was he still popping into her mind? He was yesterday's boring tragedy.

Glo had attached herself to her, always there, stride by stride, zip line to zip line. Though she smoked and drank to some excess – maintaining she was supposed to be on a "damn holiday" – she was naturally athletic and kept trim: stretch exercises for half an hour every morning and evening, followed by vigorous aerobics. After dinner, she would loll on a hammock with a gin and tonic and a Nancy Ward romance. *She is a lawyer. He is a cop. When they clash in court, they discover they share a strange passion.*

Glo entertained Maggie enormously; they had bonded like schoolgirls in a camp dormitory. But, to Maggie's mind, shoot-from-the-hip Gloria-May made an odd pairing with stern, ambitious Chester Walker. Still, she clearly owned his heart, and could melt him with a word or a touch.

Maggie bent to her creative labours at her balcony table. It was becoming a frolic to insinuate real people into her fiction: a gangly heroine, a glib villain, a shy work truck with a dark past. What role could she assign to a Southern temptress or to a square-jawed ex-Marine officer?

℘

His T-shirt smeared with grease, Jacques pulled himself from under his rust-eaten Jeep. "This is as far as this baby is going today. It's a connecting rod."

Fiona shrugged into her heavy packsack. "Let's walk."

"Let's not. We'll camp here; this is the heat of the day."

His bossiness irked her. Fiona found the fellow sufficiently capable, however sour and laconic, but she worried that he might show another face once he dipped into the litre of whisky she had seen him stow in his pack.

"Suit yourself." She marched up the track alone.

Fiona was disappointed when she reached the rushing river's edge; her plan to follow it upstream was thwarted by a twenty-metre cascade falling almost vertically from a rocky ridge. This was a mortifying defeat in the battle of wills with Dr. Cardinal; she would be forced to swallow her pride, rejoin him.

But first she would sample the pool hollowed out by the falls. She stripped off all her clothes, then arced like an arrow, feeling the cold fresh snap of the water as it engulfed her.

Not long afterwards, as she was floating, enjoying the sun on her body, she opened her myopic eyes to behold a large humanoid shape looking down at her. "The lady's even prettier when she blushes. Found yourself a nice spot."

With one fluid motion, Jacques pulled his shirt over his tangle of red hair, exposing a broad chest and a waist thickened with careless living. Unbuckling his trousers and dropping his shorts, she turned her eyes away as he hurtled into the water.

℘

Maggie reconstructed this last mangled sentence, planted a period at the end, then tended to her cramped toes. A story was definitely unfolding; the seeds of danger and romance were planted, erotic fertilizer added.

73

She put her manuscript aside at the sound of the breakfast gong. This morning's schedule included an easy meander down a valley, then an interview with Senator Walker. Because he was frequently secluded with his two advisers, Maggie's opportunities to chat with him had been brief and limited. Tomorrow one of the helicopters was returning to take Chester (he regarded that name as "wimpy," Glo had confided) back to Washington "for vital affairs of state."

Yesterday, during dinner, Maggie had merrily told him her tale of being swindled; Walker had pulled several hundred dollars from his wallet and pressed them on her, refusing to hear her protests. She accepted the money, but only as a loan to be repaid with appropriate interest. But still she felt vaguely compromised.

A champagne celebration was scheduled for after lunch: this was anniversary day. "No fancy folderol," Chuck said, "that's an order; we're just having a casual glass of cheer with friends."

The dining room was deserted except for the AP reporter, Ed Creeley. Maggie poured herself a coffee and joined him, determined to endure his cynicism.

"Got any idea why we're here, Schneider? Guy's seeking the Republican nomination; what's he doing in this shithole, trying to tie up the monkey vote?"

"Maybe it's the female vote he's after."

"That why they brought you in? To write about his romantic escape to paradise?"

Despite Maggie's repeated assurance that she was not Walker's secret hireling, retained weeks ago, Creeley insisted she was not here coincidentally: the scenario satisfied his need to find evil machinations everywhere.

"Guy's a lightweight. He got in by a fluky few thousand votes. He's a senator for one measly year and suddenly he sees himself as leader of the free world? Chuck's got as much chance getting past the primaries as a frog in a flushing toilet. Especially with that albatross around his neck."

That seemed an awkward metaphor to describe Gloria-May, but

the reporter could be right: despite her beauty and her buoyant openness (or because of it), her tart tongue seemed a political liability.

"Thank God," Creeley said, "because imagine his itchy fucking finger on the trigger."

Maggie was not particularly starchy about the occasional blunt Anglo-Saxon word, but with Creeley she endured a surfeit. He picked up on her reproving expression, lit a cigarette, and wandered out to the veranda.

As she was tucking into her half-melon, Orvil Schumenbacker, the campaign manager, came in with a lazy pudgy smile and passed Maggie a typewritten sheet. "Here are some questions you might want to ask the senator this afternoon."

"Thank you very much."

With elaborate carelessness, she stuck his notes unread in her bag, letting him know her art was not to be choreographed. She could not believe Walker was as boring as made out by the pamphlets and speech reprints that had been showered on her: a man with a "mission," bent on "restoring America's greatness." To give Walker credit, he seemed truly patriotic, though of firm, even rigid beliefs, and he was no coward; he had won the Medal of Honor for his bravery in Vietnam.

Schumenbacker excused himself as Glo slid into the chair next to her. "I have jungleitis. The next canopy I see better be hanging over a bed. After these crackers take off tomorrow, what do y'all say we scoot on down to the beach? Find ourselves a big old fancy hotel with a damn pool."

Maggie eagerly agreed: the body and the broomstick go to the beach. Maybe they could even take a kayak tour with the grumpy giant.

"Chester's sulking about me hanging around Manuel Antonio beach. I might get in a widdle twubble. I am going to have a holiday if it kills me." She turned to the waiter. "Miguel, you be a sweetie now, and put the champagne on to chill." The young man looked long and solemnly at her, uncomprehending. "El vino de bubbly. On ice."

Miguel finally trotted off after Glo mimed popping a cork and fizz coming from her glass, then returned with a glass of champagne with a cube of ice in it. "That's not . . . Oh, forget it." Glo accepted the glass and waved him away.

"Okay, Glo, what lies do you want to tell me for my article?" Maggie brought out her notepad, and asked her how she had met her husband. The setting had been a show in Vegas, which he had attended with some fellow officers. Glo had recognized Colonel Walker from a televised hearing: coolly holding his ground against angry congressmen. His eyes had been on her steadily during the chorus numbers. Afterwards, a note arrived in her dressing room, a rose pinned to it. All this on a day for which her horoscope had predicted romance.

"He was gorgeous. I went nuts. Had him in the sack after three nights."

Just before lunch, Boyer escorted Maggie to the veranda, where Chuck Walker was gently swinging in a hammock. "Forgive my poor manners, Maggie, if I don't rise. Don't know if I have the strength."

"You're forgiven, senator."

"Washington seems light-years away. They're going to have to wrestle me onto that helicopter tomorrow."

Despite his claims of comfort, he seemed to be on edge; more than mosquitoes were biting him: affairs of state, or perhaps potential affairs of spouse.

"Gloria-May tells me you two will be sharing a hotel at the beach. I think that's a fine idea, and I don't want you girls to scrimp; the entire week is on me. You make sure you keep an eye out for each other."

Maggie hid her irritation at the implied bribe to chaperone his wife. "That's very generous, senator, but I'd rather bill the magazine. Don't worry about us; I'm much too practical and Glo is very sensible."

"She does get a little frisky at times — but, hell, that's how she swept me off my feet. Now, I hope I can answer your questions without blushing too much. Never got over being shy about the intimate matters I suspect your readers will be interested in."

Boyer chimed in: "If we say off the record, it's off the record."

Maggie nodded and opened with: "A lot of people might think the middle of the jungle is an odd place for a second honeymoon. Why did you choose it?"

"Well, for one thing, it beats the jungle in Washington. I prefer real monkeys and snakes to the two-legged kind who call themselves liberals." He laughed. "Just joking. But, you know, Maggie, I feel at home in this part of the world. Spent a lot of time here in the army. Honduras, Panama, Nicaragua."

"Yes, you were helping train the Contras —"

"Off the record here," said Boyer.

"Hell, what for?" Walker said. "I'm proud of whatever small contribution I made for world peace. For democracy."

Maggie wished she had unbiased background on the senator; the publicity handouts were skimpy about his time in Central America. She knew there had been a failed vote to hold him in contempt of Congress in his military days: there had been allegations about running drugs to bankroll the Contras. When she began to ask about the hearings, Boyer again intervened. "I don't think the ladies will be interested in that. You needed to get away, senator, to have some time with your wife before the primaries."

Maggie gave up. "How did you and Gloria-May meet?"

Walker smiled, his eyes taking on a distant look as he offered a story similar to Glo's, though less sexually candid: he had wooed and pursued, properly proposed, sought acceptance from her parents, "a gracious Christian couple from the great state of Alabama."

Boyer nodded approvingly.

"I loved her from the day we met, and still do. Deeply."

The interview yielded a few tender accounts of their life together, a paean to Glo for her sacrifices in support of his political career, and a peppering of homilies about preserving family values (America was at a "moral crossroads"). While in Vietnam he had adopted – in the loose sense – three orphaned children, and paid for their schooling and several visits to the States. "We regularly correspond." He showed her photographs of two lovely women and a young man, and despite herself Maggie felt slightly misty. He became livelier, more intense, when discussing his war record. President Lyndon Johnson had pinned the Medal of Honor on him after he had rescued his platoon from an ambush in a Vietnamese rice paddy.

When they found themselves shouting to be heard over a sudden clamour of rainfall, they retreated indoors; Maggie decided she had enough to satisfy "the ladies."

In the main room, a banner had been hung: "Happy Lucky Seventh, Chuck and Glo." To bulk up the crowd, the Nieuwendoorks and their staff had joined the ceremony. Ed Creeley lifted two glasses of champagne from Miguel's tray, handed one to Maggie, saying, "Here comes a bunch of malarkey, but I have to file it anyway. Guess we're going to hear from the two pilot fish first."

Schumenbacker and Boyer tried to be jocose in offering toasts to future president and first lady, but the effect was cloying. Creeley muttered asides to Maggie: "That clonged." "These guys really know how to serve up the goo."

The senator responded with a brief oration: he was the luckiest man on earth; without Gloria-May, he could not have attained this point of his career let alone survived the trying times ahead; his only regret was they never had children. "But, off the record, it wasn't for want of trying." How inappropriate, Maggie thought; she felt embarrassed for him.

"It's been a true love, an exceptional love." The senator put his arm around Glo, who looked stunning in a mini-Armani cocktail dress. Maggie still had on her hiking boots and her khaki outfit – despite Walker's admonition to wear casual clothes, she wished she had changed into her dress.

Glo, playing to Boyer's camera, planted a lush kiss on her husband's lips, then pantomimed fainting in his arms.

"Give us a word, Gloria-May," said Schumenbacker.

"Well, all I can say is I surely wish I hadn't married such a milksop." Though Walker must have known she was teasing, he winced. "He's shiftless, no ambition." She shoved him playfully. "Love you to tiny little bits, Chester. I'm there for the long haul, and you know it, Mr. President. To long-lasting love, for God and the Republican party."

The two pilot fish smiled – Maggie couldn't believe they were so credulous as not to detect the sardonic tone. Ed Creeley grinned and joined the toast.

Glo drained her champagne, and when Boyer switched to a video camera she began mugging: still the professional entertainer. She did a bump and grind, and, with a hibiscus clenched between her teeth, danced a fandango around Walker with fluid grace. Everyone cheered, but Walker's mirth seemed strained.

Glo put her arms around her husband and kissed him again. All her audience but Creeley applauded. After a last Latin dance step, she said to Boyer, "Okay, cut, I need a drink."

"I'd like to get the real story on that dame," Creeley said. "Can't tell me she hasn't been around."

Maggie wandered off to a table where a banquet had been spread for lunch. As she picked from a bowl of fruit, she watched Glo pull Agent Johnson toward her and put an arm around him. "Loosen up, Ralph, have a drink."

Johnson declined with a smile. The other agent, Hollisson, was in his cabin with a high temperature.

Senator Walker kept checking his watch, as if he had somewhere to go. His holiday had not relaxed him much, and Maggie sensed he was revving his engine for tomorrow's return to politics.

Suddenly there came a commotion at the doorway, and Agent Hollisson staggered in, as if being flung – he was in his underwear, a blanket thrown around his shoulders.

"Ever'boddy, hands opp!" shouted a voice from behind him. "No fonny beezness."

Maggie's passing thought was that she was witnessing a burlesque – a comedy troupe had been hired as entertainment. But reality set in with the sudden invasion of five masked people waving savage-looking guns; they were dressed in jungle fatigues with belt holsters; only their eyes showed behind red kerchiefs.

A burst of submachine gun fire into the rafters sent her reeling.

A woman was screaming: Celeste. Everyone but Ralph Johnson froze in shock – he was edging behind a table, slowly moving his hand toward the firearm under his shirt.

"You, stop, hands opp!" screamed one of the masked men, brandishing his automatic weapon at Johnson. "Or I make you holes like cheese!" Johnson raised his arms. "We keel nobody," shouted the man, short and wiry and frantic. "You no make trobble, nobody he gets hurt."

After a flurry of commands in Spanish, one of the invaders put a gun to Johnson's back, and another motioned Hollisson to lie on his stomach; others produced lengths of rope and began to bind the agents' wrists and ankles.

The bandits would steal and be gone, Maggie prayed, quick and efficient. She felt faint, but was determined to stay alert; she still could not accept that this was happening. One of the group was a woman, so rape did not seem on the agenda.

Now a sixth intruder strolled into the room, with a languid, graceful gait. He also wore military fatigues and was taller than the others; the kerchief tied around his face was not red but navy blue. He held no gun but was obviously the leader: the others deferred to him, nodded as he gave orders in a low voice, his eyes sweeping the room.

"Ever'boddy lie on floor face down, arms behind back," said the short, wiry man, who seemed to be acting spokesperson. One of the gang had addressed him as Zorro.

Maggie lay down on her stomach and found herself almost bumping noses with Chuck Walker. His face was twisted with rage and shock as one of the raiders spun a rope around his wrists.

Zorro spoke to the leader, then turned to the captives. "Greetings to Senator Walker and other Yankee imperialists! We are Commando del Movimiento Cinco de Mayo. You are preesoners of war by Geneva Convention!"

"*Viva Benito Madrigal, viva libertad!*" came a shout, followed by ragged cheers from the others. Another burst of gunfire, and the CB radio shattered.

The female guerrilla grasped Maggie's wrists and looped rope around them. They were prisoners of what war, Maggie wondered, and who was Benito Madrigal? These were not ordinary thieves, but what was their mission?

One by one, she and the other guests were directed first to their feet, then onto wooden chairs fetched from the dining room, their wrists then retied behind them to the cross rails. Attempts to speak were silenced by curt orders from their captors, though they talked animatedly among themselves. They were disparate in appearance: a stooped leathery older man, a plump fair-skinned short fellow, another tall and gangly, wearing glasses – he seemed barely in his twenties, though it was difficult to tell. The woman was squat in build, ebony in colour, frizzed hair. The leader was slightly less dark skinned, his hair clipped short, military style.

Frightened and confused, Maggie obeyed directions to swivel her chair about; ultimately, after some arranging, she and her fellow guests found themselves facing forward, as if an audience to some entertainment. Next to Maggie was Glo, astonished, speechless. Chuck Walker, still red-faced, was at his wife's other side; his attempts to speak were cut off by barked orders.

The knot binding Maggie's wrists seemed bulky and inexpert; she could wiggle her hands. She had not been treated roughly, and although scared was managing to keep her head. She still felt a vague sense of unreality, as if she was living her own fiction. A fleeting thought: What would Fiona do?

Jan and Celeste Nieuwendoork were among those on chairs, but their dozen staff were made to sit on the floor, tied in pairs, back to back, wrist to wrist, shaking and sniffling and moaning in fear; behind Maggie, Celeste was crying. She could hear Walker urge in a low voice, "Everyone just be calm."

The man in the blue kerchief – Halcón, they called him – talked for a few moments with Zorro, who then studied a page of notes as if about to deliver an address. Others were collecting watches, jewellery, and money, and placing them in an empty rice sack.

"Senator Chuck Walker! Ladies and gentlemen!" Zorro was about five-foot-three, with a fanatic's hot eyes, and he seemed to need to shout. He first addressed those in the back, the Eco-Rico staff, in a mix of Spanish and English. "*Trajabores!* Exploited workers of Costa Rica! *Estamos amigos,* we are your frands. *Estamos revolutionarios, no estamos criminales.*" Addressing those on chairs, he added, "We come because Costa Rica ees dying from Yankee imperialist influence."

He studied a phrase on his handwritten sheet, then conferred with the thin young guerrilla, who, in his thick wire-rim spectacles, looked like an owlish college student.

"Manipulated," pronounced the young man.

"Maneepulated," Zorro repeated. "No longer we are maneepulated by Disneyland America. We take our contry back." He proceeded through a list of confusing complaints: their children were being exposed to the corrupting influences of American television; their best farmland was being stolen by rich Yankees, whose monopolistic practices also kept the price of rice and beans artificially high. "You know what ees costing coffee at Starbucks? – two days slavery for worker in mountains."

Through the front window, Maggie could see the short, portly guerrilla standing by the tractor. Maggie started as he fired a round of submachine bullets at its tires, then at the engine, the racket drowning Zorro's words – a tirade against the U.S. Immigration Service that seemed out of context. "They are feelthy dogs, not human!"

He ended with: "I have message for America. At thees moment, Costa Rica declares independent democratic socialist republic." With an extravagant gesture, he hoisted a half-filled bottle of champagne, gulped from it, then threw the bottle at the wall.

"*Viva Benito Madrigal, viva libertad!*" came a chorus behind him.

Halcón, the leader, stayed in the room's shadows, issuing soft instructions. Maggie was uncertain about the hierarchy of the others: Zorro seemed second in command, but when he tilted another bottle to his lips, the woman wrested it from his hands and scolded him. All but Halcón seemed pumped with feigned bravado, disorganized and jumpy.

Now the bespectacled young man addressed them in fluent English. "I am placing here the list of our demands." He laid a type-written sheet on the dining room table. "We will take two Americans with us. They will not be harmed if our just claims are met."

Halcón said one word: "*Mujeres*."

"*Si, el capitán*. Two women must come with us."

As the guerrillas deliberated, Maggie tried to become invisible. But they would not take her; she was not an imperialist — she wasn't even American.

"Señora Walker," Zorro said.

Glo's mouth went wide open. "Aw, now, look —"

"Keep calm," Walker said. "Let me talk to these people. I think I understand where they're coming from." Despite Zorro's shouted demands for silence, Walker spoke forcefully in Spanish. Maggie gathered he was urging that their demands could be negotiated.

Halcón spoke sharply to Zorro, who put a stop to the speech with a shot into the floor from his automatic pistol — just in front of Walker's toes.

"Señora Walker!" Zorro screamed.

"Easy, easy, everyone," Walker said. "I'm sure they'd rather have me." He rose awkwardly, tied to his wooden chair, and shuffled forward, remonstrating, offering himself in exchange for Glo. Zorro kicked at the chair, and Walker toppled over on his side.

Glo swore as two guerrillas set upon her: "You mangy shits, get your hands off!" They silenced her by tying a bandanna over her mouth, then, huffing and grunting, carried her outside, chair and all. Walker was shouting with fury as he struggled to right himself. "You bastards! She is only a woman!"

Zorro knocked over his chair again, then conferred with his boss, who looked fleetingly at Maggie, then gestured at Celeste. She screamed.

"No! Jan! Don't let them!"

Now Jan was talking rapidly in a choked voice, begging. Celeste fainted as two of the guerrillas began to untie her. Maggie heard Jan repeat the word *embarazada*: "*Cinco mesas embarazada, por favor, señores.*" Maggie took it to mean pregnant.

The revolutionaries seemed insistent on taking Celeste, and suddenly Maggie heard herself, to her utter amazement, saying, "Take me instead."

Another whispered conference, then the young bespectacled man addressed her: "Who are you?"

"Margaret Schneider. I'm a writer. I will . . . tell your story to the world."

She heard a scuffling noise outside, saw Glo being released from her chair, but still gagged and her wrists bound. She was refusing to rise from the ground.

Halcón butted his cigarette, checked his watch. "*Muy bien,*" he said. "*Un escritora, ella. Vámonos, amigos.*"

Freed her from her chair, Maggie was led to the door. Her knees locked and her legs gave way and she stumbled over the sill. Arms grasped her, pulled her upright. She cast one last look about at the many staring eyes. Senator Walker, who had managed to regain a seated position, was hopping in his chair toward the door, crying Gloria-May's name; grief and fury were in his eyes.

— 5 —

Maggie's watch had been taken, so she was guessing that she and Gloria-May and their six masked captors had been trudging for an hour along one of the lodge's trails, en route, it would seem, to the towering waterfall under which she had bathed a few days ago. The rain made the ground slippery, and from time to time one of the guerrillas would lose footing, and fall and curse.

Though tense with fright, she was managing better than they, taking some small comfort that her walking shoes had firm grip. Though her hands had been freed, she was tethered by a rope tied around her waist; the other end was knotted to the belt of the lanky young man in thick glasses, whom they called Buho: Spanish for owl. He spoke few words to her, but was solicitous and polite.

Gloria-May was still being limply uncooperative. A string hammock, fetched from the lodge's balcony, served as her litter, two guerrillas taking shifts at the ends. From time to time, one of her porters would slip and Glo would fall hard onto mud and rocks. She was altogether a pitiful figure, sullen and gagged, clothed only in her mid-thigh cocktail dress, wrists and ankles trussed. Hiking boots that had been retrieved from her cabin were fitted onto her feet. Before fleeing the lodge, the soldiers of the Comando Cinco de Mayo had looted the rooms.

At the head of this convoy was the older man, well over fifty, Maggie guessed, though she was unable to see his face. She had caught his name: Coyote. Slightly built, bent as if with the labours of a lifetime, he had the weathered look and manners of a campesino, a man of the country. His comrades' feet were clad in leather, but Coyote wore gumboots, and seemed uncomfortable in them, perhaps more used to walking in bare feet. Clutching a long machete in his hand, he walked warily, eyes to the ground.

Apparently, they had all assumed animal names, except for the short rotund fellow they called Gordo. She was unsure what manner of beast was a Zorro, but the little man answering to that name gave the impression of an ill-natured weasel. She particularly dreaded him, a volatile man, twice armed, with a large-calibre pistol and one of the two submachine guns. Whenever he lost his footing it swung about dangerously, and he'd mutter, "*Eewai puta*," some manner of Tico curse. When not taking turn with the hammock, he walked beside the black woman. From the reproving, familiar way she spoke to Zorro, Maggie gathered they were partnered – she remembered the woman snatching the champagne bottle from his hands at the lodge. They called her Tayra. At the lodge, Maggie had seen a photograph of such an animal, an otter-like forest forager.

Wiry old Coyote and their leader, Halcón – which meant falcon – were the fittest of the troop; the others were puffing and red-faced with the effort of their steep ascent. All carried guns except Halcón, whose only weapon was a short machete. Around his neck dangled a compass, and several keys and a small flashlight swung from a chain at his belt. On his wrist was a gold-plated Rolex – once Orvil Schumenbacker's. From time to time, he took a small transistor short-wave from a jacket pocket and held it to his ear. He rarely spoke, but his dark eyes were active, occasionally resting on Maggie, who felt their intensity.

She was curious to know what they looked like behind their kerchiefs but realized she would be at risk if able to identify them. What were their so-called just claims – she had not seen the list – and who was this Benito Madrigal whose name they had cheered? As frightened as she was, she was determined to maintain her composure, to be as compliant as possible. She had read somewhere about the proper etiquette for a hostage: remain alert, observe, be polite, don't provoke anger.

She assumed ransom would be sought and wondered how much they would demand. Surely they were not anticipating much profit from Margaret Schneider. How many millions did they think Gloria-May was worth? Senator Walker might not have great personal means, but presumably he had wealthy backers.

They must have some secure hideout, but where? This trail stopped at the waterfall, and searchers would quickly scour it from beginning to end.

She thought of her parents and brothers receiving word of her kidnapping, their dismay and horror. Of slighter concern, though it niggled at her, was that her manuscript had been left behind at the Jungle House. The plot she was living seemed more frightening and ill-boding than any she had devised. She tried positive thinking as a stress relief, seeking to persuade herself that no one had reason to harm her; this was an adventure, an exciting story to tell her friends.

The column halted, and now Maggie understood why Coyote had been treading with so much caution. Weaving across the road was a snake-like creature with legs: a skink. Suddenly, a hovering kite darted down and snatched at the tail. The long wiggling appendage broke off, and the lizard scampered into the underbrush, the raptor carrying away its consolation prize. Despite her anxious state, Maggie watched in fascination: nature had given the skink a clever survival ruse. What means of escape could Maggie devise?

The comrades of Comando Cinco de Mayo had little in the way of supplies — a few small packs laden with the stolen valuables — so they couldn't intend to travel far. In a few hours the sun would set, and surely they would not chance the jungle at night. If Maggie and Glo could somehow untie themselves in the darkness, they could slip away unseen. These out-of-condition outlaws might not pursue them and perhaps would flee, and she and Glo could return to the path at dawn. After playing with the idea, she dismissed it; they had been warned: if you try to run away we must kill you, we are sorry, *lo siento*. She wasn't sure if they meant it, but didn't want to push them that far.

Maggie noticed Halcón glancing at his watch. They were near the falls; she could hear the roar of the water. It was about three o'clock, perhaps two and a half hours since they'd left the Eco-Rico Lodge. How long would it take for help to come? Those at the lodge would likely have been able to free themselves quickly, but even husky Agent Johnson, at a trot, would be a few hours along a muddy, slippery road reaching the town of Silencio and, presumably, a telephone.

Halcón led them directly to the high, roaring falls and its deep pool. Zorro let his end of the hammock slide, Glo tumbling to the ground with a curse muffled by her gag. Maggie reacted: "Do you people have to be so rough with her? Let me talk to her. Please take off Mrs. Walker's gag."

Halcón seemed to give the matter some thought. Pulling out a pack of cigarettes, he stuck one into a mouth-level hole in his blue kerchief; the effect was almost comical, though Maggie did not dare a smile. He lit the cigarette with a wooden match, then spoke some words to Buho, who removed the bandanna from Glo's mouth. Maggie knelt and brushed the muddy hair from her eyes.

"*Viva libertad*," Glo said. "What a fucking bummer this day has become."

"Glo, your behind must be bruised purple. Let's just go along with these folks, okay? On your feet, chum." Maggie kissed her cheek, whispering closely, "Easier to escape."

Glo struggled to a seated position, glared at Halcón. "You are an inconsiderate prick." He didn't respond but seemed to catch the message, his eyes turning cold. "Okay, damn it, I'll walk."

The ropes released, Glo massaged her wrists and ankles, then rose uncertainly. Halcón instructed Tayra to tie herself to Glo's waist in the same manner Maggie was yoked to Buho. Glo offered no resistance, folded her arms, glared lugubriously through the drizzling rain at the dense jungle on the other side of the river. "Now what?" she said. "Do we sprout wings and fly?"

Halcón was craning up at the brim of the waterfall twenty metres above them. "*Dónde?*" he asked.

"*Aqui*," said Coyote, who stepped onto a boulder and yanked at a vine trailing from a heavily buttressed tree. A high limb shook and another pull released a stout rope weighted by a leather-and-metal harness. Unfurling behind it came a slender rope ladder.

Maggie felt both admiration and dismay at the forethought that had gone into stashing this equipment; she would not have thought these seeming amateurs so enterprising. Coyote had been their advance scout, she realized; the wiry campesino had likely cut a trail through the jungle to the top of the waterfall. The strategy was ingenious: no search party would think to look up there.

Coyote expertly fastened the bottom of the ladder to the tree trunk, strapped on the harness, and began clambering up, into the mist. At the top, he swung himself over the tree limb and onto the ledge at the lip of the falls.

As the safety harness came down again, Halcón turned to Gordo. The portly little man hesitated, staring upwards with a frozen smile. "*Rápido!*" Halcón barked.

Gordo's climb was less difficult than Coyote's because the safety line was being tugged from above. It looked as if Coyote was cranking a hand winch. Once at the top, Gordo raised his arms in triumph. Maggie could barely hear his shout over the noise of the falls: "*Viva Benito Madrigal!*" Zorro went up the ladder next, strapping his machine gun on tightly, acting nonchalant.

Halcón then handed the harness to Tayra, who passed it to Gloria-May with a smile. "This little outfit will look better on you, my American *amiga*." It was the first time she had spoken in English – the accent was Caribbean.

"I said I'd walk, not climb. I am definitely not going up in that thing."

"Oh, yes, missie, you are going up that *thang*," Tayra said. She and Halcón wrestled her into the harness. Glo glared at them with silent contempt. When Halcón's hand strayed near her breast, she batted it away.

"*Tranquilo, señora*," Halcón said, unflustered.

Maggie chimed in: "Yes, Gloria-May, *tranquilo*." She was sorry to be short with her balky companion, but felt they should make the best of a bad situation. They might be held captive for some time, and there would be no easy flight to freedom. The important thing was to cooperate – and stay alive. Aware she could be winched to the top if all else failed, Gloria-May reluctantly followed Tayra up the ladder; at one point Glo had to brace her travelling companion when she slipped on the wet rungs. At the top, Tayra was embraced by Zorro, who raised her arm in shared triumph.

Halcón indicated he would follow last; Maggie, wearing the harness, would go in tandem with Buho. She had worn a similar harness during the Eco-Rico canopy tour, and felt reasonably secure, but Buho was climbing stiffly beneath her, jerking on the tether, slowing her. He seemed, physically, her male counterpart: skinny, myopic, and awkward. He truly looked owl-like, staring up at her with large anxious eyes behind thick lenses, the kerchief over his nose like a beak. He didn't seem the type to cause harm, and she wondered if she could find a way to relate to him.

Halfway up, her line was pulled taut again by the slow-moving Buho and she paused to wait for him. Finding herself finally out of the earshot of the others, she spoke bluntly. "Buho, why are you involved in this? Kidnapping is a crime. I don't think you're a criminal."

He blinked, was slow to respond. "I am a fighter for the revolution. Don Benito says a revolutionary goes everywhere with life in the hollow of his hand, ready to sacrifice it at any moment." His words sounded as if pulled from a well-thumbed tract.

"Who is Don Benito?"

"Benito Madrigal, our guide and pilot, who went to prison because he struggled for justice. Now they are torturing him. This is the story you must tell to the world."

Maggie felt the tug of the winch and began climbing again. The brief conversation had lessened her fear. Her offer to memorialize their deeds in writing must have tantalized them: it was good insurance. Clearly, a prisoner exchange was one of the rebels' demands. Surely that was attainable; it might satisfy them. Kidnappings in Latin America – frequent enough to make numbing demands on the attention span of CSKN's viewers – were as often committed by out-and-out criminals as by revolutionary fundraisers, and hostage deaths were rare. These desperados were not grubbing mercenaries; they were believers in their naïve political cause.

They seemed, however, out of touch with the reality of international power politics. *I have message for America. We take our contry back.* The economic monolith to the north might feel a flea bite from the Fifth of May Commando's desperate foray.

A stunning view was spreading below: the twisting river valley, the grassy path meandering downhill, fading into the virgin forest burgeoning from the mountainsides. Under normal circumstances, Maggie would have been exhilarated by the sight, but now she was too disconcerted by her reality, which was far more hair-raising than any adventure she had contrived for Fiona.

The sun was behind clouds, but a gloom in the air suggested it would soon descend: maybe there was an hour and a half left of good ligl t. Once she was a few rungs higher on the ladder, she noticed a plume of smoke in the distance. Perhaps it was coming from the lodge, a signal to passing aircraft. Searchers may already be on their trail.

She paused again to wait for Buho. Below, Halcón was pacing, smoking, listening to his radio. She felt an anxious yank from above and resumed her climb, finally hopping onto the ledge above the falls. She shrugged out of the harness and crouched beside Glo, who was shivering with the cold of approaching evening. They gazed across the valley at the pillar of smoke breaking up in the wind. "I can't believe this is happening," Glo said.

"We just have to keep our heads, Glo. Things will improve from here. I'm sure they'll have a warm shelter nearby."

"Little miss ray of sunshine."

"Look at them – they're more miserable than you are." The guerrillas, bedraggled and grimy, had taken on long faces as they looked up the Savegre River, wider here above the falls and slower-moving. Were they to follow it upstream? Maggie saw no evidence of a trail.

"We're fucked, honey. Chester doesn't negotiate with terrorists. It's one of his campaign themes."

"These people need us alive, Glo. That's the way this kind of operation works."

They fell silent as Halcón reached the top. He pulled up the rope ladder and balled it with the safety line and the hammock, then waded upriver and stuffed all the equipment into a cavity. With some effort, he and the others rolled a boulder on top, hiding the cache from view.

The next stage of their trek was a daunting scramble upstream along the rocky bank of the river. The march was punctuated by frequent oaths as one or another slipped on the slimy rocks or had to detour into the water. For a long stretch, they had no recourse but to wade: the riverbanks were lined with prickly palms and a species of spiny tree. However physically awkward when surrounded by the trappings of civilization, Maggie found herself reasonably sure-footed in the wilderness, more agile than most of her exhausted companions. Glo, though remaining sour and uncommunicative, made no effort to slow their progress.

As the sun toiled ever lower to the horizon, the guerrillas began showing signs of anxiety, obviously behind schedule. Gordo was especially pooped, barely able to lift his feet. Buho was limping, his feet swollen. All of them were hungry. Maggie had taken only a few pieces of fruit at the aborted lunch.

But finally, where the river flattened over a bed of pebbles, they came to a sandbar. Coyote, with a groan of relief, pulled off his rubber boots and tied them to his pack. Maggie noticed footprints on the sandbar, the deeper hoof markings of horses, and the prints of other smaller animals. A path crossed the river here, she could see it winding into the forest from its banks. A campesino trail, Maggie surmised. There might be scattered farms nearby.

Halcón, scowling at Glo, issued an order. When Tayra attempted to gag her, Glo slapped her hands: "Don't touch me, you whore."

"Rich bitch," Tayra said. Zorro roughly pinned Glo's arms from behind, twisting her wrists, as Tayra tightened the bandanna over her mouth. Halcón spoke sharply to Zorro, who released his grip. Halcón then sent Maggie a penetrating look. "I am *tranquilo*," she softly said.

"*Vámonos.*" Halcón again gave the lead to Coyote, who strode barefoot up the path to the right, but halted after a few minutes, stopping the column, sniffing the air. The scent came to Maggie, too, a stink that recalled to her the pens at the Klosky's hog farm on the highway to Melfort. Coyote began talking rapidly; Maggie caught the word "*sainos.*"

"Peccaries," Buho translated. "He says they are coming to the river to drink. If there are many, they can be dangerous; they are like dogs in a pack."

Maggie looked around for a tree to climb, but those nearest were armed with ferocious thorns. The odour was growing intense now, and she could hear a drumbeat of little marching feet, human-sounding grumblings, and an even more curious sound, like teeth chattering.

Coyote led a retreat to the river, and they waded about thirty metres upstream. The sun had set; in half an hour there would be absolute darkness. Now came the pigs, perhaps thirty in the herd, black and grey with white collars and bibs. They filed down to the river, complaining and chattering.

Maggie was more absorbed than frightened by the sight. The peccaries stank like rancid farts but did not seem threatening. Zorro muttered something, then cockily sloshed down the river, and before Halcón could check him he raised his pistol. "*Chuletas de cerdo*," he said, and fired.

The shot rang like a thunderclap, one of the animals tottered onto its side, and the others bolted back up the path. Halcón directed a few menacing oaths at Zorro while fingering the blade of his machete as if for sharpness. Maggie guessed the meaning of one slang word: "*huevos*." Tayra joined in, too, with several sharp-tongued comments.

Coyote expertly gutted the dead peccary, but Zorro was made to sling the carcass on his back and endure Tayra's continuing nagging as they made quickly for the path. Here it was darker, the twilight barely filtering through the thorn trees. Occasionally, Coyote used a flashlight as he led them another mile uphill, a ridge trail. Maggie could now make out the occasional clearing on either side, ragtag patches of corn or beans, a tumbledown shack or two.

There remained barely a crack of light in the sky, but Coyote seemed more confident, showing a familiarity with the trail. It was becoming apparent he had once inhabited this little part of the world. He may have had the kind of hardscrabble life that turns peons into revolutionaries.

An owl hooted. The path dipped to a tiny stream at which fireflies danced and bats darted. Beyond a cornfield glowed a light, a dwelling, clapboard siding and tin roof, a lamp or candle burning inside. From an open window came urgent human sounds, a man and woman making love: his ascending wail, an orgasmic yelp, then his partner softly teasing him. Buho, despite his limp, increased his pace, as if embarrassed at being in the vicinity of such intimate goings-on. Maggie was ruefully reminded of her quest, so harshly suspended, for the holy grail of love.

A few hundred metres away, from another hutch, came a woman's voice, sweet and haunting, singing a lullaby. Maggie was entranced by the simple beauty of the song, by the perfectly pitched notes of her voice. She pictured a mother at the bedside of her children, beans simmering on the stove for a husband who has toiled all day in the fields. *No one knew Juanita Sanchez had a voice of molten silver. She remained all her life undiscovered, serenading the wilderness.*

Though weary, wet, and cold, Maggie was feeling less dispirited, more optimistic now that the initial, arduous stage of this ordeal had to be nearing an end. One of these tiny farms must be Coyote's; they could warm up by his fire, dry their boots and clothes.

The trail ended at an area where the forest had recently been burned. There had been an attempt to plant beans in the scorched earth, but the jungle was coming back. Maggie could make out the blackened remnants of a shack and wondered if the fire had raced out of control. Coyote paused to contemplate it, then led them down a foot-wide passage through the beans, over the brow of a rise to a gully where two small fires glowed: an encampment, tents sloppily strung up, forming a circle.

"*Viva Benito Madrigal,*" Halcón called. The password was returned first by a male voice, then a woman's. Maggie saw them now: each stirring a pot on a propane camping stove, now dropping their spoons and hurrying forward. Both were slight and youthfully attractive; neither could be twenty years old. On Halcón's sharp command, they hurriedly pulled kerchiefs over their faces. Maggie looked quickly away, pretended she had not seen their faces.

As the other guerrillas embraced, Zorro laid down the pig carcass, talking spiritedly, the hunter returned – he had recovered from Halcón's rebuke. While Coyote began butchering, Maggie and Glo were led to the faint warmth of the stoves, where Tayra took over stirring the rice and beans simmering in aluminum pots.

She extended a spoon to Glo, saying, "Make yourself useful, my lady." Glo turned her back and made an angry muffled sound.

"I'll help," Maggie said, "but please let me take her gag off; she has to eat."

Tayra looked at Halcón, who nodded. Maggie undid the knot behind Glo's neck. Upon being unmuzzled, she mimicked, "'I'll help.' Shit, Maggie, you are altogether too friendly with these creeps."

Maggie said nothing. She had won their respect by volunteering to be a hostage; she was determined to keep it.

Zorro dumped some strips of pork into the rice pot. "You help cook," he told Glo. "This is a *cooperativo.* Ev'ryboddy shares in work."

She answered, "Take a flush, you lump of shit. Y'all aren't fit to roll with a sow."

"Gloria-May!" Maggie exclaimed. "You're just making it worse for us. Use your head." Then she took Buho by the wrist and led him to the haphazardly erected dome tents. The young guardians of this campsite had not grasped how to set them up; they had used tall sticks as centre posts. A tarpaulin had been rigged to shelter several backpacks and small burlap sacks of rice and beans.

Maggie knew her dome tents ("Hike over to Harvey's Camp Capital: your store for the great outdoors") and showed Buho the simple art of fitting the stays together. The tents, she noticed, bore labels of a wilderness trekking firm: Outward Bound. Similar insignias were on the sleeping bags inside them, so it appeared all this gear had been stolen.

While assembling the last tent, she stumbled and brought Buho down with her, their feet tangling. This prompted laughter from the others gathered around, but her tent-craft was appreciated; even the testy Zorro muttered a *"gracias."*

Halcón said nothing for a moment, studying her hard. Finally, he issued some brief instructions to Buho, who undid her leash. "You are to go about freely, señorita, until it is time to sleep," Buho said, "but you must stay within the circle of tents."

Maggie turned to Gloria-May with an expression of triumph, but received only a irritated look in return.

The young female guerrilla offered Glo and Maggie fresh clothes: ill-fitting but dry jungle fatigues. In the tent in which Maggie peeled off her wet outfit were a pair of sleeping bags and thin slabs of foam. Maggie would be sharing this tent with the girl: Quetzal, she was called, for the flamboyant bird. Glo would stay tied to Tayra in another. The others would also be two to a tent, leaving one of the eight guerrillas outside as a night guard.

As they waited for the food to cook, Halcón called a meeting of, to use his term, the "*colectivo*." The phrase was intended as a salve to the others, Maggie assumed: there were seven followers and one leader, at least in the absence of the revered Benito Madrigal. They listened solemnly to Halcón, nodded, too weary to demur.

Halcón then went off to listen to his radio, and Maggie joined Buho, who was tuning a small guitar. They would be staying here only the night, he said, no enthusiasm in his voice, his body bent with weariness. "Tomorrow we begin before dawn; we must travel far." Maggie had suspected as much after counting the backpacks: one for each of the guerrillas and hostages. She had followed coverage of an abduction in Colombia of mining engineers: five months it lasted. An ordeal that long would see Maggie turn thirty, in April. She felt herself aging.

They lined up at the stoves to fill their tin plates, then gathered to eat in dry shelter under the tarp. Masks were removed, but Maggie could not see faces in the darkness. She picked the meat away, filled up on rice and beans, more ravenous than she could ever recall. After the camp stoves were extinguished, when figures showed as faint ghosts, the kidnappers, using flashlights, washed the dishes and assembled equipment to be stowed in the backpacks.

Wearily, she crawled into the tent with Quetzal and into the warmth of a light sleeping bag. From outside came the sad notes of Buho's guitar, and it serenaded her to sleep.

DEAD MICE IN THE BEER

— I —

Slack Cardinal, already into his fourth beer of the morning, tuned in listlessly to the hubbub of complaint in Hector's Bar, where the Quepos expats had gathered – a Christmas promotion, an *oferta*, Bavaria going for two hundred colones a bottle. The narrow dark space was loud with talk and filled with smoke and beer's stale odours and the peculiar smells of Quepos itself, the sewers backing up in the heavy rains.

His compatriots were depressed entrepreneurs like himself, afraid to go back to their businesses, unwilling to face the truth that nothing was going to happen this tourist season. There was no point hanging around the shop waiting for customers, he'd go home, set flame to the fires of creation, a Homeric ode of tribulation and despair. He ordered another Bavaria, held it up to the light. No dead mice.

"Viva la libertad," someone said wearily. *"Viva Benito Madrigal."*

Benito Madrigal, for Christ's sake. He was back on the front page, and Slack couldn't understand why any serious revolutionary would prize him enough to engineer a hostage-taking. A failed politician of the lunatic fringe, he was now doing time in Pavas, in the mental hospital.

Don Benito had been a public servant, twenty years of rising through the Byzantine structures of government to become deputy minister of public works. His decline and fall were as swift as his ascent had been slow. Several years ago, out of the blue, he quit his job, formed a political party, the People's Popular Vanguard, and ran a hapless campaign for the presidency, garnering all of a hundred and twelve votes. He was a spirited orator, though, and reckless, accusing the minister of public works of taking bribes from a highway contractor. The minister was cleared and Madrigal was jailed for criminal slander, six months.

No one could understand how the poor schmuck got sucked into the maws of the justice system for accusing a cabinet minister of doing business in the traditional way, bribery was a cherished custom here. Civil rights groups spoke out. Committees formed. Madrigal did his time with constant loud complaint, and walked out of jail a hero.

He did not long remain one. Soon after his release, he strode into the Palacio de Justicia in San José with an AK-47 and single-handedly held five judges at gunpoint, a sleepless three-day standoff. Muddled with fatigue, he was jumped, his weapon wrestled from him. He went to La Reforma, sixteen years, ranting about lies and conspiracies. This all happened on a fifth of May, thus spawning Comando Cinco de Mayo.

Soon he became a victim of the nation's short attention span, the media writing him off as a crackpot. He was transferred to the Hospital Nacional Psiquiatrico, delusional, people were plotting against him. He had Slack's sympathy, he often felt the same way.

He wondered how the terrorism expert from South Dakota was processing this. Would the free world collapse, senator, if some delusional wanker got traded for your wife? Or would that be giving in to terrorism, thereby requiring an assessment of new warfare options?

In addition to freedom for the martyr Madrigal, the kidnappers' shopping list included a countrywide fifty-per-cent reduction in the price of beans and the deportation of all gringo criminal elements, their land to be distributed to the *pobres*. Their motives seemed not all noble, their wish list also included fifteen million U.S. dollars. The note hadn't said where the drop should be, further contact would be made by mail addressed to the U.S. Embassy.

The good news was that the junior senator from South Dakota had put his presidential campaign on hold. He announced that during a terse unsmiling speech on CNN, on location in Quepos.

"Another five cancellations today," someone complained. On top of everything, there'd been a U.S. tourist advisory, just before the Christmas holiday rush. The warning was in fine American imperialist tradition, a gun to the country's head, tourism was its main industry. To get the advisory lifted, the Tico government had practically given carte blanche to the Americans to run Operación Libertad, as they called it.

The raid had been well staged, according to the AP reporter who got the scoop. Halcón, their leader, was said to have been coolly in control. Slack suspected the kidnappers had vehicles, a safe house in San José. Or maybe they were heading north, up through the jungle and montane, to the Pan-American Highway. If they got across that, they'd be in the Talamanca, thousands of acres of national parkland.

It would be typical of Slack's wayward fortunes if he found himself somehow suspected, perhaps seriously implicated. He had a history of being scapegoated by the CIA for the various crimes of the century, no wonder he was paranoid – suspicion would fall on him because of his liaison with Gloria-May, the not-so-secret sunset kayak tour. But maybe this was the kind of quirky fear that four beer inspired.

He tried to form an image of her tramping blindfolded through the jungle in her Armani wedding anniversary dress. He truly felt sorry for her, but she was a spirited woman, she might survive. About the other, the Canadian, he didn't know.

When he was driven outside by the smoke, his eyes watering, he chanced to see Juan Camacho pass by in his truck, glaring at him. El Chorizo had filed a *denuncia* against Slack over that minor episode in Billy Balboa's restaurant, he was suing for a million colones. Slack figured he'd done him a favour, the nose looked better now, blunter, not as rat-like.

The skies were gathering in, another pour coming today, the rainy season showing no interest in packing it in. Wettest *invierno* on record, it was the accelerating global warming, man altering weather patterns, Niños and Niñas, the reefs dying, sea life starving, deserts encroaching. When the coastal plains were gone, when only buildings rising from the sea were left, maybe the experts would figure out what went wrong.

A helicopter howled overhead, low, descending toward La Compañía, the old company town nestled in the hills south of Quepos, headquarters of Operación Libertad. Choppers had been swarming around like bees for the last three days, Bells and Kawasakis clogging the tiny Quepos airport.

A Nissan utility van was prowling slowly down the street, a suit behind the wheel, checking faces. He braked in front of Hector's, leaned over the passenger seat, and rolled down the window a crack, trying not to lose his air-conditioned air. Thirty or so, a shaved head, crisply trimmed law-enforcement moustache.

"You Jacques Cardinal?"

"Name is Wilder, Harry Wilder. I sell dog food." Slack contemplated making a run for it, into the Ramus Hotel, out the back entrance.

The agent studied a photo in his hand, comparing likenesses. "Looks like you've gained a couple of pounds. Hop in."

A low functionary, Latin-Am section. Slack had hoped they might leave him in peace. "Make an appointment."

"You have one. With Mr. Hamilton Bakerfield."

"I thought he retired." Slack slid into the passenger seat and rolled his window down, he preferred normal air. He would see Ham for old times, he'd be pleasant, that's all.

The company man was Theodore, all three syllables, not Ted. He remained mostly silent, the kind of guy who can't talk and drive at the same time, respectful of government property, slowing for the breaks in the pavement, swerving from the potholes, the roads around here like an obstacle course, a maze for Mensa members.

They went not to La Compañía but up Cardiac Hill, in first gear, the local bus coming down at them, air brakes screaming, the wheezing Manuel Antonio Bluebird. A few months ago it lost those brakes on this hill, the driver yanking the emergency all the way, white-faced passengers at the windows. As Slack recounted this episode, Theodore took the shoulder, giving the bus ample room. From the hilltop they could see the ocean, the storm coming from that direction, pinpricks of lightning.

"They're going to be out there in the rain," Theodore said. "Those two women." He shook his head. "Rough."

Slack said nothing. It was beyond remotest human possibility that he would get involved, it was laughable that they would even ask him.

They pulled into the driveway of the Mariposa, Ham had picked one of the swankier hotels, of course. As they took the steps down to a chalet clinging to the hillside, a panorama of Manuel Antonio expanded before them, Playa Espadilla, Punta Quepos, Cathedral Point. The beauty of it was ratcheted away by the sound of helicopters, three in formation, heading for the high Savegre.

In the chalet, Hamilton Bakerfield was sitting behind a table, growling on the phone, sucking on a Löewenbräu. He sent Theodore packing with a flick of his hand.

"Listen, this is my show, I've got no room for fucking amateurs. Tell your people to get back in line." He was a bull, grizzled now, kind of bent over, as if – however unlikely – life had somehow humbled him. But that was age, he must be nearing seventy. Fifteen years on, and he was just as crusty and foul of mouth. Hamilton Bakerfield, he'd trained Slack, run him, nearly killed him several times.

Bakerfield nudged the phone back onto its cradle. "The Secret Service is comprised essentially of assholes. You want a beer or are you drunk already?" He extended his hand but didn't bother to rise. His grip hadn't lost its firmness.

"That was another of your lies, the story you'd retired?"

"Special assignment. The president himself called. He likes this, it's diverting attention from his bad polls. Yeah, I'm retired. I got a place in Minnesota, on a lake, you get northern pike and pickerel. Small world, I forgot you'd gone off to live in this little shithole. How're you doing?"

"Can't get it up nine days out of ten. Thanks for the disability pension."

"You got looked after. Told you not to take it in a lump."

Slack went to the fridge, where Bakerfield had German beer, Holstens, umlauts, the real stuff. He snapped open a Löewenbräu, settled into a chair, facing Bakerfield, who was lounging, his bare feet up on a low wicker table.

"This a CIA op?" Slack asked.

"State Department. Combined federal task force. CIA, FBI, Pentagon, Secret Service. All we're short of is local knowledge."

"Don't get any funny ideas," Slack said. "I'm out of it."

"Naw, I just wanted a chinwag. Heard you had a little set-to the other night, Sawchuk."

"Cardinal."

"Oh, yeah, I forgot."

"All I did was take out a couple of thieves. One was the *jefe* of the municipality."

"And what went on later between you and Walker's wife?"

"She was coming on like a dive bomber."

"She likes real men, what the fuck would she see in you?"

"Told her I was a poet, melted her heart."

"You make it with her?"

"I spared myself the humiliation of trying."

"Well, the senator wants her back, used or otherwise. What kind of shape do you figure she's in? From your experience."

"Shape? She's a traffic-stopper."

"In terms of fitness."

"She might be able to hold out. Tell me about the other one." Slack resented all the concern focused on Gloria-May Walker. What about the Canadian, anyone care about her? A goddamn hero, she'd exchanged herself for a pregnant woman. She'd been described as skinny, maybe frail. A farm girl, though, so she might be tough and innovative.

"Maggie Schneider from Saskatoon, Saskatchewan." Bakerfield emphasized each syllable, finding the place-name droll. "Writes ad copy for a TV station there. Also other stuff, romance novels."

Slack hadn't heard that one. He thought of petticoats and satin sheets, hearts on fire, heaving breasts. Her bravery confused him.

"So what do you think about these people? Comando Cinco de Mayo." Ham struggled with the Spanish.

"In for the bucks. The jargon of revolution is just for the six o'clock news."

Bakerfield wasn't buying that. "They're commies, fanatics. This Benito Madrigal character headed up some group called the People's Popular Vanguard, Trots or Maoists, some damn thing like that. His nephew Vicente has been going to college in Cuba. He's the one they call Buho. Skinny, Coke-bottle lenses, twenty-two years old, his father's rich, owns a grocery chain."

Slack knew some of the history, it was the stuff the pulps lap up. Vicente Bolaños alias Buho had become bitterly estranged from his wealthy bourgeois father, sought revenge by becoming a communist, siding with the family outcast, his mother's younger brother. Lately, he had been heading up something called Citizens for the Civil Rights of Benito Madrigal. A few weeks ago, Vicente disappeared.

"The others, we don't have any intelligence. A couple of them could be dangerous, guy they call Zorro, for one. What's that mean?"

"A kind of possum, they get into your attic and it takes a ten-megaton bomb to get them out of there."

"Yeah, he'll be the headache, a serious agitator. He came on sulky about U.S. Immigration, so we're checking deportation records. Any idea who this Halcón might be?"

"Not a clue. What were they using?" Why was Slack asking such an irrelevant question, as if he was interested.

"Skorpions, Brownings, couple of Russian choppers, RPKs."

"Those the new Kalashnikovs?"

"Yeah, I guess you're out of touch." Slack's nose crinkled as Ham lit a cigar. He had an aversion to them, especially the big coronas, maybe Freud could explain it.

"Some of these people Nicas, do you think?" Slack asked.

"Zorro apparently had a Nicaraguan accent. Ex-Sandinista, ex-Contra, who knows? But Kalashes are a dime a dozen at the border. Glut on the market."

"Yeah, well, your pal Walker created that market."

"No pal of mine. Guy's a bit marginal even for me. You been up there, the Savegre headwaters?"

"I've tramped around there. Years ago."

He'd once lugged a hardshell on his back all the way to the Savegre cloud forest. He'd been tough then, lean. Class four up there, even five, an amazing run. But the river was impassable now, except near the headwaters, a beginners' course, class one. The high river had got torn up by a hurricane a few years ago, left clogged with fallen boulders, dead trees.

Bakerfield toyed silently with his cigar, then turned and studied some high-resolutions taped to the wall, the upper Savegre country.

"We never figured out how they got from A to B, but we found their base camp this morning, an abandoned farm. One of the local rustics rode thirty miles on a horse to the nearest town for supplies, happened to mention he'd found a mess of boot prints. We flew a crew in, but they lost the scent. Too much rain; the dogs got confused."

"You don't need dogs. Hire a campesino to look for machete hacks." Slack could imagine the search party – preppies from Northwestern or Baylor. Hire an ignorant local? What a novel idea.

"You think you might want to help us on this?"

"I'm dying to." He batted away the second-hand smoke. Bakerfield was still trying to find ways to kill him.

"Feel you've been fucked around, don't you?"

"Right up the waste tract."

"You're lucky you got anything. At the end, we didn't know who you were going to blow up next, us or them. Lots of people thought you had rolled, maybe a mole all along, ever since Cuba. Others thought you were totally nuts. And the rest figured you were just a general all-around fuckup. Count me with them, because I don't remember you ever doing anything right."

The last one had been a classic débâcle – CIA agitators in the Green Party, their names exposed, flushed faces in Washington, the French government huffily ordering the U.S. ambassador to pack his bags. Twelve years later, Slack could almost remember it with pleasure.

"Well, I guess you know what you're doing, Ham." He slugged back his beer. He could take Ham's insults. The old man was looking put out now, his goading was going nowhere, Slack wasn't rising to the bait – it was an old trick, prove what a man you are.

Slack rose. "Good luck."

"For Christ's sake, you're broke. We can come up with a few bucks, make us an offer."

"Your brain for my ass."

"I can't help wondering if you've lost it, Sawchuk. Even a lady romance writer has more guts."

An empty appeal to his vanished pride.

"The name is Cardinal. I do kayak tours." He rose and stretched. "Time for my nap. I'll take one for the road." He helped himself to another umlaut.

"You got a problem, pal."

After Theodore drove him back to town, Slack considered dallying longer at Hector's, but decided against it. A mood had come over him, maybe dangerous, another beer might send him over the edge. Had he always been this neurotic? No, it was a learned thing, all those years of working as a spook had driven him halfway to the cackle factory. And now they have the gall to ask a favour. He'd spent too many years burying those memories, he wasn't going to unearth the coffin.

He retrieved his Land Rover, and as he set out for home the skies opened. Rumbling past the squat, swearing at his useless windshield wipers, he thought he saw El Chorizo's truck parked down there, his Isuzu. What was he up to?

Then he noticed three tin shacks in a new clearing, right on his property, ten yards from his house, some young mangoes cut down, and a guapinol and a roble on which he'd been growing orchids. What infuriated him most was that they had killed a mother armadillo and her baby, they were hanging dead on a rope.

He parked, unlocked his shed, and brought out a heavy sledge-hammer. As he advanced toward the shacks, several of Camacho's minions scurried from them like weasels. He recognized a couple of them, clerks in the municipal office, Camacho's hirelings. Finding strength through anger, he knocked all the tin structures down, taking out their wooden support beams with powerful swipes of the sledge.

Then he marched in the pouring rain down a muddy road into the squatters' village, stopping when he got to Camacho's truck. With one majestic swing, he pulverized the windshield. He waited for Camacho to come out of the house he was hiding in, his brother-in-law's. He could see him at the window now, with his bandaged reconstructed nose. When he showed no signs of desiring confrontation, Slack smashed the headlights and went back home. Next time he'd use a gun.

As the rain pummelled his tiled roof, he stood hesitantly before his fridge, wanting a drink, fighting it. Though his anger hadn't drained, he found his mind drifting elsewhere, being pulled up the Savegre.

A writer of insipid romances had more guts, that galled. He wondered how quickly she churned them out. His own muse, that unyielding bitch, had found him barren, impotent, had flounced from his life. Maybe just one last cold beer, then he'd quit. He examined a bottle of Imperial against the light. No dead mice.

— 2 —

Slack had brought the big raft for this morning's excursion, the eight-seater, and he had almost a full complement, six wet customers. They'd dropped maybe a hundred feet over half a mile, a simple run for beginners, and were now in the coastal valley, the Río Naranjo curling languidly between pastures and fruit groves.

Thanks to the Fifth of May Commando, an influx of reporters had caused an uptick in the local economy, even the small hotels filling up, Mono Titi Tours getting a booking a day, media people mostly, jungle ingénues.

"Not much wildlife to point out here. They spray these fields with poisonous chemicals so you lose the birds, their eggshells become thin as paper. Doesn't affect the snakes, though. Fer-de-lances, corals, rattlers, we got 'em all. There's one here they call the silent rattler, two-inch fangs, aggressive, it'll chase you. And watch when you walk under trees, that's where the eyelash viper lurks. Eighty per cent mortality rate."

His customers nervously searched the overhanging boughs for this latest in Slack's compendium of jungle menaces. He was feeling desperate – the world's attention was focused on little Manuel Antonio, it would become a Cancún, an Acapulco, vast rows of time-shares, BMWs and Jaguars in the parking lots. The little national park would be trampled in the rush.

"We come out on Playa Rey, that's the other side of the park, and you can swim there, but watch out for the sharks, they like to hang around the river outlets."

The guy in front of him turned, frowning. "Man, you've got to be the most depressing guide in the world." This fellow was a photographer, one of the newsmagazines, a complainer. "Isn't anything right with this place?"

Yeah, you're not right, I'm not right, nobody is. Slack was suffering his regular morning hangover and terminally sore back. He had been in a funk since his session with Ham Bakerfield, those digs about his lack of balls. He'd given them eight years. He'd been captured, beaten, tortured, he'd suffered electric shocks to his groin, and it was a special occasion when he could satisfy a woman, the desire there, the apparatus working inconsistently. Fifty thousand bucks they gave him, and a one-way ticket to Costa Rica.

So a couple of women were in peril, so what? The planet had greater crises. Greenhouse emissions, a birth rate climbing exponentially, the decimation of species. Soon there would be nothing. Just wall-to-wall pet food salesmen.

At Playa Rey, a couple of his clients went into the water, struggling out to the distant waves. A long straight ribbon of sand, big curls beyond that, but it wasn't a popular beach, usually deserted, a few surfers on weekends. Not far away, near the jungled cliffs of the national park, the Río Naranjo flowed gently into the sea past a mangrove swamp. The Savegre was bigger and wilder, a few miles down the coast.

Slack led his patrons under the shade of a palm, passed out cartons of juices, then tried to find a spot away from them to sit, but a woman joined him.

"Doesn't seem much like Christmas around here," she said. Middle-aged, heavily oiled with sunblock, a print journalist from Chicago. "So where're you from, Slack?"

"Uzbekistan."

"Seriously."

"Philadelphia. I was in pet food."

"How did you end up down here?"

A reporter, answers must be appropriately vague. "Just looking for something different."

"So can I ask you a sort of man-in-the-street question? What do you think of this hostage crisis?"

Slack didn't want to get into it. "I couldn't care less."

She looked startled. "You're not concerned?"

"A fifty-per-cent reduction in the price of beans seems like a good idea."

"You *approve* of what they're doing?"

Slack had been only half-serious, but she didn't twig to the sarcasm.

"Look, no one wants to see those women harmed, but I wish they'd taken Walker instead. That guy, the last four years, he voted for every anti-environment bill that came across his desk, and every pro-poverty bill as well. Too bad the kidnappers didn't take him, they could keep him."

"Do I sense that your politics are a little to the left?"

"Yeah, I'm a Bolshevik." Maybe that wasn't funny. She started writing notes.

He escaped to the ocean, hoping to catch a wave.

Dear Rocky,

First of all, let me respond to your derisory comments about Harry Wilder. I am sorry he depresses you, but I find offensive your characterization of him as an anxiety-ridden pantywaist who can't find his own pecker. Is it not obvious that he is an archetype for today, a hero suited to this age of angst? The world cries out for losers to love.

But the peddler of Bow Wow Chow is not in fear of physical danger, oddly that's not on his inventory of potholes to avoid along life's haphazard journey. No, Rocky, what carps at him is an obsessive dread of failure, of flubbing, screwing up, events going tragically wrong. The fuckup blows another operation, get the body bags ready, Dr. Zork succeeds in his plan to destroy the world.

Your number two gripe: Where have I hidden the bodies, where's the blood? Your advice that I begin the first chapter by shooting Harry Wilder is under advisement, but I intend to give him a period of grace.

You whine that my draft chapters lack even the prospect of, as you basely put it, nooky. "A hot box lunch was draping herself all over his kayak, and the reader doesn't even get any heavy breathing out of this schnorrer." Sorry, Rock, the guy was practically neutered during the war against the evil empire, remember?

The real bitch is that I still can't come up with an opening line, that perfect smooth takeoff still lurking somewhere in the blank pages of my mind. (I tried this: *Hardly a day passed when Harry Wilder did not give thanks that his surname wasn't Dick.*) Obsessive, you say? I suffer an anal-retentive need to do something right for a change? Not right, Rocky, perfect, totally unfucked-up. I fear writing a pulp thriller can never satisfy that need.

Okay, maybe I *am* trying to sabotage this project. Frankly, it sucks air.

I am a *poet*!

Yours,

Alfred Lord Tennyson

Slack fought his way to the bar at Billy Balboa's, the place was crowded, it had been discovered by Operación Libertad – many of its agents were here, some press, too. At one of the tables a reporter was interviewing a middle-aged couple who looked out of place, not wearing the latest Tilley fashions, the guy thin with callused workman's hands, the woman matronly, both looking strained and exhausted.

Billy poured Slack a double Centenario and lifted his own glass. "*Pura vida, maje*," he said.

"Who are those two people?"

Billy looked at his reservation list. "These people are called Schneiders."

The Schneiders from Saskatchewan, the parents of the romance writer. A broken marriage, he'd heard, but they were guileless good-hearted prairie folk.

Now the woman started weeping. Slack stared hard into his glass, then tilted it back.

By ten o'clock most of the customers had departed, and Slack was alone at the bar, clutching it for support. Others swam in and out of the haze, Billy cashing out, the Schneiders finally getting to their feet. Slack couldn't look at them, he tried to drown them in his rum, make them disappear.

He waited until their interviewer led them out before heading to the men's facility. He was doing all right, able to walk, but then he stalled, because there was motion in front of him, three men approaching, or maybe it was four, all with determined expressions.

He knew a couple of these faces. One was a cop – with the OIJota, the judicial police – and this starched-looking android, where had he seen him before? Theodore, Bakerfield's gofer.

"Señor Cardinal," said the OIJota, "you are under arrest."

He tried to charge past and was tackled. He wasn't much of a match in his condition, and after about four minutes of huffing and swearing they had him down, pinned to the floor.

He wasn't conscious of much after that except being dragged into a vehicle, thrown onto a cot in the roach-infested jail, then roused from sleep, Ham Bakerfield and some of his lackeys staring down at him.

"No point trying to deal with him now. Take him home."

— 3 —

Slack woke to African drums pounding in his head. Then he noticed the smell, a mix of stale booze and rum farts, his own putrid armpits, and – however unlikely – cigar fumes. He was covered with bites. He was lying on his kitchen floor. Because he was near the stairs, he deduced that at some point he'd made a failed effort to get up to the bedroom.

The cigar smoke was coming from the hammock, where Ham Bakerfield was stretched out.

"Wish I had a camera, former double agent depicted here as a lump of shit. You got a wheelbarrow or a forklift so we can get you to the shower?"

Slack struggled to his feet, followed Ham down the stairs to the outdoor shower, holding his back, he must have strained it in the fight.

"What was that all about, that mugging?"

"A story from the *Chicago Tribune* went over the wires, offering, quote, an unusual perspective from a local tour operator. It's got your picture and everything." Ham read from a printout: "'Cardinal, a self-styled Bolshevik, claimed he supports the cause of the kidnappers.' We had to take you in for questioning as a possible accessory."

"Yeah, right, I'm colluding with the enemy. Christ, I was just joking with her."

Ham grunted. "Nobody got the joke, including the senator. He thinks you staged it."

"I *staged* it?"

"It's a damn good cover. I straightened him out."

Slack couldn't even guess what he was talking about. "Put out that cigar, it's making me sick."

He peeled off his clothes and stood under the spout, feeling the cold shock of his piped mountain water. Ham flipped him a bar of soap. "Take a shampoo and a shave, too. I want you looking vaguely human when you meet with Walker. He said to me, 'Bring me that soldier, he has the right stuff.' He wants to make sure you can lay off the gargle, though, you were fricasseed when he last saw you. You look like a dartboard, pal."

The bugs liked the taste of Slack, his blood sweet with alcohol. Mosquitoes, *purrujas*, mites, spiders, they must have all dined on him last night. A towel wrapped around his midriff, he went to the propane refrigerator for a cold straightener. But the beer compartment was empty.

"It's down the sink, Slack."

Slack snarled at him. "I thought you stopped running my life."

"You don't have a fucking life. Get one." Ham softened his voice, opted for a conciliatory approach. "You've got to start believing in yourself again, Slack. You can do this, you've got the training, you've got the local knowledge, and suddenly you've got the perfect cover. I only admit this to myself in the privacy of my bathroom, but you're not as dumb as people think. So you can get straight and try to be a hero or you can just fucking decay. There's money, Slack. The senator's friends have put together a private fund. A hundred grand for trying, triple that if you get her back into the loving arms of her husband."

Slack was tempted. Three hundred large – if he got lucky – could buy a little chunk of peace, away from the squatters, a new start. Even the hundred was good, the consolation prize if he screwed up. "Employed or on contract?"

"A contract, but we do everything as a team, you're not going off on one of your side trips to outer space . . ." Ham reined himself in. "Sure, any way you want it."

Slack stared out the window at the tin roofs across the road. A vehicle was waiting, the Nissan, Theodore at the wheel. He couldn't shake the memory of the sad faces of those two down-home folks from Saskatchewan, Margaret Schneider's mom and dad. He kept seeing the strained white knuckles, the tears. Suddenly he hated himself, his cowardice, his obsessive fear of failure.

"All right, I'm in."

"How long's it going to take you to get into some kind of shape?"

"I've been running." Except maybe the last three mornings. But he did have his wind. There was a pot-belly that had never been there before, it didn't seem permanent. In what kind of shape was his head?

"But you give up the sauce. As of now. You see this guy over here?"

Leaning against a wall, a dark-skinned man in khaki shorts, short but wiry, legs like thick cables. Where had he come from? Had he been here all along? Yeah, he was a shadow, one of those guys who click in and out of view. Joe Borbón was his name, a Cuban from Miami, mid-thirties. He didn't offer to shake hands, just sat there looking Slack over, as if assessing him for the killing points.

"Joe here's a black belt, fourth dan. You aren't going anywhere near the suds unless you kill him first. Or he kills you."

The guy was maybe a hundred and sixty pounds, slicked hair, glasses that were probably phony. "Think you could do that?" Slack asked him.

Borbón showed no expression. "No problem."

"Yeah, well, you just keep out of my way."

"I don't plan to be in it." A toneless voice.

"What is this joker, one of the robots they build at Langley? Little electrodes, one for stalking, one for murder?" Slack sighed. "Let's go."

Theodore took them around Quepos by the old road, then headed off the highway into the palm trees. The idea was to avoid detection by the media, so the meet was to be at Pueblo Real, a condo complex by the lagoon across from Damas Island. Jorge Castillo, the minister of public security, had a weekend getaway there. Castillo himself would be present, along with Senator Walker.

Most of the units were empty, the development had never taken off, too far from the beaches. Castillo's digs were on the second floor, overlooking the pool and the weedy field that was supposed to be a golf course.

Slack walked into a blast of cold air, the conditioners roaring, he abhorred chemically treated air. Walker shook his hand, a stiff grip, his eyes raw, posture rigid. Castillo was wrapped conservatively, suit and tie, a bland mandarin with a law degree, a masters from Cornell. His grip was soft.

"Let's just clarify our roles here," Walker said. "Ham Bakerfield is in charge. I know a little about guerrillas and jungle warfare, and I think I know how the minds of these characters work, but I'm a little too emotionally involved, so I'll be content to stay in close and be an adviser."

An adviser, Walker had given himself a seat at the front table.

Ham said, "Right, senator, and, ah, of course we have to respect the fact we're on foreign soil here, friendly soil, and Minister Castillo is essentially the man at the top."

Ham was doing his diplomatic best. Castillo, who was known to have presidential ambitions, appeared resentful of Walker's patently colonial attitude but he remained polite. "May I offer you gentlemen a refreshment, perhaps a coffee or juice?"

While their host went to the kitchen to give instructions to his help, Slack subsided onto an empty couch, sat back, closed his eyes. Everything was throbbing. He tried to control his shaking.

"Is he going to be able to take on this assignment?" Walker asked.

"We don't need any foot shots, Slack," Ham said. "We can't afford a mistake."

"Just give me a few days. It'll probably take them a week to make contact, anyway. They'll want to organize a safe set-up first."

He opened his eyes to see Jorge Castillo leading in the maid with her tray of coffees and fresh-squeezed juice. He turned to Slack and began a florid speech in Spanish about how all Costa Ricans were enraged at this *desafortunado* event, which was a blot on the good name of the motherland, a nation long at the forefront of international peace efforts. Slack guessed he was testing his Spanish, and expressed his agreement in similar rococo fashion.

Castillo returned to English. "Do I hear a Cuban accent?"

"Spent seven years there."

"These kidnappers might not relate well to a gringo."

"I'm a Tico. I vote in the same elections you do."

Castillo's face expressed uncertainty as he redirected his gaze from the surly customer on the couch to Bakerfield and Walker. "With the greatest of respect, I am concerned that Señor Cardinal may not be the person for this task. Archbishop Mora has again volunteered. As you know he also intervened in that matter three years ago, with the Swiss women. They were ultimately released."

"Yes, but the kidnappers got paid off, didn't they?" said Walker. "We don't want that, that's surrendering to them."

Castillo spoke firmly, "Archbishop Mora insists he will be available. He is trusted by all Costa Ricans."

"Yes, Mr. Minister," Bakerfield said, oiling the water. "We should definitely keep him available. But in the meantime we have a very able man here in Mr. Cardinal. He's specially trained in these things."

Slack slowly sat forward, stretching the ache from his arms and shoulders. He was feeling a little better, the shakes dissipating.

"I want to see a signed contract."

"You'll get it. Okay, Double-o-seven, this is the deal. We're proceeding on the assumption this meeting did not take place. The press don't know anything about your past, nobody does. We'll bring you in after a few days, reluctantly, after we finish building the cover. You'll be a left-leaning layabout with a kayak business, but we'll say we need you for your jungle expertise. With luck, they'll accept you as their contact man, the courier of money."

"Yeah, but let's start with the martyr of Cinco de Mayo," Slack said. "Where is he? In the Psiquiatrico hospital, right?"

"The doctors call it paranoid schizophrenia." That was hard work for Castillo, he retreated to Spanish: "He is on medication. Two weeks ago he wrote this letter."

He handed Slack a clipping from *La Nación*, Madrigal's complaint about the harsh conditions he was enduring. It seemed rational enough, except for the line, "They are trying to read my thoughts."

"Apparently, some of his friends have taken this nonsense seriously," Castillo said.

Slack continued in Spanish. "Don Jorge, it would help us if Madrigal were released from the hospital and placed in better circumstances. Then I will meet with him."

Ham was looking petulant, wishing they would talk American. But Walker was following this, musing it over.

"I take Benito to them first," Slack explained, "an offering of trust."

They thrashed it out more, Ham liking the idea, adding decorations. Walker remained silent until the end, then spoke stiffly about his concern for his wife. "I take it we're all agreed there'll be no action until she's safely removed. After that, I don't care if you napalm them."

Castillo looked horrified, and stuttered in protest. "Senator Walker, my friend, you understand that Costa Rican law does not allow foreign soldiers or military equipment. We have many skilled people who can help Señor Cardinal. We can solve this problem peacefully."

"Sure," said Walker. "Of course, we'll do it peacefully. Whatever works."

Slack could tell he'd rather use napalm. No small part of a presidential wannabe's reputation was riding on the prospect of blasting a bunch of amateurs into oblivion.

The process of rehabilitating his body began that morning, the sun already high as Slack ran the sands of Espadilla. A few dozen bodies were stretched out, white sun-blocked skin, tourists, U.S. agents enjoying their off-shifts, a petite young woman stretched out on a towel who caused an Esperanza flashback. Also running the beach, a hundred yards behind him, was the shadow, Joe Borbón.

He'd had to accept Borbón as part of the deal. The signed contract said Slack was to use his "best efforts" to help free the two women under the advice and direction of Ham Bakerfield. That was vague enough, it left room for what little personal initiative he might muster.

Several surfers were sitting on their boards, riding the swells out by Final, the north end of the beach where Slack made a tight loop and headed back to the park entrance. Borbón passed him going the other way, expressionless, the wind-up man. A few naked people were on discreet display here, nudity being vaguely tolerated at Final.

Slack was in majestic pain, but pressing himself, maybe he could just burn it away fast, the need, the addiction. If only he could keep the dogs of defeat at bay, the fear of failure that continually nipped at his heels. It was a loser's complex — can't make a living, can't keep a woman, can't get it up — and it was getting worse, almost patholog-ical, soon he, too, would be claiming they were trying to read his thoughts.

Fifty yards on, a family was attempting to body surf, three kids and their parents, probably on holiday from San José, and just as Slack was plodding past them he heard the mother cry out. Their older boy, brave for a Tico, or maybe just foolhardy in his adolescence, had caught a rip, and was fast being sucked out to sea in a current of boil-ing brown water. Even more foolish was the father, who — like almost every Tico Slack had met — could barely swim, and in his rescue attempt was being pulled beyond his depth, the rip catching him, too.

Slack plunged in as a wave crashed over him, swam first for the boy, who was panicking, gulping water. He pinned his arms to stop his thrashing, then swam him to the side of the rip and hauled him to shore.

By this time, the father was fifty yards out, and Slack dove in again. The man was going down when Slack finally got to him, and it was no easy task to swim while carrying him on his back. A crowd had gathered by the time he was able to lay him on the sand, and he motioned the spectators away, then gave the man mouth-to-mouth. He finally spewed out the seawater, coughing, gasping. His wife flew at Slack, and hugged him as she wept. Joe Borbón stood at the edge of the crowd, no expression.

Slack didn't wait for further thanks. One of the U.S. agents had shouldered through the crowd, and as soon as Slack saw father and son were being well tended to, he continued his run.

❧

That afternoon, accompanied by his faithful Cuban watchdog, Slack was ferried by chopper to the Eco-Rico Lodge. There wasn't much to see, all items of evidence bagged up and taken, the place temporarily shut down, abandoned but for caretakers. The bad guys had tossed all the cabins, scooping about thirty-five thousand in cash, jewellery, and Rolexes, nothing bulky. Chuck Walker thought they had even nicked a vial of Gloria-May's expensive perfume, L'Eau d'Issey. Margaret Schneider's so-called Jungle House had got hit, too, five hundred dollars the senator lent her after she had fallen into a typical tourist trap, she had entertained Walker with her tale of being ripped off by a silky seducer. Her writings had been strewn all over the floor, notes for a *roman de romance*, Slack should probably glance through them.

The Cinco de Mayoists had been messy but quick, they had scouted the place well. They seemed to know the layout of the grounds and the trails beyond, maybe they had had inside help.

Slack slipped away from Joe Borbón's sight long enough to borrow a dirt bike, and raced off to survey the area, up a trail that deadended at a waterfall. He couldn't figure out how the kidnappers had got up the river, but their base camp had been not far from the Savegre and three thousand feet higher.

They flew off to that camp next. There, a ridge trail fed into a few scattered campesino farms, small plots burned out of the jungle in dry season, a time of year that depressed Slack, fires raging through the helpless forest. But Mother Nature had avenged herself upon the arsonist, his shack had been razed.

The ground team was led by Yale Brittlewaite, African-American, grizzled hair and beard, retired Vietnam snake-eater. "The ridge ends another three hundred yards up, and we haven't found any paths they could have hacked out of here, no squashed ferns, no machete cuts."

Cinco de Mayo had shown a laudable concern for the environment – the only scrap of garbage left behind was a torn tent label, it had been traced to a break-in a month ago at the San José warehouse of Outward Bound, the wilderness trekkers. The night guard claimed to have slept through it, he was still being questioned. Otherwise no prints anywhere, no clues, *nada*.

Slack wanted to talk to some of the locals, but Borbón tersely reminded him: no unofficial contacts. It was time to go home, face an evening of punishment, it would start with a hundred push-ups. He was determined to prove himself, even if only to the extent of his limited expectations. This morning's deed of valour, his rescue of two lives, had spurred him on, maybe it was the new start he sought, the opening paragraph of a reformed life.

NO TIME FOR SORROW

— I —

After four gruelling days as a captive of the Comando Cinco de Mayo, Maggie's terror had dissipated, supplanted by a weary malaise. Her physical discomfort was bearable, though her legs ached from the daily forced marches and her skin was pebbled with insect bites and reddened with cuts and scrapes. It had rained often, and her clothes were smeared with mud from her many slips and falls. She endured without complaint the shifting weight of an unwieldy backpack.

She was tired but not as exhausted as several of the guerrillas, who were out of wind and puffing, constantly demanding rest stops, slapping at bugs, tugging at their tight kerchiefs, grunting curses, *"Hijueputa!"*

Each day they had climbed higher, and now were at a cooler altitude, in a dripping, moss-rich forest of buttressed giants, sunlight filtering through their leafy reaches. Maggie wondered if they were lost – Halcón often ordered a halt, checking the compass he wore as a pendant, frowning, muttering.

Occasionally, Coyote, in the lead with a machete, was forced to cut a path through the undergrowth, but here, beneath a canopy that starved ground cover of light, was only forest litter. Maggie had taken fixes from the sun: they were going roughly northeast, with many detours when they followed one of the raging creeks. They would descend, then climb, dip and climb again – a zigzag path intended to make pursuit difficult.

They had sighted humans only once, shortly after leaving the original campsite: a man leading a horse down the trail, his wife and two children astride it. They had flattened themselves in a cornfield, where they remained unobserved in the morning twilight. Then they had retraced their steps to the Savegre River, struggling up its bank for three hours before Coyote took them into the forest, slashing a narrow trail.

Only at night when the moon was hidden did the rebels of Cinco de Mayo remove their kerchiefs. Maggie and Glo were not restrained while in their tents; no one expected them to stray off and risk the terrors of night in the jungle. In any event, one guerrilla was always on guard outside, the men taking four-hour shifts.

Maggie continued to share a tent with seventeen-year-old Quetzal, who liked to practise her English. When they were alone in the tent, even with a candle burning, Quetzal went without her kerchief, aware that Maggie had already seen her face. Though she offered confidences – often intimate – she professed not to know where they were going, and seemed more interested in talking about film stars and pop musicians than in changing the world. She had found love, that frangible, elusive concept, and had eyes only for the young man who had been with her at the supply base, Perezoso, meaning sloth. During rest stops he and Quetzal held hands and often kissed: they seemed immature, mundanely performing the stock roles of revolutionaries in love.

Since Tayra was Gloria-May's tentmate, Zorro enjoyed a nightly respite from his partner's scalding tongue. Maggie had been impressed to learn from Quetzal they had been married for twenty years. They were both Nicaraguans; he was from Managua, she was Afro-Caribbean, from the east coast, a descendant of the slaves brought there two centuries ago. They had met in the war – both Sandinistas, Maggie assumed, though Quetzal wasn't sure. Tayra was the troupe's hardest worker, running the field kitchen, cleaning and packing up afterwards.

Although no longer tethered to Buho – in reward for her good behaviour – Maggie remained close to the scrawny young man, the gentlest of the crew, often speaking solicitously to her in his formal, precise English. He occasionally lectured her, using phrases like "doomed bourgeois society" and "educating the masses by deed," proclaiming sombrely that "political conflicts are not settled by talk, as the liberals believe, but by struggle." He was, as she had guessed, a student, studying for a degree in economics at Cuba's national university. He played mournful tunes on his guitar in the evenings. His boots were ill-fitting and he walked in discomfort.

Wiry, stooped Coyote was the best of Halcón's soldiers, the sole revolutionary here with jungle skills, expert at slicing through the ferns and spiny shrub and thick lianas. But life had dealt him a bad hand. According to Quetzal, he had been a squatter, turned embittered when the rural guard threw him and his family on the road with their pots and pans and soiled mattresses. His wife and children had gone off with another man. Afterwards, he had tried homesteading – until his shack was gutted by fire.

Though Halcón smoked a cigarette at every pause, he had better wind than his comrades. He never addressed his two captives, and had few words even for his mates. Maggie was intrigued by this laconic man, with his dark, darting eyes and military haircut. What secrets were hidden behind that blue kerchief? If Quetzal knew any of his history she didn't share it. As for the mysterious Benito Madrigal, he was currently in a mental hospital: a radical politician who had once run for president. Quetzal, formerly his housemaid, claimed he was a visionary, a great orator, a man much misunderstood.

Halcón was matched in stamina only by his two captives, the complaisant Margaret Schneider and the snarling Gloria-May Walker – too proud to beg Halcón for a cigarette, she had quit smoking: good for the lungs, bad for an already nasty disposition. Glo had refused to carry a backpack, and between bouts of vituperation marched sullenly behind Tayra like a dog, a rope around her waist.

Glo had a particular distaste for Zorro, who leered at her whenever his wife was not watching. When Tayra caught him doing so, she severely dressed him down. Zorro endured Tayra's complaints and insults silently, though with an edge of irritation. It worried Maggie that Halcón had entrusted him with their entire arsenal; the two sub-machine guns and five pistols were bundled in his pack.

Late on the third day of their forced march, they entered a cloud forest: giant trees so weighted with moss and ferns and epiphytes that many had collapsed. At times, the going became treacherous, as they scrambled over deadfalls, among branches where Coyote prodded for snakes, through an understory thick with large-leaf herbs and prickly shrubs that lacerated their legs through the fabric of their pants.

Finally, the path became easier, a serviceable animal track. Here, the terrain was relatively gentle, the forest floor carpeted with dead leaves, but they were moving slowly, Coyote warily stirring the leaves with his machete. He had an almost instinctive sense of where snakes might hide, but the several they encountered had simply slithered away.

Everyone froze at the sound of a helicopter, a distant chuffing that soon receded. They often heard search aircraft passing directly over them, unseen above the treetops. Maggie felt sure that some-where to the south, a ground party was advancing. Expert followers would soon locate one of the trails they had made: machete cuts, boot prints in mud. In the meantime, until rescued or otherwise released, she would think positively: this was a unique adventure, inspiration for a gripping novel.

Coyote, his machete whispering through the undergrowth, was now leading them single file up a twenty-degree incline, followed by Halcón, then Maggie, and the tandem of Tayra and Glo, the five others straggling behind, fat Gordo at the rear, panting hard.

The column abruptly halted, closing like an accordion. "*Matabuey*," Coyote said in a hoarse voice. He was shaking, stepping slowly back, then he started running down the hill, the others scampering after him, a chain reaction. Glo, tugged by Tayra's rope, fell, and Maggie paused to help her to her feet.

"What's going on?" she asked.

"A bushmaster, *matabuey*," Buho said in a trembling whisper. "This means bull killer." He translated Coyote's rapid-fire Spanish: "He says it is very fast, and will pursue." Coyote had his machete at the ready. Zorro had retrieved an automatic pistol from his heavy pack.

Maggie had encountered rattlers on the prairies, but had not heard of snakes seeking human prey. Her curiosity overcame her qualms and she retraced her steps, climbing onto a high cradle formed by a twisting liana. From this perch, she spotted the diamond-backed snake, at least three metres long and only ten metres away. It yawned, showing a chilling set of fangs. Maggie would have bolted had she not seen a bulky protrusion in the area of its stomach.

"*Qué pasa?*" someone called.

"It's not moving. I think it just ate." As she spoke, the snake did begin to move, turning in a long, lazy spiral and winding slowly into the forest. She felt awed by its grace and savage beauty. "We're okay," she called. "It's going."

They seemed uncertain at first, but Halcón prodded them forward. Maggie could not tell if, behind their kerchiefs, they appeared sheepish as they silently rejoined her. Glo was scornful: "The brave soldiers of the Fifth of May. *No hablo cojones.*" Her Spanish might have been flawed, but the message was reasonably clear.

As they recommenced their slow upward journey, rays of the lowering sun pierced the foliage above. Maggie was the first to see the quetzal – with its streaming green tail feathers, scarlet and snowy white beneath. The entire column stopped and watched as it snapped a lizard from a branch, then sailed into the mist.

Under more comfortable circumstances, Maggie might have been enraptured by this expedition: a diversion from her mundane world of hawking farm machinery or extolling the sizzling steaks at Spiro's Eighth Street Grill. Coyote had shown them tracks of a jaguar and a tapir. Tanagers and trogons regularly darted past them, birds of such brilliant plumage that at each sighting Maggie felt a momentary lifting of gloom.

Maggie heard groans from the group ahead, who had reached a wide rocky ledge. She grasped a tree root, swung herself up beside them, and found herself looking down the rim of a forested ravine; distantly from below came the sound of rushing water, the upper reaches of the Savegre.

Halcón checked his compass, then drew a cigarette from his pack of Derbys. While he conferred with his team, Maggie sat beside Glo and whispered, "I don't think we are where we're supposed to be."

"You can fucking definitely say that again. These yo-yos couldn't follow the south end of a northbound mule." She called, "Hey, you, Buho."

The young man came over. "Can I be of help, señora?"

"I feel grubbier than a rat in a swamp – let's carry on down to where there's some water."

"I am sorry, Halcón says we should camp here."

"Look, you go over there and tell that son of a bitch to admit he's got y'all completely lost. He's leading you nowhere, Buho, so maybe it's time for the rank and file to rise."

"Do not underestimate our captain, señora."

"Tell him my husband is going to have his love appendages hanging off a barbed-wire fence." She said this loudly, intended for Halcón, who glanced her way. She shouted at him: "Fetch me some goddamn water so I can wash up. It's no way to treat a lady, you lump of mule shit!"

Until now, Halcón had taken her abuse with an almost unsettling composure – but he finally reacted. He strode toward them and addressed Glo in clear English. "Be a lady, then I will treat you that way. This is not the Royal Plaza Hotel." A deep voice but flat, without tone or emphasis. "But as you see, the sun, soon it will set. The river is half an hour. Here we will camp."

Halcón turned to his comrades and issued quiet orders. Backpacks were shucked, tents removed. From this high vantage point, Maggie could see the hazy blue of the Pacific Ocean, the sun flattening on it like a bright orange egg. She watched solemnly until it was a pinprick of light; before dying it shot out an intense green spark that made her blink in surprise. It seemed a cryptic message, perhaps of hope.

The three men erecting the tents suddenly began a wild dance, lifting their legs, slapping at their ankles.

"*Hormigas rojas!*"

Fire ants – Maggie could see tiny forms swarming the men as they raced into the trees.

Zorro performed a feat of bravery, running to the tents, picking them up, hurrying to safety. Tayra bent and brushed the ants from his ankles: a rare moment of caring interaction between them.

Glo called: "Where did you learn to pick a campsite, Halcón, the Boy Scouts?" He did not respond.

The site abandoned, they began filing down the ravine along a switchback animal path, a descent marked by much tripping and sliding and grasping at roots and branches. Darkness was settling upon them as they reached the edge of a fast-rushing creek, a *quebrada*, in Maggie's growing Spanish lexicon.

Overlooking the stream was a rock bluff. Maggie's eyes widened at the sight of an extraordinary object resting on it, a ten-ton granite cannonball, a spherical stone at least two metres in diameter and so symmetrical it had to be the work of man not nature. All but Coyote, who was leery of it, gathered around its perimeter, staring with awe, stroking it.

"This is a sign," said Buho.

"Of what?" Maggie asked.

He frowned. "I am not sure." But he explained the sphere was likely sculpted by the peoples of pre-Columbian times; many had been found in Costa Rica, though their purpose had never been determined.

A breeze whispered through the trees. Coyote backed away several metres from the sphere, muttering anxiously.

"He says he can hear their voices, they are warning us of danger." Buho shrugged. "We must forgive Coyote; he comes from a tradition of false beliefs, of superstition."

Gordo seemed less concerned, insisting that his fellows boost him onto the stone, where he rose to his full five feet and four inches and raised a fist. "*Viva Benito Madrigal*," he said. Of all the guerrillas, he seemed their hero's staunchest fan.

The bluff was a natural campsite, hidden under vine-entangled trees, and Halcón, dismissing Coyote's objections, ordered the tents be raised near the sphere. Maggie, as usual, took charge of the task, gathering stones to weigh down the tents. She listened for the warning voices of ancient aboriginal spirits but heard only the haunting call of a bird: poo-oor me, it seemed to say.

The stoves were lit for the *gallo pinto*. The plain daily fare – rice and beans for breakfast, lunch, and dinner – was putting Maggie's taste buds to sleep. She had passed up chances to vary the diet: Coyote occasionally caught crawfish and river shrimp and even trout, using berries to lure them to the point of his machete. On their second day, he had snared a turkey-sized bird, a curassow, but she had picked the bits of meat away from her *arroz con curassow*.

The stars were out by the time the camp was set up. Maggie found Glo by her tent; her bindings had been released and she was pulling off her boots, which parted from her feet with a sucking sound. She turned them upside down to dry and shouted at Gordo, who was standing guard, "Get me some hot water!"

"Glo, I think you might be better turning on the charm."

"I'd throw up."

"Try it, Glo. You might not have to spend all day at the end of a rope."

Maggie found her way in the darkness to the glow of the stoves. She joined Quetzal, picked up a wooden spoon, and began stirring the beans. The young woman, who had already removed her kerchief, smiled at her.

She called Maggie *valiente* because she had not fled from the snake. Maggie shrugged off the compliment: Quetzal, too, was brave, to have joined this revolutionary commando. Quetzal said she had been inspired to do so by the words and deed of her former *patrón*, Benito Madrigal.

Her boyfriend, Perezoso, had enlisted in Madrigal's *movimiento* by a different route. While canvassing as a Jehovah's Witness, he had been invited into his house, where Quetzal was staying. "For him and me, was love at first sight." Abandoning religion, blinded by his passion for Quetzal, Perezoso joined the revolution. His parents were middle class, but Quetzal was an orphan raised by the church.

In the near darkness, Maggie worked her way through the campsite to fetch Glo to dinner. Halcón was in his tent – she could hear his short-wave, the news in Spanish, too muffled to be made out. She had a vision of her family gathered at the farm around the radio, listening for hopeful news. If only she could get word to them . . .

Below, illuminated under the stars at the edge of the stream, she glimpsed a bare rising leg, Glo's contorted torso. Maggie descended from the ledge.

"Haven't you been getting enough exercise?"

Glo carried on, twisting, bending. "You'll never have a problem, you're so naturally wiry. This is where the muscles start to waste." As her hand caressed her inner thigh it was caught in the beam of a flashlight aimed from the ledge above. Maggie heard a thick-throated gasp.

"Shut that off!" Glo shouted.

The flashlight continued to play on Glo's legs, and she picked up a stone and sent it spinning at the beam. The flashlight fell; a shout of pain: "*Puta!*" – the high-pitched voice of Zorro. And now he was scrambling down toward them.

In the glow of the fallen flashlight, Maggie made out his unmasked face: narrow-jawed, his moustache so thin it seemed stencilled on. He shoved his way past Maggie and made a futile grab for Glo's shirt. She sidestepped him, swung her fist, and struck him in the face. He stumbled backward and fell into the creek.

Now others were arriving: more flashlights, exclamations. Glo was yelling at the fallen Zorro: "You touch me again I'll knock your teeth out, you Tico trash, you peeping Tom!"

"*Ya basta!*" Halcón shouted, and the gabble around them ceased. He was the only one wearing a kerchief – even at night he rarely removed it. He spoke to Glo, "What happened?"

"That little toad tried to attack me."

"Zorro, *qué pasó?*"

Zorro seemed dazed, still sitting in the water as he offered his version – Maggie gathered he was explaining he had been assigned to guard her, and was struck by a stone for doing his duty. "*No la moleste!*" he cried.

Halcón turned to Maggie. "What is the truth?"

She said bluntly, "*Moleste, si*. That's exactly what he tried to do to her."

Buho and Coyote helped Zorro from the water, and in the crossing light beams, Maggie could make them out: Buho with a long, pitted face, protruding upper teeth; Coyote with the tired, lined expression of a man constantly burdened. Also nearby was Tayra; her features seemed more American aboriginal than African: sharp nose, high cheekbones. She was holding a frying pan in one hand, a soapy cloth in the other. Gordo, also standing by, had the nondescript look of an overweight clerk.

Halcón insisted on hearing the details. When Maggie told him how Zorro had trained a light on Glo during an innocent but intimate moment, Tayra glared at Zorro and said something sharp. When he was brought dripping into their circle, Tayra hefted the frying pan. He cursed and stalked away.

Halcón turned to Maggie and simply nodded, as if to say that the matter had been satisfactorily concluded: the offender's spouse would mete out appropriate punishment. His dark eyes remained on her, and she felt her pulse quicken; those eyes were magnetic. He disappeared into the gloom, and Maggie sat and tucked into her *pinto* and allowed her thoughts to tempt her into the realm of the forbidden.

A whisper in her ear disturbed her from her sleep: "Go in freedom, Maggie, you have won my heart." But the image was a fleeting one. Where was Jacques when Fiona needed him? *He was the only man who knew the Savegre . . .*

After dinner, Halcón – as if to make up for Zorro's rudeness – personally delivered a stewing pot filled with warm water, along with a bar of soap and two towels.

"Aren't you such a gentleman," Glo said, still snide and imperious. "Now, how about building us a fire so we can dry some of these wet things."

"A small fire," Halcón said. His acquiescence surprised Maggie: fires were forbidden under clear skies; they could be seen from the air.

"And I need a tampon, okay?"

This reference to women's needs seemed to fluster Halcón. He hesitated, put out his cigarette, and pocketed the butt: even such minor items of litter were packed out with the garbage. Quetzal soon came by with a tampon for Glo, and by then Maggie could hear machetes hacking at branches for kindling.

After their sponge bath, Maggie and Glo sat near their tents, wrapped in their sleeping bags. A few metres away, a bonfire crackled and clothing had been spread to dry. The men huddled there, weary, grimy, each with a week's growth of whiskers. Halcón was by the fire, too, his hands gesturing relentlessly as he talked to his compatriots. Buho was strumming his guitar and humming sad Latin tunes. Near him Quetzal and Perezoso cuddled. Glo had taken to calling them Romeo and Juliet.

The ambience was eerily romantic, calming, further dissuading Maggie from the harrowing notion of escape – her present peril seemed far less frightening than the dark offerings of the jungle. But danger could come from anywhere: a botched rescue attempt, a gun battle, a stray bullet from an itchy-fingered gunslinger on a SWAT squad. Or Glo might engineer a dangerous escapade that could result in them being injured, even killed.

Glo swatted a mosquito. "I'm going in. Buenasnachos."

Left alone, Maggie watched a blur of moths dancing near the flames, listened to the guitar and the gurgle of the creek – and to a haunting repeated sound: a night bird or insect. "Plink," came the one-note liquid tune, "plink, plink." She was reminded of water dripping on tin.

She felt regret that she was without tools to write. But how could she compose romantic escapism when life at its rawest was in her face? And what a sad tale her novel seemed in comparison to this harrowing adventure. Fiona Wardell was little more than a blur for her now. Maggie could not decide if her heroine, faced with this plight, would allow herself to be as co-opted as her creator – or would she be tough and spunky like Maggie's real-life companion?

Gloria-May constantly amazed her: the lack of fear, the tartness. An interesting past, the loose fast life of Las Vegas, had emboldened her.

Lost in contemplation, she was only dimly aware of the fire flickering out, the guerrillas gathering their packs, retreating to their tents. After Buho departed with his guitar, there came just the sounds of night crickets, and that mysterious plink, plink. Mesmerized by the night, she failed to notice Halcón standing next to her, and she started when he spoke.

"I saw you were alone."

"I was thinking about a book I'm writing. Please sit down." Maggie had long waited for this chance to know him better. She had a sense of him as driven by forces he might not understand – but nevertheless urbane, even charming when he put his mind to it.

He continued to hover above her. "And what kind of book is this?"

"It is about love and adventure in Costa Rica."

"Will you tell the truth of our country? How we are all peons to the pirates of Wall Street. Or am I the bad guy?" His voice had lost much of its flatness, was more mellifluous.

"Maybe not."

"Or a fool. A romantic fool – do you have room for this person in your fiction?"

"If he is also a handsome hero." As blatant as that sounded, she had decided to play to his ego.

He finally sat, pulling out a cigarette. They were alone but for Perezoso strolling about the sphere on night watch.

By the light of the match he struck, she could see his dark Spanish eyes above his bandit's mask; they seemed to dance to the rhythm of the flame. Watching him insert and light the cigarette through the hole of his kerchief, she could not suppress a smile. "Tell me about this romantic fool," she said.

He took a deep pull on the cigarette. "I can tell you a story; it might sell many books. A life outside the law in a struggle always for justice for my country. Romance, yes, I have known that, and much adventure, too."

My *contry*. The way he said that, the way his hands darted as he talked . . . A powerful sense of déjà vu overcame her. She recalled words spoken only a week ago: *Maybe you will find room in your book for a lonely history professor.* Her mouth formed a wide oval of shock, and for a few moments she was unable to speak.

"Is the story also about a thief?"

Her words were met with silence.

Anger welled in Maggie, despite her consternation. She wanted to slap his face, and could barely stop herself from doing so. She sputtered: "You . . . you two-faced lying *snake!*"

"*Qué?* Snake? I do not understand."

"This is too *bizarre*. You . . . you *puta!*" She didn't know what the word meant, but it was obviously a Tico curse. She tried to settle herself, make reason of this. The pickpocket professor, Pablo Esquivel, had metamorphosed as captain of the Comando Cinco de Mayo.

Now she remembered his mimicry of the Laughing Falcon at the restaurant – he had called this bird, this *halcón*, the masked bandit of the skies. She had missed that clue and been treated to the full *guaco* once again.

She fought to compose herself and spoke resentfully. "I guess you thought I had come straight from the cornfields. You left me nearly broke. I was mortified when you abandoned me in that restaurant with all the people staring."

He pulled off his blue kerchief. In the glow of cigarette and distant dying embers, she could make out his finely sculpted face, his wide handsome moustache, his easy Latin smile. "We needed your donation for a last-minute budget crisis. The caretaker at Outward Bound demanded more than our agreement called for."

Maggie took several deep breaths to calm herself, and tried making sense of why a man she had banished to daydreams and fiction had returned to haunt her reality. If she wrote this in a book, no reader would believe it. It was too far-fetched, too *coincidental*.

"Maybe the plot goes like this. The villain sees a pretty señorita walk from her hotel and follows her to the university."

A pretty señorita: still the thieving gigolo, still utterly attractive despite the recent cropping of his collar-length hair. This pseudo-professor with all his savoir faire and cool audacity was nothing more than a common rogue, a thief, and a kidnapper. Did he have credentials as a revolutionary or was he posturing at that as well? She spoke sharply: "And why would you be hanging around my hotel? You wanted to check me out – you knew I had signed on for the lodge." Had he sloughed off her denial of being rich and famous? Had he thought a large ransom could be earned?

"This is a clever thought, but I think it belongs in the world of detective fiction."

His evasiveness persuaded Maggie not to pursue the matter, but she was confounded – how would he have known she was staying at the Pensión Paraíso?

"Let me tell you something, Maggie. It is not easy to speak of this. Perhaps you will think it is, how do you say, a line, a come-on, but you have won a place in my heart. You are, to me, a woman not merely of outer beauty but of great inner beauty, not like your companion, with all her peevish vanity. You are also a woman of courage, *valiente*. So compassionate in offering yourself in place of another. That I will never forget, when you said, 'Take me instead.' And it is my hope that maybe one day I will bring you to understand me, and to forgive me, and to know that this difficult time is a means to a great humanitarian end."

During this speech, his voice, no longer disguised, regained its full range of tone. Though still stunned, perplexed by his return engagement in her life, her wrath had much abated. She would be better able to forgive his crimes if she could believe he had acted with benign motives. Then came an inner voice of warning: He is a master of the glib phrase, he is merely seeking to disarm you, to make sure you cooperate.

"A *puta*, by the way, is a prostitute. The phrase you hear, '*hijueputa*,' was corrupted by common use from '*hijo de puta*,' son of a whore. I think that is what you meant to call me."

She was still trying to settle her mind, bring herself back to the harsh reality of her plight. What was the soundest course of action here? She decided she must hold to her plan to befriend and disarm him.

Perezoso, the night guard, hearing their low conversation, came to investigate. Halcón sent him retreating with a few sharp words.

"They have to understand, I am their captain – that was the arrangement. One must be firm with these people; they are amateurs, lacking experience in the hard life of a revolutionary."

"But you will lead them to the promised land."

"*Si Dios quiere*. But you must not think that we seek personal profit. It is not a crime that we commit – that is an empty word. Ours is a political act. The true criminals, the true terrorists, are those who sit at the tables of power, and the warmonger Senator Walker wants to sit at the head."

"So why didn't you take *him*?"

"Who would want him back?" That seemed flip, unresponsive.

"The real reason is that you think women are easier to control."

"I wish I had found that so."

"This is how you make a political statement, kidnapping women." Maggie remained skeptical. "You don't hope to get rich from it?"

"Only the poor will be rewarded."

"With what? How much money are you demanding?"

"Fifteen million."

Maggie was staggered by the sum. "That's impossible."

"Walker has wealthy friends."

"You picked the worst possible target. He'll never negotiate."

Halcón shrugged. "If we win freedom for Benito Madrigal, that may be profit enough."

He was prepared to bargain; Maggie felt relief. "Who is this messiah?"

"A man of honour. They have placed him in an asylum, claiming he is *loco*, but that is one of their many lies, that is how they stop his tongue. We do not know what tortures he has been subjected to. One day you will meet him, briefly, perhaps, during an exchange. But, Miss Schneider, understand this well: though we are not murderers, in the end we must do what we must do."

That created a chill and a silence; Maggie thought it wise to change the subject. "The sounds of the night are beautiful. What makes that plink?"

"*Un martillito*, a tink frog. It is very tiny for such a big sound."

The night was hushed but for those bell-clear tinks and the sibilant whispers of life in the trees. She shivered, not from the cold – she was still wrapped in her sleeping bag – but from his closeness. Despite her unease, she had begun to feel more *valiente*, confident enough to ask a favour. "Is there paper here? A pen or a pencil?"

"And you would write your novel?"

She spoke as brazenly as she dared: "You inspired me, Halcón, with your story about the lost Spanish mission. How true was that? Captain Morgan, the treasure boats."

"The mission truly existed. This story of buried treasure is one of the great legends of my country, and all great legends are based on truth, yes?"

"Is that what you're doing now – creating a legend?"

"Life creates its own legends, Miss Schneider, and a life worth living creates history. Napoleon defined history as 'a set of lies agreed upon,' but I am not so cynical. The chronicle I write may be only a footnote, but . . ." He shrugged. "Life is a drama with many dangers; that is how I prefer to see it, to live it. I once wasted myself in an office – but that is another, duller story." He looked contemplative, squinting into the smoke from the last puff of his cigarette.

His brief treatise had bared much about himself. Maybe he was, in reality, a historian who had read deeply of Napoleon, perhaps of other conquerors – and he appeared to share the personality complex coined in Napoleon's honour, seeking fame, his own legend.

Not wanting him to leave yet, hoping to learn more, she blurted, "By the way, you will be in my book. You *could* have been the hero, but you lost the job."

He laughed. "The thief of love. I cannot deny I enjoyed the stolen kisses; nor can I deny what my body felt. You were very pretty in the soft light playing on the waterfall."

She wondered if this was just his typical blarney. Yet she had felt that pressure against her groin; they had both been aroused.

"Fiona Wardell was very disappointed in the light-fingered history professor."

"Fiona – ah, the heroine of your book. And now who will she find to love?"

"His name is Jacques Cardinal. Unfortunately, he has problems. But he'll have to do." She told him she had borrowed the name from the owner of a kayak business in Quepos. "A drunken ruffian."

"She will be sorry she rejected the professor."

Relationship between captor and prisoner had taken on an oddly familiar character. Maggie was picking up innuendoes that added to the confusion she was feeling about him. She was finding it difficult to restructure him as a commando leader, to erase a former picture.

"But why would you not write the truth? Here is your work of literature. Here, under the stars, with this small band of men and women who dream of better worlds."

"I dream of other worlds myself, Halcón, when I write; it's my therapy. But I did promise to tell the story of Cinco de Mayo. I can do that, too." She sensed he sought celebrity – probably his followers did, as well.

He stood. "One must not deny talent. And I will not deny a lady of such charm and of such . . . forthrightness. Is that the word?"

"Your English is very good."

"I lived many years in the wastelands of America."

Soon after Halcón left, Perezoso came by the tent with the reward for her collaboration: a pencil, a few sheets of blank paper, and a candle. Quetzal groaned in her sleep and rolled over.

Maggie wasn't immediately able to write; Halcón was too much in her mind. A man of many layers, as bright and urbane as he was brazen and defiant. She must stay on guard against the pull he exerted: she was fascinated by a sense of danger that seemed to glow in him.

She must not forget she was in peril; she was in uncharted jungle with a gang of revolutionary dreamers led either by a charlatan or a naïve utopian of the far left.

But surely he was committed to a revolutionary's ethics. After all, he had surrounded himself with like-minded men and women; they had performed a daring political act, a raid on a guarded redoubt of a notorious senator. If he sought just financial gain, he could have picked a softer target of greater wealth.

She must remind herself he was acting outside the law; however dashing a villain, he was a kidnapper.

She closed her eyes and tried to visualize Fiona and Jacques and Spanish gold . . .

❧

When Fiona lightly dug into the earth she realized the object she had chanced upon was not another rock. Carefully, she picked around the broken lid of a clay pot. As she began brushing the dirt from it, she felt a rush of excitement – a year had been scratched upon its surface: 1671.

Despite the pall placed on this expedition by her bearish companion, she was thrilled to be at the threshold of a brilliant success. She beckoned to Jacques, and he rose from his own toil some distance away.

As he bent beside her, he said, "You're beautiful."

She looked sharply at him.

"I was talking to the pot lid." He favoured her with the mocking smile that had begun so much to vex her.

❧

The broken lead tip of her pencil wobbled and fell out, and she gave up, dissatisfied with her meagre effort. The two characters were lacking joy. She disliked caustic Jacques and was not sure if, ultimately, she could picture him throwing himself in adoration at Fiona's feet. She might well be sorry she rejected the professor . . .

But she was annoyed even more by Fiona – after a long hiatus between creative renderings, she had become a bore, and so had the plot. Her artistic juices were drying up. The likely cause: she was living a chapter of her own life far beyond her creative dreams. How could her imagination ever match this reality?

She would write a truer tale: an account of her jungle ordeal, one that honoured her commitment to be fair to Cinco de Mayo and Halcón. Anyway, publishers would be far less interested in buried treasure than the perils of Margaret and Gloria-May. The women's magazine for which she had been cajoled to write might serialize it.

She blew out the candle and stretched out next to Quetzal and remembered again those two long kisses in the gardens of La Linda Vista.

— 2 —

Maggie woke at dawn to screams, and quickly crawled from her tent. She recognized the voice: Gordo, who sounded almost beyond terror. As she looked behind the tent toward the stone sphere, she was stunned to see a gigantic boa constrictor wrapping itself around Gordo's leg, its mouth clamped on his left boot.

Her campmates rushed from their tents, a melee of movement and noise: "*Culebra grande!*" Maggie was frozen, horrified, as Gordo struggled with the snake, which was at least four metres long. He tried in vain to crawl free, then managed to pull his pistol from its holster.

He fired two great blasts that echoed through the jungle valley. The snake freed its teeth from Gordo's boot and jerked wildly, thrashing, banging its tail against the huge round rock. A moment later, Coyote decapitated it, and there came a sickening spume of blood. Maggie watched aghast as the dying boa continued to writhe and as Gordo, grunting and gasping, crawled free, his left boot streaming with blood.

Maggie felt faint at the sight of the injury, of all the blood, the entire awful spectacle. She stepped slowly backwards, almost stumbling against a tent. Tayra, still dressing, quickly emerged from it, then Glo's head poked out from behind the entrance flap.

"Jesus freaking Christ, what was all that?"

Maggie explained. She assumed Gordo had fallen asleep under the sphere while on guard duty; the snake had seen his chubby leg protruding. "I think he shot himself in the foot."

"How symbolic." Glo ducked inside to dress while Maggie joined the group squatting around the injured man. None had paused to tie kerchiefs over their faces. Coyote was looking stern: had he not warned them about the dangers of the jungle?

As Buho came rushing from a tent with a first-aid kit, Halcón sliced the boot from Gordo's damaged left foot and peeled away his blood-soaked sock: it was indeed a bullet wound. Everyone stood about helplessly for a few moments, then Glo burst from her tent, strode toward Gordo, and bent to examine the wound. "Okay, one of you useless pansies get some water – warm water, heat it. Get his foot up in the air, pass me the goddamn gauze."

Maggie looked on with awe and admiration as Glo went to work, staunching the flow of blood with gauze, applying an antiseptic solution. One of the two bullets had missed, but the other had shattered the bones in the arch of his foot.

Gordo continued to moan; Halcón began demanding answers from him, his temper frayed. If Maggie understood Gordo's response, he was denying that he fell asleep, though no one seemed to believe that, and Zorro loudly scoffed.

Finally, a pot of warm water was delivered and Glo washed the foot, applied more antiseptic, then wrapped the wound with bandages. Halcón looked around, frowning, and, aware that the entire group had been seen by the hostages in clear daylight, he didn't order them to put their kerchiefs on.

After the tents were struck and the camp was dismantled, Halcón called a meeting of the *colectivo*. They crouched in a circle around Gordo, whose propped-up foot was in a bulbous bandage. At one point, Zorro seemed about to cuff him, but Halcón snapped an order and Zorro lowered his hand.

Maggie joined Glo outside the perimeter. "Where did you learn first aid?"

"Down where I come from, you see a few gunshot wounds. I felt sorry for that fat little critter. You know what? These bozos look better with their faces covered."

"Except for Halcón."

"Doesn't turn *my* crank, honey. The guy's right out of some 1940s B movie."

"I had a long talk with him last night." Maggie was about to expand on that, but the circle broke and Halcón strode up to them.

"Señora Walker, I will thank you, but we must ask you to share some of the load today."

She raised her middle finger. "That's what I'm sharing."

"I am starting to worry that Senator Walker may not be so pleased to have you back."

"Y'all can kiss my ass."

He turned to Maggie. "Remind your friend she is not on the plantation with her shuffling Uncle Toms."

"I don't think you're doing the right thing, Glo," Maggie whispered.

"I'd rather get fucked standing up than take it lying down."

"Make friends, not enemies. That's what I was doing last night with Halcón."

"You cotton to that smarmy greaser?"

"Well, no, but . . . he's the same guy who robbed me in San José."

Glo's mouth fell open. Maggie said nothing more because Tayra had joined them; she began tying the rope around Glo's middle. "I'm sorry, but I have to do this."

Coyote had fashioned a crutch for Gordo, but he needed to be carried as they followed the creek downstream for a few hundred metres. Halcón regularly took them wading up or down the creeks that bisected their path to confuse search dogs that presumably had sniffed clothing at the Eco-Rico Lodge.

A troop of spider monkeys swung past them, low in the trees, and while everyone else stopped to watch, Glo came abreast of Maggie, then flung a small garment into the bushes. No one else noticed, and though Glo's strategem struck Maggie as a wasted effort, she gave her a conspiratorial nudge.

The climb up the other side of the *quebrada* was slow, Buho and Zorro having to wrestle Gordo up the hill. When he tried to walk with his makeshift crutch, he managed a one-legged hop. At difficult spots, they carried him. He seemed weak with shock, and blood was seeping through the bandage.

During breaks, Maggie recounted to Glo last night's odd tête-à-tête with Halcón, urging her to find reassurance from his words, to join her in being a team player, offer to carry a backpack. Glo just shook her head. "I've done enough."

Maggie was feeling far more sanguine since her conversation with Halcón. These idealists were unlikely to harm them; they seemed more a threat to themselves. Halcón's revelation that they were using her and Glo as trade bait for Benito Madrigal encouraged her hopes for a safe outcome. Flirting with her like that, praising her – she couldn't deny he had obtained the desired effect, though she told herself to resist his pull.

Her captors seemed to lack Maggie's fortitude, some of them muttering complaints as the day began to wane and turn colder. The forest here was of immense oak trees festooned with moss and red-tinted bromeliads, the understory thick with stunted bamboo. The thin air was demanding on the lungs and, burdened with Gordo, they took frequent rests. Coyote would then sharpen his machetes on a flat file; their edges were dulled quickly by the dense undergrowth.

As the afternoon grew late, frequent patches of fog obscured their route – but also hid them from a helicopter that buzzed for a few moments overhead. They had heard, but not seen, three of them today, plus a few winged aircraft. Though they were hidden by the canopy, they would go still or hide behind trees, and a hand would be clapped over Glo's mouth.

Gordo had to be hauled by rope up the steepest inclines; his expression had turned zombie-like and he whimpered incessantly. Buho, his feet rubbed raw by his boots, winced with each step. Perezoso, the young Romeo, had been bitten in the cheek – apparently by a small venomous spider – while plucking a spray of wild ginger for his Juliet. The poison had got into his glands, and he looked like he had a severe case of the mumps. Quetzal seemed too exhausted to offer him solace.

Eventually, they climbed above a sea of cloud stretching to the far horizons and felt the warm relief of sunshine reflecting from the clouds below them. But the terrain was steeper here and the flora scrubbier; dense ferns and thick-stemmed shrubs challenged the machetes stubbornly. Their clothing, tattered and shredded by the unyielding foliage, was coated with prickly burrs. This was the *páramo*, the shrubby barrens of the Central American highlands – Maggie found it the cruellest test yet of her four days in the wilderness. Ahead, dominating the view, was a mountain of almost twenty-six hundred metres. She overheard someone mutter, "*Cerro de la Muerte.*" She shivered: the mountain of death.

After another hour, they were merely inching along, Coyote near collapse. Buho finally fell under Gordo's weight, and pleaded for a rest. Halcón checked his compass, then his watch, then the lowering sun. Maggie sat beside Glo on a rock and they numbly watched a trail of leaf-eater ants toiling up the hill, as if showing them the way, demonstrating grit, carrying burdens four times their size.

"Fat boy needs a doctor," Glo said loudly, "so why don't y'all take us to town."

No one responded, but uncomfortable looks were exchanged. Tayra began bickering with Zorro, who turned from her and spoke a few bitter words to Halcón; others joined in. Even dour Coyote, as he sharpened his machete, was looking at their leader in a displeased way. Glo lowered her voice: "I think the masses are rebelling."

Halcón said nothing, just looked penetratingly at each in turn. Most dropped their eyes. He rose, took the machete from Coyote, and began hacking an uphill path with long, sweeping strokes. The rest of his ragged company remained seated, their heads low, staring at the earth, panting in the thin air. There was no sound but the swack-swack of the machete.

Maggie was not sure why she decided to follow him, but when she did so, the others, to her surprise, staggered up, one by one, adjusting their packs. Gordo, with unexpected pluck, pulled himself up with his crutch. They silently tagged along, higher into the *páramo*, where evening mists had begun to form ghosts in the air.

Halcón stopped only once to catch his breath and trade machetes, then powered his way up yet another steep rise. He led them finally to a less forbidding terrain, topped by great clumps of bracken, the fronds fluttering in a breeze that fragmented the thickening mist. From the distance came a low, sullen roar, increasing in intensity as they slashed their way through the ferns. Maggie thought at first they were approaching another waterfall – but they were in the high country where streams were only trickles.

Halcón suddenly halted, and the others gathered beside them. The roar had taken on a metallic grinding sound. He waved everyone to the ground. Into a gap in the fog, just above the foliage, a large rectangular shape appeared from the left, a semi, she realized, moving slowly uphill. "Transportes de Centroamerica S.A.," read the painted letters at the top. Now came a sound of shifting gears, the truck accelerating, then swallowed by the mist.

It was followed by several wooden chairs that were roped together and seemed to float through the air. In close order came two men sitting on sacks of coffee beans, a fluttering flag on a car aerial, and a row of faces behind the windows of a bus. Maggie realized they had reached the continental divide: this was the Pan-American Highway, which ran up the spine of Costa Rica.

She heard another vehicle, a small car from the sound of it, race by in the opposite direction.

Suddenly, Glo flashed past Maggie, vaulting over the bracken, racing for the road, the rope dangling behind her – she had jerked it free from Tayra. Halcón sped off in pursuit and stepped on the rope, causing her to tumble. She sprang up, but he leaped, tackling her, the momentum carrying them into a tangled bush of lavender roadside flowers.

Halcón, his hand over Glo's mouth, raised his head, then ducked quickly as a truck came from the right, down the hill, air brakes hissing.

Crouched behind a gnarled tree, Zorro appeared agitated, waving his automatic pistol. A flycatcher above him emitted a sudden loud "Seek-a-*ski*-er," and as it dove for an insect, Zorro whirled and fired a shot into the air, an ear-splitting crack that echoed down the hillside. Maggie could see Halcón's startled face rise and turn in their direction. Zorro, frantic now, waved to the others to retreat.

Maggie was not about to defy the rattled Zorro, so she retreated down the hill, quickly overtaking Gordo and those assisting him. After a few minutes, she stopped at a level, well-protected area; the others scurried to join her.

Gordo fell, grabbing at his foot in pain. Coyote slashed down some bracken clumps to widen the clearing and they all dropped their packs; they were out of breath, gasping, tense.

As several minutes passed in silence, worry gnawed at Maggie. Glo could well have been injured when brought down so heavily by Halcón. Had the two of them been detected? That shot had been incredibly loud.

Finally, down the path came Halcón, Glo over his shoulder, her ankles and wrists tied, his blue kerchief gagging her mouth – it seemed painfully tight. Zorro followed, watching their rear, trembling, clearly in an anxious state.

Glo's eyes were sparking angrily as Halcón knelt and laid her on the ground. He expelled a deep breath and looked wearily at Maggie. "How far are we from the road – two hundred metres?" His handsome features were marred by scratches and the welts of digging fingernails.

"Even farther."

He checked his watch: five-thirty. "We must hope that shot wasn't heard. I think we should take our chances here until the night."

"Then what? Over the road?"

"That was the idea."

"What's out there?"

"Nothing and no one. Beyond that, only the mountains of Chirripó and the Talamanca."

Was the plan to continue even higher? That would be almost impossibly taxing – how would they survive the cold? "We didn't come out where we were supposed to, did we?"

"A small miscalculation."

Here was the captain of the Comando Cinco de Mayo engaging his prisoner in a casual conversation while the troops politely stood by. Maybe Halcón had lost faith in his revolutionary soldiers.

Glo was still lying next to them, squirming. "What are we going to do with this one?" Halcón asked.

Maggie thought it odd that he was openly consulting her; the relationship of captor and captive seemed to have perceptibly shifted. "Let me untie her, Halcón. That gag is too tight, it's hurting her."

He touched his hand to his face. "This woman has claws like a tiger. Leave her hands tied. Since she is not sharing our work, she will not share our food."

As he strode off to give directions to the others, Maggie leaned down to Glo and began undoing the kerchief. Glo's cheekbone was red, deeply bruised. "Are you okay? That was foolish, Glo. Don't tempt danger. You could have been shot."

Glo's first words were obscenities, but softly muttered. Then she spat. "The pig. He hit me."

"You got your digs in."

"Oh, shit, she's sorry for him. Whose side are you on?"

"Our side." A fierce whisper: "Dammit, if we're going to do anything, we need them relaxed, and now you pull this stupid stunt."

Maggie ceased her whispering because Halcón was looking at them. She freed Glo's ankles.

Halcón gazed about the clearing. "Zorro, *venga,*" he called.

Zorro emerged from behind a wind-clipped shrub. Halcón extended his hand, palm up. Zorro shrugged, working up a wan, penitent smile. Halcón's index finger wiggled: come here. The rest of the crew stepped back, creating a path as Zorro, the smile breaking down, came forward, then placed his automatic on the palm of the outstretched hand.

Halcón hefted the gun, and for a moment seemed tempted to strike Zorro with it. But he kept his temper, saying not a word, stuffing the automatic in a side pocket of his pack, then pulling out a map.

The silence as he studied it was broken by a soft taunt by Tayra at her chastened partner. That prompted others to join in on a condemnation of Zorro and his itchy trigger finger. Tayra, guarding her role as Zorro's chief scold, then began disputing with the others. *"Silencio!"* Halcón ordered, glaring them into stillness.

Night was quickly falling. No tents had been erected, nor had they dared light the stoves, but along the way Coyote had collected some pejibaye and heart of palm that sufficed for a light meal. They would need what was left of their strength for the night; Halcón had told them to prepare for a long but not difficult march – they would be proceeding for some distance along the highway.

Maggie drew him aside. "Come on, Halcón, Geneva Convention, you have to let Glo eat."

"I agree only if her mouth is used for nothing else."

Glo heard this. "I don't plan to use it to kiss your ass either. Don't you ever try to hit me again, pal." She seemed about to pursue the point, then suddenly sagged. "Oh, fuck it . . ." She raised her hands, a gesture of surrender. "Okay, *capitán*, I'm sorry. I just reacted. I've been scared out of my goddamn britches. I promise to be a good little girl from now on." She reached out to touch the scratches on his face. "Did I do *that?*" Halcón jerked his head back.

He gave Maggie an inquiring look, as if seeking confirmation that Glo had entered some less dangerous phase. He then bowed slightly to Glo. "I regret having struck you, señora. It was not something I enjoyed." He left them to tend to Gordo.

"Now you're coming on just a little strong. Work up to it." Maggie felt like a stage director.

"What are they going to do with that fat little varmint? They can't just keep dragging him along. Those wounds will fester."

Gordo was nodding as if receiving instructions; a pat on the head from Halcón elicited a brave smile. Halcón seemed born to lead; somehow he had whipped this ragtag band into a bumbling version of the merry men of Sherwood Forest.

Glo wriggled into her sleeping bag. "Christ, it's freezing."

Maggie had endured worse; she was from Saskatchewan. What were they making of this in Saskatoon? *Coming up, the latest developments in the desperate search for CSKN's own Margaret Schneider, but first a word from our friends down at Koroluk's Implement Mart.* She must try to persuade Halcón to send word that she and Gloria-May were safe.

As Halcón went off to listen to his radio, Maggie settled beside Buho, who was picking out a tune on his guitar and singing softly in his croaking voice. "This is a song I wrote," he told her. "A hymn to Benito Madrigal. We are blood; he is my uncle, but more father to me than my true one, who is a capitalist running dog."

Maggie was astonished at his harshness of tone toward his father. She sought to find out why he had rejected him, but Buho preferred to talk of the teachings of his favoured uncle.

"In this song, he is reminding us that throughout history a small minority was always called upon to show the way. Benito has taught us that a fighting group can only come into being through struggle. That is how we write history – by shedding our blood for others." He was like a talking manifesto.

"Buho, what's the history of your *comando?*"

"We are named the Movement of May Fifth in honour of Benito. Before, we were something else."

He seemed hesitant to continue, as if fearing he might betray secrets; he rose to confer with Halcón, who removed his radio from his ear. Buho's petition was greeted with a nod. When he again sat beside her, he seemed more relaxed.

"Once we were the People's Popular Vanguard. You have heard of it?"

"Not exactly, no."

"We were ignored by the press, of course. That is how they isolate people with progressive views. The Vanguard was a legitimate political party. Benito Madrigal, he was our candidate for president – this was six years ago. We were fools; we tried it their way. But the two parties of the oligarchy had all the money. They made sure we didn't win a seat. After, we were bitter and divided; there were factions among us and our followers dwindled. And then my uncle brought us together with a desperate, brave action, striking at the heart of our unjust, decaying system."

As he told a tangled story – a libel action and a hostage crisis at a courthouse – Maggie dimly remembered an item on Channel Ten's *Eye to the Universe*: several Costa Rican judges held hostage by a former presidential candidate. He was ultimately disarmed and arrested without bloodshed.

"Now they have created a lie that he is insane. They have tortured him, wired him to machines – this was in the newspapers. After his brave act, we were united again in our determination, but we were drifting in the wilderness, without a plan. Then *he* came along. Halcón." He pointed at the saviour, who was now conversing earnestly with Romeo and Juliet as well as Gordo.

And where had Halcón come from? Everywhere, it seemed. He had been in Peru with the Shining Path. He had been in Colombia, organizing bands of the rebel left. It was said he had been in Africa: in Libya, the Congo.

One day, he made contact with the remnants of the People's Vanguard, arriving unannounced, "encouraging us, firing us up, speaking the true language of revolution. A brilliant new leader." Buho's voice dropped. "A man of better tactics than Don Benito, I admit. He has a clearer vision. He holds the traditional ways in scorn, the old politics. He has moulded us into a fighting revolutionary force."

֍

The hours passed with growing tension as they listened to a distant rumble of traffic from the road. Halcón was offering no indication when they might venture onto it.

It was about midnight, and the sky was as clear and massed with brittle stars as on a cloudless winter night on the prairies. A crescent moon yielded a startling light, revealing forms around Maggie, huddled or lying in sleeping bags. In one of them, Perezoso was moaning with the pain of his spider bite and Quetzal was whispering words of comfort. Maggie was concerned for them: they were far too young to be involved in this hazardous intrigue.

Gloria-May was dozing off. Halcón was pacing and no longer conserving his cigarettes. His uncharacteristic tension fuelled Maggie's own anxiety about what the night was to offer and dissuaded her from approaching him. She remembered how he had pressed kisses upon her neck at La Linda Vista, their bodies tight against each other. *I cannot hold inside what I feel.* How would Danielle Steele write it? *As he drew himself into her, she felt flashes of lightning erupt within, bursting into flames that consumed them both.* Could it ever be that way? Could love and eros combine in such brilliant fire?

She had felt a taste of that legendary fire, a tantalizing nibble, as they had kissed. She had felt overpowered not just by desire's hot jolt, but by a profound closeness to a deeper mystery, to the secret of love itself.

There came a sound as clear as a clarion in the still night: "Chup-wheer-purr-*wheew!*" The warning shriek of the nightjar reminded Maggie she must keep a wary distance from the captain of the Fifth of May Commando.

As the nightjar fluttered off into the darkness, the night fell silent. Silent night: Maggie had not thought much about Christmas, only five days hence, more or less – she was beginning to lose track of time. Barring a sudden miracle, the festive season would be shared with the Comando Cinco de Mayo. How were plans coming for the family dinner at the farm? She pictured them gathered around Aunt Ruthilda's thirty-pound tom turkey. Surely her mother had relented and insisted that Woodrow join them.

Don't be depressed, she told herself, the *valientes* do not show distress. Stay alert, concentrate on honing survival skills. But she couldn't help thinking of the sadness of Christmas at Lake Lenore . . .

She realized she was softly sobbing, and removed her glasses to wipe away the tears. She must not succumb; she must be much stronger than this.

But Halcón had noticed, and was now standing at her side. "Is there anything I can do?"

"I was thinking of my family."

He sat down and touched her hand; she was so startled that she almost withdrew it. His fingers rested lightly on hers.

"But of course you will return safely to your family – you are our chronicler to the world. That is why I chose you."

She found his words reassuring but confusing. "Your first choice was a pregnant woman."

"In the end, we would have chosen you, but this was my test for you: I wanted you to volunteer."

Maggie was glad he turned silent; she needed time to absorb this information. He had planned her abduction, perhaps from the first time they met. He had known, even as he kissed and thieved, that she would be his captive, that they would come together again . . .

The nightjar voiced its strident song: "Chup, chuck-weer!" She would heed its warning: be wary of men who kiss and run. She slid her hand from beneath his, then regretted her abruptness. She would not wish him to think his offer of comfort had been rejected.

"You're shivering. Wrap this around you." She extended a loose fold of her sleeping bag, and he drew it around his shoulders. Now their bodies were touching and she had to clear her throat before speaking. "Tell me your story – this life outside the law."

She started as his hand brushed her thigh; he was working at his pocket. He pulled out his pack of Derbys and tapped one out. The spark and flame of the match were reflected in his eyes.

"It is not easy to begin." He squinted forlornly into the smoke.

"You told me it would sell many copies."

"Maybe not. Who enjoys reading of such sad things?" He shrugged. "When I was a little boy, an *hijo*, they came and burned our home. They raped my mother."

Maggie gasped. "How *awful*. Where?"

"Here, in this proud democracy of Costa Rica. The story I am about to tell you has been suppressed."

He told a ghastly tale that caused her skin to prickle. His father was an honest farmer and an outspoken communist. One night, a band of drunken fascists – among them, several members of the Rural Guard – pulled into their farmyard and set fire to their house, beating a brave father who resisted, gang-raping his mother.

"The government, it did nothing; it covered up and blamed the attack on foreigners, Nicaraguan cut-throats. No arrests were made."

Maggie felt him shudder. He seemed unable to continue, overcome by deep sadness. But he abruptly shook off his childhood ghosts, looked at his watch, and stood up. "It is the hour of departure. There will be other nights when I can bore you with my stories." He called out, "*Vámonos.*"

Feelings of horror and revulsion continued to assail Maggie as they made their way single file along a stretch of newly laid pavement, down hairpin twists. She tried to concentrate on their route, but was rattled, unable to shake a stark picture of a child witnessing such savagery. Many would not have emotionally survived the trauma; many would have turned cruel, scarred with bitterness. To his credit, Halcón had directed his fury toward an uprooting of the evils he saw infecting humankind.

It was the dead of night and traffic was sparse but for an occasional van or international transport. At the first glimpse of headlights, Halcón would motion the column off the road, and they would hide among the scrub and bush until the vehicle passed. Glo, despite her pledge of cooperation, had been gagged again, her hands tied.

Between stops and starts they moved with speed, no longer burdened with injured Gordo, who had been left behind in the care of Romeo and Juliet. The three of them had changed from their jungle fatigues into slacks and shirts, then hid themselves in foliage by the shoulder of the highway. They would wait there till dawn, then flag a bus for the town of San Isidro and its hospital. They would make their way ultimately to San José, where the commando had an apartment. All this, Halcón told Maggie as he walked alongside her.

She doubted that Halcón was befriending her solely because he enjoyed her company. He wanted something from her. She would be the portrait artist of the Laughing Falcon, the teller of the tale of his tragic early history, of his life as a rebel. She had not failed to detect a swagger of pride, of Napoleonic arrogance – but these seemed minor faults. All great leaders have robust egos – he was entitled to his literary recognition.

But he was fretting now. "We have to keep our fingers crossed. I am worried about those three. They are not among the brightest our country has produced."

"Will Gordo be able to pull it off? Won't the police be curious about a man being treated for a bullet wound in his foot?"

"He will describe an accident while shooting pigeons, a common occurrence here – few in my country are trained in firearms. Even if he is suspected, there is no proof against him, and I have not revealed to him – or anyone – our ultimate harbour."

"And where is that?"

He merely smiled.

After an hour of downhill plodding, a few clearings began to appear on either side of the road, and Maggie could make out an occasional rustic tile-roofed farmhouse, often with a yard light. Other properties seemed deserted, as if their tenants had given up trying to till this barren soil.

Halcón halted them across the road from one such clearing, and under the dim glow of the thin moon studied an unlit structure set fifty metres behind a barbed-wire fence. A mile down the road were some scattered lights, perhaps a village. He checked his map – Maggie had peeked at it once: a scaled chart of the Savegre area. "*Bien*," he said, satisfied. They ducked into the bush as a pickup rattled by, then crossed the highway, climbing over the fence into a field.

Soon they were on a dirt track that led to a crumbling building of mortared stone, maidenhair fern growing along the walls — a former house or small barn, deserted but for a few squeaking bats. Was this where they would be held? It seemed too close to the country's major highway. And Halcón had mentioned Chirripó and the Talamanca.

"We will rest here," he told her. "But only until dawn. There must be silence now."

While Maggie removed Glo's gag and untied her, the guerrillas, all but Halcón, nestled into sleeping bags. She could see him in the glow of match or cigarette, watchful and restless, listening to his radio, which was turned low.

Maggie lay down between Glo and the wall. Noiselessly, she tore a page from her pad, and with the lead loosened from her pencil wrote in bold capital strokes: "BOTH OK. NOT HURT." She signed it and was about to tuck it away in a hole in the mortar, then hesitated. Did she not owe it to the authorities to elaborate?

She felt confused about where her duty lay and struggled awhile with her dilemma: should she be aiding these revolutionaries? She thought of the terror Halcón had undergone as a child, and how justice had then become his holy cause. Should such a noble motive be subverted by her?

She pulled herself up sharply — she must not be blinded by sympathy into not doing the right thing. She added to her note: "Chirripó, Talamanca. Injured man, short, fat, San Isidro Hospital." She decided not to mention Romeo and Juliet; she wanted no harm to come to them.

Maggie quietly worked the paper into the niche, pulling back her hand just as Halcón clicked on his pocket flashlight. But he was just looking at his map.

Denying the demands of sleep, she lay still through the remaining night, tense with worry that the note would be discovered as the crew tidied up before packing out.

Shortly after five, as there came through a window the first slight paling of the eastern sky, Halcón began rousing his comrades, and they rose groaning. Tayra nudged Zorro, who seemed unwilling to rise. He was an almost tragic figure now, broken in rank and given to long, morose silences. To Maggie's relief, only a cursory effort was made to pick up their leavings.

Halcón confused Maggie by guiding them not forward into the dark forest rising to the north, but back down the rutted track toward the highway. Daring the use of a flashlight, he found a gate leading to the road. They heard a distant complaint of engine, a change of gears, as Halcón quickly shepherded them across the pavement, into a ditch, over a knoll, and down a rock scree.

They rested for a moment at a spring bubbling from the rocks, replenishing water bottles. The sky was pinking now, the stars struggling to hold their light. Why were they returning south instead of north and east, Maggie wondered.

Halcón ordered Glo's wrists to be unbound. "We will need all our limbs for this. *Vámonos, amigos.*"

He led them single file down the creek bed below the spring, a steep, twisting path strewn with rocks. These were hard and sharp beneath their feet and caused many stumbles. When Buho sought escape onto the mossy lip of the *quebrada*, Halcón ordered him back in line. There would be no boot prints to follow here, no trail of machete cuts.

The descent became precipitous; progress was snail-like, the soldiers of Cinco de Mayo moving with cautious terror, slipping, ripping their clothes, rocks tumbling away beneath their feet. Zorro wrenched his shoulder in a fall. Tayra's hand bled from a cut.

Glo, however, finally freed of all restraints, was nimble and sure of foot. Maggie, though weary, dug into wells of strength and maintained pace with her, close behind Halcón.

The next rest stop was on a boulder overhanging a spindly waterfall. They had dropped a couple thousand metres, and the growth was lusher here. Below them spread a richly green panorama of rolling hills, and, at the farthest beyond, in faded blue, disappearing in mist and cloud, the great reaches of the Pacific Ocean.

"Chirripó, Talamanca," she had written. Were her note found, her rescuers would set out in a wrong direction.

Halcón was lying on his back, his shirt off. There was something in his smile that reminded Maggie of a smug, self-satisfied cat.

"So where are we?" she asked.

"The valley of a tributary of Río Naranjo."

"Are you planning on getting us lost again?"

"We were never lost."

Maggie had the sense he had suspected she might leave a note. They had slogged four days northeast to the doorstop of Chirripó National Park and now were doubling back. Had he hoped Maggie would drop a misleading clue? Though his eyes were closed, the sly smile remained.

DO NOT TRUST ARCHBISHOP MORA

— I —

Slack rose before dawn, put coffee on, and went out to the patio to do his push-ups. The dense dank air vibrated to the chatter and trill of insects. It was drizzling, a cloud-blackened night. The *temporal* had lasted three days, now going on four, almost constant rain, several prodigious dumps.

It was day nine of Operación Libertad, though more apt would be Operation Frustration, the storms sweeping continuously through the mountains, obliterating the trail, the spoor, the dogs now useless. Even the best campesino trackers had failed.

Returning to the dark kitchen, he nearly knocked over the fifty twelve-packs of beer piled against the wall. Six hundred beer on the wall, they'd arrived out of the blue. Slack had thought at first it was some kind of Christmas present, then began to suspect he was being tested by Ham Bakerfield, but it turned out the man he had pulled from the ocean was the brewmaster at Cervecería de Costa Rica. Pilsen, Bavaria, Imperial, Slack had vast tempting riches.

But he had abstained, discovering there was a nubbin of toughness still within him, a small piece of grit. He had rescued someone. Maybe he could do it again, *si Dios quiere*. If God was still in the miracle business.

Slowly he became aware that Joe Borbón was in the room, there, standing against the kitchen wall. It was always eerie, the way Slack could sense his near-invisible presence.

"You want some coffee?"

"I don't drink poison." He preferred some kind of brown syrupy goop, a health concoction.

"What's up?"

"We found one of their camps. The old man wants to see you."

Borbón, who wasn't much for small talk, went out and began strapping a couple of inflatables onto the Rover. Since Joe would be hanging around without apparent reason, Slack had been given permission to put him to work, helping with the tours. That way, they could meet openly, and Slack could spar with him, get some help with the weight training.

While waiting for his coffee to brew, Slack thumbed through the pile of papers and reports on his desk. "Operación Libertad," they were stamped. "Classified." Under the sullen dawn light he studied one of the photos of Gloria-May Walker taken at the lodge. She was stunning in her swirling skirt, her show of dancing leg, a hibiscus between her perfect teeth. Walker was in the background, looking awkward.

The colonel's official flack had also managed to capture Margaret Schneider, romance writer, in a couple of unguarded moments. Making notes, interviewing Walker in his hammock, her eyebrow raised as if in disbelief. In another photo, Glo was posing with Maggie Schneider at the hot springs, her arm around her shoulders. Bosom pals. The Canadian woman wasn't exactly what you'd call voluptuous, she was built like a high jumper. Despite her cropped hair and thick glasses, she was more pretty than plain. Comely, even, when she smiled, which she was doing here, easy and cheery.

She'd mailed a postcard to her mother from San José, a picture of the Opera House. "Dinner date tonight with world's most gorgeous man." That dinner had cost her eight hundred bucks.

Slack had wanted to talk to her parents, but that was not permitted. Officially, he was still waiting to be called in. He wasn't sure that was even going to happen because the minister of security had gone off on his own tangent with a nationally broadcast plea to the Cinco de Mayoists, urging them to start negotiating, offering Archbishop

Mora as an emissary. That put Ham Bakerfield on a slow burn, he had no time for amateurs.

So Slack had been hanging about Quepos, pretending it was business as usual, though yesterday an interview had been arranged with one of the big networks. Again, Slack expressed support for the kidnappers' goals, sympathizing with Benito Madrigal, denigrating Chuck Walker. This was a part of the job he liked, there was a theatrical vein in him somewhere. After it aired, he was again taken in for questioning. Friends began to shun him.

༄

Ham Bakerfield seemed oddly impassive, a cop collecting data, as he watched Esperanza slide from the mud below the mangroves. Crocodile, six feet, fanged, possibly dangerous, sign here, you're hired. "I named her after a woman I used to know," Slack said. She was always around here, a scary treat for the tourists. "Stay behind me."

They manoeuvred their kayaks around, and followed Esperanza as she wove down the narrow channel to Estero Damas, a Quepos lagoon sheltered from the pitch and toss of the ocean by the sandy islands of Big and Little Damas. The landward side was choked with mangrove swamp.

"Her brother ate a dog a few weeks ago," Slack said. "Over there, on the island. Owners were fairly pissed."

Ham just grunted. He was doing okay for his age, able to keep up, shrugging off the discomfort of the sporadic rain. Lightning was crackling over the ocean, the skies pulsing with the energy of yet another coming thunderstorm.

"Where did you find their pit stop?"

"Beside a creek in the high Savegre. Interesting artefact there, a stone sphere, some kind of pre-Columbian sculpture."

Slack's interest was piqued, he had seen a few granite spheres at the National Museum, but never in the wild. Costa Rica's first peoples used to roll them down the rivers to the plains for reasons no one understood, maybe tributes to their demanding gods. "How did you stumble on the site?"

"We sent climbers up the river with ropes and pylons, it was steep. The guys who read the site said it was an overnight. Someone shot a snake, the buzzards had got at it pretty good, big one, a boa constrictor. A slug from a 7-mm parabellum. Not much else, a cigarette butt, some rocks probably used to weigh down the tents. From there they must have gone up the creek bed."

Slack listened to the burps and grumbles from the massing clouds. He wanted to see this prehistoric sphere, and he needed action, it might alleviate his drying-out pangs. "How about flying me up there?"

"If it ever clears."

"Any word from the kidnappers?" Ham had people hanging around the post office to intercept any notes addressed to the U.S. Embassy.

"None. We've set up Benito Madrigal for you, we have a nice place for him, a house in San José, maid service, home-cooked meals. He's on medication, seems okay. I'm stalling the security minister — he wants to send the archbishop in to see him, that could gum everything up. Madrigal liked you on the TV, he wanted to see the print interviews. I can't believe this is actually working, but he wants to meet, comrade to comrade. We're trying to fix that up for tomorrow."

Slack had memorized the brief on Madrigal, unmarried at forty-nine, degree in economics, a former top mandarin. The cramped little San José office of his People's Popular Vanguard had been tossed but found deserted, every scrap of paper spirited away. A couple of party adherents had gone missing and were likely involved in the plot. The few others who could be found claimed to know nothing.

"What does Benito say about this kidnapping?"

"He is proud of his comrades. He knows they will be 'connected.'"

A bright thick spear of lightning. They headed up the lagoon, trying to outrace the front, losing by about a hundred feet, drenched by the time they got to the dock. Ham's driver extended an umbrella for his boss, and Slack headed back into the choppy waters and up a channel, where Joe Borbón was waiting for him with the Rover.

They received a good weather report later that day, so Borbón drove Slack to a pick-up point in La Compañía – Operación Libertad had installed itself in one of the sprawling frame buildings of that former bastion of imperialism, the United Fruit Company. The front was moving through fast, sending out trails of ripped, ragged clouds dissolving into blue sky over the ocean.

Borbón parked on the old banana dock by a Bell 205. He seemed reluctant to part from his charge, but Slack promised to be back in an hour.

The crew rushed him aboard – there were some holes over the high Savegre, they could get him in if they hurried. Slack felt his stomach drop as the helicopter rose, and he watched field and meadow grow small below him, along with the grid of palm oil trees that surrounded Manuel Antonio, an island within a monoculture sea. The highlands ahead had not yet been touched by man, and maybe that's where he should escape to, live up in the mountains, have his own waterfall, a natural pool, a deck where he could listen to the songs of the forest.

For how long? Wherever he went, others seemed to follow, like the rats of Hamelin. When he led them to paradise they tromped upon it, flattened the land, built upon it. But hadn't he done the same? We are all enemies of the earth, choking her to death.

Environmental angst. He was feeling it more acutely now that he wasn't drinking and blotting out the world. On the other hand, his senses had been sharpened, he could see more clearly, enjoy as he hadn't for years the thrill of looking upon the splendour of the pulsing green living sea below, the dense canopy layered with strands of cloud and mist.

The helicopter swooped into an opening above the Savegre, the pilot searching for a landing spot. There wasn't any, just a narrow cleft above a creek, and standing there, on a ledge by a huge granite sphere, the honcho of the ground searchers, Yale Brittlewaite. Slack watched the rope ladder unfurling, almost tangling in the trees. One of the crew told him it was time to do his Tarzan act.

Gingerly, he crept down the rungs, until he was dangling about twenty feet above the sphere. He got some momentum going, swung himself to a liana, pushed off against the trunk of a strangler fig, and somersaulted onto the ledge. Brittlewaite was talking into a radio, unimpressed with Slack's derring-do.

"Crawl up about another fifty yards and call in."

"Roger."

Slack ran his hand over the sphere, it was almost smooth as marble. What secrets did it keep, what rites had been performed around it fourteen-odd centuries ago? The Bruncas used to offer virgins to the gods, had it seen human sacrifices? If only it had a mouth to speak . . .

Brittlewaite explained that his crew was inching up the creek, looking for the kidnappers' exit point back into the forest. "Those cowboys knew what they were doing, they didn't disturb the growth."

"You think they're that smart?"

"Someone is."

"If they're that smart, maybe they backtracked, went downriver."

The heavy stench of the rotting snake hung in the air. Vultures waited impatiently in the trees for it to be released to them again. He could see where the moss was disturbed at a rocky campsite, the remnants of a bonfire. This had probably been their fourth overnight stop, they were maybe doing six zigzag miles a day, maybe heading all the way up to the high country, the scrubby *cerros*. A pick-up point on the Pan-Am Highway, that seemed likely. Slack couldn't believe they'd still be outside in this weather, however well equipped they were.

He had time to do a little scouting on his own, the copter wouldn't be back for half an hour. He rubbed the sphere for luck, maybe it had occult power, a kind of Blarney Stone. He decided to go downriver, because maybe the kidnappers *were* that clever. Halcón was a "cool customer," Walker had said, "totally in control," so he wasn't some brain-dead camp follower of Benito Madrigal. A man in control, Slack was envious.

The water was up with all the rain, and the valley narrow here, compressing the creek into a series of swift cascades. A cyclone of small yellow butterflies swarmed into the air, then disappeared down the gut of the *quebrada*. Slack was feeling all right, enjoying nature's palette, his back stiffening a bit, that was all, the thirst not gnawing at him too bad. The fear of screwing up was still there, that was the one monkey he couldn't dislodge.

Slack scrambled over a series of boulders and around buttress roots leading to a gap in the forest. Just downstream, pinned to a fallen branch . . . what have we here? Panties. Slack picked up the tiny garment with the end of a stick, it was silky, maybe satin. Victoria's Secret, said the label.

Somehow, this didn't seem Maggie's brand of underwear, so all credit to Gloria-May. Hansel and Gretel had only dropped crumbs. He examined the nearby foliage – trampled ferns and machete cuts in the heliconia: yes, indeed, she had accurately marked the spot where her captors had led her into the forest. The stone sphere was guarded by the ghosts of good karma, after all. He called out to Brittlewaite, who came quickly with some of his group.

"Maybe you're smarter than I thought."

Slack assumed the word had gone out, a general all-around fuckup was among them. His orders were to go quickly in and out of here, but the hell with it, he was hot on the trail. He wasn't some kind of neophyte, he'd tramped all over Costa Rica, the coastal lowlands, the Talamancas, the high Atlantic rain forest.

So he pressed himself into service with the search party, and they began a hard climb up into a cloud forest luxurious with streaming banners of moss, thick lianas twisting toward the canopy, the mist rolling through the boughs. These virgin woods seemed mystical to Slack, but also hearty and generous, filled with energy, growing, struggling, sucking in the carbon, exhaling the oxygen of life.

After a slow several hundred yards the trail became easier to follow, it was as if the Cinco de Mayo had become tired, careless about covering their tracks – or in a hurry. So was Slack. The day was wasting, Brittlewaite and his crew were just poking along, examining every little mark and footprint. He marched past these slow frontrunners, and soon found himself far ahead, alone. There was no rain and little fog, so he made quick progress among the giant oak trees, sparser now, dwarf palms growing in the light gaps between them.

He stopped suddenly, thrilled by the liquid fluted song of a *jilguero*, the black-faced solitaire, the famous chanseur of the treetops. He had never seen a *jilguero* in the wild, though he had once angrily freed one from some moron in the caged-bird trade. Another trill, an undulating melody. Trying for a sighting, he meandered into the dense understory. He thought he saw his bird take flight, but wasn't sure, didn't see the orange markings. Then, more distant, it sang a Chopin-esque étude from somewhere high among the mossy twisted boughs.

After trudging through the forest for another twenty minutes, following the siren song of the *jilguero*, he finally saw the small bird on a twig, slate and orange. It erupted again with song, but he applauded too loudly and it flew off. When he turned back, he found it wasn't so easy to retrace his steps. After an hour of trying, he gave in to the annoying truth that he didn't know where the hell he was.

The day was becoming short, and he could feel a chill through his thin cotton jacket, a *papagayo* blowing from the northwest. His back was starting to ache. He had no radio, no compass, no machete, and, it was becoming obvious, no brain. This was not a time to panic, he would continue upwards, toward the inter-American highway, it was somewhere up there, crawling across the top of the country. The *jilguero* serenaded him again, taunting him.

At sunset, scratched by spines and thorns, his hand bleeding where he'd stumbled against a saw-toothed bromeliad, his bones aching from cold and exhaustion, his back throbbing, Slack climbed above timberline. He was in the high *páramo* now, he realized dully, bunch grasses, flat-topped shrubs sculpted by the wind, branches like grasping hands, all forming a thick, sticky net that seemed to grab at him, he was moving about thirty yards a minute. Once, he almost stumbled over a coral snake, bands of yellow, red, and black slithering past his boots. The ghosts of the granite sphere had lured him here, were laughing at him.

The sky had begun to glow fiercely, pink and russet. What a fool – if he survived this, Ham would be on him like a bulldozer. He had heard helicopters, they'd probably been searching for him, and he'd be blamed for losing precious time better reserved for Op Libertad.

Stop, reconnoitre. That windswept peak to the left, that had to be Cerro de la Muerte, the mountain of death. Oddly, despite its ill-boding name, the ancient volcano's closeness gave him renewed hope, Slack had once climbed it, a clear summer day when both oceans were in view. Somewhere near was the highway, and a path from it to the peak. He took a deep breath and made his way through the elfin forest and foot-sucking bog of the *páramo*. As the sun vanished he felt the first drops of rain.

Two hours later, he staggered onto the road, guided by a cacophony of horns, and now, as about fifty people stared down at him from a Tica line bus, he was squatting on the road, regaining strength, wondering why vehicles were backed up for miles down the road, why their drivers were honking and cursing.

A hundred yards up the hill, where the road curved back into view, he saw lights, a barricade, people toiling around it, a helicopter behind it. He had no alternative but to go up there and face the music.

Ham started in as soon as they dragged Slack up into the big Kawasaki, scorning his explanations, raking him over for fifteen minutes as he shivered, wet and chilled and gashed, under a pile of blankets. Brittlewaite was here, too, they'd reached the highway three hours ago, while the sun was up. Outside, the traffic was moving again, vehicles being waved through, one lane at a time.

"He goes la-la'ing off up the primrose path alone, what a horse's ass. We work as a *team*, that way you don't get lost for seven hours up your own rectum."

"Look at it as a test of young manhood," Slack mumbled. He'd followed his nose right into Gloria-May Walker's panties, found the trail, give him some credit.

Ham turned to one of his minions. "Get him a fucking change of clothing. The guy starts following a bleeping *bird*."

As Slack was thinking how a beer would go down just fine, he noticed Joe Borbón watching him from the back of the aircraft, waiting for a good excuse to off him. Slack might even welcome that right now, the way his spine was torturing him. He was bent like a pretzel as he struggled into a dry shirt and pants.

"We must have gone past you while you were bird-watching," Brittlewaite said, grinning at him. "Thought you were ahead of us."

Brittlewaite had found another campsite near the road, called into head office, blocked the highway, and searched it for exit points. About a mile and a half downhill, in an area where some small farms had been hacked out of the shrub, they'd found tracks leading to a ramshackle farmhouse, abandoned, falling down.

That's where they'd found a Christmas present. "BOTH OK," Maggie Schneider's note said. "NOT HURT." Slack had felt relief when he'd read that. But then she'd written: "Chirripó, Talamanca." Something she'd overheard? Maggie Schneider had spunk, somehow she had wheedled pencil and paper from them. But if they had gone into the vast wilderness of the Talamanca, the search would be immensely difficult.

"Injured man," she'd also written, "short, fat, San Isidro Hospital." About thirty miles away, in the valley of El General, the town was its commercial centre.

Ham's pitch descended to a mere grumble. "What were those assholes at that hospital doing, they couldn't report a wounded man. Okay, let's get down there so Slack can get those cuts treated before we lose him to gangrene, we should be so lucky."

Slack could tell Ham was feeling better, he'd probably even enjoyed his tirade. No harm had been done but to Slack's body, his pride, and his already damaged sense of accomplishment.

"Just get me a chiropractor, I'll be all right."

"You need a head doctor."

❦

Records in the admitting office of San Isidro Hospital revealed that the likely suspect was one Herman Rebozo, at least that was the name on the *cédula* he'd produced. He'd come in four days ago, apparently after flagging a bus, and left the next day with a cast on his foot. A nurse remembered him leaving in a taxi with a young man and woman, accomplices maybe, members of the Eco-Rico raiding party.

Slack and Ham waited in an examining room until the surgeon who'd seen to Rebozo was fetched from his home. He was surprised to learn he'd been gulled by a kidnapper, who was in his estimation dull-witted, *un hombre muy estúpido*. He had repaired a bone splinter in Rebozo's left foot, a bullet wound. The patient didn't have much to say except that he'd accidentally pulled the trigger of his .22 rifle.

"He told me a hunting accident. These happen all the time."

Ham snorted. "Yeah, right. Well, three characters including a little fat guy with a cast on his foot shouldn't be hard to track down, so we'll do the rounds of all the taxi drivers in this burg, also the hotels."

The doctor looked after Slack's cuts, then examined his back. As his fingers probed Slack's spinal cord, he yelped.

"I believe what you have, señor, is a slight spinal misalignment."

Slack was taken to a private ward, where he lay down heavily on the bed, depleted.

"You and your spine are having breakfast tomorrow with Benito Madrigal," Bakerfield said.

"Hey, Christ, I've got to get some sleep."

"You're not getting paid to sleep. We want you to get onside with him, persuade him to broadcast a message to his comrades not to harm the women." He handed Slack a battery-powered tape recorder. "You going to be able to relate to this psychotic?"

"For me it'll be a piece of cake."

"Don't fuck up."

Slack had the look of a bent octogenarian as he followed Bakerfield out the door of a Cessna at San José's Pavas airport. Though exhausted, he hadn't slept well, his brain replaying that moronic rollick through the jungle, now everyone in the operation was laughing at him.

Slack was displeased to see Chuck Walker seated in the waiting van, he wished he'd go away somewhere, let the real cops do their job. "Contact has been made," Walker said. "Envelope intercepted at the post office, addressed to the embassy. This was in it." He held up a gold hoop earring. "It's Glo's. Goddamn, let's get on this. Next time it could be an ear."

He handed Slack the envelope and a lined sheet of paper, both darkened with fingerprint dust. The postmark was San José. In Spanish, penned in block capital letters, were greetings from Comando Cinco de Mayo. Four choppy sentences: "Our demands remain firm. We will not negotiate. Lives of political prisoners are at risk. We will meet with Archbishop Mora when we are ready."

"We will not negotiate" – a standard negotiating ploy. Halcón was just being a good businessman, not in a hurry. Totally in control. Doubtless, the wounded foot-soldier, Rebozo, had put it in the mail. Last night, investigators had traced him to a San Isidro bus station, where a cab driver had dropped him off. Now he was probably some-where in the crowded Central Valley, among millions of people.

"We're not negotiating either," Walker said. "Let's figure out a way to dump this interfering cleric."

They were taken first to the sprawling compound of the U.S. Embassy, where Ambassador Higgins, after some effusive greetings, began fawning over the senator, congratulating him for a "great jump-start" toward the Republican nomination. A *Newsweek* poll had him number four with a bullet.

The embassy's press attaché was hanging around, so Walker pro-vided a sound bite: "I think Americans know I am down here fight-ing a more important war than an election campaign, however high the office."

In the eyes of the great American public, he was a hero, he'd offered himself to the guerrillas, pleaded with them to take him hostage in place of his wife. Slack found it hard to digest, a guy reputed to be a sure loser had announced he was no longer campaigning, and now he was accelerating through the pack.

They were ushered into a swank office where Slack was introduced to the head psychiatrist at the Psiquiatrico, Dr. Ignacio Bleyer, a jowly gentleman with a Sigmund Freud beard.

"The man you are about to talk to is a particular favourite of mine," he said. "It is not often one sees so much varied delusional material of a persecutory nature. He sees plots everywhere."

Slack nodded. He had some first-hand experience, his mother, neurotic, refusing to leave her house, everyone a threat, she had suffered an abnormal fear of authority. "All right, he's potty."

Bleyer looked down at Slack with an expression of professional disapproval. "I would prefer to term his condition as a borderline psychosis of the paranoid type."

He continued with a dissertation to the effect that Benito Madrigal had been suffering a mild form of paranoid schizophrenia long before he was jailed. He was charismatic enough to have gathered some ingenuous followers into his People's Vanguard for his quixotic run for the Costa Rican presidency.

"Clearly, he was in an extreme paranoid phase when he held the judges hostage. Regrettably, following his incarceration, the symptoms have not lessened. Señor Madrigal does, however, enter periods in which he is able to reason and to relate to others. The use of Clozaril enhances such occasions."

"Okay, you keep him doped up. What state is he in now?"

"Reasonably stable. Unfortunately, he has been rejecting his medication, claiming we are trying to poison him."

"Will he know who I am?"

"He has been following events carefully and has seen you many times on television, we have arranged that. We can only hope he will not reject you as he has others who have tried to help him."

On the way out, Slack gulped down a couple of muscle relaxants.

A neurotic and a psychotic, how was this going to work out? Head-to-head combat, Slack's shaky reality against the multi-faceted world of the imprisoned martyr of his own failed revolution.

As they were about to leave the embassy, Walker drew him aside. "If you find your way into this nest of terrorists, Slack, I want you to do what you have to do."

"What do you mean?"

"Do I have to be specific?" An impatient tone.

"I'm afraid so, senator."

He went close to Slack's ear. "Waste them. I want them dead. Every one of those bastards. It's the only way we deter this kind of crap. You won't need much of an excuse. We can put whatever spin on it we want."

"Yeah, well, we'll see what goes down." Slack felt a bilious lump in the pit of his stomach.

∾

Benito Madrigal was sequestered in a house in the upscale Los Yoses area, eastern San José. Slack's driver pointed to a substantial brick home set behind a vine-entangled wall. It served well as a prison, like most fine houses in San José it was barred against thieves. The curiosity seekers hanging around out front probably included media, so Slack was taken immediately into the garage, which connected to the house.

An OIJota was waiting for him just inside, two others in the kitchen, playing dominoes, one of them with a headset, so Slack assumed Benito's room was wired. The other cop pointed to the living room door.

Slack unlocked it and quietly peeked in. The room was fairly dark, the front-facing windows shuttered, though a floor lamp was on. The walls weren't padded, but the furniture was, a sofa, a few armchairs, a deep-pile carpet. A console TV sat in the corner, a stereo on a shelf. It all looked homey, unthreatening.

Benito Madrigal was seated on the sofa, reading a book. He seemed thinner than in the photos Slack had seen, umber-skinned, a

Lenin-esque smoothness of scalp with a fringe around the edges. In his pressed trousers, white shirt, red-patterned tie, and glasses, he still looked like the high-ranking bureaucrat he once was.

Slack brewed up two mugs of coffee, then entered cautiously, placed them on the table before Madrigal, who immediately jumped up, as if frightened.

He said, in Spanish, "Who sent you?"

"You did. My name is Jacques Cardinal, Señor Madrigal."

Benito studied him for a long time. "Cardinal. Yes. I am aware of you. If it is you. One has to be careful, there are many spies and pretenders."

"I'm real, Don Benito."

After he studied Slack's *cédula*, the creases of doubt disappeared from his thin face, and he gripped his hand with unexpected fierceness. "The one who supports the cause of Cinco de Mayo, and has been arrested for it. I didn't believe they would allow you to see me – I suspect their motives."

"They say you will not speak to anyone else. I think I know what their motives are, they want to do a prisoner exchange." Slack was going at this carefully, sizing him up. He didn't seem so bad, a little paranoia is a healthy thing.

"They will never let me go. They consider me dangerous. I have evidence of corruption in the highest places. I am a prisoner, yes, Cardinal, but a prisoner of war – the great war of ideas and beliefs." He had a sonorous voice with good carry, he'd been a forceful orator.

Slack produced his tape recorder. "They gave me this. They want you to record a message for your comrades in the field."

Benito checked to make sure the door was firmly closed, then spoke in a low, urgent voice. "Be careful. They can hear everything." He was right about that, maybe he wasn't so crazy. "In the hospital, they connected my head to a machine, that is how they do their brainwashing. Do you know how to disconnect the wires?"

Slack wasn't sure, did he mean wires in his brain? He went to the stereo, examined a suspicious lead into the wall, then yanked it out. "That should do the trick."

"*Bueno*. They listen, they try to analyze my thoughts."

When they sat opposite each other, Benito pushed the coffee away. "It is dangerous to drink this. They are always trying to administer drugs. They sprinkle potions into my food to stop me from thinking clearly."

However disturbed, he was no fool.

"Cardinal. Your name has great significance, it is the colour of the revolutionary martyrs' blood. You are Jacques the Red." He laughed. "And who is this man they call Halcón? Is he reliable?"

"You have not met him?"

Madrigal shook his head. "No."

"No one knows much about him."

"He seems ambitious. That is not necessarily a bad thing, if it is not personal ambition."

"His desire is to free you, Don Benito. And we must let him know you are safe and well, and ready to join your comrades."

"First, the state must pardon me of all crimes, that way they cannot arrest me again. That is the law." Benito picked up the tape recorder, examined it as if expecting to find some hidden lethal device. "What do they want me to say? Are you sure it's not a trick?"

"They want you to name a mediator. They are very anxious to use Archbishop Mora."

Benito's eyes narrowed. "Why?"

Slack leaned to him, conspiratorial. "I think they have some kind of hold on him."

"*Claro*. So he is working for the other side."

"Yes, the forces of reaction."

"I have never trusted him."

"They could be setting a trap for your comrades."

"You are right, Jacques Cardinal. We must warn them."

Slack was getting along uncomfortably well with Benito, it worried him that he had so little trouble entering his world, they shared something. He reached into a pocket for pen and notepad and began writing out a brief script. "If we word this right, the media will be sure to broadcast it."

When Slack placed the paper in front of him, Benito adjusted his glasses and began to read aloud: "'I give comradely greetings to Comando Cinco de Mayo.' Yes, excellent. 'I am being treated well and soon will be with you . . .' But do they dare release me, Cardinal? I know too much." He lowered his voice. "Senator Walker also has an ambition – to dominate the world through the multinational corporations that support him."

"I share your concern." Benito had it pretty well right.

He leaned toward Slack's ear. "He maintains a secret militia force."

"How do you know?"

"I have seen this with my inner eye."

Had Cinco de Mayo any idea what they were bartering for? They must have thought the claims of mental illness were lies of the state.

"The government says you will be released if you instruct our comrades not to harm the two women."

"They must be desperate indeed." He continued reading Slack's message: "'I urge you to send word immediately that our political prisoners will not be harmed. Do not trust Archbishop Mora.' Surely that is not what they want me to say."

"No, but you must tell the truth, you must warn your people about Mora."

"Our comrades will hear this on the radio?"

"I will make sure of it. I will send it out to all the stations."

"They could alter my voice."

"But I am your witness." Slack turned on the recorder. "Read it in your normal voice, Benito."

One of the guards took this inopportune time to come in with *gallo pinto* and eggs and mini-boxes of cereal. He set plates and cutlery before them.

"What is it this time?" Benito snorted. "Truth serum in the corn flakes? Did you piss on the *huevos*?"

The OIJota glanced at the wall, the dangling cord Slack had yanked from it, and glared at him. "How long are you going to be?"

"Just leave us alone, okay?" Slack said. As the guard made his way out, he added, "And keep that door shut, stop trying to listen in."

"Bravo," said Benito. He shoved his plate away and returned to the note. "It says I am being treated well. But sometimes they poison the *pinto*. Can you see how they are weakening my body? I am losing weight."

He was probably quite hungry. So was Slack, he'd had a juice at the embassy, that was all.

"To be safe, Benito, let's switch plates." He moved them about, took a forkful of Benito's eggs, they tasted fine, no arsenic.

Benito still looked uncertain, but his hunger got the better of his suspicions, he began eating voraciously as Slack again urged the tape recorder toward him. "This is our chance to get the word out, Benito, read it into this machine."

But Benito began rambling. "The fifth of May, it is significant, yes? The second odd number following International Workers' Day. In La Reforma, they laughed at me. Ha! Now the laughing has died to a stillness. The government fears I will expose the corruption that infests it, and at least one minister is trembling in his shoes."

That would be his former boss, the head of public works, who had Benito jailed for slander. Slack liked the vibrant speech, he could see how Benito could collect a few green followers.

"Your supporters are waiting for word from you. Give them the news that you are well." He straightened out the paper in front of Benito.

"Yes, but I demand to meet with the president. He must grant me a pardon. I am not a criminal, Jacques Cardinal, what I did was for my country. And he must fire the minister. There is no reason for blood to be shed if he does that."

Getting this message recorded was turning out to be no easy task. Slack was fagged, his exertions of yesterday were catching up to him, and those muscle relaxants were making him woozy. In fact, he felt . . . drugged. As the last of the *huevos revueltos* journeyed toward his mouth, he had an unpleasant thought, they had probably doctored Benito's food, some kind of potent sedative. He set his fork down. He felt dismay mingled with light-headedness, as if he was moving out into some strange gentle space.

"Let's get the message recorded, okay, Benito?" He heard his own voice as if from a distance, drawn out, drawled.

"Yes, we must get word out to the cadres, they are waiting." He was standing at the window now, opening the shutters. "Raise high the banners, comrades, the national revolution has begun!" Slack heard a single cheer from outside, either he was hallucinating or Benito had a fan.

Slack fumbled for the recorder, but his aim was off, his hand nudged the device over the table edge. He went down on knees, saw that the two AA batteries had spilled out. He had trouble getting them back in, figuring out which went where. He felt very tired.

He sat on a couch, trying to make sense of the recorder and its batteries, one would be positive, the other negative. He tried to stay awake . . .

Someone was pulling at Slack, shaking him, speaking urgently in his ear. "You've been here two hours, what the fuck's going on?" What *was* going on, he was lying prone on a couch. He rolled over, looked up into Ham Bakerfield's scowling face.

"He told us not to disturb him," an OIJota said.

In the background, a commotion. "Do not trust Archbishop Mora!" The voice of Benito Madrigal, the scene was beginning to focus. Slack sat up, saw Benito cowering in a corner of the room, shouting into the tape recorder. "Repeat! Do not trust Archbishop Mora!"

Dr. Bleyer was trying to calm him down. "Relax, no one will hurt you."

As Slack pulled himself to a wobbly standing position, Benito tossed the miniature recorder to him. "Spread the word, comrade! Be brave, don't give in to them." He batted away Bleyer's extended hand. "It's too late, you swine! It's out! The word is out!"

— 3 —

Joe Borbón wasn't at the Quepos airport to greet Slack, so he took a taxi, the driver giving him suspicious looks all the way. He had lost whatever credibility he had in this community, even the gang at Balboa's was avoiding him now. Elsewhere, however, the guerrillas had earned support, especially among the poor and the anti-American left.

To add to Slack's unsavoury reputation, a false report had gone out to the media claiming he was wanted in the U.S. for passing counterfeit currency. That had been Slack's own idea, though, the kidnappers might relate better to a fellow outlaw.

The media couldn't get enough of Benito's taped message, they'd been replaying it all day. Somehow, Madrigal had got the recorder working after Slack conked out, had read the script with frantic gusto. The sole slightly worrying note was Benito's ad lib with its hint of paranoia, the archbishop was a spy for the capitalist oligarchy. Meanwhile, Monsignor Mora had withdrawn his name as intermediary. The security minister had expressed regret. Slack assumed the Tico government was unhappy with the machinations of Bakerfield's team.

In pulling off this miracle, Jacques the Red had kept his handlers' faith alive, though he'd undergone some painful ribbing for eating the wrong breakfast. Praise came from the humourless Chuck Walker, who seemed ever more staunchly behind him. "Way to go, soldier." Soldier. He was growing to hate that. Waste the bastards, he'd ordered.

His house seemed unusually tidy, swept out. It was Borbón's doing, like most over-trained agents he was a cleanliness freak. He'd got rid of all the beer, too, Slack had told him to give it to a charity for Christmas.

He made himself a sandwich, then spread out a foamy on the patio and lay on it, resting his back, wondering if there was poetry left in him – but what chance of inspiration amid yapping dogs and crowing roosters? He noticed a few families had started to put up more substantial homes in the *precaria*, footings, forms, concrete block. They were digging in, making the squat a *fait accompli* before the lazy courts could move on it. One of the buildings had been made into a store, a *pulpería*, a Borden's truck in front of it, a Pepsi van arriving.

The squatters seemed to be holding a Christmas party, they were whooping and laughing, three different radios loudly competing, salsa, jingle bells, saccharine songs of love. Slack clenched his teeth.

He heard a diesel engine outside, burping, subsiding. After a few minutes, he said, "Joe, you here?"

"Just doing dishes. I don't like ants."

"Where did you deliver the beer?"

"Across the street."

Free beer, that's why they were celebrating. "Dammit, I said give it to a good cause."

"They're selling it, raising funds to build a church."

Slack wanted to weep.

"This is something you asked for." Joe materialized beside him, handed him a packet, copies of some Nancy Ward novels plus Margaret Schneider's notepad, left behind at the Eco-Rico Lodge. Her *Birds of Central America*, too, notations scribbled in the margins.

"Did they put the pinch on this Rebozo guy yet?"

"Nope."

"Has he been IDed?"

"A little fat nothing guy everyone calls Gordo. Former government payroll clerk. Worked under Benito Madrigal. Got politicized, joined the People's Vanguard." A long speech for Borbón.

"What about the couple he was seen with?"

"*Nada.*"

"Did the ground party pick up the trail?"

"Nope." That was it. Joe disappeared somewhere.

"Chirripó, the Talamanca," Maggie Schneider's note said, Slack was having trouble accepting that. How would they supply themselves in the middle of nowhere?

He listened for a while to the howling *rancheras* coming from across the road, broken hearts, lost love, *vaya con Dios*, my darling. If Joe hadn't carted out the beer, he'd be tempted to tie one on.

He leafed through a couple of Maggie Schneider's books. *When Love Triumphs. No Time for Sorrow. Return to the House of Heartbreak.* "Her breath came in quick starts as his hand teased at her shoulder strap." He read on, feeling mildly voyeuristic, as the couple hotly coupled, lips, hips, and swelling breasts, rapturous surrender. He was embarrassed to feel a slight tremor in his pants.

As he flipped through *No Time for Sorrow*, a theme seemed to surface. "Had Emma, despite her ventures up many blind alleys, finally stumbled upon the wellspring of that imponderable rapture called love?" Emma, a comely crisis worker, was afraid of flying, Tod was a stunt pilot.

He opened the notepad, fluid slanting letters, paragraphs crossed out, begun again. He had asked to see it when he'd learned, to his surprise, that nobody had bothered to read her notes through to the end. "Romantic twaddle," Ham had said.

The pages of her work-in-progress were filled with the stop-and-go adventures of one Fiona Wardell, a voluptuous alter ego, he assumed, altogether a scary creation. *She was not interested in pandering to the weak egos of shallow men who feared strong women.*

But here she was looking for a vanishing warbler, an admirable cause. But no, a few pages later the mission changed. A lost treasure, a Spanish mission on the Savegre River, where had she got that? One of his friends, a Quepos historian, subscribed to that theory, but many scoffed.

This was interesting: several pages of hurried scribbles, relating, it seemed, to an encounter with a certain Professor Pablo Esquivel and his, "Forgive me, I cannot hold inside what I feel."

What he was feeling for was her U.S. dollars. Something tugged at Slack about this coming-together with a Tico flim-flam artist, its bittersweet symbolism, the kiss of the Laughing Falcon, the flowers of Yesterday, Today, and Tomorrow . . .

Her postcard to her mother had mentioned a "gorgeous" professor, so likely she was incorporating real events and characters into her book. Suddenly he had bizarre proof of that.

You're Jacques Cardinal, aren't you?

"Slack," he said, slurring the name. "That's what they call me around here."

He pried his eyes from the page, looked around to see if he was still on planet earth.

Her impression was of a man either bored with life or defeated by its challenges. . . . Close up, he smelled rancid.

How had she got close enough to smell him? Had he met her? Where, in what alcoholic stupor? She'd spent a day at Manuel Antonio, they must have bumped into each other.

There seemed little likelihood that much could be salvaged of the nobility he once possessed. Her portrayal of him smarted, but he read on, fascinated. What had she done to him, this Cardinal fellow was a lout.

He raised his eyes from the page. Someone was at the soirée across the road who shouldn't be there. That someone was Joe Borbón, shaved, shampooed, long-sleeve white shirt, hitting on a dark-haired damsel. Here was fodder for romance writer Nancy Ward, the killing machine plucking a hibiscus for Juan Camacho's kid sister. He tried hard to swallow his rage.

Rocky,

    I'm sending along another packet of pages of *Harry's Wild Adventure.* I gave up trying to follow your testy urgings to rewrite Agent Wilder as more macho; I simply don't possess the cooking skills to follow a recipe for the type of cardboard caricature demanded by the mass market. I *intend* that Harry bums you out; he is the creation of a depressive poet's mind. Give him a break – he's the local pariah, the town drunk avoids him, even the bugs don't like him any more, he's suffering from acute alcohol deficiency. He volunteered for this plot, didn't he? He's risking his life for R. B. Rubinstein's standard fifteen-per-cent commission.

    As Dr. Bleyer might put it, the patient is so conflicted with self-doubt and loathing that he has begun to separate from reality. Has he dipped into his mother's gene pool? Or is mental illness contagious, did he catch it from the leader of the People's Popular Vanguard? When he was seventeen, was he traumatized beyond repair by a decaying mouse in a beer bottle?

Reality has become so tenuous that suddenly Harry finds himself trapped within someone else's novel and portrayed, I regret to say, as a person one might regret knowing. Looking into the mirror of her pages, he sees, in fact, an asshole. What ugly fumbling encounter had inspired her to create this Frankenstein's monster? Though our hero sifts through the sands of memory, he cannot find this woman hidden there.

How dare she putter with Harry's heart in her search for the wellspring of love? And what's all this malarkey about a lost mission? Let it stay lost, dammit – all the Spanish gold in the world is piffle as against the infinite worth of Buff-Breasted Blue Warblers. A lost mission? That's Harry's story.

Since the standard motif of the romance novel requires the heroine to rehabilitate a sub-human lout, maybe there is hope that Dr. Wilder might yet salvage the nobility he once possessed. How disappointed Fiona will be when she finally drags him into bed only to find him incapable of satisfying the burning desire she has fought so hard to deny during the previous nine chapters.

"That's all right." Fiona smiled sweetly, barely able to suppress her laughter. *"Lots of men can't."*

Poor old Harry. He has taken to spending much time lying restlessly in his hammock, staring at the photograph of this skinny bespectacled farm girl from Lake Lenore, Saskatchewan. That jaunty smile, those knowing eyes, those dangling adjectival clauses.

I wish I knew where this is heading, Rock. I'm afraid for my character; he's going to choke, I know it. I already feel beaten by the competition, I'll never be able to *summon the fortitude to enter one last saloon, as usual smelling of must and stale spirits and urine.*

Jacques the Red.

THE DARKSIDE OF THE MOON

— I —

The night was black but for a faint hope of dawn and a wedge of waxing moon shining palely on seven exhausted, grimy figures trudging down a path in the lowland forest. They had come upon this trail yesterday after their quick and dangerous descent, and had camped near it, catching a daytime nap while a thunderstorm raged. As the clouds fled and they struck their tents, Maggie had watched the sun set gloriously over the infinite Pacific – now, after eleven hours of this moonlit march, they must be near the coastal plain.

Buho had given up on his boots and was faltering along the muddy path on blistered feet. He was in added distress – he had blundered into a tick-infested bush and was now scratching himself ferociously. He was given no time to stop and pick the ticks away: Halcón was urging them to quicken their pace, concerned they might meet early risers. Zorro was in too much pain from his wrenched shoulder to carry the heavy pack of weapons, so Coyote had taken on that burden, relinquishing his own pack to Glo – she was heeding Maggie's advice to seek comity with the rebels.

This was a trail well travelled, and Maggie sensed Halcón had passed this way before, reconnoitring the area with Coyote. Although continuing to share confidences with Maggie, he had remained coy about their destination. Halcón had planned superbly – and with speed: Glo's Eco-Rico holiday had been sprung as a surprise on her only weeks ago.

He was a few feet ahead of Maggie, a dim outline in the moonlight, and when he stopped suddenly and turned around, she carried into him, stumbling. His hand went out to steady her, and they engaged in a clumsy dance to gain balance, a step forward, a step back. It took him a moment to realize his palm was against her breast; he withdrew it abruptly.

The collision, she realized, occurred because Coyote, who had been walking fifty metres ahead, had hurried back to urge them from the trail. "*Viene un hombre,*" a man is coming. They hid in the foliage while a flashlight approached: a barefoot campesino leading a wheezing Brahma bull with a rope tied to a nose ring. Maggie crouched close to Halcón, and despite her anxiety and her almost numbing fatigue, felt flushed, her breast prickling where his hand had cupped it.

Maggie feared that Glo might bolt or cry out, but she remained still and silent until the man and the bull passed out of sight. She and Maggie had not lost hope they might yet be able to escape. That chance might come soon because the trail had begun to connect a scattering of human outposts, farms bordering the Naranjo River, swollen from the December rains.

As the eastern horizon began to glimmer with light, the trail gradually metamorphosed into a road that might, in dry season, bear four-wheel vehicles. Indeed, there was evidence of fresh tire tracks, a stirring in the mud where wheels must have spun before the driver surrendered and reversed down the hill.

They came to another clearing, with a campesino home: sheets of tin, wooden slats. The road closed up again within a canyon of trees, but as they rounded a bend, Maggie could see a distant flickering of light, too high up to be a flashlight. When they passed a farmyard, she saw an incandescent bulb on a pole.

Halcón hurried them along even faster; the sky was turning pink. Above, Maggie saw a limp power line. Here was a utility pole, and here a barbed-wire fence leading to a six-foot-high gate of welded rebar. Behind it was a narrow two-storey concrete structure.

Halcón flipped through a ring of keys, then opened the padlock of the gate, directing everyone inside the grounds. Glo at first hesitated, looking warily at the squat concrete tower with its rickety outer staircase and barred windows. Maggie wondered if they would dare lock them in such a depressing prison.

Halcón spoke to Coyote, who put a handgun in his pocket and hauled his pack up the stairs, unlocking a wooden door to a small room with a window overlooking the road. Halcón explained: "This is a bodega. Tools are stored below and there are quarters above. He will be the watchman."

Maggie could hear the roar of the Naranjo River more distinctly as they descended along winding parallel tracks. A hundred metres on, a night-flowering plant was pouring out a dizzying perfume; bats were fluttering about its long white trumpets. Here were bananas, citrus, papaya, a tropical orchard hemmed in by the vine-choked jungle. Farther on, Maggie saw the outline of a dark mass etched in the rays of twilight, a two-storey house in a grassy clearing.

"You have arrived at the dark side of the moon," Halcón said.

The front of the house was faced with rock cemented into concrete; the walls appeared not merely lumpy but lopsided – as if the builder had not known how to use a plumb line. The second floor looked like an afterthought; it probably held a couple of bedrooms. The roof was white-painted steel, bolted to fasteners in the rafters.

The windows at the front were heavily barred with half-inch steel curlicues and hearts. Behind the grills were sturdy wooden shutters. A plate above the heavy-timbered front door read, "Darkside of the Moon."

Again Halcón fished through his keys; after opening the door he reached inside – and lights went on. Maggie was forced to blink, the glare of the electric bulbs seeming unnatural. A bat squeaked by and flew out between the shutters that Halcón was opening.

He gestured Maggie and Glo inside while Buho stripped and sat under an outdoor shower and tried to pick off the ticks. Zorro and Tayra went off to the orchard to gather some fruit.

The house quickly lost its sense of gloom as Halcón walked its inner perimeter, pulling open all the shutters. A beautiful pale morning light streamed through wide arched windows, through which they could see the dense forest and hear the rumble of the river.

"You will each have a room to yourselves." Halcón indicated a rough cemented staircase that led to the upper bedrooms. "The only toilet is downstairs. To amend, I can offer a hot-water shower."

After Halcón returned outside to confer with his squad, Maggie and Glo wandered through the house, speculating in low whispers about how Halcón had acquired this house. Aside from one bedroom at the far end, the entire main floor was open, only a low concrete divider separating the kitchen from the living space. The kitchen was well equipped: a propane stove, a softly buzzing fridge. A back door was secured not just by a lock, but by lengths of rebar welded to the metal doorframe.

The staircase, which was almost comically out of plumb, was built into the front wall. The other sides of the house featured several wide arched windows, all barred – more hearts and curlicues – but open to small visitors. A violet butterfly wobbled in through one window and out another.

"This is a *hiding* place?" Glo said.

"A little airy, isn't it?"

The living room held several wooden chairs, three hammocks strung from rafters, and cushions scattered on the floor for extra seating. Numerous books and magazines were lying about. Other diversions included a stereo and a fourteen-inch television, with a coat hanger aerial. Interior walls were fouled with guano; the dusty, streaked tile floor demanded the attentions of a mop. Maggie, a compulsive house cleaner, knew she could not relax until that was done.

"Filthy, but . . . Glo, this could be *lots* worse."

"If you don't mind living in a Yellow Submarine."

The walls were painted garishly with wide rectangular blocks of yellow, orange, blue. A Trekkie might have lived here: a poster on the wall showed *The Enterprise* zooming through a constellation. She and Glo speculated that the owner, presumably a Pink Floyd fan, was a drug-addled escapee from North America, his vacation home inno-cently rented out to desperados.

Upstairs, they checked out the two bedrooms separated by a nar-row corridor, the interiors dusty and spotted with bird leavings, bat droppings, and dead insects. Glo chose the larger room facing the back, with the queen-size bed. Maggie preferred the room facing the front: a single bed but also a writing table and a view of the orchard and green-clad mountains. On the brick patio below, Zorro was opening up several collapsible wood-and-leather rocking chairs, and Tayra was halving oranges and sweet lemons at a concrete table.

Downstairs, their tour took them to the tiled bathroom − the floor and ceiling were far from parallel, and the sink counter took yet another direction. The shower stall was in a large uncurtained corner, and looked enormously tempting.

"Flip you for it," Glo said.

Maggie turned on the tap; the water came brown initially, then clear. "First, let's make this prison a home. God knows how long we're going to be here." She began filling a plastic pail.

"The unstoppable Maggie Schneider." Glo took up a mop.

Halcón and the others returned as Maggie was beating down cob-webs. Though the guerrillas protested their weariness, they were ulti-mately shamed into participating in a thorough cleanup that lasted into the afternoon. Buho brought a ladder from Coyote's bodega and dusted the beams and rafters; he and Zorro washed the walls. Halcón swabbed out the downstairs bedroom, which was to serve as his pri-vate quarters. Tayra scrubbed the kitchen.

Maggie saved her own room for last. Her arched, barred window reached almost to the ceiling from a two-foot-high sill, and with the shutters open afforded a cooling breeze. The door had a heavy dead-bolt lock, which pleased as much as surprised her. Less gratifying was the paint job − a jolting orange and yellow.

Her labours done, she set off for the shower. Downstairs, Buho and Zorro were in a coma-like sleep on hammocks; Halcón was nap-ping, too, on an air mattress beside the locked front door.

This was not a palace, but no dank, rat-infested cellar, either. Maggie's ordeal could yet have a happy ending – as long as the rescue team were not headed by some cowboy charging around with six-guns blazing, bullets ricocheting everywhere. Surely their liberators would be calm and careful: they had well-developed routines for hostage-takings.

Still, she felt she might be in more danger from her rescuers than her kidnappers, though she had concerns about Zorro's shaky state of equilibrium – especially because Halcón had returned his pistol. The other firearms had been wrapped in burlap and placed in a lock-closet under the stairway, along with valuables from the Eco-Rico looting. Zorro's gun stayed buckled in its holster, but she often saw him fondling its grip. He was not one to live with loss of face, and had become skittish and moody after being shamed in front of his comrades.

As she stripped in the bathroom, she anxiously studied the electric shower head, a contraption jury-rigged with wires and electric tape – but the walls of the stall were wet, so others had recently tempted fate and not been electrocuted. When she turned the shower on, the lights dimmed.

On a shelf were soap, shampoo, and a clean washcloth, which Maggie put to hard use, finding heaven under the streaming hot water. The window was unshuttered, so Maggie could see Tayra outside, a doughty slave to duty, working through a hill of laundry at a concrete pila. At night, Tayra would be stationed between the two upstairs bedrooms; Maggie or Glo would find it impossible to slip out without awakening her. The door to the outside would be locked, anyway.

Maggie towelled her body dry and turned to the mirror to brush her hair. Revealed was a sinewy, tawny body that had lost little weight despite the rigours of the last week, though her breasts had firmed up and her thigh muscles were well-toned. She affected a supermodel pout and struck a pose for the catwalk. "You were *muy linda*," he had said, "in the soft light playing on the waterfall."

Wrapped in her towel, she went upstairs. She had earned a long siesta.

2

Maggie was awakened by the rolling sputtering song of a house wren and saw it dart above a timber bracing just outside the window, where it was welcomed with a chorus of peeps. A nest, babies! Now she knew the source of the little drippings that she had scrubbed from the orange wall. The wren took flight to a nearby lime tree, then burbled another song.

She felt refreshed – how long had she slept? For a few hours, she realized; the sun was behind the trees, soon to set, throwing rays like spears between the boughs. She had not locked her door and saw, hanging to dry beside it, her undergarments and her two sets of clothes, freshly washed and placed there by Tayra. The army fatigues were torn almost to shreds, and the knees and elbows were unravelling from her khakis also. They were still damp, but she slipped them on. She felt like Raggedy Ann.

In the kitchen, Glo was helping Tayra, demonstrating her new-found team spirit, putting the finishing touches to a fruit salad: pineapples, bananas, papaya, citrus.

Before dinner, the *colectivo* – four without Coyote – held a brief meeting at the far end of the room. After vigorous debate, a decision was reached and announced to the hostages: they would all eat in front of the television set.

"We have agreed, with one abstention," Buho proclaimed, "that we will allow the guests of our commando to watch the six o'clock news." Halcón shrugged, obviously the abstainer. He was prepared to let the comrades have their little victories.

Maggie settled on the sofa beside Glo and attacked her plate of fruit salad while Zorro fiddled with the dial. He could find only one channel that offered more than fuzz and swimming colours, but it was one of the major San José outlets: Canal Siete. The headline item involved a vandalism of a front-yard crèche: it had been kicked apart, a plaster Mary and baby Jesus stolen. ("This event has shocked the nation," Buho translated. "They should be thrown in jail," muttered Tayra.) For balance, a happier story: a poor family winning a lottery after having had to borrow money for Christmas gifts. Buho translated with appropriate feeling.

Maggie was beginning to wonder if the hostage-taking had become yesterday's news when the Channel Seven crew cut to a taped interview with a man named Jorge Castillo, the minister of public security. Halcón began making notes.

"This is about us," Buho explained. "Archbishop Mora has withdrawn an offer to intercede, and Minister Castillo is offering a list of five others." Stills of these offerings were paraded.

"Priests and politicians," said Halcón. "Not an honest man among them." He was grouchy; he was out of cigarettes.

"He is pleading with us to make contact," said Buho.

Maggie started as she saw herself: another still, one of the photos taken at the lodge, her mouth agape as she interviewed Walker; then Glo filled the screen, wearing her cocktail dress and a comical come-hither look.

She complained, "Damn, I look like a cheap hooker."

"We are asked to confirm the two ladies are safe. This request is from, they call themselves Operación Libertad, but it is coming also from . . . here is Benito, my uncle." Buho sat upright.

In an old clip, Benito Madrigal was shown at a political rally. Following that came words that sounded of an urgent plea. "This is a message to us; it is Don Benito recorded from yesterday." Buho's words took on a high, excited pitch. "*Gracias a Dios*, he is saying he will soon be with us, and we must keep our guests safe, and . . . also he is saying, 'Do not trust Archbishop Mora.' He warns the archbishop is working for the other side. He is very sure of this."

Maggie found the admonition to shun the archbishop odd. Apparently so did Halcón, who was frowning, still writing. During a commercial break, the four guerrillas talked spiritedly in Spanish about Benito Madrigal's advice. They seemed encouraged if not elated by his words.

The next item caused her an odd sensation, something between déjà vu and a jolt of recognition, though she had never seen the man being interviewed: known to her as Jacques (Slack) Cardinal, her own not-so-fictitious character created out of bar chatter. He seemed not to have shaved for a week; he *looked* like a hard drinker, a tall shaggy man, loose of limb, a tousled crown of red hair peppered with grey.

"This man, he is a strong sympathizer to our cause." The *gerente* of Mono Titi Tours listened to questions with impatient shrugs, answered in Spanish in a cantankerous voice, almost bellicose. Buho clapped. "He says Senator Walker is a dangerous fool."

Glo was gaping at the screen with incredulity, but Halcón was laughing. "How delightful is literary irony. This is your character, Maggie, your very own Jacques Cardinal. I like this man, this ruffian, as you call him."

Glo looked sharply at Maggie – an intense message Maggie could not decipher – then hid her consternation under laughter. "Jesus, somehow the media found some dumb donkey to take your side, Halcón."

"Thank goodness *he's* not on their list of go-betweens," Maggie said, and felt a sharp nudge from Glo's elbow.

Maggie yawned her way up to her room soon after dinner. Glo joined her a few minutes later, bolting the door behind her.

"Honey, I'm going to tell you something top secret. Maybe I should have told you earlier, but it came from bedroom talk with Chester. That real-life character of yours, Slack Cardinal, he's not just your ordinary jungle buzzard. Chester found out he spent some years with the CIA doing undercover shit."

"Are you putting me on?"

"He's been hiding out here – Jacques Cardinal is a pseudonym."

"Hiding from whom?"

"Everyone, he said. I reckon an infiltrator of terrorists makes a lot of enemies. They retired him after he screwed up big-time; he caused a messy ruckus with the French government."

"You are talking about the Quepos *pisstank*?"

"The one and only, my sunset tour guide. I was right curious about his history, and I asked him a whole lot of questions. He got as nervous as a sore-tailed cat and I promised I'd keep his secrets."

A spy who had retired under a cloud, a former infiltrator . . . Maggie was having difficulty readjusting the picture; it did not want to hang properly for her.

"A 'strong sympathizer to our cause.' I reckon I know what's going on, Maggie." Glo suggested a scenario: the CIA was seeking to plant Slack Cardinal inside Comando Cinco de Mayo, or at least setting him up as an acceptable go-between. They broke off discussion when they heard Tayra coming up the stairs.

"Not a word to your pal, Halcón, okay?" Glo left to help Tayra haul up her bedding.

No, it would not be wise to mention any sunset kayak cruise, nor to hint at the subversive role Cardinal might play. All Halcón knew was that Glo had encountered Slack in a restaurant – Glo had regaled them about the kayaker quarrelling with her husband and laying low someone from their party. When Maggie reflected, she could see that Halcón would view the episode as being to Slack's credit.

Maggie lit a candle on her writing table, then pondered: a disgraced former spy? How intriguing – but was he hiding from the world, as Glo had intimated, or from himself? I like this ruffian, Halcón had said. The captain of Cinco de Mayo might profoundly err and take the bait.

She had found a writing pad downstairs and had already begun to record her impressions of the last ten days. Dr. Fiona Wardell would go on sabbatical while she composed a truer, more electric tale. But she could barely raise her pen; she was fatigued almost beyond measure from her day of toil and her nightlong gruelling trudge. *Creative Writing 403: A bad writer has a hundred excuses not to start. A good writer has only ten.* Where to begin this twenty-first-century odyssey? Where better but the here and now . . .

It is December twenty-second, a pitch-dark night, and only a fluttering candle illuminates these opening words of the bizarre adventure I am living. I find it almost impossible to conceive that only eleven days ago I was pouring hot coffee into the frozen lock of my car door, my nose pinched red by the

harsh winds. But now I am caressed by warm breezes that suffuse the air with the perfume of angels' trumpets — flowers that unfurl unseen in the tropical night. From the buzzing jungle come the trilling of crickets and the moans of the Río Naranjo.

Yet I am in a prison and my life is in danger. I must never forget that. The music of the night is lulling, and I am so exhausted . . .

— 3 —

On the morning of the third day of my confinement at the Darkside, I rise to birdsong and I stretch and look out the window. It is raining again, but bees and butterflies are dancing among the citrus blossoms and my wren is singing. Yesterday, during Spanish class, several capuchins came by to see the humans behind the bars: white-faced monkeys, or cariblancos, *as Buho calls them. Glo and I tried to coax them closer, but they held back shyly in the trees.*

Tomorrow is Christmas Day, but it will surely be far from a traditional one. My memories are of skating on the pond, gifts piled high and mincemeat pie, Aunt Ruthilda in the kitchen, my mother directing traffic. But Lake Lenore seems far away, impossible and unreal . . .

Maggie put aside her notepad and rose from bed, pulling on panties that had probably survived their last washing — the elastic spent, one cheek hanging by a thread. Her shorts were also wearing out; someone had better provide new issue soon or she would be baring her bottom.

The morning sun was throwing barred patterns on the walls: her watch read seven-fifteen. Halcón had returned it to her after sorting through the valuables in the lock-closet. Peeking over his shoulder, she had seen the guns; Halcón's short-wave radio was there, too, also a Polaroid camera.

Downstairs, she found Buho preparing the day's lesson — the young man was teaching Maggie and Glo Spanish for three hours every morning, using an old textbook they had found. *Buenas tardes, señor. Donde está el baño?* He was an excellent teacher.

Glo was reclining in a tasselled hammock, reading. "'The portals of success could open for you,'" she quoted, "'but think twice about seizing the first opportunity.'"

"I beg your pardon?"

Glo showed her a book she had found while rummaging: *The Complete Annual Horoscopes*. She read: "'Don't give in too quickly to the many signs of attention coming from that special person.' That must mean Zorro." He didn't hear; he was still slumbering in another hammock.

Tayra was in the kitchen scrambling the last of their eggs; Maggie began squeezing oranges. The fridge had been full when they arrived, but with so many mouths to feed, supplies were running low. Maggie wondered how they planned to restock. One does not simply wander down to the nearest *pulpería* and order five kilos of rice – a buying spree would raise eyebrows and loosen tongues. Already, a local farmer had briefly engaged Coyote after catching him urinating from the bodega staircase. Coyote had explained he was a caretaker for absentee landlords.

"He speaks the common slang," Halcón had assured her. "No one will mistake him for a member of the revolutionary elite." At any event, the authorities were not looking here for their suspects. Maggie had sent them wandering off into the Talamanca forest.

The house looked clean-scrubbed now, the tiled floor made glossy by a second coat of wax. From the windows hung polished crystals, slowly turning in the breeze, dappling the gaudy walls with the purer colours of the spectrum.

After breakfast, Maggie and Glo sat down with Buho. Lesson three, Anna and Carlos go to a restaurant: *Te gusta la salsa picante?*

❧

The rain had relented, and Halcón was outside, playing solitaire at a concrete table. Lacking cigarettes, he had been of brittle temper, but his edginess did not translate into a lack of dexterity. His nimble hands expertly riffled the deck and he made a clean one-handed cut. His card skills, he'd told Maggie, had been sharpened in Caribbean casinos, where he had been a dealer and a croupier. Soldier of fortune, gambler, aficionado of history, of the arts – he could walk into any salon and be embraced by the most priggish of its snobs.

It came as no great surprise to her that he admitted to a postgraduate degree in history. But he had rejected the soft life of an academic, becoming an adviser to the Zapatistas, a fugitive, hunted by the Mexican army, forever moving camps, hiding in the homes of poor peons. Chile, Guatemala, South Africa – where had he not been? Sometimes, though, he became confused about his dates – he had himself lying near death in a Bogotá hospital when, according to an earlier account, he was serving with Cuban soldiers in Angola.

Maggie could not bear to imagine how many women he had slept with; she had not coaxed his romantic history from him but would not have been surprised if he was on the run from a former partner. She found anomalous and strange that he continued to confide in her. He seemed to enjoy flirting with her, too. But however flattered she felt, she knew she must constantly check her feelings; there had been erotic fantasies, followed by self-rebuke.

She called to him: "Can I pick more fruit?" She had been allowed a guarded outing yesterday.

"Yes, but let me help." Halcón rose and unclipped the keys from his belt.

Glo paused from her splits and stretches in the living room to call to Halcón: "When's my turn?"

"Tomorrow, Señora Walker, I will give you a tour of the gardens." He was invariably formal with Glo, and, like a dog once bitten, had steered clear of her after their wrestle beside the highway.

Glo's comportment had been excellent since their arrival here: much teasing and suggestive banter but no unpleasant eruptions. Zorro had not managed to grow on her, but she hid her antipathy behind a condescending smile. He was awake now, staring slack-mouthed at Glo, braless in a faded cotton T-shirt. Yesterday, in his presence, she had complained: "Well, damn, I've worn out all my undies. I surely don't enjoy going around without anything underneath."

Maggie did not know why Glo insisted on playing this risky game, taunting the excitable Zorro. Especially right now while Tayra, with a plate of food for Coyote in the guardhouse, was standing at the front door waiting to be let out. She gave Zorro a look that could draw blood.

Halcón led Maggie across the patio into the orchard, under a spreading orange tree laden with fruit. A nearby lime tree was in white, sweet-scented bloom.

"I will be your ladder," Halcón said as he knelt. Maggie hesitated, unsure of protocol. "Climb onto me," he ordered. He lowered his head, and Maggie hoisted herself on top of his back, and, for whatever unlikely reason, underwent a reaction akin to that of fear of flying. He grasped her waist, ducked his head between her thighs, and bore her upwards on his shoulders, but staggered back a step. Trying to stay balanced, Maggie wrapped her hands under his chin. Her shirt rode up and a tuft of his jet-black hair tickled her bare skin.

Wordlessly, taking deep breaths to slow her heart, she straightened up, pulled down her shirt, passed the basket down, and began handing him the oranges she plucked. He had not shaved for two days, and his stubble prickled her thighs, but with his neck cradled tightly against her pelvis she was feeling other, warmer sensations.

She was forced to close her legs around him as he walked her to another bough, his hand gripping her above the knee. She was facing the house now, and could see Glo upright in her hammock, staring at them. Maggie wiggled her fingers and tried to smile.

The basket full, she slid from him with a leg-flailing lack of grace, landing on her behind. She refused his hand and hurriedly turned from him, began picking up a few stray oranges.

Together, they carried the filled basket to the concrete table, where he lit one of the cigarette butts he had saved on the trek. "What do you think about this Jacques Cardinal?" he asked. "It is like an omen that this character was plucked by you for your novel and now appears to us again. This strange man with a kayak business, he is brave to speak so loudly on our behalf. But you say he is a drunkard."

Maggie was in a dilemma: should she encourage Halcón to take the bait, or would she be endangering lives? She was not at all sure that she wanted someone with a history of causing diplomatic crises to barge his way into this already-risky situation.

"I think he could be a dangerous friend."

"Why would you not trust him?"

"Someone called him a walking disaster."

"I sense a rebel spirit in him – though perhaps he is not too bright." He gazed thoughtfully at the distant mountains. "You have not yet been to the river."

He led her toward an opening in the forest, where stone steps curled down a steep rocky knoll. The river was a hundred metres distant, sounding with unremitting thunder as they neared it. Then came into view a roaring cascade, water spouting over a two-metre ledge before seeking escape between giant boulders, its course widening in the shallows below. They sat together on the bank.

"In the summer, it is smaller, and there are places to bathe, but with the rains it is dangerous."

"I'll believe you. But it's beautiful."

"You add to it."

He was looking intensely at her; she felt giddy.

"You are so *simpática*, Maggie. Your courage in these difficult times has helped raise my own spirits."

Her mind did not quite go blank; she saw events clearly, but some external force was acting on her. She turned to him and kissed him on the mouth, and was then unable to pull away. He neither responded nor withdrew, and she disengaged and quickly rose.

Stunned at her audacity, she ran back up the steps, stumbling in her haste. He followed at a distance in silence.

Blushing crimson, she dared not look him in the face as she retrieved her basket of oranges and waited for him at the door. But he said nothing as he escorted her inside, lighting another butt.

Glo, who had returned to her stretches, made matters worse by saying, "And what have *you* two been up to?" Maggie responded with a stiff smile.

She fled to the bathroom feeling almost faint at the thought of the brash act she had committed. This was a wake-up call. Maggie was modern, mature; she was not about to succumb to those wild emotions she wrote about under the name of Nancy Ward. She took a few deep breaths and tried desperately to obliterate the kiss from her mind. It didn't happen.

∾

Tense with embarrassment, Maggie sat as far as she could from Halcón, unable to meet his eyes as they settled over dinner to watch the evening news: the odd family, four terrorists and two captive tourists, paying homage to the electronic Cyclops. St. Nicholas, according to a satellite tracker, had departed the North Pole and was on a bearing for Central America. The announcer traded a smile for a scowl as he turned to Operación Libertad and the hostage crisis. The search was now being concentrated in an area north of the Pan-American Highway. Buho interpreted: "It is believed the kidnappers spent the night in this dwelling."

They watched footage of police examining the dilapidated structure in which they had waited out the night. Surely they must have found her note, but no mention was made of it, or of any injured man having been taken to hospital. Maggie wondered if Gordo and his young companions had slipped the net.

Suddenly, there was her mother – staring nervously at the camera, her dad next to her, shifting in his chair, uncomfortable, his Adam's apple bobbing. Maggie began swallowing hard, too, as Beverley and Woodrow Schneider took turns pleading for their daughter's safety, beseeching the kidnappers to look within their souls for charity in this season of good-will.

Maggie burst into tears just as they cut away to commercials and stumbled up to her room, where she fell onto the bed and buried her face in a pillow. That had been taped on location, in Quepos.

Glo came to her a minute later, her eyes also wet. "The season of joy," she said, carefully closing the door.

"I'm okay. I'll get over it."

"That had Buho wiping his eyes, too." She sat on the bed and stroked Maggie's hair.

Halcón announced himself outside the door. "*Upe. Con permiso.*" Glo let him in. He was holding the Polaroid camera. "I will prove to them that you have not been harmed."

He sat them down, moved close, and aimed, and there came a click and a flash.

❧

A growl of engine awoke Maggie in the night, her eyes blinking open to the play of light on her wall, a bright beam diffused by leafy branches. Then the headlights were switched off and the engine was cut. The glowing dials of her watch told her it was three-fifteen.

No lights came on in the house, but from the window she could make out the vehicle under the fattening moon: an old Jeep, Zorro walking toward it. He turned and looked in her direction, and she ducked but continued to peek over the sill.

When the driver opened his door, a cab light momentarily went on, and she could see he was blond, his ponytailed hair falling to mid-back. Here was a gringo confederate – might he also be the Pink Floyd fan?

It came to her suddenly who this man was: the ear-ringed manager of the Eco-Rico office in San José. *I used to run tours for these guys; now they got me down here clicking slides, man.* How had he introduced himself? Elmer Jericho, devotee of interstellar travel. He was clearly a veteran of the sixties, perhaps of antiwar demonstrations. Had he helped plan the kidnapping?

Jericho and Zorro began unpacking sacks and boxes and propane tanks from the vehicle and lugged these to the house, taking eight trips. A light came on below: a yellow glow on the patio. She heard conversation, too low and distant to make out, but mostly between Halcón and Jericho. Relief supplies included cigarettes, she could smell them. Another odour wafted up: marijuana.

Twenty minutes later, their meeting concluded and Jericho left, shouldering a heavy packsack, which she guessed contained the goods ransacked from Eco-Rico; no doubt they would be sold on the San José black market. Thousands of dollars had been taken, too. With the guerrillas generously endowed and supplied, she and Glo could be in for a very long stay at the Darkside.

Solved now was the mystery of how Halcón knew she was staying at the Pensión Paraíso. Ruefully, Maggie recalled jauntily telling the history professor how she had bamboozled this late-life hippie into believing she was on assignment with the *Geographic*. The two of them had probably discussed her in some detail before Halcón put her innocence to the test at the restaurant in Escazú.

— 4 —

Maggie rose at dawn, anxious to confer with Glo. She waited until she heard Tayra descending, then slipped out and knocked softly. "*Upe.*" Maggie found much to admire about this Tico word, "oopay" – combining a warning of arrival, a greeting, and a request to enter.

She found Glo half-dressed, forlornly examining a threadbare pair of pants reduced to cut-offs. After they exchanged Christmas hugs, Glo asked, "Where did we put the needles and thread?"

"You might be able to junk those pants. Santa Claus came by last night."

In the back room, where the river drowned other noise, Glo had slept undisturbed, so Maggie told her of the nocturnal visit of Elmer Jericho, the commando's man in San José. Undoubtedly, Jericho had described to Halcón in detail the Eco-Rico layout, provided maps, even told him where the Secret Service men were quartered.

Glo finished dressing as she listened, and looked puzzled. "Jericho. Where did I hear that name?"

"Probably at the lodge."

"Maybe I remember it from bible class. I don't care if he's Moses as long as he brought underwear. Look, sweetie, while we have this moment, do y'all mind if I say something personal?"

"About what?"

"*El capitán*, the Throb. You have this yearning look in your eyes."

"What do you mean?"

"You're developing a damn thing about him." Glo was a quick read; Maggie hid emotions poorly. She dared not mention her foolishness of yesterday, the kiss by the riverside.

"I'm just playing him along. Being crafty, staying on his good side." She feigned a careless shrug.

"Just remember he could be your executioner. That's a threat we both face if they don't get paid."

"He'd *never* do that."

As Maggie descended the stairs, she glanced uneasily at Halcón, who was at the far end of the living room with Buho, pulling out clothes from boxes.

From outside came sounds of Tayra and Zorro quarrelling while they washed clothes at the *pila*. With the passing of days their bickering had become aural wallpaper.

In the bathroom, she observed a tall stack of toilet rolls, a massive resupplying that offered further proof their stay could be much extended. The prospect of several more months in Halcón's company was both tantalizing and discomfiting. She must be on closer guard; she had shocked herself to her senses yesterday. She had no doubt shocked him, too – but perhaps she was making more of the matter than it merited. And was the attraction so one-sided? *Simpática*, he had called her. She and Halcón were in a state of friendship, that was all; indeed, that was bizarre enough.

Halcón and Buho were engrossed in wrapping objects with coloured tissue. Before Maggie could approach, Halcón said, "Give me ten more minutes."

In the kitchen she found a pot of brewed coffee: freshly ground and tasting of high-quality beans; Halcón, an aficionado of light roasts, had invested in an electric grinder. Sitting behind it were a bottle of brandy, several cartons of Derby cigarettes, piles of canned goods, dozens of bags of pasta. On the counter was a burlap sack with fresh vegetables, produce that needed to be kept cool – but the refrigerator was almost at overflow, three frozen chickens commanding much of the space. Here was wine chilling, here a quart of eggnog.

She watched Halcón and Buho working with scissors and ribbons, and when Glo joined her for coffee, she said, "I think they're planning to give us something for Christmas."

"How absurd is that?"

Halcón finally waved them over. "*Feliz Navidad.*"

Buho offered similar greetings, and extended a small, prettily wrapped gift to Glo.

"I feel awful – I didn't get y'all anything." She unwrapped a vial of perfume: L'Eau d'Issey; it was apparently a fragrance Glo favoured, because she looked surprised. "How did you know?"

"You were wearing it on December the seventeenth," Halcón said.

The day of the kidnapping. Maggie was confounded by Halcón's apparent expertise in perfume until it came to her they had likely found the vial in Glo's cosmetic bag at the lodge. Halcón presented Maggie with a bulkier parcel, and when she unwrapped it she was taken aback by his prescience: it was the perfect gift, *Guide to the Birds of Costa Rica*. She grasped it to her chest, chirruping her thanks, feeling ridiculous.

Glo was gracious but formal, thanking them, shaking their hands. Maggie followed suit, dropping her eyes as Halcón's hand grasped hers. The occasion seemed to demand a more demonstrative reply. "I'll make a special Christmas dinner. I'll do those chickens. I know a recipe for stuffing with rice and – we don't have peaches; we'll use papayas."

Halcón spread out an array of women's clothing. "I was too bashful to ask for your measurements, so I hope they fit." Several garments still had store labels affixed to them: simple unpatterned skirts and shirts and shorts and undies and pairs of flip-flops. Jericho had also brought a mosquito net: Glo, on the breezeless side of the house, had complained of bites.

"Did we awake you last night?" Halcón asked Maggie.

She felt he would detect too bold a lie. "Yes, I heard a car pull in."

"A friend who is assisting us. I will talk to you about this later."

He was called away to unlock the door for Zorro, who marched in with an empty clothesbasket, looking sour and truculent.

"Attention, class." Buho clapped his hands. "Lesson begins in five minutes. Today we will study irregular verbs."

❧

Refusing all offers of help, Maggie toiled alone in the kitchen that afternoon. In addition to stuffing, there would be carrots, potatoes, yams, a fruit salad — a thimble of brandy to add zest — and cheesecake for dessert.

She looked up from her chores to see Halcón and Glo outside her window, returning from the walk he had promised. Glo beckoned him to join her at a table, where she picked up his deck of cards and began shuffling them. "I heard you play a little 'jack, Hal."

He sat across from her and she spun some cards in his direction. Halcón seemed surprised at Glo's adeptness; she had confided in Maggie that in Las Vegas, between dance productions, she had dealt a lot of 'jack, as she put it. She had spent eight years in nightclubs and casinos.

"Hit me," Halcón said.

Glo flipped him a card. "You're busted, honey."

"That card did not come from the top of the deck."

"I'm out of practice."

Maggie was pleased to see their truce had firmly taken hold. Halcón looked up to her window and smiled, as if sharing a silent confidence.

She turned to see Zorro sidling into the kitchen. He was the glitch in an otherwise agreeable day, with his constant tippling of brandy — the bottle was down by four inches. Now he was reaching again for it.

"Zorro, get away from there." She was unafraid to boss him; he knew she had Halcón's ear.

"*Un pequeñito.*" He poured not a little one, but a good two ounces. His eyes seemed glazed; he departed with a weaving gait.

200

She hid the bottle in an alcove by the window. Zorro was temperamental even when sober; drunk, he could become unstable. She was about to call upon Halcón to deal with the problem, but he and Glo had wandered to the banana grove, where he was severing a stalk with his machete.

Maggie watched as Zorro climbed into a hammock with his drink and a comic book he had found, *Escape from Planet Xenith*. He promptly fell asleep. Maggie relaxed. Halcón, hefting the bananas, led Glo to the door, where they hung them from a rafter. Tayra was snoring peacefully. Buho was strumming carols on his guitar. In an almost surreal way, it was beginning to seem a lot like Christmas.

❧

Dinner was delayed until after the television news: the search for the terrorists and their captives had been extended to the Panama border area. Halcón appeared skeptical – he was suspicious of everything that emanated from Operación Libertad. With little fresh to report, the major news feature was an interview with the infamous Slack Cardinal at the Mono Titi Tours office. He seemed slightly bruised, was wincing.

"Señor Cardinal was attacked on the streets of Quepos by four men," Buho explained. "An employee came to his aid. All four of the attackers were taken to hospital."

At one point Cardinal responded in English, "I know who loosed those fascist goons on me, and I'm going to break his . . . neck." Halcón laughed as the penultimate word, an adjective, was bleeped.

After the news, they sat around a laden dinner table decorated with flowers. Maggie's cuisine was greeted with toasts and compliments from all but Zorro, who avoided conversation, sitting stiffly in his chair, his eyes eerily blank. After two glasses of wine, Maggie, too, was feeling a light-headedness, complicated by the closeness of Halcón sitting beside her.

There was little conversation at first. Buho kept glancing shyly at Glo, who picked at her plate and was unusually quiet. Tayra was keeping a sharp eye on her tipsy husband. To fill the silence, Maggie began a spirited reminiscence of the prairies in winter: skating on the lake, snowball fights with her brothers, tunnelling into snow forts. Tayra seemed fascinated – she had never seen snow.

"About all it's good for is skiing," said Glo, who had spent her winter off-days at Tahoe.

Halcón had skied in the Andes. "It is majestic in those mountains. I will very soon return." Maggie wondered if he kept a retreat there.

Zorro finally spoke, volunteering to deliver the plates prepared for Coyote. He had difficulty rising and almost spilled the platter as Halcón ushered him out. Tayra watched him with half-veiled eyes.

A few minutes later, after Maggie returned to the kitchen to grind the coffee, she discovered that the brandy had disappeared from the alcove by the window ledge.

When Halcón answered her summons to join her, she told him of Zorro's heavy tippling. "He has a gun. Why on earth did you give it back to him?"

"A gesture to save his pride, maybe a foolish one. I warned him he must keep it in the holster."

"How well do you know him?"

"Two months."

"My Lord, is that all?"

"I did not meet these comrades before then, until my return from exile in Cuba." Halcón had mobilized them very quickly.

They called Tayra over. The news was not good: "He gets bad when he has a few drinks."

After waiting for Zorro for twenty minutes, Halcón dispatched Buho to search for him. Maggie could not understand why Halcón hadn't gone to the gun closet to arm himself or why he did not seem overly concerned.

Halcón drew Maggie off to his room, which was cluttered, clothes hanging from a chair by an unmade bed, a filled ashtray on a chair. She itched to tidy it up.

"I sense you are opposed, but I have decided to make contact with this man Cardinal."

Maggie brushed some lint from the bedsheet and tightened it. She was not sure how to react. It must have stood well with Halcón that Cardinal had warded off an attack by the so-called fascist goons – he had seen his own mother raped by such men.

"You will laugh, but I think our meeting is preordained."

Maggie flicked a brown leaf from the bed; it took wing, a butterfly, a perfect imitation, a pretender like Halcón and Cardinal.

"Naturally, our friend who came last night will check him out."

Halcón's attention was now drawn outside: Buho was approaching, walking backwards, each of his hands raised slightly. From the shadows came the swaying figure of Zorro, talking rapidly.

Maggie quickly followed Halcón out to the main room. Glo had already moved a few cautious steps upstairs, and Maggie considered following her, but something about the scene held her where she was. It did not seem that Buho was being threatened. As the men came into the light from the windows, she could see that Zorro was pointing his gun not at Buho but at his own head.

They paused by a window – behind which Tayra was standing, looking appalled. Maggie could make little sense from Zorro's rush of words, delivered in theatrical tones. He seemed to be tabulating a list of grievances.

Halcón, looking more annoyed than concerned, stood at the open door while Buho slipped back inside. "He wants her to be kinder to him or he will kill himself," he explained. "I don't think it is too serious."

Now Tayra was responding, softly at first, then with more emotion, and as their dialogue continued for several minutes both of them began to vent tears. Abruptly, she rushed outside, her arms outstretched, and embraced him. As Zorro hugged her in return, Halcón carefully disengaged the gun from his hand.

"You have to understand," Buho said. "They are very much in love."

Maggie was touched; there was a wonky tenderness to this scene, two Nicaraguan warriors clutching and crying while being led into the house.

They had met, Buho said, on the field of battle. "She was with the Sandinistas; he was a Contra. Afterwards, he was her prisoner, and love bloomed and he saw the light and joined the great cause for social justice."

"Gag me," Glo said, and ascended to her room.

Halcón was in a prickly mood as he joined Maggie to seek her counsel. He was determined to banish Zorro to the guard tower, to relieve Coyote. Maggie told him to forgo any reprimands until tomorrow.

"They are husband and wife, for God's sake, Halcón. They haven't shared a bed for a long time, and they need a night of closeness."

"That is a reward for bad behaviour."

Not far away, the couple were whispering and holding hands. Maggie continued to speak bluntly. "A night together might relax him, then we'd all feel more comfortable. I'm sure Tayra would welcome it. Look at it as a Christmas present. Keep the troops happy."

He nodded. "I have your point."

"Glo has a double bed; I'll sleep with her."

"It is Gloria-May Walker you prefer to sleep with?" He strolled off, leaving Maggie to work through the implications of that unnerving question.

Maggie and Glo faced each other on the bed, their legs curled under them, a flickering candle between them. Maggie wore a long T-shirt, but Glo only panties, the brownness of her limbs in startling contrast to her white torso. She was frowning over Maggie's notebook: the passages recounting Halcón's dramatic history.

"You sure he's not setting up scenes to make himself look good in your book?"

"I can't believe he's that conniving." He might have dressed up his tales, but it was no great human error to want to be immortalized: a Garibaldi, a Robin Hood, a Scarlet Pimpernel; he was engineering a great escapade.

"You're blind, honey. The Throb stole your poke, stole your ass, and now he's snaffled your heart."

"That is *not* happening. Yes, I do admire him. He's a man who rose above childhood pain. Sure he's a renegade, but he's interesting and vital; he's a natural leader, unafraid to consult."

"Yeah, right. Just remember to keep your panties dry when you're consulting, you hear? Or riding horsy on his shoulders."

"I'm *totally* in control." She sought a change of subject. "He's going to sentence Zorro to the guardhouse for the next month."

"Next *month*?" Glo groaned.

"I think the negotiations to get us out of here will take some time. But at least they're going to start. That Jericho character, their outside man or inside, or whatever, is going to make contact with Slack Cardinal."

"Does Halcón tell you *everything*? With Zorro out of here, what's that make you? Second in command, I reckon. I hope you haven't said anything to him about the kayak man."

"Of course not." Maggie watched a moth, a mimic with eyeballs on its wings, flutter outside the mosquito net. From her own room, across the hall, came the sound of a squeaking bed.

"That should keep him from slobbering at the bathroom window for a while," Glo said.

"Oh, Tayra has him under her thumb. He's actually just a harmless bag of bluster. She pretends to be a hard-boiled radical, but she's just a pussycat underneath, too."

"Yeah, I guess if you have to be kidnapped by someone, why not the good folks from Cinco de Mayo. We treat our hostages right."

"I'm worried less about us than them. If it comes down to some violent stand-off against a SWAT team, God, these poor . . ." She faded out because Glo was frowning and shaking her head. "What's the matter?"

"Chester's attitude will be, let's blast these assholes off the face of the earth. If he has his way, that's what he'll do, and Chester is used to having his way."

That cast a spell of gloom. Maggie watched a firefly crawl along the netting, blinking green and white. The sounds from the next room had subsided.

"They should just pay these people something and send them off to Cuba," she said.

"Chester's too ornery to do that."

In that case, Maggie decided, she must get word out that the kidnappers were well meaning; they must not be harmed. Maybe the key was Jacques Cardinal – Halcón must be persuaded to let her talk to him, to demand assurances.

But Glo offered a grim scenario: "It'll be too late. They'll follow Cardinal out here. This place has huge windows, there's nowhere to hide. They'll have floodlights. They'll have about ten sharpshooters; they'll each have a target and orders to kill."

"Gloria-May! For God's sake, don't talk that way. We're *not* going to let anyone get hurt."

"Snipers – that's how Chester will do it. I know how he thinks; I've been married to him too long."

Her last sentence hung in the air for a few moments. She looked so sad and beautiful, the candlelight playing on her breasts.

"Too long, Glo?"

"You know what I mean. Hey, I love him; we're just on different wavelengths." That seemed an understatement: she had loathed the politico-military world into which marriage had plunged her, had expressed herself as hating every second of her two years in Washington.

"You knew what you were getting into."

Glo sighed. "I was twenty-seven. I thought I was over the hill. I'd seen what happened to some of the other girls. I was too scared to walk away from the altar."

"What do you mean, the other girls?"

"Oh, you know, friends in the business." Their conversation abruptly ended. "I'm tuckered out. I'm crawling in."

Maggie blew out the candle, and they covered themselves with the sheet. She was tired, too, but jangled by thoughts of the disastrous events Glo had augured. Should she warn Halcón? *Do not trust Slack Cardinal, he is an infiltrator, a spy . . .* But that could ruin a well-planned attempt at a bloodless rescue. Glo had been posing the worst possible outcome. Surely they would want to negotiate first.

She tried to shut off the turmoil in her head, focusing on the night sounds, the whistle and whir and chirping from the jungle, the grumble of the river. An owl hooted. Or was it a moan from the other room? The bed began to creak again.

The erotic energy emanating from across the hall made Maggie restless. She could tell sleep was not coming easily for Glo, either; she kept shifting positions.

"You ever try it with another woman?"

Maggie was startled by the question; it seemed fraught with hazardous prospects.

"No." That time with her cousin didn't count, an adolescent examining.

"I'm not going to suggest we try it; I was just thinking . . . Cooped up here, those guys grunting and thrashing all night, how can you not think of sex? Ever do a threesome?"

"No, and not many twosomes, either."

"I did more than my fair share . . . Are we off the record?"

"Of course."

"I don't want this appearing in a damn book that's going to be in every store window."

"Don't *worry*."

"I specialized in Japanese guys, suits from Tokyo, humongous expense accounts. Some of those old boys would pay incredibly large for two girls."

"You were a *prostitute*?"

"Less crassly put: an escort, my dear, with an exclusive gold card listing. Seven-fifty a pop – that was real money then. Yeah, honey, I did some bad things. Freckle-faced runt of fifteen, I wasn't wasting any more of my life in Tuscaloosa. I was going plunk straight to Hollywood to fuck a producer, get into the flicks. Only instead I got stuck in the desert, and had to hustle a bit, and I found it paid. Did it for a few years until someone realized I could also dance. Graduated from honky-tonk bar to chorus line."

Maggie did not know what to say. "Glo, that's outrageous."

"Don't you whisper nary a word. I don't know why I'm telling you this."

"Obviously, Chester doesn't know."

"And no one *he* knows knows. Just a bunch of rich Japanese know; maybe the entire board of directors of the Sony Corporation knows, and they're not saying. To Chester, I was just a sweet southern belle with a sense of rhythm trying to raise money for college tuition."

"I don't know what to say. I feel actually . . . honoured you told me."

"Because I trust you. More than my own sister. If I had one. Always wanted a sister." Maggie pressed Glo's hand. The gesture was returned with a hug and a kiss.

Various Views from the Edge
of the Precipice

— I —

Slack wedged his Rover between a pair of almond trees and cut the engine. The beach was deserted tonight, everyone heading down to the New Year's Eve *baile*, a popular salsa band from San José at Maracas, the dance hall by the Palma Tica dock.

Memo's, a beach food-and-booze outlet, was closing up, a waiter turning off the lights, but this is where Slack's anonymous caller said they would meet. "Say in about an hour, it's about something that's big in the news, man." That was at ten, now it was just after eleven, no sign of him, he was probably a crank.

Slack hadn't planned on going out tonight, revelry would disturb his equilibrium. The folks at Operación Libertad wouldn't be doing much partying, either, there'd been several useless forays into the Talamanca, all blind alleys. A few days ago, another note arrived at the U.S. Embassy: "The five names are rejected. We are deadly serious, please be serious, too." The word "*mortalmente*" – deadly – was underlined in red.

The note was accompanied by a Polaroid of the two captive women in ragged clothes, holding hands, Gloria-May forcing a smile, Maggie melancholy, her expression wistful. Most of the background had been cut away with scissors, but the women seemed to be sitting on a bed, so they were no longer out in the weather – but in what hideaway? The Central Valley seemed likely, the note had been mailed in San José.

Op Libertad had responded by broadcasting a plea to the gang: offer your own list of mediators. Should Slack's name appear on it, he would reluctantly accept.

Where was the mysterious caller? Slack walked around the cement tables to the water, high tide now, an exhausted breaker swishing by his sandals. The moon was full, its silver light prancing on the waves. As he sat on one of the outdoor stools, the waiter, Miguel, glanced at him. Slack recognized him from the squatters' village, he figured to be a jerk, one of Camacho's many distant cousins.

He was pleased to be able to sit and nurse his bruises from that street fracas, a bunch of drunken cretins egged on by El Chorizo. Slack hadn't been sure he could handle them all by himself, and had to admit that his shadow had finally proved his worth. But tonight Joe Borbón had been given leave from guard duty – astonishingly, the killing machine had proved capable of the higher emotions, he'd gone sweet on that girl from the squat, Camacho's sister, he'd escorted her to the New Year's Eve soirée.

Miguel approached. "I am sorry, we are closed, Señor Cardinal."

"I'm waiting for someone." Was he going to order him off the premises? It might take some gall, this establishment was trespassing on the public beachfront.

"But I would like you to have this." Miguel extended a litre of Ron Abuelo. "It is to thank you for your support of our church."

The fifty dozen cases of beer. "Yeah, thanks."

As Miguel departed, Slack looked dejectedly at the bottle, it looked alluring. This was the Roman calendar's great night of cele-bration, the thirty-first of December, the end of a bad year, Borbón was a couple of miles away. But he kept his perspiring hands off the screw cap. His portrayal in Maggie Schneider's book as an ignoble drunk still rankled. A farm girl turned copywriter, composing roman-tic slurp as a sideline, why had she targeted *him*?

He heard a crunch of foot on dried almond leaves, and turned to see someone in the shadows, watching him. Tall and thin, a long ponytail pulled tight behind his ears, mid- or late-fifties. Slack had an uncertain feeling he'd seen him before.

The man approached with a lazy shuffling motion, he was wearing a T-shirt that proclaimed, "Don't sweat it." From the thick roll-your-own pressed between thumb and forefinger came the fragrant odour of cannabis.

He extended it as he sat. "Toke?"

Slack hesitated. He didn't handle pot very well, but it wasn't on the prohibited list and might dull the need for drink. He took one short sweet suck, and realized this stuff was potent, not the usual seedy junk available around here. He passed the joint back.

"You don't know me, but I heard a lot about you, a guy who don't take no shit, who sings his own tune." He spoke with a relaxed drawl. Slack *had* seen him, or a photograph. "Heard you was wanted on some kind of counterfeit beef, how's that going?"

"Bum rap. They got me mixed up with someone else."

"Yeah, I bet. You gonna offer me a drink of that?"

"Help yourself."

"Hey, man, happy new year." Don't-Sweat-It unscrewed the cap, wiped his lips, slugged back a healthy dollop of rum, and belched. "Check out that moon. I figure it's stingy of the universe to give us only one. Jupiter's a hog, it's got sixteen."

"Those are the breaks." Slack was feeling uncomfortably stoned.

"They're all different, them moons of Jupiter. Some are almost all gas. One of them, Io, has got volcanoes. Spews shit into the sky."

The moon expert tamped down his bomber and pocketed it. Slack could hear the thump of electrified bass all the way from the Quepos dock, the volume turned up as midnight approached.

His companion didn't get straight to the point, instead carried on about how impressed he was with Slack's recent public utterances. Slack was a radical, just like him, he was right about that Senator Walker, the guy was a piece of shit. Slack murmured his agreement, he sensed he was being scouted out, a kind of loyalty test.

"You really a Bolshevik, man?"

"Yeah, *un rojillo*."

"So you're asking, what's this all about, right?"

"I'm listening."

"Let me put it to you straight. I got a friend of a friend who knows a friend in the body trade. As in, like, he's willing to trade a couple of bodies for a certain revolutionary hero plus fifteen million in change and cheaper beans, though it'll be pretty hard to enforce that one, I bet they let it pass. Anyway, he's looking to find some responsible businessman to volunteer to make this happen. I don't know nothing about it, actually, I'm just passing information on I've sort of heard."

"Why would I be interested in helping out?"

"'Cause your heart's in the right place. Good cause and all. And also there could be a little palm oil in it for you." He tilted the bottle back again, passed it to Slack.

"Not right now." Abstinence was requiring courage, Slack wanted to celebrate, it looked like he'd hit the jackpot.

"You know, a percentage, a finder's fee, six points, something like that. A guy could walk away a rich man. Now, I'm not saying I know these people real well, but if you're interested, I could maybe pass your name up the line."

"Why me? Why not you?"

"Hey, I'm a little too close to this scene. I'm gonna trust you, and if this gets repeated I'm going to say you're full of shit. The thing is I work for that Eco-Rico Lodge, and of course that could put a lot of unjust suspicion on me. Name's Elmer, that's all you gotta know."

Despite his slight marijuana fog, Slack was able to sort through some of the files and photographs they'd implanted in his head. Elmer Jericho, Vietnam vet with medals, old Costa Rican hand, kicked around Central America for twenty-five years. Most recent employment, eight months at Eco-Rico, ran some of their tours, did shifts in the San José office. Looks older than his picture. Clean bill of health, said the interviewing agent. "Harmless brain-dead hippie, no priors, no bad friends, openly admits to use of soft drugs and LSD."

They'd passed over Elmer too quickly, which was odd, because he seemed the sort of guy the straight-laced agents of the CIA would put high on any list. They'd given Slack a deaf ear with his theory about someone working inside, casing the lodge.

"The question I ask is, if your name was proposed as a kind of broker for this deal, would you go along? Like, for the right vig."

Vigorish, there was definitely a mercenary flavour to this business. Ham Bakerfield still insisted they were politicos. Some of them, maybe, the naïve believers, probably not Halcón, definitely not this guy.

"The cops hate my guts, not a chance."

"They got no choice, man. They're saying, okay, you don't like our list, give us yours. So maybe Cinco de Mayo comes up with a list, and there's only one name on it. And here's the kicker, that counterfeit rap? Hey, man, I bet they bury the papers on that one."

The redesigning of the secret agent had worked superbly, Elmer was hot after the product. "What would the drill be?"

"I don't know, maybe they'll figure it out as it goes along. The main thing right away, as I see it, they want this Benito Madrigal, one of them guy's is his nephew. And I guess they'll make sure you're not being followed or wired or nothing, and then I imagine they'd sort of blindfold you and take you to . . . wherever. Where those women are. And then you negotiate for the other stuff. And then somewhere along the line, you show up with a suitcase full of bread. You rescue them two wenches and come out of it a rich hero. What I can't figure is how you can lose on such a deal."

"I could get stiffed."

"How? Who's carrying the dough? Take your cut in advance, man. Think about it, six pieces of fifteen million, that's some real walking-around money. Plus you strike a blow for freedom."

Slack was almost sorry he was such an upstanding citizen, the deal proposed would tempt a lesser man. Walk into the Cinco de Mayo nest with the blessings of the U.S. and Tico governments, stash away a small fortune in an offshore account.

"So I guess they'd want me to be a tough negotiator."

"Yeah, you got the idea. Way I hear it, there's not going to be much wriggle room. Hell, for that guy Walker, fifteen mil is peanuts, Santa has been real good to him."

True enough. Walker's team had organized a Keep Chuck Running movement, and suddenly the non-campaign for the Republican nomination was taking off. Investing heavily in him were some well-heeled private interests in tune with his Neanderthal views. But worse, Mr. and Mrs. America were also responding, widows were sending their pension cheques, children were digging into piggy banks to keep Chuck in the race for high public office.

Comfortably quartered in a sumptuous suite at the Cariari Hotel near San José, Chuck Walker, according to the latest polls, was now number two in the hearts and minds of registered Republicans, he had momentum. Only in America, it's why Slack loved the good old U.S.A., it was Hollywood. The civilized world would owe him a favour if he got those women freed fast, screwed up the senator's campaign, eliminated the sympathy factor.

He realized he wasn't focusing on Elmer's words, the pot was a bad idea. Elmer was still making his pitch, a good salesman, though Slack wished he'd just drop the transparent pretence. He was probably in it with Halcón about fifty-fifty.

"The suits say, okay, we're forced to go with this Slack guy, but how can we trust him? We'll have to pay him off with some coin. You see, that's a scenario these Cinco de Mayo guys have probably figured out. They want to make sure they look after you better. It's like I say, a no-lose deal."

"You mind standing up?"

"I'm clean."

"Just want to check. There's a few people who'd like to set me up."

Slack went through a show of patting him down for recording devices. "Okay, thanks. I'm in for twenty per cent."

Elmer seemed taken aback. "Maybe they'll think that's a little extreme."

"You want a strong negotiator? Try me."

"It's not my call, man. I'm just, like, a courier of information."

A long pause, Slack looked at his watch, almost midnight. Earth's lonely boring moon was rolling behind a veil of thin cloud. This was going too well, Elmer wasn't much of a deep thinker, easy to handle.

"They might double the six."

"Twenty per cent. I don't have an inch of wriggle room, Elmer."

Elmer grinned. "Man, you're too much. I'll pass on the suggestion."

"Stop the bullshit, you're into this up to your ears."

"Well, shit, I knew we had the right guy."

Elmer extended the bottle. Slack gave it a careful study, no dead mice. Then, abruptly, he seized it and took a swig. It was the dawn of a brave new year, goddammit, and he was about to pull off the perfect undercover scam. He'd get that albatross from around his neck, the label of all-round fuckup.

A distant din of celebration. Horns honking.

Slack raised the bottle again. "Happy new year, partner." One last drink for auld lang syne.

Slack knew generally where he was, somewhere in the old section of San José, barrio Amón, in a saloon that brought anxious memories of a dungeon where he'd been tortured years ago, in the Arabian desert. In fact, this place *was* called the Dungeon, heavy architecture, stone walls, the cellar of a century-old building.

Elmer knew this town, he was a kind of San José boulevardier, and he called this joint one of his "stash" bars, places that don't get mentioned in all those earnest guidebooks, off the main streets, barely legal.

It looked like lots of payola had passed under the counter to keep this one open, an all-nighter, full of grifters, a guy wandering around selling coke like he had a licence, numerous business-women. One of them was sitting on Elmer's lap, dyed-blonde, skinny legs. Another was wedged beside Slack on his bench, reeking of perfume, her hand caressing his thigh, her purple nails playing with the frayed cuff of his shorts. Loretta, she called herself, a sultry black Tica from Limón. He really didn't want to encourage her, he was unsure he could carry out his end of the contract, his nuts had been fried in that dungeon. Or maybe he was just finding excuses, a team of neurologists had examined him, couldn't find anything disconnected down there.

Anyway, he was too drunk to perform, he'd split the Ron Abuelo with Elmer on the way up, a romp up the old Puriscal Road in Elmer's beat-up Jeep, laughing, toking, debating the nature of stars and planets, and he'd been chain-drinking Haig and Haig since he got here. He was having trouble figuring out how drunk he was, somewhere at a level below outright staggering, though he hadn't tested himself on his feet for a while. Those fingertips tracing tiny circles on his skin were keeping him frozen to his seat.

Slack tried to rationalize. He needed the break, it seemed like eons since he had kicked back and shed life's myriad worries. Let the planet save itself for one night, kidnapping and subterfuge, he'll deal with that stuff when the sun comes up.

And it was important to stay tight with this Jericho character, vital to broaden this new and excellent friendship. Elmer was picking up the tab tonight, generous with the take from the Eco-Rico Lodge. The guy was smoking through a pack of Marlboros, talking non-stop, he had good Spanish. He also knew his drugs.

"Ecstasy, that's just rabbit food for Yuppies scared to get high. Same with Dex and ludes and all that shit. Ergot's still the only thing. Owsley, haze, flying A. Acid, man, LSD-25. No one's come up with a better product. I must've done a thousand trips." He turned to his companion, cooed something in her ear, she punched him playfully on his shoulder.

Slack started to drink more heavily as Elmer entered into negotiations with the whores, suggesting a package deal, extras included. Slack wasn't keen on the project, you can't fake an erection.

"So let's find a couple of rooms, man. I'm paying."

Slack tried to figure a way out of this. He knocked back a last desperate whisky straight. He had to focus hard, his eyes were seeing double Elmer, double Loretta, and, by the bar, the blurred outlines of the bartender, who was engaged with a burly, bald gentleman who looked like he was having his hand greased, maybe the local bylaw inspector.

Suddenly Loretta was burying herself behind his shoulder, and then he saw that the bald guy was approaching their table, looking pissed off.

Slack tried to make sense of what Loretta was whispering into his ear. "On the virgin's name, I took only what was fair. He's a cop, he thought he could get it for free."

The policeman started swearing at Loretta. "You thieving nigger bitch, where is my money? Give me your purse!"

The fellow was being boorish and uncivil, an off-duty *guardia*, a cop on the pad, cheating the girls. This character really put Slack off, he would give him some words of advice. "Stick your head up your *cujo*, you prick."

At that, the whole bar went silent, everyone watching and listening, Elmer nervously shifting in his chair, Loretta still cringing behind his back.

When the cop made a grab for Loretta's bag, Slack stood up, snatched his wrist, and cracked him in the shin with the toe of his boot. Then, as the policeman performed a one-legged hop, Slack kicked the other leg from under him, and with his hand to the back of his neck propelled him face down onto the table. He could hear the nasty crunch of brittle nose bone.

He stepped back, shocked at what he had done, he had overreacted, his judgment impaired. He saw blood begin to pool. The cop wasn't moving.

"Let's get out of here," Elmer said.

Slack hesitated, checked for a pulse, it seemed to take forever to find it. The cop began to stir.

"C'mon!" Elmer was already on the move.

Loretta was still pasted all over Slack as he staggered out into the cool night air. He saw a glow in the eastern sky.

— 2 —

The view through the window was of fields and rolling hills under the shadow of Irazú volcano, so Slack knew he was in the mountains somewhere east of San José. He vaguely remembered an ambulance hauling him out here yesterday, it was a private clinic, attendants prowling about in white garments.

The light from the window hurt his eyes, and so did the sight of Ham Bakerfield staring quietly down at his multi-hued body, an abstract canvas of blue and purple. Joe Borbón was off in a corner, looking dejected, Ham must have dealt him a tongue-lashing.

Slack remembered little of what happened after he left the Dungeon. Somewhere, in the distant reaches of his mind, resided a foggy scene in which he got pummelled, but alcoholic amnesia spared him the details.

He'd lost track of Elmer, though he had a sense of Loretta having been with him in a dingy hotel room. He couldn't recall if he miraculously rose to the occasion. Nor did he remember being rolled by her, though that must have happened, because he'd lost six toucans from his wallet, close to a hundred bucks.

Ham lit a Churchill. "You able to talk now?"

Slack hadn't been able to do that for two days, he'd got one in the throat, though most of the pain was coming from his two cracked ribs. The Demerol helped.

As best he could put it together, the cop whose nose he'd broken had gathered up a few of his cronies from the station, figured out where he was, or maybe Loretta squealed, and they barged into the room. Without even the courtesy of advising him of his rights, they proceeded to settle their dispute out of court.

"How did you find me?" he croaked.

"By the smell. Hurt much?"

"Only when I laugh."

Slack assumed they'd done the rounds of the hospitals, he recalled stumbling into one before the ambulance took him out here.

"Almost predictable, the babysitter takes one night off, the trained agent goes on a tear, sneaks up to San José, gets rolled by a hooker, and ends up on the floor of some flophouse smelling like a garbage truck and looking like it just rolled over him." Ham blew out a cumulous cloud of smoke. This was a care facility, there had to be a rule against polluting the air, but Slack was too weak to complain.

"So give me the Purple Heart," he rasped. "I'm in deep, I'm inside."

"What we got here is a team player who keeps scoring in his own goal. You could have called in, hero."

But Slack could see through puffy eyes that Bakerfield was smiling, trying to rein in his mirth.

"What the hell, looking at you, I got my sweet revenge. You sure this Jericho guy trusts you?"

"Like his mother."

Yesterday, during one fairly lucid moment, Slack had been able to jot down Elmer Jericho's name, along with the notation: "Inside job. Don't touch him." This morning he had managed to scribble out a fuller report.

"Didn't think we were dealing with any gringos."

"It's a con game." Despite the pain of the swollen larynx, Slack delighted in rubbing it in. "What I said from the start."

"He checked into work this morning, the Eco-Rico office. We have eyes on him."

"Stay away. I put a lot of work into this guy."

"I got to admit the Einstein who had his file didn't do a prize job of backgrounding him. Now we find out he was into some teak plantation scam a few years ago, selling ten-thousand-dollar shares for a square foot of dirt. Ex-Special Services, did you know that?"

"Said he was in 'Nam."

"We're checking the land registry, see if he owns a house where the two women might be."

"Good luck, registry's a mess." It had taken Slack a month to locate the title to his own property.

"When are you supposed to connect with him?"

"Ten days."

"How about quicker?"

"Dying here, Ham."

"You'll die when I give the order, pansy. You got a few lumps, that's all. I want you up and walking by the morning, we'll brief you then."

As Borbón followed him out, he gave Slack a hurt look, as if he'd been betrayed. Cozying up to the squatters, the windup Cuban got what he deserved, he missed a good fight.

Slack's multiple swellings had subsided somewhat by the next morning, and since all his limbs seemed to be functioning he passed up the offer of a wheelchair and limped out to take some air on the back patio.

The small clinic specialized in tucks and lifts, he'd seen a few customers wandering around with face straps, men and women, vanity was gender neutral. The facility was in the hills above Tres Ríos, under the precarious shelter of Irazú and its hissing vents. Slack guessed they located it here because of the nearby hot springs, where they had guest cabins, you could hide out until your skin grew back. He wouldn't mind doing a few facelifts of his own on those unsporting peace officers who jumped a drunk. But maybe he'd asked for it, let it go.

It bothered Slack that he couldn't seem to get from point A to B in this rescue op without causing damage to himself, but his pain was dulled by the satisfaction he had pulled off a major coup. Not that Ham Bakerfield would ever openly applaud it, you could tie a ribbon around the entire Cinco de Mayo, present them on a platter, and he wouldn't twitch an eyebrow.

He eased himself into a plastic lawn chair. Borbón was out here, pouting, refusing to acknowledge him. Otherwise the ambience was pleasant enough, flower-choked trellises, Mexican tiles, the sun out, summer finally here. Down the hill, a pastoral scene, a herd of Holsteins being ushered from a farm gate, a Land Cruiser waiting to get by.

The vehicle finally worked its way through and pulled into the parking area, then Ham and Chuck Walker emerged and began trudging up the path. Slack had it all worked out, what he was going to propose to them. He would have to abide Walker and his many helpful hints because the senator would have to okay his plan.

He greeted his guests with a limp wave and sent Borbón off to fetch coffee. Walker insisted on grasping his hand, squeezing the bones. Maybe Slack had got in a punch or two the other night, his hand was sore.

"Excellent work, it looks like we recruited the right man." But for some reason Chuck didn't look happy, worry lines marking his face. Maybe he was disappointed that the show was nearing final curtain, he wouldn't be crowding America's front pages much longer. "You're sure this character – Jericho, is it? – wasn't just bullshitting?"

Ham answered for Slack. "I don't think that's likely, senator. This just came in." He handed Slack a page of lined paper: "*Cinco de Mayo desinga Señor Slack Cardinal.*" The verb was misspelled.

Walker was playing devil's advocate: "Is it genuine? Could it be a practical joke? No photograph, no proof it's from them."

"Elmer Jericho wrote this," Slack said. "He's the genuine article, senator." It was painful to talk, because of the cracked ribs he dared not take a deep breath.

"He sounds somewhat lacking in the brain department."

"Blown out on dope."

"Well, I hope we can pull it off."

"Think there's any chance of doing this in one shot?" Ham asked. "Just follow you in there?"

"No, I should reconnoitre first, see the lay of the land."

"Okay, I think you're right. But you're to be blindfolded, isn't that the idea?"

"And checked for wiring. I'm going to have to work this Halcón guy a bit."

"So you won't be armed," Walker said, disappointed.

Slack ignored him. "Ham, can we get Benito Madrigal out of that house without a media carnival?"

"I think we can smuggle him out. He's in the hands of the local authorities, they'll have to be brought into the picture."

"I don't want Minister Castillo or any of his ineffectual Ticos involved," Walker said. "Well-meaning, but they don't have the know-how."

"Can't be avoided," Ham said. "Madrigal is acting up, wants a full pardon before he'll agree to be released. Guess that can be arranged, too."

"I'll also need a shitload of *dinero*."

Slack waited for the reaction, and was met with a silence that held while Borbón passed around mugs of coffee.

"I understood we would not be donating to the cause of left-wing terrorism," Walker said.

Slack shrugged. "A good-will offering, senator. Say, a token five hundred thousand dollars."

Walker seemed in a state of shock. "That's totally unacceptable."

Slack spoke hoarsely, ordering himself to ignore the pain, he had to make the strongest possible case. "Maybe that's not going to be enough. Six hundred. Senator, they may just jump at that, it might be enough, and then I get the women out of there. Even if it's not enough, it's a hell of a down payment. The money will be safe, they won't be able to run off with it. Then they'll be softened up for my next visit. With backup."

Slack didn't really think the Mayoists would accept six hundred free and clear, but maybe he could use it for Maggie Schneider, get her out of the way in case there's rough stuff later. They had no reason to hold her. No discredit to her, but she wasn't worth anywhere as much as Glo. He dared not let Walker know what was in his mind, the Canadian woman was nothing to him, he would go cold on the idea.

She had looked so sad and pretty in that Polaroid photo, a hardy, spindly prairie flower. *Close up, he smelled rancid* . . . She'd be on her knees thanking him, though he'd remember to shower first.

"It seems a very risky investment."

"Bait money, senator. It'll set this whole thing up, they're going to think I'm their best pal. And the next time I go in there, I'll be packing, a snug in my boot, how's that?"

"And you take them out."

"If necessary." Slack gave him a fixed look, didn't bat an eye. Let him think he'd do it.

"Your call, senator." Ham's face was shrouded in smoke, but Slack could tell he didn't mind, it wasn't his money. "He'll have to be wired on the second go-round, and he'll need first-rate backup."

"Snipers," Walker said. Then he shook his head, still antagonistic to the idea. He had a big war chest, the Keep Chuck Running fund was rumoured at around forty million dollars, Walker could look bad if he refused to invest a small portion in Glo's freedom.

"Tell you what," Slack said, "the three hundred you'll be paying me, I'll throw that in. You ante up the same amount."

Walker began pacing. "I hope I'm being fair, Slack, but, ah, it seems to me you've had a few misadventures along the way, and . . ."

Slack stood up, winced, staggered a step, a demonstration of what he had suffered on Walker's behalf during the course of these misadventures. He got close to him.

"Senator, you're risking no more money than me, and I'm almost dead broke. I'm also risking my life – for the woman you love."

That pulled him up. This was the kind of appeal Walker could understand, he prided himself on his honour, an old-fashioned principled conservative. Slack sensed his heroic offer had hit home. Walker himself was no coward, a decorated officer, he'd rescued his platoon behind enemy lines.

He patted Slack on the shoulder, gave him a squeeze. "I take your point, soldier. I'll discuss the matter with some friends, see if we can come up with the extra three on top of what we'll owe you."

Ham was looking at Slack with renewed respect. "Okay, sounds good, anything else?"

"Expense money. I'll need about ten grand, I'm not talking colones."

"I'll make out a requisition. Maybe we can clean this up quick. Do we have to wait ten days for you to contact Jericho?"

"That's what he said. *I* need ten days."

"Give him what time he needs," Walker said. Astonishingly, he seemed to have bought Slack's expensive plan, he'd expected to be bargained down.

"You running more checks on that name, Pablo Esquivel?" he asked Ham.

"We're looking into it."

Slack was working on a theory.

3

La Esmeralda, downtown on Avenida Segunda, was a venerable San José eatery, packed with musicians, home of the Mariachi Union, also a hangout of promoters, speculators, and fixers, crowded now at two p.m., still lunchtime. Ham Bakerfield had put some people on the street, but Slack had told them to stay well downwind.

The big room echoed with guitar music and the loud gabble of the country's vast underground economy at work. You could get the best rates on the U.S. dollar here, passports for sale, *permisos*, Swiss watches. You could buy or sell just about anything in San José, a connection town, you just had to know the right person.

They'd fixed up Slack a bit at the clinic and he didn't draw anyone's attention as he strolled in, looking for Elmer. After ten days, much of his bruising had subsided, but the cracked ribs remained a potent reminder of the perils of drink; negative conditioning works.

He spotted Elmer waving at him from the back. Slack had called him on a tapped line at the Eco-Rico office, hinting at developments. Elmer had suggested the Esmeralda. "We better not be talking on the phone." If he was that nervous, why weren't they meeting at a more clandestine location? Slack was having trouble figuring out these people.

Someone was with Elmer, short and stout, and as Slack approached, he got a better look at him, noticed a cane leaning against his chair. Herman Rebozo of the wounded foot, his cast had been removed, the bullet wound couldn't have been that crippling.

"Looks like they got you pretty good, buddy. This here's Herman, but everyone calls him Gordo."

Rebozo didn't seem to like the teasing nickname, and looked uneasy, distrustful, his handshake didn't have much oomph. The moustache and beard were new, needed a few more weeks to fill out. Ex-payroll clerk in the civil service, fervent believer in the Great Dead God of Marxism, plus he'd run away from a wife and six kids. You'd think she'd be bitter, but interviewers hadn't found her a fountain of information.

Elmer called for a round of beer, Slack said he'd stick to coffee. He and Elmer had a few laughs over Slack's run-in with the cops, Gordo not following, he had no English.

"You ain't had any second thoughts? You know, about the project."

"Like you say, how can I lose? Things fuck up, I'm just a guy doing my best to help out."

"Gordo here, he's officially running the show out of San José, that was his orders from Johnny . . . ah, from the war office. I'm just a lowly go-between, far as he's concerned, you gotta bear that in mind."

Who was Johnny? Slack assumed he meant Halcón.

"I'm afraid this patsy ain't too sure about you." He said in Spanish to Gordo, "Señor Cardinal, he supports the goals of the revolution."

"You will bring our leader to us?" Rebozo asked.

"I will do my best, *compañero*."

He wasn't sure Gordo was buying it, he didn't seem too trustful of Elmer, either, maybe doubting his revolutionary credentials.

"Gordo's gonna be your main contact person except in emergencies because I can't be front and centre. So what's the news?"

"The news is good." "The U.S. Embassy got your note and they've already been in contact with me. You spelled *designa* wrong."

"I never won no spelling bees."

"That's the kind of goof could get us in shit, they might think Spanish isn't the first language of the guy who wrote it." Gordo was looking lost, so Slack switched to Spanish. "The man who talked to me hinted some accommodation could be made. I assume that means they're willing to pay."

"Who was it?" Elmer asked.

"Some geezer named Bakerfield, a friend of the senator. They offered me twenty thousand and expenses and said they would forget a mistake in my past. I said I would think about it."

"You are sure they are not deceiving you, señor?" said Gordo. He was as bad as Benito Madrigal, paranoid, Slack was going to have trouble bringing him around.

"When they release Don Benito, we will know they are sincere."

"Maybe. We will see."

"When they call me again, I will insist they give me not only Don Benito, but a down payment. I'm going to ask for a million dollars."

"Good luck on that one," Elmer said.

"Just watch me."

Elmer grinned and said in English, "You know, after this is over, you and me should maybe work on a few other projects. I think we got some chemistry happening."

Slack massaged his aching neck, sipped his coffee. Despite Gordo's wariness, he was pleased with himself, basking in the sunshine of accomplishment.

"Okay, this is the arrangement: they will not release my name to the press – they don't want reporters hanging around, and neither do we. One thing they will insist on is a photograph, me and the two women, or else they're not dealing." He asked Gordo, "So when can you take me to them?"

"I don't know the way, I have not been told." He was obviously miffed at that.

Elmer returned to English. "Gordo don't have a clue. It's way out in the country, I'm gonna have to give him directions." He paused in thought. "No, that ain't gonna work, Gordo's kind of dim. Okay, the three of us have to meet in a secure place and sneak out under darkness."

"You forgot Benito."

"Oh, yeah, that's a nuisance, how're we gonna bring him along? Well, we'll work it out – you make your personal deals with them, come up with that down payment, and then you'll be contacting Gordo here and he'll know where to find me." He gave Slack an address for Gordo, Barrio Mexico, a working-class area.

The plan seemed riven with holes, unplanned-for contingencies, an amateurish gamble for high stakes. Could they be operating so loosely, or was he missing something? Still, the hostages offered good security in the case of mishap, maybe that's what they were banking on.

"Hey, remember you gotta tell them if they follow you or do some dumb thing like that, they don't get them women back." Elmer slit his own throat with a forefinger. "In pieces, that's how they get them back."

The gesture did not seem flip, though Slack wondered if they had the balls to carry out the threat. But for the first time, he noticed something cold and mean in Elmer's eyes.

— 4 —

Slack stayed on in San José, in a fourth-floor suite at the Gran Hotel. Walker usually showed up for the daily briefing there, seeming ever more strained but not butting in too much. He'd talked to his friends, the six hundred thousand was coming from the U.S. by diplomatic pouch.

The hotel was by the busy Plaza de la Cultura, and Slack often wandered out to mingle with the crowds watching the fire-eaters and puppeteers. He'd been given a .38 snub and offered a car, but opted for a motorcycle, a big 1500 c.c. Honda touring bike, easier to wiggle through the congested inner city.

He felt he was ready, but the handlers thought he needed a few days on fundamental matters such as memory training for the minutiae of the kidnap scene. Somehow, he was expected to memorize the route and collate evidence even when blindfolded.

He'd been almost a week in San José, and Joe Borbón was back in Quepos, trying to get into the pants of Camacho's sister and keeping Mono Titi Tours afloat. It would look odd if the office was closed in high season. Should anyone — reporters, former friends — ask as to his whereabouts, Joe would say Slack was sick. If they pressed, he was in a dry-out clinic.

Though Joe would not be dogging his steps during the risky next stage of Operación Libertad, Slack worried someone else might try to shadow him. If they screw everything up by doing that, they'd better not blame the fuckup.

The one hitch was getting Madrigal sprung, Minister Castillo insisting that proper procedures must be followed. "In this country, we are guided by the rule of law." The security chief was miffed he was out of the loop, his people rarely consulted. But though he was a pain in the neck with his little obstacles, he finally seemed to understand that this hemisphere's colonial power was in charge of Op Libertad.

Eager to get the show underway, Slack volunteered to do battle with the Tico bureaucracy, to get the pardon issued, Benito out of custody, his personal belongings released. Otherwise, it might take weeks for some dawdling official to work his way through the red tape, manufacture of which was the major industry of the Republic of Costa Rica.

He criss-crossed the city on his *moto*: the courthouse registry for the required forms, over to another public building for tax stamps, an hour finding the right wicket, up to the corrections ministry to get Benito's wallet and his *cédula* released, back to the security ministry for the pardon, the document crossing a myriad desks, various officials examining, initialling, discussing, finally applying rubber stamps.

At other stops, supporting records were missing, misfiled, or *in trámite* between offices. Finally, near the end of his third full day, he found himself crawling to the front of one more line, one more counter, one more functionary, a prim no-nonsense woman who sniffed at the paper he produced and said, "I see no *permiso* from the Judicial Police."

"Just sign it, please." He smiled through clenched teeth.

"Sorry, señor, it is not authenticated, you must return tomorrow. We are closing now."

"I'm not waiting until tomorrow!" he yelled.

As she was about to ring down a metal shutter, Slack pulled open his jacket and showed her his Smith .38. "Sign the goddamn paper!"

She did so with a wavering hand, stamped it, and frantically closed the shutter as Slack raced outside to his Honda.

That evening, after some searching, he found Herman Rebozo's apartment on a nondescript lane in Barrio Mexico, north of the Coca-Cola Station, a neighbourhood of decaying concrete structures scarred with graffiti, narrow sidewalks of broken paving stones.

It was a walk-up, a staircase leading to a small flat. He chained his *moto* to the stair rails, it wouldn't last five minutes outside.

He wondered if others were hiding here, the young couple who had smuggled Gordo in and out of the San Isidro Hospital. One of them had been identified, a teenaged boy whose parents had finally reported in, concerned that their mixed-up kid might be involved. About the girl, Slack knew nothing.

He knocked lightly on the door and it opened a crack, an eye peeked out, and a chain was released. Gordo quickly ushered him in.

The place was cramped but tidy, some old furniture, doorways leading to a kitchen and a bedroom. The sleeping cot beneath the living-room window appeared to have been in use, Gordo's two cohorts were sleeping in the bedroom – its door was open a crack and he could hear whispering.

"You were not followed?"

"No one can follow a motorcycle in San José."

"You have met with them again?"

"Yes. They will give Don Benito his freedom tomorrow."

"Why are you so sure?"

"I have the papers." He brought out a thick envelope, spread the documents on the dining table.

Gordo had served a dozen years as one of those faceless civil servants under whose dominion Slack had so recently suffered. He would enjoy these documents, he would understand their beauty.

His portly host slipped on his reading glasses and pored over the papers, studying all the hard-earned stamps and signatures. He seemed impressed enough. Slack waved a bundle of bills at him. "This is ten thousand. I will have sixty more like this."

"Why do they trust you with all this money?"

"This is nothing to them, a piss in the ocean. We have not asked for enough."

Gordo frowned, the explanation didn't satisfy him. Slack peeled off a couple of thousand for him, pocketed the rest, his walking-around money.

"Should I bring him here?"

"No, that would not be wise, in case you are followed."

"All right, you, me, Elmer, we'll meet somewhere Friday at six. I'll bring Don Benito on my motorcycle. At rush hour it will be difficult to follow me."

Gordo took a deep breath. It was a time of decision. He was either running the show here, as Halcón's trusted deputy, or he was just some two-bit payroll clerk. He had to make a leap of faith in Slack Cardinal.

"I will decide where we meet. I have purchased a truck, a delivery van." Gordo limped off to fetch some scaled maps, fished through them. The one he spread out showed the Escazú hills, south of San José. "Up here, we can see for kilometres down any road. We will know if you are followed."

They spent some time working it out, selecting a remote gravelled trail that climbed all the way up the *cerros* before descending to a valley in the south. Gordo recalled a *pulpería* with a Kimby Chicken sign at the entrance to the gravel road, and, about three miles farther, near the top, a turnoff to a viewpoint. That was where they would meet tomorrow at sunset.

Slack didn't argue, kept saying, "*Claro, claro.*" This was fine, let Gordo demonstrate his leadership capabilities.

A sound came from the bedroom, a rustling. Slack saw an eye peek out.

"Who's in there, Gordo?"

"It is not important. You will be searched, that is understood? You will also be blindfolded. Those are my orders, however friendly you may be to our cause."

It was that phony story about the counterfeit felony that prompted all this hostility, the worst nightmare of a payroll clerk. "*Claro,* Gordo."

The little fellow straightened himself to his full height. "You will be privileged to meet Halcón, who is a great revolutionary. He has fought for the Zapatistas in Mexico and for our comrades in the Colombian struggle. Together with Don Benito, they will form a dynamic partnership."

"I must warn you that they say Benito has been sick," Slack said. "You should be prepared for that."

"The pure air of freedom will cure him."

Slack moved to the bedroom door and swung it open. "Comrades, I don't like being spied on." The room was tiny, basically a bureau and a bed, a young couple lying on it, sitting up quickly now. They were kids, teenagers, how did they get messed up in this?

"How old are you?" They were speechless, sitting stiffly, as if caught in some shameful act. "Sixteen, seventeen, what?"

"They are useless," Gordo said. "All they do is eat and screw."

But apparently they also read. Here was an open book, a Chilean collection, Neruda, Mistral. Slack was tempted to sit down and read with them, share this good poetry. They looked so innocent, Slack couldn't picture them lugging submachine guns through the jungle.

"Both of you should be in school. Pack up and get out of here." Slack peeled three thousand from his roll, snapped a rubber band around the bills, tossed them to the girl. "Do you have passports?" Both nodded. "This is the number of an important woman in Havana, a friend." He scribbled a note on the inner flyleaf of their book. "Go separately, and don't fly direct, if they've identified you they may be watching the Cubana counter. Take the bus to Managua and fly from there."

Slack couldn't tell if Gordo was impressed by his high Cuban connections. He still had many friends in Cuba, had slept with this particular important woman. At any event, Gordo seemed relieved to send these youngsters on their way.

"There is a bus that leaves tonight," Slack said.

Wordlessly, the two of them began to pack, they seemed in a little awe of him.

Gordo didn't offer tea or cookies, so after studying the map, memorizing it, Slack saluted them with a raised fist and went down to his *moto*.

He had trouble getting to sleep that night, his blood running cold with the fear this was going much too well, there was a nasty glitch

lurking out there somewhere. He was equal to handling the likes of
Elmer and Gordo, but how would he stand up to Halcón?

❧

Dear Rocky,

If by some miracle you are now in possession of the
enclosed pages, it will mean the thieves who infest the Tico
postal service didn't consider them worth the effort to snitch.
Since the target for trash lit consists primarily of lip-movers,
may I suggest you enclose the dialogue in speech balloons and
throw in some line drawings and a pack of crayons. I have
bowed to your lust for violence by kicking the shit out of Harry
Wilder several times, but – somewhat like that big inflated
clown we used to spar with when we were kids – after every
thump he springs back, chin out for more.

Harry has comfortably buttered his way into the high
command of Dr. Zork, and tonight he is to buy freedom for the
woman who immortalized him as the town tank of Quepos.
Though he seems on top of his game, spectres of impending
failure infest his mind – he has a history of international
débâcles and general all-around fuckupness . . . and he knows
the canon demands brutal twists.

In the meantime, for my opening, I am playing with
something simple but which pulls the reader in: "Harry Wilder
scoffed at rumours of a secret military base in the high
Savegre." Or, more simply, "Harry Wilder knew a red herring
when he smelled one."

Please send a letter bomb to that illiterate fop at Permanent
Press who turned down *Hymns to a Dying Planet*. Made him
feel suicidal? Fuck him.

Jacques.

— 5 —

On the morning of Friday, January 21, the day of Slack's rendezvous
with Gordo and Elmer, Ham Bakerfield showed up at Slack's hotel

with all his doubts and worries. "How's this going to work out? You got a raving lunatic on your bike, he could freak out, jump off, do anything."

Slack was in the washroom, Ham standing by the door, watching him shave. Slack had decided to dress up his act for Maggie Schneider, fool her, she'd be expecting some drunken roué. His hair was much too long, falling over his ears, he would see a barber, too, just a trim, he didn't want anyone to think he worked for the government.

"Maybe you're going to have to sedate him."

"And how does *that* play? You're on steep roads, you got a drugged-up guy behind you trying to hold on who could fall asleep any moment." Ham began fiddling with a cigar.

"So fix up a harness, I'll strap him to me. You're not lighting that in here, pal." Slack stepped into the shower.

When he got out, he could smell the fumes. He hauled on his pants and walked past Ham to hurl the balcony doors open.

"How're the ribs?"

"Bearable." Below him, in the square, a marimba band was entertaining tourists, their numbers had been increasing, the U.S. advisory had been lifted. "You're not going to have a fleet of search copters out there, Ham. Elmer made a threat."

"Yeah, I worry about that guy. Found out he did deep penetration stuff in Vietnam. One of his jobs was to take out community leaders who belonged to the Cong."

Slack felt a chill; Elmer was a seasoned killer.

"After Vietnam, there's a big gap. Worked for a security service in Ohio for a few months, then disappeared. Four years later he's in Costa Rica. It's almost like a bunch of files on him went missing."

"Soldier for hire? Nicaragua?"

"Maybe, he seems that type. Be careful, don't underestimate him."

"You trace any property to him?"

"Nothing so far."

"Get a line on this Professor Pablo Esquivel?"

"Yeah, Minister Castillo claims he has something for you, he's on his way with some character who used to be one of their chief investigators. He quit a few years ago because of some scandal, so be wary of him."

He warned Slack not to be specific about his route into the hills. The security ministry was a sieve, they didn't need an army of reporters following them.

⚮

Jorge Castillo arrived just after breakfast, looking pleased with himself, announcing there had been a "break in the case." With him was a pear-shaped fellow in his fifties who was introduced as Frank Sierra, a fastidious look to him, a pencil moustache and darting, dark intelligent eyes. He gave Slack an embossed business card: licensed investigator.

"Mr. Sierra is one of our best minds," Castillo told Slack. "Sadly, we lost him to private practice."

"I would prefer to characterize it as voluntary exile from the ministry," Sierra said in flawless English, giving Castillo a cold look.

"Ah, yes, that's Frank's dry sense of humour. A little problem in the past, all forgotten." No one bothered to elucidate, and Castillo clapped his hands, as if to dismiss this awkward subject, maybe Sierra had been too honest a cop, a sin in Costa Rica. "To the matter at hand. We believe we have learned who Halcón is."

Bakerfield addressed Sierra, who was obviously here for a reason, he had the dope on Halcón. "What you got, Frank?"

Castillo answered for him, "My ministry may not have the resources of the CIA, but we have our methods." He was angling for the Liberación Party nomination for Tico president, if they pulled this off, he wouldn't want his own role to go unnoticed. "It was brought to my attention that Mr. Sierra, when he was in our service, was in charge of a file on a Professor Pablo Esquivel. Naturally, I sought him out. He spent all yesterday burying himself in papers, didn't you, Frank?"

"I think appropriate credit must go to Mr. Cardinal, who insisted this lead be followed." Sierra had a curlicue manner of speaking, slightly pontifical, amusing. "Foolishly, or out of vanity – from which

234

he suffers grievously – my old friend Johnny Diego overused an alias." He pulled several computer printouts from his briefcase, charts and all, he was a paperwork freak. "I have been Inspector Javert to his Jean Valjean. Several times he slipped through my fingers."

Esquivel, he explained, was one of a myriad of different names the man had used. Juan Santamaria Diego was his real name. "He has never been any kind of communist or revolutionary – that is just his latest guise. His parents are coffee growers from Cartago, honest, sensible people of comfortable means. Of the four siblings, he was the only bad seed. He showed brilliance in school, the only handicap to his studies being a distraction caused by the ladies. He was much pursued."

He showed Slack a surveillance photo taken a few years ago. A dark, slim, smiling man, dapper in a business suit, entering a building. About forty, long of hair and wide of moustache, piercing black eyes.

"Ten years ago he ran a language school, advertising himself in *The Tico Times* as Professor Pablo Esquivel. He is a man of some charm, and one might even call him charismatic, so it is not unremarkable that he built up a clientele of wealthy gringas eager to improve their Spanish."

Within a year, Halcón had managed to fleece these lambs for eighty thousand dollars: phony paper, shares in moribund companies, sales of unregistered land, own your own personal acre of teak forest.

Slack told himself not to gloat. A confidence trickster, to use that fine Victorian expression. He remembered the name, Diego, from the newspapers, a complex fraud trial several years ago.

"He lived well, and did much travelling and entertaining until he began to feel the heat we were applying. Then he moved for a while to the Caribbean, then Panama. When he returned, he began running an illegal game here in San José, poker and blackjack. After we broke that up, he began a time-share enterprise at Playa Hermosa, overselling the units several times. One of his most successful exercises in chicanery was later performed from America – for several years he lived in California raising funds for rain-forest preservation. Subsequently, an audit revealed administrative expenses to be over ninety per cent."

Halcón had been doing fine up to now, as far as Slack was concerned, but this one lost him points, a rain-forest scam.

"He eluded the FBI, returning to Costa Rica under an assumed name."

"He ever get nailed?" Ham asked.

"Only one charge has held, for which he earned a year's imprisonment. He has been skilful in the use of the courts, and has paid for the best lawyers. He happens to be one himself."

Slack's chest still hurt when he laughed. "A *lawyer?*"

"With a degree from my alma mater, the University of Costa Rica. But why should you be surprised?" Sierra smiled politely. Slack got the point, Castillo was a member of that unloved profession.

Slack wondered why a law degree, a licence to steal money legally, wouldn't be enough for Johnny Diego. But maybe bilking clients was too boring and easy, he held wider ambitions.

"What was his last hustle, before this?"

"Also kidnapping, but of expensive cars."

"Good money in that one," said Slack. Holding Cherokees and Audis for ransom, threatening to sell them for parts unless the owner dropped off a boodle somewhere. One of Slack's friends had had to buy back his Range Rover for twenty thousand, it was worth eighty to replace. Slack felt a bout of laughter coming on. He failed to suppress it, and paid the price, had to hold his chest as he told the story.

His friend's car had been stolen again by the same gang, the leader phoning to demand the standard fee. When the victim complained about unfair business practices, the thief promised to run a check on his computer. Afterwards, he apologized and said the vehicle would be returned. "It is our policy, señor, not to steal the same car twice."

Sierra laughed, too. "Yes, I am sure that is our friend, Halcón. His sense of humour may be more warped than his sense of ethics. He is legendary, a national hero to some. To be ruefully honest, I am one of his keenest admirers. It strikes me as curious that the ministry didn't come up with his name sooner."

Castillo made an elaborate shrugging gesture. "He was not on our list – we didn't expect this of him."

"That is understandable," Sierra said. "Johnny Diego has not used violent means before to attain his ends. I can only speculate as to how he infiltrated the Popular Vanguard. One assumes he observed how remunerative were several recent kidnappings in Mexico and Colombia – these have enjoyed a statistically high rate of success."

Slack nodded. "And he began looking for a big score. And for some idealistic dupes he could use to provide cover and free labour."

"Very likely."

Slack could see it: the quixotic followers of Benito Madrigal would be a rich field of talent, however naïve. Johnny slicked his way into their ranks, laid it on with a shovel until he looked like the second coming of Che Guevara, and mobilized them into the local red guard.

When Slack asked if Halcón could be linked to Elmer Jericho, Sierra pulled out a government form.

"In records filed by Flamingo Teak Plantations, S.A., now bank-rupt, Mr. Jericho is shown as a salesman. The president, chief execu-tive officer, and sole shareholder of that business was Johnny Diego."

Likely, Jericho had brought Halcón the play: major American politicos, a remote jungle retreat. He would have warned Johnny of the risks. *I don't know, man, you got Secret Service guys, you got guns and all that shit, could be hairy.*

Slack figured that hairy was what Johnny liked. A fraud artist, but emphasize the artist, he was putting on a rave show, the perfect score, a headline-grabber featuring a reactionary senator – his little Marxist commando had almost been designed for such a task.

Ham seemed anxious to cut this short, Chuck Walker was due by with six hundred thousand friends. "Gentlemen, we will have to excuse you. Some, ah, delicate business to attend to."

Castillo looked displeased to be so summarily evicted. "I am curi-ous, what is the plan for this evening?"

"That's what we're working on right now," Ham said.

Castillo asked to be kept informed. Ham promised he'd do that every inch of the way.

Frank Sierra agreed to drop by after Slack absorbed the files on Halcón, then rose and grasped his hand. "I am honoured to be associated with such a fine lyric poet." To Slack's astonishment, he produced from his jacket pocket a slim volume of poetry: *Various Views from the Edge of the Precipice*. "I found this while rummaging through a dusty bookstore."

Slack had salted the book around a few outlets in San José, but had never heard of anyone buying a copy.

"I would be delighted if you would sign it."

Slack muttered some feigned self-deprecations as he signed with a flourish: to my esteemed new colleague.

Walker arrived accompanied by a tall bespectacled technician and a Secret Service agent carrying a suitcase with the six hundred large. The tech was a chiphead from the Langley labs. They hadn't heard Slack clearly? No transmitters.

"Did you propose it to him?" Walker asked Ham.

"Not yet." Ham was fishing out another cigar.

"Please," said the technician, "no smoking, the device is very sensitive."

He held up a tiny bug on the end of his index finger, a silicon chip in a plastic capsule. "Transmits to a radius of eight miles. Subminiature battery, a faint signal, but a portable machine will be tuned to its exact frequency."

"I said no hearing aids."

"Here's the thing, Slack." For some reason, Ham was finding this awkward. "Okay, they'll strip search you. But if you were to, ah, insert this in a place where they won't be looking –"

"Up *yours*."

Ham shrugged. "Okay, save the idea for later."

The electronics engineer, pouting, pressed ahead. "You could have Agent Cardinal simply swallow it."

"Look, you twink, I'm not an agent, so I'm allowed to use my own brains. I'm not putting some battery-powered piece of high-tech junk in my stomach."

"The capsule –"

"Oh, fuck, get this guy out of here."

"Okay, easy does it," Walker said. "This is Slack's call, he's the first-string tackle here, the fellow whose ass is against the goal line. My only concern is that there's a lot of money on the table."

"I'll try to protect your investment," Slack said.

"The main thing is Gloria-May," Walker said. "And the other woman, of course."

He seemed edgy, maybe because the media back home were starting to hop on him. As he climbed higher in the polls, the spotlights had begun to cast a harsher glare. The press may also have found his soft underbelly – they were looking at Gloria-May, too, hints of unsavoury habits and low-life friends from her years in Vegas.

Slack opened the suitcase and did a riffle count through a couple of the banded bundles, all in hundreds. He checked others at random, making sure they hadn't slipped in any smaller bills.

"I won't be needing this." He handed Ham his piece. "Remember to put some horse tranquilizer in Benito's soup. Six o'clock?"

"He'll be there," Ham said. They would be bringing him to the U.S. Embassy compound in an unmarked vehicle. Slack would leave by another gate, with Benito in close embrace behind him on the Honda.

"Okay, if we're all finished, I'd like to take a nap before Frank comes back. Long night ahead."

"Who's Frank?" Walker asked.

"Someone we're going to check out," said Ham, leading them out the door, then pausing, talking low to Slack. "I don't like the way Sierra sucked up to you, crawling through a bunch of bookstores looking for a surefire way to make an impression. These Keystone Cops must have blurted out your name to him. He'll leak everything to Castillo, we'll have Ticos in our hair, reporters everywhere."

"Don't be so damn paranoid."

Frank Sierra's knock at the door aroused Slack from a fleeting dream of being mired in futility and failure. As Frank pulled files from his briefcase, Slack ordered up some coffee, then went under a cold shower to wake up. He returned to find Frank reading his notepad, checking items off with a pencil.

"That voluntary exile thing – what's that all about, Frank? Your gripe with Minister Castillo."

"Some years ago, he abruptly moved me from the investigative service after I picked up an aroma of drug-dealing and bribery emanating from one of his fellow ministers. Exiled to the Siberia of a remote hamlet, I resigned. The bitterness has subsided."

Over coffee, Slack shared a few of his own indignities at the hands of scheming higher-ups. Garrulous at the best of times, even when sober, Slack found it easy to talk with this erudite man.

"To business at hand." Frank flipped through his notepad. "I have just spent a most useful hour with the wife of Herman Rebozo."

He explained that some delicate prodding had opened her mouth, rancour at her husband finally spilling. He had abandoned her and six children "for his stupid revolution." Gordo's house had hosted meetings of the Popular Vanguard, regularly attended by a Nicaraguan couple whose names she did not remember, but they were Sandinistas, experienced in war.

"Of him, called Zorro, one must be especially careful, Señora Rebozo recalled him as hot-blooded. He is resentful of Americans – apparently he once sought refugee status in Miami, claiming to be a Contra, but was deported." Another of the regulars was a dispossessed farmer who constantly complained about Americans stealing land from Ticos. "Others drifted in and out, but these were the core."

Inocentes all, but it was Halcón who would be across the table, the lawyer. Frank had a few ideas about how to handle him, appeal subtly to his vanity, don't play cat and mouse, be open and friendly.

Slack showed him the suitcase full of money. "The grand gesture," Frank said. "Johnny will appreciate it."

"I'm hoping to buy Margaret Schneider with it."

"An excellent start." Frank began to pace, deep in thought. "My friend Jacques, I must say there is something about this business that smells of overripe cheese. Have you also detected it?"

Slack had also had such thoughts. Frank's musing made him wonder about cheese — it's what you put in a rat trap. He'd been used before as a fall guy for the CIA, they weren't above setting him up for another kick in the ass. But for what reason?

"I can't locate the source of this niggling concern," Frank said. "I am of a suspicious bent — it is too much in my nature."

— 6 —

The sun was sitting low in the west as Slack was waved into the compound, his face masked by a bike helmet and goggles. A utility van with dark windows was waiting there, along with a couple of agents, Dr. Ignacio Bleyer, and Benito Madrigal, who was looking about in a vague, uncentred way.

"Regrettably, all this excitement has aggravated his condition," Bleyer said. "He and reality have at least momentarily gone their separate ways. Medication has made him very groggy, however, and he may sleep through much of your journey." He passed Slack a bottle of yellow pills. "Every four hours, two of these."

Benito seemed not to recognize Slack until he took off his helmet and goggles, but then his face lit up. "Ah, it is Jacques Cardinal, it is you I have to thank."

"You are a free man now."

He held the door for the woozy Benito, who had difficulty getting out. He hugged Slack, who felt good about that, they would get along fine.

Benito whispered in his ear, "They said I have been pardoned. Can we believe them?" Slack showed the official pardon to Benito, who seemed unable to focus on the papers, maybe Bleyer had dosed him too heavily. "Where are we going?"

"To join your comrades."

Benito frowned, seemed to be having trouble grasping his grant of freedom. Then he nodded. "Sí, claro. It is a prisoner exchange, is it not?"

Slack set a helmet on Benito's head, secured him with harness and safety strap, then made sure the saddlebags were also buckled tight. He would be riding into the sunset with six hundred thousand dollars and a drugged schizophrenic, the commando could make of their saviour what they wished. On his return, he hoped to have a different passenger, she would feel remorse for her libellous depiction of him, but he would laugh it off.

Slack took the back roads, south into the hills, an area of scrappy farms that began to peter out amid clumps of trees and scrub. For a while, Benito gripped Slack tightly around his waist, then relaxed and fell asleep, missing out on the big sunset, the sky flaming out, painting the darkening fields.

Whence came that scent of overripe cheese that Frank Sierra had picked up? Slack would henceforth maintain a healthy distrust of Bakerfield and Walker. They *might* have sent followers, they would want fuck-up insurance on Slack. They could call on the cream of FBI shaggers, they would have a big moon to light their way. But when he stopped his engine, he heard no sound of distant motor, just the brisk breeze soughing through the trees, a papagayo from the north.

He unhooked himself from Benito, dismounted, checked behind fenders and bumpers and wheel wells for hidden devices, went through the pockets of his slumbering passenger. Satisfied, he resumed his journey.

The land was cruelly eroded here, carved by paths of wandering cattle. Shanties clung to the hillsides between mansions of the rich. No planning, everything helter-skelter, it was painful to see his adopted country become a bourgeois wasteland.

Here, a remote outpost of civilization, the *pulpería* with the Kimby Chicken sign. He turned onto a poorly gravelled road that led to the lip of the vast crater of the Central Valley, San José spread out behind him, a carpet of lights. No one was tailing him, no sound of engines or rotor blades.

He almost missed the lookout, then his lights reflected on a vehicle parked beneath a balsam tree, a one-ton van with a square oversized box. Gordo's truck was a nondescript clunker, grinders like these cluttered the nation's highways. As he pulled up beside it, Elmer emerged from the cab, followed by Gordo.

"Hey, man, *como está?*" Elmer said.

"*Pura vida,*" said Slack.

"Far out, you sprung Madrigal."

Gordo was holding a .22 pistol. "Put that away," Slack ordered sharply. Gordo slid it into his pants pocket and made his way to Benito's side. Slack undid the safety harness, and Benito slid from the bike into Gordo's arms.

Benito came around enough to mumble a greeting, then staggered sideways, leaned against the truck, and glided to the ground.

Gordo gasped. "What have they done to him?"

"Looks gonged out, man."

"I think they dosed him up," Slack said.

"They are filthy dogs. Benito, my friend, it is me, Herman Rebozo."

Benito's eyes opened slightly and he mumbled, "Beware the enemy within."

"Benito, it is me."

He fell asleep.

"He gonna be all right when he comes down?" Elmer asked.

"They will pay for this," Gordo hissed.

When Gordo unlocked the back door of the van and slid it open, Slack could see the truck was loaded with provisions: vegetables, canned goods, boxes of corn flakes and dried pasta. On top of these were two inflated air mattresses, poolside toys looped with rope.

"You get to ride in comfort," Elmer said.

They wouldn't need to blindfold him, the back of the van was windowless, a tin cage. They hefted Benito onto one of the air mattresses, then Slack moved some boxes around to make room for the Honda.

Gordo objected. "Something could be concealed in it, a weapon, a transmitter."

Slack sighed and wheeled it down the slope into a thicket of wild cane, it should be safe there until daybreak.

"I want you to search Señor Cardinal. Make him take his clothes off."

"Hey, Gordo, relax," Elmer said. "Go sit in the truck."

Gordo seemed about to take umbrage at being ordered about, but he just pulled up his sagging pants and climbed behind the wheel.

Elmer bent his elbow around Slack's neck, a tight hug. "Don't worry about that worrywart, he can just sit there and pull his weenie. What's in those bags — you score some folding off those guys?"

"Six hundred grand."

"Hey, man, that's incredible, top shelf."

"But I'm expected to get something for it. Some gesture. One of the women, at least, Maggie Schneider."

"I don't follow. Why don't we just keep the dough and both women and say, 'More, please.'"

"We have to show we're square, otherwise they'll stop dealing. Gloria-May Walker is worth millions."

"Let's see what Halcón says. Listen, you gotta piss, better join me, we got a long road ahead."

They strolled to the edge of the escarpment, Slack hauling the saddlebags with him. Elmer peeked in one of them, fingered the money, pulled out a sample. "This is looking like a very sweet deal. So where you going after you make your nut off it?"

"Staying right here, I guess."

"Thailand, man, that's where I'm heading. They don't give a shit for nothing over there, and they got some mondo reefer." He lit a joint. "See that up there, near the Dipper? That's Mars, man. It's got mountains three times as high as Everest, volcanoes, canyons deeper than we got on earth."

Elmer continued to fill him in about Mars as they shared brotherly release at the edge of the escarpment, their streams descending into the great glowing bowl of the Central Valley.

❧

Elmer had given Slack a flashlight before locking him in, and he used it to probe for holes, finding several cracks, all too narrow to see through. Then he found a larger aperture, near the roof, about the size of a fat peanut, but he could make out very little, it looked like foliage rushing by.

They had been travelling for three hours along paved mountain roads, falling and rising, curling and meandering, the pavement deteriorating to gravel, dust finding its way in, causing him to choke. Benito, however, lay peacefully on his mattress, a whinnying noise as he slept.

They must still be high in the cordillera, he could feel the chill. Forget the memory training, Slack hadn't a clue if they were going north, south, east, or west. Otherwise, things were going *too* well, it was almost worrying. He hadn't screwed up for two weeks so maybe he was due.

Now they were on a dirt road that for the most part seemed to descend. They were moving more slowly, branches brushing the walls of the van, a track for four-wheelers that coiled through the mountains, not intended for clangers like this. The rig could lose its steering at any moment, Slack could be in a tomb.

The van braked, and Slack, who was trying to stand, fell clattering against the piled boxes. The vehicle began moving slowly again, gingerly engineering its way into and out of a deep rut, then groaning up an incline. When Slack looked through his hole all he could see were stars.

The jolt had awakened Benito. "Where are we?"

Slack played his light on him. He was sitting, his glasses in his hand, rubbing his eyes.

"We are in a vehicle, Benito. We are taking you to your people."

"But we are being followed."

"How do you know?"

"I have acute sensory receptors. Also, I must tell you, in all honesty, I have a problem of a personal nature. The true revolutionary should not be embarrassed by normal bodily functions, so I tell you I have to take a shit."

"A shit."

"The demand is urgent."

Slack crawled to the front and banged loudly on the tin wall several times, and finally the truck came to a halt. "We've got a problem here!" he shouted.

A moment later the door opened a crack and when Slack explained the situation, Gordo helped Benito out, he was more alert now, his tranqs wearing off. "The drugs they force down my throat, they act like a laxative."

Gordo scowled. "The pigs. They should all be hanged."

"Who are you? I know that voice. Why, it is my friend, Herman. So this is no dream."

"No, Don Benito, this is reality, *gracias a Dios*." He helped him off the rutted trail to a spot behind a large rock.

As Elmer poked among the supplies for toilet paper, Slack did a quick field study. They were below the cloud forest, at about five thousand feet, he guessed, from what he could make out of the climate and vegetation.

Tall trees obscured the valley bottom, but to the south was a gap through which he could see moonlight glinting on a pie-slice of ocean. Which one? The stars and moon told him he was facing southwest, toward the Pacific. But it could be the Gulf of Nicoya, they could be in Guanacaste, in the Tilaran mountains, anywhere.

Operation Defecation succeeded without mishap. Benito, looking much relieved, said, "Now, if they follow, all they will find is shit."

Gordo didn't know what to make of that, Elmer found it funny. Benito's words, however, struck Slack as clairvoyant. Had they slipped more than drugs down Benito's throat? He relished the image of the chiphead from Langley bending down to examine a transmitting turd.

"We must keep moving," Benito said. "It confuses their beams."

"I don't understand," Gordo said.

"If you try too hard to understand it becomes impossible."

Gordo thought about that. "Yes, I see your point, Don Benito."

"Can you read my thoughts?"

"I don't think so."

"*Bueno.*"

As this colloquy continued, Gordo looking increasingly baffled, Elmer drew Slack aside. "It's like he's flashing on acid, man."

"He's been in a hospital, he's schizophrenic."

"Jeez, these simple souls think that's just bullshit, I half convinced myself. A bowl of fruit salad, that's what we got here. What a weird blast of fate, man."

The moon, now low to the horizon, rolled out of a bed of wispy cloud, illuminating Gordo's distraught features, he had given up trying to make sense of Benito's words. "He says they have altered his brain patterns. Obviously, he was broken under torture." He squinted hard at Slack, suspicious, looking for someone to blame. "In case he has a problem again, he should ride up front. You will return to the back."

"You're the boss, Gordo."

"Let's get this carnival back on tour, man."

❧

Slack spent the next two hours playing with a dark suspicion that Ham Bakerfield wasn't playing the game according to the agreed rules. He *hoped* Benito had shit out their damn bug, a form of anal poetic justice.

As the truck wound its way down from the hills, the road improved, gravel again, a valley bottom. A strong flickering light outside, a smell of smoke, the remnants of a slash-and-burn fire, cattle farmers razing the jungle, leaving their burns to smoulder all night. Such scenes played out every dry season, cowboys standing around sucking on their sugar cane, hypnotized by the flames. It was a kind of murder, we're devouring the wilderness as we gobble our Big Macs and triple-patties.

The air became dense and sweet, a rich rain-forest smell, which meant they were definitely not in the dry north country. No, this felt very close to home, the Central Pacific zone. Through his peephole, Slack could see fields flow by, the occasional yardlight, maybe a farm. Now they were on a clanking metal bridge. Half a mile farther on, the truck slowed, and he glimpsed a few lights burning, a village. A sharp left turn. The road became rough again, rocks spinning from the tires. They were ascending once more, up a river valley.

This configuration of bridge, village, and river near the Pacific coast seemed all too familiar. Slack had an almost instinctive sense he had many times travelled this route, hauling kayaks past a burg called Londres, up the Naranjo River. After fifteen slow minutes over rocky bumps and shallow pits, he was sure: he would know this route in his sleep, the rockiest country lane this side of the cordilleras. He could hear rapids as they dipped, and through his peephole saw the truck's lights striking a rusted oil drum, Mono Titi Tours' garbage receptacle. This *was* the Naranjo, his very own kayak launch point. He wasn't ten miles as the crow flies from his own bloody home.

After another twenty minutes of tortuous progress, the truck wheezed to a halt. Slack felt a shift of weight as someone got out of the cab, he heard muffled conversation, and after a few moments the creak of gate hinges. He remembered trucks hauling gravel and concrete block up this way several years ago, recalled a metal gate, a bodega, but had never seen the house, it was buried in the woods. The vehicle resumed its progress for about a minute, then the engine was turned off. More conversation.

He lay down, pretended to be asleep as the door opened. The moon had fallen below the horizon, and the night was black, the stars hidden by trees. He caught a scent of angels' trumpets and citrus blossoms. Distantly came the moans of the river.

He was momentarily blinded by a flashlight beam. "Rise and shine, old buddy," Elmer said.

Slack groped about for his saddlebags, flung them over his shoulder. The beam was directed down, lighting his way onto a patch of grass. Otherwise he could see nothing but moving shapes, several people.

"*Viva Benito Madrigal!*" A joyous shout.

"Yeah, man, you can have him." Elmer sounded weary, Benito had worn him out.

"Announce me to Halcón," Benito called out. "But be careful. We may be near the Americans' secret base."

"Yeah, right," Elmer said. "Sorry to keep you in the dark, Slack, but *el capitán* figures if you can't see nothing, you can't say nothing, like when the boys uptown try to quiz you."

The narrow circle of light on the grass began to move, and Slack followed it to a brick patio. The shadowy mass nearby might be a building, but it was nearly impossible to tell.

"*Apaga la luz, por favor.*" A gently spoken command, a voice that reeked of self-assurance. Halcón, Johnny Diego, he seemed to be sitting down.

The flashlight was extinguished, and Slack swore as he stumbled against a folding chair, his legs tangling in its rungs, and his first thought as he went sprawling onto the bricks was that this was a snare they'd rigged up. Spy-trap.

But no, Elmer was helping Slack to his feet, chortling.

"A grand entrance to our humble hideaway, Jacques Cardinal," Halcón said. "I must apologize, those fold-up rockers are a menace. When you're safely in them, however, they are comfortable. It's a pleasure to meet you, sir."

"Pleasure's all mine." Slack righted the chair and eased himself into it. Whose pad was this, he wondered. A *norteamericano*, he guessed, a pal of Elmer, his tropical hideaway.

"Hey, Halcón, man, we got a problem with Benito Madrigal." A scraping sound, as Elmer sat. "I got a whole load of him driving down here. He's on a different planet, not one I heard of."

They could hear him, maybe thirty yards away, demanding that people identify themselves. Someone was attending to him, speaking in a squeaky pleading voice. Buho, maybe, the student, Benito's nephew.

"I was hoping the press had exaggerated," Halcón said. "He is that ill?"

"My question," said Elmer, "and maybe you want to ask yourself this real seriously, is what the fuck are you going to do with him?"

"Who are you?" Benito shouted.

"It is Vicente."

"Vicente, my dear nephew! And my brave Sandinista warriors! Ah, now we are a fighting force again. Let us inform the president we will take up arms if the minister is not dismissed."

Elmer snorted. "It's gonna be like having the mad hatter around here, man. Tell him what you got in the bags, Slack."

Slack took a deep breath, he was about to test Johnny Diego's sense of honour.

"A six-hundred-thousand-dollar down payment, in return for Maggie Schneider. They understand Mrs. Walker will be more expensive."

After a silence, Halcón said, "Amazing. And they trusted you with this?"

"My life wouldn't be worth a sparrow fart if I stole it."

"I would not have expected such initial generosity from them."

"It makes sense to sell Miss Schneider to them," Slack said. "Reduces your burden. You'd never get that much for her alone, her family has no money. If they're willing to pay that much for Maggie, they'll go well into the millions for Gloria-May, she's your real ticket." He hoped he wasn't overplaying his hand, but they had to see he was making excellent sense.

Benito was still carrying on. "Where is my headquarters, my office?"

"He's supposed to take a couple of these every four hours," Slack said. "Downers." He gave Elmer the pill bottle.

As Elmer shuffled off in the darkness, Halcón sighed. "This is sad, about Comrade Madrigal. Why can't things go smoothly, Mr. Cardinal?"

"There's always something. Call me Slack."

"Elmer says you are a man of goodwill, Slack. Also that you drive a hard bargain."

"That's in our mutual interest, isn't it?"

"He must have been drunk when he agreed to twenty per cent."

"He was stoned."

"When isn't he? But Elmer is not so lazy of mind as he pretends. He says he trusts you. But the American government also seems to trust you. Do I trust you, too?"

"I guess you have to take chances in life, Halcón."

"You could be more reassuring, my friend."

"Look, there's no point in kidding around. Comando Cinco de Mayo – it's brilliant, I give you credit. I know where I am, near the Naranjo. You're about the last gringo house on a dead-end road. I don't think you have any choice but to trust me."

A silence. Halcón struck a wooden match, lit a cigarette. He didn't try to shield his face, and Slack saw the sardonic smile. "I think it would be a mistake to underestimate you, Slack."

"You have everyone else bamboozled. To the cops, you're dangerous revolutionaries."

Halcón's laughter seemed open and generous, not contrived. "A Bolshevik – I had to smile at that. You share our noble motives to the tune of twenty per cent."

"It's a bargain already."

Halcón's hand reached out and Slack gripped it firmly. "Maggie had her doubts, but I had an instinct that I would find you a person *muy amable*."

Maggie had doubts? Why was she even consulted?

"Throw those pills away," Benito called out. "I know what's in them. I'm thirsty, someone please get me a soda, and I want to see it opened in front of me."

Halcón turned business-like. "Slack, I wish we had more time to enjoy each other's company, but the night is slipping away. You require to be photographed with our guests, that must be done. We must settle on a maximum, though reasonable, figure. You've met with them. How high will they go?"

"For Gloria-May Walker?"

"Yes, we will put the matter of Miss Schneider aside for the moment."

"I'm not sure, maybe five or six million if we guarantee to move fast on it. More than that, they'll probably wait us out, hope you'll make a mistake. Walker isn't afraid of spinning things out, he's begun to realize human crises win votes."

"Feeding that man's ambition is something I hadn't counted on. They say he is cold and conniving – married to a woman like Glo, it makes no sense."

"He's an extreme guy, all the more reason to pull this off." Slack had to remind himself he was working for the forces of law and order. It would actually be a lark to pay these guys off, let them get away, there goes the campaign, down the toilet, a politician who won't deal with terrorists gets tubed by them.

People were shuffling about, moving sacks and boxes into the house, as Slack and Halcón discussed tactics and figures, moving fluidly between English and Spanish, trying to come up with a fair figure, suggesting negotiating ploys. "Always get them to name a figure first, triple that, agree halfway," said Halcón. "It's a formula that seems to work."

"We can promise one-day delivery?"

"Two, *maje*, to be safe." *Maje*, pal, they were getting on like long-lost lovers. "To give us time to disappear. Then Glo can be picked up here."

"And Maggie will go with me tonight."

Halcón remained silent, thinking about it. "The problem is this. Like you, she has a very good idea of where we are. Unlike you, she has no reason to be shy about saying so."

Slack hadn't factored that in. "This place may be getting a little hot, anyway. Anywhere else you can go?"

"Yes, of course, we have backup locations. Elmer can tell you where, but . . . Let's see what Maggie has to say about it."

Slack was content with that, let Maggie have a vote.

"Can you get access to the media?" Halcón asked.

"What would you like me to tell them?"

"Maggie has written a note, it was her suggestion, actually. It will explain that any funds we gain will be distributed to the poor."

Slack could see the benefit, the tactic would marshal public support, someone stumbling onto their scam might be less than eager to turn them in.

Elmer rejoined them. "How are we getting along here?"

"I have found a brother in spirit," Halcón said. "We are considering five million for quick delivery."

"Yeah, quick is the right idea, you don't want to be living with that squirrel too long. I put four of those pills in his grape Fanta, maybe he'll dim out again."

"Slack, there's one more awkward matter before I fetch our guests. The authorities must understand we are willing to carry out the ultimate threat. Do you think you can make that clear?"

"That you're prepared to kill them?"

Halcón seemed uncomfortable, maybe preferring a euphemism.

"Don't worry," said Elmer. "I'll do them."

A chilling reassurance, it produced a long, tight silence.

"I think if you promise them we are *all* prepared to die, that should be enough."

Elmer yawned loudly, strolled off. "I don't want to be seen by them women."

Halcón's chair creaked as he rose. "I'll bring our two subjects separately. Oh, one more thing. Obviously, they mustn't be told about our little, ah, partnership arrangement."

"There you go, *maje*. Underestimating me."

A moment later, he could hear a lock turn. A light went on inside, gleaming between openings in the shutters, they had power here, all the amenities. He could make out the house now, huge arches, grillwork, the structure lopsided. Behind him, in the trees, a shadowy figure, a glint of metal, an armed guard.

Slack hoped there'd be no last-minute hitch. For instance, Gloria-May may have told Halcón she'd met Slack, described the episode in Bar Balboa, maybe even the sunset cruise. It could prove awkward if he pretended they were strangers.

It was Gloria-May whom Halcón first fetched. She was wearing a short nightdress and seemed confused, as if startled from sleep, but when she saw Slack she smiled. Halcón was behind her, holding a Polaroid camera. He flicked off the interior light as he relocked the door.

"Well, who have we got here?" Glo said, then didn't allow him to answer. "I remember you. Didn't I see you in that little restaurant at Manuel Antonio? Got into a big argument with my old man, as I recollect."

"Yeah, I guess I was pretty fried. Slack. Slack Cardinal."

"That's right. Don't you run some kind of boat charter?"

She was quick. "Kayaks."

"So you're our negotiator. What do you reckon I'm worth?"

Slack was astounded by how blithe she was in manner. Clearly, she hadn't been mistreated. If anything, the opposite.

"Some works of art are priceless."

"Aren't y'all just too suavé. Where do you get your corn, fresh out of the garden?" She affected a sultry voice, addressing Halcón. "You got a light there, handsome?"

"We must make this quick, *mi hijita*." A casual term of endearment, Halcón had charmed them mercilessly. He held a match for her cigarette, and by its light Glo located Slack, approached his chair.

"You going to take our picture, Hal? Me and this big old hunk?"

Suddenly, Glo was in his lap, an arm around his neck, her cigarette in his face. He didn't know what to do with his hands, gingerly put one on her waist. She smelled sweetly of night sweat and something aromatic, maybe yesterday's perfume.

"Cheese," she said. The bulb flashed. Her smile seemed equally blinding, an athletic pose, a two-fingered salute and a leg raised high, toward the camera.

"Must you look so happy?" Halcón said.

"I want everyone to know we're okay. I want y'all to say that, Slack." She gently pinched his cheek, she was too hot and hip for Slack, too damned intimidating.

She got to her feet, serious now, the flirtatious lilt gone from her voice. "Tell them not to be coming here with guns and tanks. We want this whole thing settled peacefully, tell Chester that, tell him I'll surely divorce him if someone gets hurt."

"That's clear enough. Any other message?"

"You can tell him I'm being treated like a lady."

With the aid of a pen flashlight, Halcón watched the print emerge from the camera. Glo joined him, close, their bodies touching. She chuckled over the photo.

"An excellent close-up of a bare foot," Halcón said. "But we can make out your faces well enough." He handed the photo to Slack. "Glo, I must take you in now."

She didn't argue. "Toodle-oo, Mr. Kayak Man. Maybe we can run a river some time." The light went out, metallic sounds of a key in the lock.

Everything went quiet, just the night buzz, then a cough from the man standing guard in the trees. Halcón had only a handful of followers here, not counting Elmer and Benito, all probably green-horns, but who knows how they would react if panicked? No heavy artillery, he'd definitely insist on that, hustle the women out, then just surround these guys and wait them out. It almost seemed a pity to pull this stunt on them.

This time as the door opened, the light did not go on.

"This way," said Halcón. "Take my hand."

"I'm over here, Ms. Schneider. Follow my voice." Slack sensed her trying to locate him, then felt her bump into his chair, her hand brushing his face, a gentle touch.

"Are you Mr. Cardinal?"

"Slack," he said. "That's what they call me." He hoped she remembered that was a line from her manuscript, but there was silence from her.

"We can release you, Maggie," Halcón said. "They have paid six hundred thousand dollars for you."

"You're joking!" This wasn't said with astonished delight, she sounded almost miffed.

"Christ, it's not enough?" Slack said. He wasn't creating a fabulous first impression, that probably sounded sarcastic to her, he was coming on like the bitter antihero of her novel.

"And what about Glo?"

"That's a different story," Slack said. "She'll come later."

"When?"

"That all has to be negotiated." She was no longer touching him, but he sensed her above him, standing, she was quite tall. "We're doing this in stages."

"No, we're not. Do you think I'm capable of being that fickle to a friend? I'm not just going to walk out on her, not for all your money."

"Run that past me again. Real slow."

"We're sticking together, Mr. Cardinal. Maybe you've never heard of the concept, but it's called friendship. We've been up and down mountains together, through jungle and up snake-infested streams, and at times we've been absolutely terrified, and when we weren't crying we were laughing. We've given each other strength. We're not afraid."

It was a big firm speech. Okay, Slack could see it her way, more credit to her, loyalty being such a rare commodity.

"Anyway, I can't go." Her voice lost some of its resolution. "I'm writing a book about this whole thing. I haven't reached the final chapter."

"I was worried about this," Halcón said. "Maggie, please think about it."

"You're not getting rid of me that easily."

Halcón turned on his pencil flashlight. "Can I see the money?"

As he approached, Slack undid the straps of the bag, then handed him the wads of money. Halcón played his light on them, fished around, ran an expert thumb through one, then sighed.

"It is with an aching heart I must return it all to you. It has never been my policy to breach a trust."

Slack was taken aback, the grand gesture, tit for tat.

Maggie commenced a breathless speech: "Now you see what you're dealing with, Mr. . . . . Okay, Slack. I'm not sure if I like that name, I prefer Jacques. Anyway, Halcón's not what you expected, is he? You thought of some cold-blooded revolutionary. No, he's not, he has ideals, he's been everywhere, fought in important struggles, and you can question his methods but not his objects, because every-

thing you get from Mr. Walker's rich friends, and I hope it's a fortune, will be donated to the poor." She pressed a paper into his hand.
"I wrote this out, and it also expresses some of my feelings about
these people, how well meaning they are."

What had we here, another Patty Hearst? He pictured her with a
submachine gun, holding up a bank to fund the people's revolution.
Five weeks of bonding had done this.

"And I want you to pass word to my parents. Tell them to relax,
because I'm in great shape, just fine. And tell them to get their lives
together, their *marriage*."

"Okay, Ms. Schneider."

"I'm not through. If you have any idea where we are, I will hold
you in absolute contempt if you tell anyone. Glo says they'll send
snipers, that's how her husband would like to end this, in blood.
Dammit, these are *good* people, maybe some of them are out of their
depth, but . . . they'll have to shoot me first."

Slack gained his feet, then twitched as the camera flashed. He saw
her finally, her eyes large and defiant behind her glasses, slender and
mop-topped, radiant with courage.

He fumbled for her hand, then whispered in her ear, "I will be
back for you, Maggie Schneider."

PRISONER OF LOVE

— I —

It is the twenty-fourth of January as I enter my fifth week of internment at the Darkside of the Moon, three days since Benito Madrigal was deposited here in all his fragmented glory, three days since that big, shuffling redhead whispered his promise to return for me.

Mr. Cardinal seemed confused by what he witnessed here (and how stupefied he looked when the camera flashed). I can only hope he has managed to relay my message that those in charge must reject violent solutions. If the man has any receptive powers at all, he must have grasped that my hosts are harmless.

To give him credit, he has complied with our terms: my note has been read many times on the air, and I have seen it in close-up on Channel Seven. No mention was made in the media, however, of his role as go-between or of the tribute offered — and rejected — for my release. Nor, oddly, has the grant of freedom to Benito Madrigal been made public. I am sensing, from the people-on-the-street interviews, that public opinion is shifting in the commandos' favour, in particular, the sympathies of the poor.

We are still waiting for Jacques Cardinal's next visit, hoping he will not be followed, uncertain whether events will end with a bang, a whimper, or waves of fond farewell and misting eyes. But I am more optimistic now, for the opposition (as I have almost begun to regard them) seems eager to come to terms; my worth alone has been assessed at more than half a million dollars.

I remain convinced I took the right course by refusing to part from Gloria-May; I would never dream of leaving such a dear friend to face danger alone.

(I will continue to insist that my expressed desire to stay to finish this book was quite secondary.)

Our remaining days here may be short. Halcón has agreed we should move to another refuge that the commando maintains. (I am not at liberty to say where.) Detection has become a concern: Zorro, while stationed at the gate, contended yesterday with a couple seeking recruits for God, and has previously turned away campesinos selling melons and manzanas de agua. Twice, on consecutive nights, a thief has tried to climb the fence, only to be run off.

For the balance of my stay, I will continue to be a slave to the routines that allay the boredom of the long, long wait and the discomfort of fractious eruptions to which people in close quarters fall prey. I rise each day at dawn, attend my Spanish class ("Cómo amaneció?" they say — not "How did you sleep?" but "How did you wake up?"), followed by a spate of cleaning and sweeping, a nap, a guided stroll about the grounds, and the Channel Seven news over dinner.

While doing so I often picture a scene at home: my brothers at the farm, Aunt Ruthilda and Uncle Ralph, watching the Channel Ten Eye to the Universe. "Good evening, it is day thirty-eight of the Costa Rica hostage crisis," the announcer is gravely saying. "The ordeal continues for Saskatoon's own Maggie Schneider . . ."

Afterwards, I ascend to my room to scribble — by candlelight, because no electric bulbs are allowed upstairs. But I write in spurts all day as well; these notes are being composed in the afternoon, downstairs where it is cooler and where Halcón is taking his siesta on the hammock next to me. He looks sad in sleep, his handsome brown face creased, his eyelids moving — occasionally his lips, too, as if forming words. I wonder what dreams come to him. He often shows up in mine, and I awake disturbed, my mind in disarray . . .

She hoped he would wake soon, because it was four o'clock when she usually took her turn outside. Glo preferred her outings in the mornings, exercising on the patio or strolling about the gardens with Halcón. He never allowed them outside together; he remained strict about that.

From across the room, she could hear Benito muttering to himself, probably about Halcón making secret signs. This was one of his oft-voiced complaints; every hand gesture by Halcón or nod of his head was a cause for suspicion. Maggie was not as convinced as his nephew Buho that his schizophrenic disorder had been induced by capitalist-lackey doctors in the state hospital.

Benito had finally begun to take to Maggie, who had extended him many kindnesses. He had been leery of her at first because of her practice of writing as she wandered about the house. The ever-patient Buho had explained she was less a prisoner than a friend, that she was compiling notes for a book about them, about the guerrillas of the Fifth of May. "It is the story of the struggle, Don Benito."

He had the appearance of a bespectacled balding intellectual, and often communicated as one. Though delusional, he occasionally showed a startling lucidity, and some of his speculations – delivered in heavily accented English – were oddly incisive. ("Jacques Cardinal, he plays a sinister game, but he is the only outsider we can trust.")

She was determined to befriend Benito, to seek interesting quotes, for he was one of the central characters of this drama, its inspiration. It bode well that earlier today he hinted, in a conspiratorial voice, he had important secret information for her book. It concerned her, though, that he was so antagonistic toward Halcón. "He still thinks he is running this show. Soon, I make my move. Don't put that in your book."

The bland-looking economist had assumed the right to command upon his arrival: issuing orders, demanding his own room, a desk, a secretary, the prerogatives of leadership. Halcón gave him his bedroom, and when Benito did not settle down he locked him in it for a day. Then Buho had a talk with his uncle, and prevailed upon him to maintain a lower profile. It was clear to all but Benito himself that the once charismatic leader of the Popular Vanguard had been demoted to the sidelines, an object of pity and even softly spoken humour.

Halcón was awake now, staring at the ceiling, frowning, as if deep in thought, perhaps about the logistics of their impending move. She had concurred with him that they should all migrate to his alternative hideout on the Caribbean coast; they would leave in the truck with Gordo, who would be returning in a few days.

She simply did not trust Jacques Cardinal enough to stay here longer, to risk his penchant for débâcles. She hoped this former double agent would not turn out to be a double-dealer. She still had not told Halcón the truth about him – Glo had made her swear not to; it was a dilemma. Still, Halcón's faith in the go-between seemed not entirely misplaced: Cardinal knew the location of the Darkside; if he had betrayed them, surely there would be signs of police activity.

Halcón finally rose and went to the bathroom – without once looking at her. She had the niggling sense he was purposefully avoiding her – he had recently become more cautious with her, had toned down the teasing and flirting. That kiss on the riverbank was never spoken of; it fluttered over them like a banner, obvious but as unmentionable as dirty underwear. She was baffled by her intense attraction to him, fearful of playing the role of love's fool. Her long search for the meaning of that most passionate of emotions seemed to be dissolving in turmoil.

As a protective measure, Glo persistently drew them apart, monopolizing Halcón, playing cards with him, diverting him with humorous comments and anecdotes. She had continued to counsel Maggie: screw your head on straight; pull back or you're heading for the big fall. Maggie tried to tune into her friend's voice of reason, to persuade herself the lure she felt was not true romantic love but a secondary emotion.

Keep a firm grip on that wandering heart, she repeated to herself. This surely was not love in any true form. But what else could it be? She remembered the many reports of those who had fallen afoul of the fixation known as Stockholm Syndrome – it created unnatural bonding; the emotions played tricks. But she knew herself; she was too strong to fall prey to such thinking.

"'Be wary of your hidden desires.'" Glo was lying on an air mattress with her *Complete Annual Horoscopes*. "'Giving in to temptation may cause serious regret.' Who wrote this book, some total depressive? That should be *your* horoscope." She was smoking again, panhandling cigarettes from Halcón.

"What *is* mine?"

"Aries. 'Do something silly today. You may be pleasantly surprised at the effect it has on others.'"

"I'll wait for inspiration to strike."

Halcón was pacing about the room, still deep in thought. Maggie was entitled to her yard time, a right imbedded in custom. She swung from her hammock and tinkled the copper chimes by the window. Halcón returned to this world, unlocked the door, and ushered her out.

During these daily sojourns, Maggie had taken to tending the flowering shrubs and picking blooms for the house. Halcón still wore a far-away expression as he watched her snipping at the ginger and jasmine and anthurium. "I have seen heliconia by the river," he said. "Would that add to the display?"

She had not visited the river since the ignominious kiss. Glo had made a few excursions, though, and told her that its flow had abated. She followed him down the rock steps, refusing the hand he offered, managing the steep parts by herself. As she clambered toward the waterfall, she was reminded of how beautiful it was here. ("You add to it," he had said.)

Bright red claws of heliconia stretched toward the river from the shade of a pejibaye palm. This time she accepted his hand, following him over the slippery rocks, watched as he drew his long knife from its sheath and sliced across the stems.

"It almost seems a sacrilege," she said. "Take just a couple."

As she stepped forward to receive them, she stubbed her foot on a rock and lost her balance. For a moment, she teetered, whirling her arms like windmills. He reached out for her but failed to find her hand, and she splashed into the water.

The current carried her a few feet to a barricade of boulders, and she clutched at one as the stream poured by. But the river was shallow here, only a metre deep, and she was able to gain her feet. The initial cold shock of the water dissipated quickly, and she found the frothing current refreshing. She reached for Halcón's hand and tugged gently.

"Come on in."

"I am not so good a swimmer." He sat on a stretch of sand nearby.

After playing in the swift current for a few minutes, she climbed out and joined him, lying on her back to dry under a sun still hot at five o'clock. Her halter-top was sticking to her, her nipples shamelessly erect. Halcón did not seem to notice.

"You seem very subdued," she said.

"I am thinking about how we must soon go away."

Their alternative refuge was another large house, on the Caribbean side. He had not been more specific.

"I think I'll miss the Darkside," she said.

"We are too comfortable; that is when we become careless."

"Where will you settle when this is all over?"

"I have a place."

"You're not going to tell me where?"

"I tell you too much."

He leaned over her to shelter a match from the breeze, lighting a cigarette, his eyes squinting, his cupped hands inches from her bosom. She felt her throat constrict, her speech tight: "This has been . . . a really strange time for me."

"For me, too, Maggie. It has caused me some problems. With my *emociones*."

What was she to read into that? But he remained mute, staring at the smoke curling above his nicotine-stained fingers. She sought words that might cause him to open up, to reveal those emotions, to confirm or deny that she was a source of at least some of them. "Do you remember when I kissed you? Here, by the river."

"Of course."

She sat up. "I want to . . . I need to explain it. You'd been so kind to Glo and me . . . You still are, and . . . you're a very attractive man."

She was flushed with embarrassment, yet found herself unable to resist touching his arm: dark, sinewy, lightly haired. He shrugged. His smile was helpless and apologetic, but his eyes were like pulling magnets, and she felt herself being drawn into them, and she could no longer restrain herself and moved toward him, to his lips.

"Oh, God, I can't help myself, Halcón."

But their lips did not touch; he pulled away and fended off her reaching arms.

"No, Maggie, we cannot allow this to happen."

Maggie was ablaze with the shame of this abrupt rejection; she struggled to her feet, tears rushing to her eyes. "Oh, wow, I feel so ridiculous."

"Please understand, it is because of the feelings I hold."

"Yes, well, let's never *reveal* them."

She flew up the steps, but slowed before she neared the house; she would feel even more wretched if everyone saw her tears. She stood for a moment, wiping them with her fingers. How scandalously she had acted; how utterly humiliated she felt.

Lying on her bed, her door locked, she mentally lashed herself. Making another blunt overture to Halcón – had her brain turned to mush? Why had she not just raced from here with Slack Cardinal, back to civilization, to reality, to her senses? The agitation within her was terrible. She had to face up to the disastrous truth: she was a prisoner of love. She could no longer even pretend to deny it.

So this was how the miracle felt. This was the wild, mindless rush of feelings that she had tried to conceive, on paper and in reality, all her teen and adult life. She had never dreamed love could come with such power. She was no longer its keen researcher but its blind victim, too bewildered even to try to grasp the forces that had drawn her into its tangled nets.

She remembered a pact she had made with herself in snowy Saskatoon: that she would find romance in paradise, a sublime conjoining of spirits that she could share with Fiona Wardell. Not for a millisecond had she contemplated her heart would fall to a revolutionary Marxist kidnapper. She was twice his prisoner.

But how well was she focusing? Perhaps she was overreacting and had misread Halcón's gentle rejection. Clearly, he held feelings toward her beyond ordinary friendship. Why should she assume he was not struggling with his own feelings? His attempt to deny his *emociones* would explain his brooding and restlessness, even his avoidance of her. In all good conscience he could not misuse his position as her captor; that was the reason for his rectitude.

Into the falling evening came the call of the nightjar: "Chup–chup, *weer!*" She pressed her hands to her ears.

— 2 —

Maggie spent the following day trying to pretend she was not at all rattled, substituting false gaiety for the confusion she felt. She laughed too loudly during Buho's Spanish lesson when Glo's teasing made him blush. She avoided looking at Halcón for fear she would turn a brighter red.

Afterwards, Buho played sad tunes on his guitar as Glo, taking her turn outside, danced, languid and graceful, to his music. Halcón was with her on the patio, shuffling his cards, again in brooding thought. It seemed odd that he so casually ignored Glo's displays of physical attributes; likely, he found her abrasive, lacking the old–fashioned femininity that Latin men preferred.

She had not mentioned to Glo that she had practically offered her body to Halcón, and did not wish to hear more stern advice from her. Of recent, Glo, too, had been acting strangely: wistful, lost in thought, almost as uncommunicative as Halcón.

When it became Maggie's turn to join Halcón outside, she declined with a careless wave of her hand. "I need to sweep up around here; this place is starting to look like an ant nest." She wielded a broom for a while, but continued to feel awkward in his presence.

She fled to the kitchen, where she had promised to show Tayra how to make perogies. She flew into the task, and, to keep her thoughts from wandering dangerously down to the banks of the Naranjo, pep–pered her with questions about Central America's Caribbean coast, the culture of its people. Suddenly she found herself weeping.

"I think, young lady, you are in trouble."

Everyone knew.

☙

"It is a kind of *tamal?*" Buho asked, inspecting one of the perogies.

"What is in them?" Benito said, poking at them with his fork.

"Benito, yours came out of the same pot as the others," Maggie said.

All but Coyote, who was taking a turn at the gate, were eating from their laps around the television set, waiting for the news. Jorge Castillo, the security minister, had called a press conference for this evening.

"This is a great delicacy," said Buho. "It is the *plato típico* of Saskatchewan?"

"Not really." Maggie held her eyes to the set, concentrating on a commercial: a Tico version of Honest Brod Kipling at a display of Toyotas.

Benito was still staring at his plate. "In La Reforma, they put fluorides in my food."

"We do *not* put fluorides in the perogies," Maggie said.

There came a groan from Buho as an older man in a business suit glowered at them from the screen. "*Mi padre.*"

It was the fourth time they had seen Tomás Bolaños on television. This was yet another plea from Buho's wealthy father to his son to end his foolishness. Señor Bolaños had the appearance of one who was scornful of dreamy romantics, who might think his guitar-playing son was not capable of entering the hard world of business.

"Again he says he loves me and wants me back." Buho spoke with a strangled voice. "He says he will get me the best lawyers."

His eyes had filmed over; Maggie could not think of a way to comfort him. But Benito stood and patted him on the shoulder. "He is a bourgeois philistine, my brother-in-law," he said.

The announcer apologized: the security minister's press conference had been delayed but would soon be presented live.

"What are they up to?" Halcón muttered.

"I will not listen to the lies of these puppets of the state." Benito stalked to his room with his plate.

As filler before the press conference, Canal Siete showed a video clip of Senator Walker accepting flowers from a five-year-old girl, hugging her, then marching briskly to a parked helicopter. Buho translated the voice-over: "Though Senator Walker is leading in the New Hampshire primary, he has sworn to stay in Costa Rica in his relentless hunt for the leftist terrorists, and here we see the senator joining in, as he has every day."

Now Chuck Walker was in close-up by the open portal of the aircraft, speaking Spanish through a lapel-clip microphone. "He is saying that if we hurt Glo in any way he will pursue us to the ends of the earth." Now Walker spoke in English: "My darling, if you are anywhere that you can see or hear this, I swear to you upon my dying breath I will bring you home safely." He jumped into the helicopter and its propellers began to whirl. He saluted from the window.

Glo saluted back, poker-faced.

"I also will protect you," Buho said tautly. "Here finally is Castillo." The minister was behind a wide desk arrayed with microphones; he appeared ruffled and red of face, as if he had just been in a quarrel.

Buho summarized: "He is saying the Comando Cinco de Mayo has been taken in by our captain, and the public should not be fooled the same way."

Halcón cut him off, rising. "There is nothing new here. They know what our terms are."

"Yes, Halcón, but he is talking about . . . who is Johnny Diego?" Buho showed consternation as a head-and-shoulders photo of Halcón was inset onto the screen: unshaven, loose tie, jaunty smile – it had the look of a mug shot.

Halcón angrily switched off the set, cursing in Spanish, then making a fervent speech seemingly in defence of himself while accusing the government of slandering him. Maggie had never seen him in such a hot temper.

Later, while doing the dishes, Maggie and Glo watched Halcón in animated conversation with Buho, Zorro, and Tayra at the far end of the house. Benito remained outside the circle, watching them skeptically, as if witnessing the hatching of a new conspiracy.

Clearly, Halcón had been identified; his true name was Johnny Diego. What had the minister been saying that had caused him to become so wrathful? From what Maggie could make out, Halcón was cancelling television privileges; he was instructing Tayra and Zorro to remove the set to the bodega.

Halcón came to the kitchen to pour himself a coffee, calmer now, but his smile strained. "They are truly desperate. They have made up crazy stories about me, claiming I have a long criminal history. That way, they try to divide us."

"As a result, we are united as never before," said Buho, standing behind his leader.

"What stories?" Glo was smiling, an eyebrow raised.

Buho laughed. "They say he is a dishonest lawyer who has been in jail. Our captain! With this scandal, they try to win back public support. They know lawyers are hated in Costa Rica."

Now Maggie understood Halcón's fury: Operación Libertad had concocted a clever scheme, an attempt to isolate Halcón, to plant seeds of distrust within his ranks and stem the tide of sympathy for the guerrillas.

Just then, the roof began to rattle, the metal chimes sounding, the crystals swaying. Maggie started, and thought of running for cover. But the earthquake was minor, and after a few moments all was still.

"The gods are uneasy," Halcón said. "Maybe it is a message, a warning."

They spent the remains of the evening in nervous anticipation of the next shudder. Maggie had already experienced several; they usually came in series. But though no aftershocks occurred, somewhere a power line must have snapped; the house grew dark with the coming of night. The flickering of candlelight made the house seem eerie; Buho's doleful guitar plucking was not raising spirits or lessening the tension in the air. Glo had gone upstairs, and, thankfully, Benito had settled into bed, while Halcón, now relegated to a mattress in the main room, sat on the staircase, smoking his way through a pack of cigarettes.

Maggie suppressed the impulse to go to him, to touch his face and soothe the lines from his brow. What could be troubling him so deeply? Not the government's slanders, which seemed too obvious a ploy to have plunged him into such gloom.

He might well be thinking of her, perhaps regretting having spurned her. The likelihood that he shared her feelings seemed more compelling the more she thought about it. That he was undergoing such inner battle gave him credit; an ignoble man would surrender to lust.

As she climbed the stairs to her room, he touched her ankle, star-tling her. "About the matter yesterday," he said softly, "I was compli-mented. In normal times I might have responded with too much eagerness . . . but these are not normal times."

"Thank you. I understand."

That was enough for him to say, more than enough. She felt her way up the stairs in the darkness, almost tripped on Tayra's bedding, made a tangle-footed entrance into her room.

A candle was burning on Maggie's writing table, and Glo was seated at it, smiling as Maggie made her noisy arrival. "Do you reckon the delivery man is in on it, or did the Throb con him, too?"

"Excuse me?"

"Jericho, Elmer Jericho. The walls don't come tumbling down, because I still can't remember where I heard that name. Anyway, what do you think about our Johnny Diego? I mean, isn't that a stitch? He's the flim-flam man, he surely is."

"Glo, did you actually swallow that? Don't be so naïve."

That caused Glo to burst into laughter. "Who, *me*? Oh, honey, you are a caution. You've got to be the sweetest, most innocent thing since the Lord made puppy dogs." She held a cigarette to the candle, then stuck it between her teeth, grinning. "He's a clip artist. He conned everybody, took off their shoes and socks without their knowing it. Oh, yeah, the great freedom fighter – closest he's been to a revolution is watching clothes in a dryer."

Maggie understood Glo's stratagem: she was trying to poison her against Halcón and cause a rupture between them. She was not offended; Glo had her best interests at heart.

"All those home movies he's been producing for you, about his thrilling life: what bullshit. I've seen some real sharks in action, working the rubes from Des Moines in the casinos, but this guy surely is the all-time home-run king. Also got balls like an elephant."

Maggie laughed lightly, humouring her.

"Maggie, you forget? This is a guy who had his fingers in your fucking fanny pack while his tongue was in your mouth."

Maggie would not let such grossness upset her. From somewhere outside came the bell-like call of a tink frog – how she loved that sound: first heard the night Halcón unveiled himself, when he told her she was *valiente*.

"He's a no-limit poker player, honey, I know this guy. He won six hundred grand and he's throwing it in their face, calling them. I kind of sassed him out when he caught me slipping a card from the bottom of the deck. That takes quick eyes and a lot of experience at doing the same. He's a bodacious sting artist."

"Well, does that turn you on?"

"Yeah, gets me *real* hot. Baby, baby, bonk your head on something, loosen up the brain. He's not the one for you. You don't want to introduce him to your folks. You're not going to be showing him around the farm at Lake Lenore. He ain't interested."

That was brutal, and Maggie had to still her temper. She had not been rendered totally blind by her feelings; she was aware of her situation, and moreover had few expectations.

"Even if some of what they said on the TV is the truth, it's a warped truth. Sure, he's been in jail – he told me that himself. He's a social activist; one time they arrested him for leading a demonstration, and they beat him afterwards. You don't really know him, and I think you're just a little jealous. He's been very sincere with me and enjoys my company; I'm sorry if that bothers you. He told me yesterday he was confused by his feelings for me."

"Oh, Maggie."

— 3 —

Maggie struggled up from her hammock to watch the cumulous clouds billowing toward the Darkside, fully headed, distended with their watery burden. There had been no rain for two weeks, so its coming would be a respite from ceaseless daytime heat.

Glo was taking her turn outside, performing sit-ups near Halcón's table; she seemed more graceful and feline each day, every unnecessary ounce trimmed from hips and thighs. But Halcón, as usual, was showing not even a bored interest in her. Staring up at the brooding sky, he was agonizingly beautiful in silhouette, his expression soft and dream-like.

Over the last three days, the intoxication of love had begun to manifest itself in troublesome ways as Maggie swung between periods of paralysis, then of uncontrollable energy. She would storm through the house with mop and scrub brush, then wander about with her pad, writing words that did not make sense. Where was the bliss they claimed was love's avid companion?

She avoided Halcón as if he were a man with a deadly contagion, fleeing to her room when he was about, taking her turns outside with Buho, Coyote, or Tayra. Halcón, in turn, respected her need for distance and found fewer occasions to consult her; it was apparent to him, to all, that Maggie had gone emotionally overboard.

Glo had stopped trying to bring her to her senses, though she continued to disparage Halcón: he was a slick shyster, this Johnny Diego, without conscience. Maggie hotly defended him: the charges against him were false – that is how the state isolates troublemakers.

"Good lord, it's the invasion of the body snatchers," Glo said. "You're beginning to sound like Buho." Glo had been looking somewhat blank-eyed herself of late, less ebullient – but the tension of waiting for Cardinal to return with a response from Operación Libertad was causing strain to everyone.

"Without the house keys, he is nothing," said Benito, who had sidled up to her and was squinting at Halcón over the rims of his glasses. Maggie had succeeded so well in her efforts to befriend him that she had won the role of honourary co-conspirator. "He is afraid to be exposed as a fraud; that is why the television was removed. Only he, the usurper, is permitted to hear the radio."

But Maggie could appreciate Halcón's point of view: the government had taken a sly offensive, a propaganda blitz intended to divide and discredit Cinco de Mayo. "Let them think we are listening to this nonsense," he had said.

Glo was standing outside by the table, trying to interest Halcón in a game of casino, but he shrugged her off, still sky-gazing. "There is something going on between them," Benito said. "I can see this by the way they avoid to look at each other. How can you be sure she is your friend?"

Buho joined them, extending to his uncle a glass of water and two of the pills he was required to take every several hours. Getting them into him was always a task, but they did seem to soothe him.

Benito declined the offering with a brusque shake of his head. "Why always do you follow me?"

"*Lo siento, tío*," Buho said with a sigh. Also afflicting him was his burden of disappointment in the martyr of Cinco de Mayo.

Benito called out to Halcón; Maggie could not follow their brief exchange and asked Buho to translate. "My uncle asked, why does not our list of demands include to fire the minister? Halcón responded that it is an excellent idea."

"He is trying to humour me," Benito said.

Halcón was studying the sky as if expecting answers to come with the rain. From the south came a tendril of lightning, followed by a throaty low roll of thunder. A gust of wind caused the chimes to tinkle. A flock of parakeets swooped and chattered above the house, then settled onto a tree, battening down for the storm.

"Soon will come another earthquake," Benito said.

"How can you be sure, uncle?"

"I am cursed with a third eye that sees the future." He ignored Buho and bent to Maggie's ear. "They plan to assassinate Jacques Cardinal; I have seen this in my mind's eye. Did you write in your book that Archbishop Mora is working with the fascists?"

"You are bothering the señorita." Buho led Benito away, and Maggie lay back in her hammock and picked up her Spanish text. Ana and Carlos go to a restaurant. *Qué quiere usted? Huevos revueltos, por favor.* Scrambled eggs described her brain; she wondered if there was a translation for a fool in love.

Halcón was standing now, drawing Glo's attention to a curled grey shape in a balsam tree. What at first appeared to Maggie to be a termite nest revealed itself as a sloth when it began inching along a branch.

She watched it for several minutes; its lethargy induced drowsiness, and soon she fell asleep.

§

She awoke to grunts of thunder followed by a loud crackle, then a great crashing of cymbals. Rain was falling, slanting in the wind, and the chimes were loudly lamenting. Tayra was moving about the house, sliding shutters closed.

"Leave mine open," Maggie said.

"You will get sopping wet," said Tayra. She called to Zorro to help. "You, the lazy one."

Still disoriented from sleep, Maggie listened to Zorro and Tayra feuding, then sat up and looked outside. The concrete table was deserted, and the wind had spilled the playing cards onto the patio.

"Where are they?" said Buho as he came beside her at the window. "They have been gone for an hour." It took Maggie a moment to realize he was talking about Glo and Halcón, and then she reacted with concern; she hoped Glo had not dared a risky escape down the river.

The house suddenly began to shake violently, the roof clanging, jars falling from shelves. "Oh, my God," she exclaimed, concerned that this could be a major shock. She tried to flee the hammock, but her feet became tangled and she fell to the floor. Just as she freed herself, calm returned, and there were only the sounds of chimes and swishing branches.

Buho assisted her to her feet; his face was pale and his words were halting: "This was predicted by my uncle. Do you think it is true that he has a sixth sense? They have truly altered his brain patterns with their tortures."

As Tayra and Zorro untwisted from their paralyzed embrace beneath the stairs, Maggie went about the house picking up. Benito was sitting on a chair, unworried. She hoped Coyote was safe in his tilting bodega, but she was more concerned about Glo and Halcón. She grasped the wrought-iron grill and looked up into the thick grey sky, waiting, feeling inexplicably numb. The rain became a downpour: a tumultuous hammering on the metal roof that drowned all other sound.

Finally they appeared, racing up the path from the river, both of them laughing, Glo clutching Halcón's hand but releasing it as they came into view. As Halcón sifted through his keys, Glo composed herself by the doorway; her dress was pasted to her like cellophane wrap.

Inside, they parted with haste that seemed contrived. Glo passed by Maggie without a glance, and walked quickly up the stairs. There were mud streaks on her bottom, on her thighs.

"This rain, it caught us by surprise," Halcón said as he peeled off his wet shirt. "Did everyone feel the *temblor?*"

Maggie hastened to the bathroom, feeling nauseated, her body shaking. She put her head under the shower, and let it run cold upon her face. Leaving, she collided with Halcón, who was waiting to change into dry clothes. "Excuse me," she said, shouldering past his bared brown chest.

Then suddenly everything went blank for her. She whirled on him and swung her hand hard against his face, a slap that cracked like a whip. "You bastard!"

She marched down the hall in a searing rage, pausing only to pick up *The Complete Annual Horoscopes* from a table and hurl it at him as he stood staring at her, his mouth agape. "You lying *shit!* Both of you!"

Buho emerged from the kitchen with a plastic pail of slop for the compost. He put it down and extended a restraining hand, but she batted it away, shoved him to the side, picked up the pail, and emptied it on Halcón's mattress: plate scrapings and grease, pineapple skins and chicken bones cascading over his clean sheets and his maps and papers. She hurled the pail at the wall, and a streak of brown scum splattered across the *Star Trek* poster.

Benito, still sitting, spoke calmly, "I am sorry, but did I not say? All the time they have been plotting, and now we know they were screwing each other."

"Shut up!"

"Yes, uncle, please," said Buho, "you make matters worse."

She strode up to Buho, fists balled. "You want to get it on with Gloria-May Walker? Go ahead! She's ready for *all* comers! Maybe she'll teach you a few tricks!"

She strode toward Tayra and Zorro, who had been watching raptly from their station by the stairs. "Get the hell out of my way."

Upstairs, she stood for a few minutes at her door, taking deep breaths. Her world slowly came into focus, but she had only a blurred memory of the last few minutes. She realized her hand was stinging fiercely; dribbles from the compost were running down her legs and arms. Waves of nausea were still rising, and she steadied herself against the wall, willing her head to clear.

She entered Glo's room to find her taking a deep draw on a cigarette, staring out the window, still in her wet clothes. Glo turned to her startled; a smile froze on her face as she saw Maggie's sparking eyes. But she pretended nonchalance. "That was a hell of a shake. I did a total Maggie Schneider, fell on my ass into the river. What was all that commotion downstairs?"

She began disrobing. Her bra strap was twisted, a hurried job of dressing.

"You lying, false-hearted slut," Maggie hissed. "Who made the first move?"

"Now, honey, don't get into a snit."

"Snit? I'll show you a snit! I'm livid! You hypocritical bitch!" She banged the window shutters closed so their voices could not be heard below.

"My God, little miss ray of sunshine shows she has a darker side. You are in a most disagreeable lather."

Maggie fought off an impulse to strike her, kick her, throw her damned stinking ashtray at her. But all her strength suddenly went; she felt sick to her stomach and slumped against the wall. "Damn you. You're the one who kept saying, 'Watch yourself.'"

Glo took her time to answer, stuffing her wet clothes into a bag, picking up a bath towel. "Because I don't think you can handle it. I can."

"You were protecting my innocent heart — what sheer *bullshit*."

Glo spoke defiantly. "Damn right I was thinking about you. Nothing else was going to wake you up."

"Where did you screw him? On that sandbar by the river?"

Glo raised her arms, as if in surrender. "Oh, Christ, I don't know what came over me; maybe I've gone stir crazy. Penned up here for six weeks, even Zorro was starting to look good." She wrapped the towel around her. "I have to get my head together about it. Let's talk later. I'm going down for a shower."

Maggie followed her into the hallway. "You're nothing but a cheap whore and you always were." Glo didn't respond, and Maggie kicked at the doorjamb, sprinted to her own room, and dove onto her bed.

— 4 —

Maggie was unable to sleep that night, or most of the next day, dozing only in fits and starts, jolting awake in confusion, then sitting up and staring blankly outside into the sadness of the rain. Yet another night and day passed like that, the clouds grunting their displeasure, Maggie rarely leaving her room, hugging the window bars, her hair dripping from windblown rain, drops rolling down her nose.

Cutest upturned nose this side of Dixie, Glo had told her. *Maggie, y'all are looking more fetching by the day, so tanned and lithe.* Glo had ridiculed the notion that Maggie lacked physical appeal, insisted she must grow more confident with men. *You're gorgeous, honey.*

She developed a fever, and Tayra tended to her with soups and herb concoctions, not raising embarrassing subjects, maintaining a pretence that Maggie had the grippe.

Benito was her only other visitor. "I am telling you, when two people do not look at each other they are in league. Halcón and his lover, they are scheming to take everything. For a writer, you do not observe well what is going on." Clairvoyant Benito had been right: *How can you be sure she is your friend?*

During trips to the bathroom, she would see her fellow inmates of the Darkside staring and whispering. Maggie was not alone in heartbreak; Buho seemed gripped by a powerful depression, his lanky figure huddled over his guitar, an image from Picasso.

The rain finally relented on the third day of her torpor, and by early evening the clouds were dispersing. Her fever had relented and she was even feeling a little sadness lift with the clouds – and then spotted Glo and Halcón slipping off together: walking toward the rear of the house so that they might creep unseen down the river trail.

Maggie lay down and stared at the orange wall. When she next looked out, forty minutes later, they were on the patio, Glo whirling through her routines with elaborate nonchalance, Halcón ignoring her, playing solitaire.

As the clouds began to break apart, there came a brilliant rainbow, arcing over the distant hills from the rose-tinted sky: a scene of such unanticipated beauty that Maggie found herself smiling; it seemed corny, out of a bad movie. A slate-coloured robin trilled for vespers; a red squirrel scampered among the branches of an inflorescent mango tree. She strained to think positively: all beauty had not disappeared from the planet; her wounds were not mortal – she had been forced to come spinning back into the real world, saved from a humiliating emotional disaster.

Then, with a stabbing pain, came his mellifluous voice: *You are, to me, a woman not merely of outer beauty but of great inner beauty.* How smooth he was, how patronizing; his eyes had always been set on Glo. *We cannot allow this to happen. I have problems with my emociones.* Bright-eyed, self-deluded Maggie Poppins had dared to think she, not Glo, had caused such problems.

How could she possibly render this sickening true-life twist onto paper? *My Highly Embarrassing Story*, by Margaret Schneider: the gullible writer of romances, having surrendered her chance for freedom, has the rug pulled from under her by Ms. White Trash of Tuscaloosa. She envisioned people lining up for book signings with smirks on their faces; they had read the hilarious reviews. *I just loved the book, the way you let it all hang out.*

She should just do that, display her wounds for all to see.

This evening, I am unable to set down my thoughts in rational order. Events have occurred which I am almost incapable of describing. But if I am to be loyal to my readers, I must now admit to a most awkward plight: I am caught up in that state lamented by all those syrupy country songs. I am miserable in love.

Though the issue will no doubt be bruited about, I am not suffering Stockholm Syndrome, that quirky empathy captives feel for their masters. Surely only the weak succumb to such self-enslavement, currying to a protector for safety. What I feel is untainted by any instinct for self-preservation, though it is warped in its own way, misshaped by anger, by powerful feelings of betrayal.

Logic — never mind the stars — had destined what was unthinkable, unrealizable, to end in heartbreak. It was a love that should never have been, could never have been consummated. I have to swallow that, but it is a bitter tonic nonetheless, and I can only pray that the jolt of recent awareness will help repair mind and heart.

How damnably fickle is friendship . . .

Maggie stowed her notes as the door opened and Glo peeked in, grimacing. "*Upe*. Can I come in?"

"If you must."

Glo closed the door behind her, and lay back on Maggie's bed and shut her eyes. "Sorry."

"I'll survive." For a few minutes Maggie played with her pen, waiting for Glo to state her business, but finally broke the silence. "It's the callousness, the deceit, acting as though he didn't interest you in the least."

"At first he didn't, not at all. I thought he was a phony snob, a dilettante playing a game of Robin Hood. When he turned out to be a gambler by the name of Johnny Diego, it just hit me what a damn classy character he really was. What a hustle, what a brilliant play, conning the Popular Vanguard like yokels at a carnival."

"I suppose it's been going on for a while."

"We thought we were just teasing each other. I don't know what happened. That earthquake . . . Honey, the earth actually moved; it was too profound. I'm real sorry, baby. I didn't know how to break it to you." Another harsh silence fell between them. "I rationalized. I told myself I was saving you from the heartbreak he would cause you."

"I'm toying with putting it in the book. Or do you want me to hide your dirty laundry?"

"Spill it all. You know what? I don't care. You have to write the truth because that's the way you are: honest. You're a heap of work, honey. You're so damn guileless and generous and straight, so fucking good and loving, that I want to scream. What's with this broad, I ask myself. I, on the other hand, am *not* an honest woman – write that."

"Good, I want to."

"Go ahead, I'll take it as a favour – Chuck won't get to be president and I'll never have to be first lady. Can you see me serving tea in the White House to the Pro-life Ladies' Guild of Podunk, Oklahoma? Hobnobbing with bank presidents and slumlords at fundraisers?"

"Then that's what you deserve. I *don't* feel good or loving; I'm angry and I'm jealous. I had a chance to leave here; I didn't because I was worried about you, I cared for you."

"I truly am sorry, sweetheart."

"I'd like to be alone."

❧

Churning dreams scattered as Maggie was woken by an altered pitch in the night: an approaching sound, low and guttural. Sitting up, she saw headlights blinking through the trees: the white delivery van, Gordo at the steering wheel, alone.

Muffled voices came from below, then she heard the clank of keys and saw shadowy forms on the patio: Halcón's crew carrying bags to the truck.

Now she heard Halcón and Tayra conversing outside her door. She opened it, and was able to make out Tayra descending the stairs, Halcón clinking his keys. "It is time," he said.

"Why is it so dark?"

"I have cut the power. We are abandoning the Darkside for the Caribbean coast. Are you feeling well enough to travel?"

Maggie just shrugged.

Outside, Zorro was pumping air into mattresses with a foot pedal, then throwing them into the back of the truck. However tempted she was to ride off on one of those mattresses, she knew that if she remained in the pull of Halcón's gravity she would crash again.

"I will leave while you get dressed."

"Come in for a minute."

He hesitated, then entered.

"I won't be going with you, Halcón."

"I do not blame you for being angry at me."

"I'm more angry at myself." She sat on the edge of the bed.

"This is not how you planned to write it."

"Actually, I haven't got the ending figured out yet. This isn't fiction; I can't control reality. I can only hope for you, Halcón. I'll even pray for you – though I'm not that firm a believer."

She felt the bed shift as he sat at its end. "I believe. The universe is too strange and wonderful to have happened by accident. There must be meaning; otherwise there is nothing to hang on to, only anarchy. What am I carrying on about? Have I heard you right? Of course you must come."

"I will stay here, Halcón."

He sighed. "But you would not be alone; Benito Madrigal must also stay. He needs medical help. That cannot be denied."

"He isn't dangerous; we relate well. I'll look after him."

"My comrades would feel uneasy if we did not lock you inside. And there will be no electricity."

"We'll use candles. There's propane; there's plenty of food."

"I have run out of arguments. I have disappointed you deeply. I regret that with all my heart."

She stood and grasped a window bar, steadying herself, looking down on the play of light and shadow from the headlights of the truck.

"I wasn't hiding it very well, was I?" She could make his features out dimly and saw sadness.

"I am to blame; I did not discourage you. I found you most attractive – but for me, you were a lady, and I feared dishonouring you. As a modern woman, maybe you do not accept that, but . . . it's my old-fashioned attitude."

"Why is it so different with Glo?"

A helpless shrug. The answer seemed too obvious: Glo was street-smart, vivacious; she made a fit with him that school-teacherish Maggie Klutz could never match. "I'm twenty-nine, and you're the first man I've truly loved. I guess I waited too long, and it built up, then came crashing down on top of me."

"I am honoured. A few times I have felt the sting of love, and each time swore the tragedy would not be repeated."

"I used to be afraid of you, but I never disliked you. Glo did at first, though, and you shared the feeling. What happened?"

"God knows." He rose and came beside her, and they stood silently at the window. Gordo, still with a slight limp, was packing a submachine gun and several pistols in the cab, behind the front seat.

"In two or three days, I will send a message telling them where you are."

"I don't suppose you'll have to tie Glo up."

"She will come without protest."

"Protect her."

"With my life. There will be dangers ahead, and I admit to some relief that even as brave a spirit as yours will not have to risk them."

Maggie found herself smiling, however weakly: this honey-tongued rogue remained relentlessly charming to the end. "What is the plan now? Or do you dare tell me?"

"But I must. Of all persons, I trust you most closely, my prisoner but also my confidante. So I ask of you, when you have the ear of Slack Cardinal, give this message. Tell him Limón, Sloth Park, at nine o'clock on the night of this coming Saturday. Tell no one else."

"I promise." She was right to assume that she would remain his friendly conspirator: she had lost her heart to him. She again wanted to tell him: do not trust Slack Cardinal. But let his paramour deliver that warning.

Outside, the truck engine had started.

"What's going to happen, Halcón?"

"I am no longer sure. My thoughts are confused by . . . well, it is better left unsaid. *Hasta la vista*, Maggie. Now we must begin a long journey. We will find our way to heaven or to hell as God wishes." He took her hand, kissed her fingertips, released it. "Ciao."

"*Buena suerte*," she said.

She listened to his footfalls on the stairs, then heard the front door being locked. She saw two shadowy figures walk toward the van, talking, smoking; she heard Glo's throaty laugh. She felt devitalized, drained of feeling.

THE LOST MISSION OF HARRY WILDER

— I —

Dear Rocky,

Here's some more mash for the pulp mills. I have written out the health freak, substituted a new sidekick, and introduced Harry to an acid head, a black-moustached Snidely Whiplash, and the author of *When Love Triumphs*, *No Time for Sorrow*, *Return to the House of Heartbreak*, and *The Torrid Zone*, as her masterwork was titled before she entered into the uncertain world of non-fiction.

She wasn't what Harry expected. Her defiant expression was burned into memory when the camera flashed in the night, when he looked into her eyes. He saw something in them too vital to be the dull glow of Stockholm Syndrome – the woman was madly in love with the putative villain of this piece. This is a form of literary irony, Rocky, in case you didn't get it.

Operationally, Harry is in so tight with the bad guys he barely has room to fart. Things continue to go too well for his comfort; he keeps wondering how he's going to blow it. He isn't sure where this plot is going to take him, but he suspects he is to be thrown to the wolves again; he isn't going to get the money, he isn't going to get the girl, he's going to get it up the ass in the end. I have had a ghastly premonition that you are going to have it your way; there will be blood, Harry's blood, a lovely flow of it. If I don't come up with an ending, you'll know the blood was mine.

Cheers,

Harry

P.S. I don't know why the red herring insists on smelling like overripe cheese. Maybe Zork *does* have a secret army.

≈

Slack showered the sea salt from his body, not a bad day, two tours in the morning, another just finished. Twelve days had passed since his visit to the Darkside, and he was sliding back into familiar routines, but this evening he was feeling the nervous edge of anticipation: the ransom monies had finally been put together, Elmer Jericho would be making contact tonight – by phone to Bar Balboa. He wasn't sure the proprietor would be there, he'd seen Billy in town, lit up like neon, one of his all-day drunkaramas.

His own lines were tapped, so he'd given Elmer the number at the bar and a time, eight o'clock, two hours from now. He hoped Elmer had got that straight, he'd been almost comatose during the drive back to the hidden *moto*. Slack had to take over the wheel while Elmer and Gordo slept.

Physically, he was in reasonable shape, he hadn't been beaten up for a few weeks, his ribs no longer felt as if they had been roughly welded together. Only one snag had marred his return to Quepos – the discovery that Joe Borbón was cuddling in a bedroom with Camacho's kid sister, an inviting young woman who had invited her uncle and cousin over to sort through Slack's belongings. He had walked in just as they were grubbing among his CDs.

He'd fired Borbón on the spot, which is why Slack was now doing all the tours – a hassle, he'd had to hire a local layabout for some of the driving chores. Ham, too, had been disappointed in Borbón: the pursuit of love softens you, that's how stone killers lose their edge.

Frank Sierra was Slack's new henchman, they'd met clandestinely several times, trading suspicions, speculations – they shared something deeply felt: a brooding distrust of their overseers. Slack had straight-faced lied to Ham, telling him he hadn't a clue where he'd been taken, a campesino farm in the boondocks.

Senator Walker had looked shocked when presented with the photo of his wife hamming it up on Slack's lap, and nearly popped a collar button when Slack dumped the full refund on a table. Ham Bakerfield suffered one of his rare losses of composure, sputtering, "Never seen anything like this. Never. Who does this guy think he is?"

Johnny Falcon. What style, give this man the gold medal for chutzpah.

Everyone had been amazed at how deep Slack had penetrated. Walker, his faith in the master spy oiled and greased, had been spurred to come up with four million. Halcón would be happy with that until he was collared about ten minutes later.

He pulled on cut-offs and went out to the balcony to take a piss in the general direction of the squatters' village. The big shudder a few days ago had collapsed some shacks, but they were going up again. Foundations for the church were being poured. You got a church, ipso, you got a town – Slack was feeling the fight go out of him, resigned to it, world over-population had arrived at his front door.

A tourist microbus was parked outside Billy's restaurant, and Slack could hear noises of confrontation from within. About a dozen men and women were crowding the bar, giving Billy a bad time, the Chattanooga Kinsmen Club, according to their badges.

"Go away," Billy shouted. "We are closed." He seemed barely able to stand, eyes glazed over, smelling like a fermentation plant.

"Look here now, we *reserved*. We have drink vouchers."

"Maybe tomorrow we open."

"We would like to speak to the owner of this establishment," said an amply endowed woman, a Kinette, Slack thought that's what they were called.

"He's not here, lady."

"We made reservations with a Mr. Balboa," said the tropical shirt. "Is that you?"

"No, it's some other guy."

His chef and headwaiter were conversing at a table, unsure what to do. The waitress, a young woman with an insatiable addiction to inane chatter on the telephone, was tying up the line. "Okay, back to work," Slack told them. The cook butted a cigarette and returned to the kitchen.

He helped Billy onto a cot in the back room, then promised the rebellious customers an extra round on the house. The Kinsmen, happy to see a white guy take charge, took their coladas and margaritas off to the balcony and began taking photos of the sunset, which was turning out to be a non-event, a cloudless sky, earth's life-sustaining star plopping onto the horizon like a ripe tomato.

Elmer might be trying to get through, Slack hollered at the phone junkie, interrupting her breathless account of her second cousin's unexpected pregnancy. When she didn't hang up immediately, he drew a finger across his throat.

He checked the reservation list, all seven tables booked on a Tuesday night. Two names stood out, Woodrow and Beverley Schneider, Maggie's parents. He was supposed to instruct them to mend their marriage, but he'd been forbidden to approach them. "They're out of the loop," Ham had said.

Four old toughs came in, tried to claim the best table. Slack apologized, it was reserved, and settled them elsewhere. These were new faces, older and beefier than most of the bulls around here, but lawmen of some kind, you could always tell, the swagger, the shifting flickering eyes, the presumption of authority. Maybe this was a SWAT squad, they had that look about them, maybe marksmen.

The bar stools began to fill, a few locals, some media types, one of them Ed Creeley, the AP reporter who'd been on location at Eco-Rico, they shared a distaste for Senator Walker.

"Double Black, straight up. I think he's going all the way, Cardinal."

"God help us."

"He's got a lock on New Hampshire, sending organizers streaming into Florida and Alabama. Huge in Texas and the sun belt. All he needs is for those loonies to rape his old lady, something like that, he'll ride in on a tsunami of sympathy. He's even better off if they snuff her." He lowered his voice. "Nobody's got the guts to publish this, but there's been a grand jury leak out of Nevada, word is she used to hang with parties of dubious reputation, washed their money at the tables."

When Woodrow and Beverley Schneider entered, Slack ushered them to the table he'd saved for them, a view across Manuel Antonio bay, lights flickering in the distance, the stars switching on at the last glimmer of sunset. He held Beverley's chair, lit a candle, introduced himself.

"You're the Bolshevist," Beverley said, she had seen him on the TV. She was wider and shorter than her daughter, attractive if she weren't scowling. She quickly butted her cigarette and rose. "We're leaving."

"Now, Bev, don't get riled up." Woodrow was a tall drink of water, all loose bones, the less aggressive of the two, obviously. Maggie inherited her spunk from her mom.

"He's a damn communist."

This was getting off to a bad start. "I'm totally on your side, Mrs. Schneider. Nobody understands my sense of humour. Really, it started off as a joke, I guess I'm the only one who gets it."

"Well, if that's the case, you cut off your nose despite your face," Beverley said.

Slack continued apologizing, fulsome in his praise for their daughter, he really admired her, if there was a Nobel Prize for heroism she'd get it. Somewhat mollified, Beverley reclaimed her seat. Slack told them to order whatever pleased them most, dinner was on him, it was the least he could do.

He dared not hint that Halcón had reeled her in, that she was wiggling on his hook. Not naïveté but bold innocence, that was the crime of this seeker of romance from the wheat fields of Saskatchewan. A rare specimen, a caring person, worried about her parents, loyal to her buddy.

"Table number four," he told the waitress, "bring them champagne, everything's on my tab."

Ed Creeley was well into his cups, building up his own hefty tab buying drinks for media pals. He was still going on about Chuck

Walker, railing about his war against the godless Marxists of Nicaragua, about the Contras he'd trained in the violent arts.

Half those fuckers are street muggers and bank robbers now. And after you take off the uniform and the silver eagle, Chuck's just another pissass drug dealer. How do you think he financed merce- naries if it wasn't dope? Remember the epidemic in the eighties? The streets of L.A. were paved with the crack cocaine his boys flew in." The congressional witch-hunt, the senator liked to call it, had been about allegations he and his boys had helped the Contras run the pipeline from Colombia.

"Speak of the devil," Creeley said. The senator himself had just come in, flanked by two Secret Service agents and trailed by Orvil Schumenbacker, his campaign manager, and Clay Boyer, official gas attendant, in charge of pumping out the press releases. Walker looked puzzled at seeing Slack behind the bar. More agents came in, fanning out.

As Walker pressed flesh with some American tourists, Schumenbacker bellied up to the bar, smiling and fat, you couldn't tell where his chin left off and his jowls began. "Heard there's some great food happening here. Table for three."

"Sorry, they're all reserved."

Schumenbacker chuckled. "I guess you don't recognize that gentleman over there." Walker was now laughing with the four grizzled bruisers, there was some backslapping going on, a scene of camaraderie.

"I don't care if he's the king of Siam, we're booked."

"Maybe you can ask this fine fellow." He gave Creeley a punch on the shoulder. "Ed, haven't seen you since we got invaded by the body snatchers. Great story, you get my note?"

"Hey, Orvil," Creeley said, "you're looking kind of white. Just crawl out from under something?"

Schumenbacker's smile didn't dim. "Northern tan, Ed, northern tan. Be the first to know, Senator Greer's coming on board with most of Kansas. Listen, why don't you tell this gentleman who his special guest is?"

"Why don't you tell us if Gloria-May Walker used to run errands for Vinnie the Monk DiLucchi?"

Schumenbacker finally lost his smile, his lips puckering like they'd sucked on a lemon. Walker wasn't paying attention, he was still with those four gorillas, Slack guessed the hidden war, the so-called military advisers to the Contras, they called them Walker's Rangers. Was he putting together his own team?

Now Walker was coming over to glad-hand some of the reporters, but his progress was halted by Schumenbacker. A quick briefing, and Chuck frowned, then went red and taut, and suddenly he was in Ed Creeley's face.

"You print any shit like that I'll kick your fucking ass from here to Honolulu."

"Senator, let's go." Schumenbacker had him by the arm, pulling it, agents went on ready alert. The colonel's aides made a try at recovering their good humour, a brave effort at laughter, Boyer telling the reporters it's been a strain for Walker, how can you blame the guy.

Slack was called away to the phone. He listened to coins drop as he watched the senator's party leave with an offering of shrugs and smiles, the room now buzzing with conversation.

It was Elmer. "Hey, man. *Qué tal?*"

"*Pura vida.*"

"You cool?"

"I'm cool, what's up?"

"You settle up with the, ah, trust fund yet?"

"They'll give us four."

"Out of sight."

A reporter was tugging at him, another waiting, both wanting the phone, anxious to file the Walker temper tantrum item. Slack cupped his mouth into the receiver. "Let's not fart around. Let's do it."

"Friday night okay?"

Three days from now. "Darkside?"

"Yeah, you remember how to get there."

"Yep. You got my home number?"

"Hey, man, you said not to use it."

"Disguise your voice. Just say, 'Friday, usual place, usual time.'"

"Got it, that's just to confuse —"

Slack cut him off. "*Hasta luego.*"

— 2 —

The Swedes just ahead of Slack claimed to have had some river experience, but they were constantly in trouble. He had a full complement today, mostly Scandinavians, a couple of Yanks, an Australian. They were two to a duckee, the inflatables. Slack was in a hardshell, their sheep-dog, trying to keep them moving.

He churned back to the Swedes, they were hung up on a rock. "Back right!" he shouted. "Back paddle!" He came alongside and tugged, and their inflatable finally swung about, then shot the three-foot drop. The other duckees, waiting at an eddy, started to move downstream again.

He'd done a gentler tour yesterday, a paddle around the pretty beaches tucked behind Punta Quepos. That was for a private party of two, the Schneiders, who'd seemed puzzled at the attention paid them. Slack found out they were sharing if not a bed at least a hotel room, that was a good sign. Much of their conversation was about Maggie, of course, and he had to bite his tongue to avoid telling them he had met her, that she was well, was thinking of them.

Maggie, it turned out, lived in a suite overlooking the Saskatchewan River. Skating, bicycling, birding, an outdoors person, unattached. Beverley's flow of words and imagery seemed inexhaustible. "She's too choosy, she's going to miss the boat if she waits until the cows come home for Mr. Right to gallop up the road."

Slack had read Maggie's novels, Mr. Right didn't gallop, he wasn't a cowboy, he was a clean-cut academic, cultivated, slightly mocking in manner, a virtuoso in bed. Slack had none of these faults.

He had to rescue the Australian, he'd spilled when his duckee took the wrong channel, a narrow sluice between two boulders.

"Feet first, on your back!" he shouted as the man began to flail, the current carrying him, Slack pursuing, finally hoisting him aboard his boat. Thankfully, this was the end of the white water, all class one from here.

Tomorrow, in the morning, a copter would take him to San José, a final briefing at the resort where Walker's entourage was staying. "Friday, usual place, usual time" – that's what Ham's tappers heard on the line. Everyone was convinced Elmer meant the Escazú Hills at dusk.

The river widened as it took a broad turn where a crescent of sand had been deposited, Slack's staging area near the road. He shepherded his clients to shore. "Watch for the sand fleas, they bite like crazy. Stay out of the grass, there's chiggers here, too, they lay eggs under your skin."

Slack could see Frank Sierra sitting in his rented Suzuki four-wheel, reading a book. Slack catered to his customers, laying out sandwiches and beer and soft drinks, then joined him. He could tell Frank had something, he looked too pleased with himself, twirling an end of his moustache.

"The property in question," he said, "extends from the Naranjo River into the mountains across the road, comprising eighty hectares. It was purchased four years ago as raw land for a hundred thousand dollars by one Abner Krock, who built the house. He is shown in government records also to have an address in Denver. His current address, however, and for the next twenty years, is San Quentin, California."

Slack watched his kayakers slather on the bug repellent. "Drugs, I'll bet."

"Precisely. He was among three Americans, two Colombians, and a Puerto Rican who were arrested on an airstrip at a cattle ranch not far from here. The cargo of three hundred pounds of cocaine was destined for America, and this was a U.S. Drug Enforcement sting. All were extradited but one, a man who said he was present at the scene merely by happenstance."

"Jericho."

Frank nodded. "I thought it odd that although the others also claimed to be innocent bystanders, he alone escaped justice. One is prompted to surmise that some quiet intervention was undertaken."

"In words of one syllable, Frank."

"Friends in high places."

"Maybe he just did a deal, rolled over for them."

"He incriminated nobody. Any deal, perhaps, was for future favours."

"Why wasn't all this in Jericho's file?"

Frank raised a speculative eyebrow. "The same friends in high places? It is indeed odd. The agent who did the initial check on Mr. Jericho felt constrained not to talk to me."

"That's bullshit – who gave that order?"

"He preferred not to say."

Frank wasn't in the loop. Slack wasn't in the loop. Whose loop was it, anyway? Whose neck?

— 3 —

From the balconies of the senator's adjoining suites at the Cariari Hotel, Slack could see the volcanic range that guarded the Central Valley, the foothills bare and brown. The golf course, though, was green, a sprinkler system. Walker was about to tackle it, he was practising on the carpet with a putter and a plastic cup. Ham and his tactical team were here, too, counting money, stuffing thick wads of U.S. hundreds into two duffle bags.

"You'll be armed, I take it," Walker said.

"No guns." Slack had retrieved his Smith .38 but given it to Frank.

Walker missed a putt, gave him an exasperated look. "You're just going to walk in there with our four million dollars and no protection?"

"I don't want to see anyone with hardware. I'm going to give them the dough, I'm going to grab the women, and I'm getting out of there, then you guys ask them, nicely, please, to surrender."

"I can't see it being that easy." Walker gruffly threw his putter into his golf bag. "I recall these characters as being somewhat gun-happy."

Slack had let the senator down. "Where am I going to hide a piece? They did a good job feeling me up last time."

"We'll have a tag team behind him this time, senator," Ham said. "And he'll also have the little beeper."

Slack had been confused when they asked him if he was circumcised, now he wished he had been. An indelicate hiding place, but his objections had been overruled, the tiny capsule with the transmitter would be taped to his glans, his foreskin rolled over it.

"Think you can avoid getting a bone on?" Ham asked.

Slack didn't think he would have that problem.

From the balcony, Slack watched Walker tee off, good form, a long, looping slice but still on the fairway. His companions took their turns, Schumenbacker, a couple of agents, plus the gorillas who were at Bar Balboa the other night.

Slack called Ham away from his tactical team. "Those four aren't campaign workers."

Ham squinted through his dense cigar fog. "The senator said he was bringing in some extra help. I told him we don't need it, we don't want it."

"I think you better start thinking of putting a lid on the senator from the great state of Nicaragua."

"He's been warned."

"I'd like to see those guys picked up and held."

"You tell me what law they're breaking."

"Those are some mean mother-fuckers, Ham. They kill innocent people." Including journalists, Chuck's Rangers had engineered a bombing near the Costa Rica border, a political assassination gone awry. "Chuck doesn't trust me to waste the bad guys, so he's signed up psychopaths to do the job. You getting the picture, Ham?"

"I'm directing the fucking movie. On a warrant from the U.S. president. Walker ain't calling any shots."

Slack would just have to watch his back and do things differently. Plan A was to follow Bakerfield's book. Plan B allowed personal initiative. "What about the Ticos?"

Minister Castillo had gone on air, outing Johnny Diego, despite Ham Bakerfield's roundly stated objections. Now Castillo was licking his wounds, the White House had phoned the Costa Rica president, told him to butt out or they'd buy no more bananas.

"They'll get briefed when it's over. One of the networks has been greasing Castillo's people for advance tips, they're liable to have the press swarming around us like fish flies. Your fan, the poetry lover, he's not gonna know. Okay?"

"Sure." Slack tried to look grave and innocent.

"A dozen people know, and they're all in this room."

Slack slouched onto a couch beside a member of the pursuit team, a young woman in bike leather, a Harley jacket, a cocky smirk.

"Listen up," Ham said. "We're presuming an identical pattern to the last time. Slack meets them at that lookout point, leaves his motorcycle there, goes off in their van. Meantime, we've done a copter drop, Pedersen and Szabo are hiding in the bush there, watching. They get on the radio, tell us what route the targets are taking. There are only five exits from those back roads onto the highways. We'll have those points covered, it'll be dark by then. We have five pursuit vehicles, two will overtake the truck, riding point, three stay behind, and I don't want them seeing the same headlights in the rear view all the time."

"You forgot me." The woman beside Slack, lounging back, cowboy boots on the coffee table.

"Slack, I want you to meet Agent Kitty Conroy, twice women's dirt bike champion in . . . where?"

"Kentucky."

Slack eyed her carefully. "A pleasure."

"Same."

"Let's return to go," Ham said. "Kitty follows Slack out of town. She keeps him in view until she gets to that dinky Kimby Chicken store up there, then calls into control."

"Why do we need her?" Slack said. "You know where I'm going."

"You're carrying four million fucking dollars, that's why."

The ransom money was on the bed, in two duffle bags to be strapped to Slack's *moto*. He'd checked the bills, they weren't the products of a high-end colour copier, he'd felt them for the familiar crackle of cotton-linen fibre, examined the security threads and watermarks, the details of engraving, randomness of serial numbers.

"Okay, let's talk about site control," Ham said. "We need to check out any escape routes so we can seal off the area."

Slack wondered if he had the skills to shake off the Kentucky dirt bike champion, to enact Plan B, his own precarious plot to effect a rescue unaided by the U.S. State Department. The ominous presence of Walker's Rangers had firmed up his resolve.

He would just damn well pay Halcón off, it was money well spent, wasted otherwise on the Keep Chuck Running fund. Then he'd ride out of there on his *moto* with Glo behind him and Maggie in front, and call Ham from the nearest pay phone, giving Halcón maybe half an hour.

Op Libertad could lump it. He'd been hired to save those women, that was the deal, nothing in the small print about doing it cheap.

❧

At five o'clock, as the sun was nestling into the southern cordillera, Slack was on the *autopista*, weaving through heavy traffic backed up behind a stalled bus, normal San José rush hour on a Friday. The duffle bags were bulky, it was a task to squeeze between the vehicles, but he was making headway. So was Kitty Conroy, fifty yards behind him on a stripped-down racing bike.

They'd had a friendly chat, bike talk, Slack used to ride a big hog in the old days. He'd professed to know only one route to Escazú, through the heart of San José. He had an edge, he knew the city, its busy sections, its maze of one-way streets. There were no dirt bike trails in San José.

"Let's see how good you are," he'd said. She'd answered, "Give it your best shot."

He took to the shoulder, found his way blocked by a bus, wiggled around it, bolted ahead of a grunting van, no problem for Kitty Conroy, slipping right through the tight fit. Now, Sabana Park was stretching off to the right, the Nissan dealership, the art gallery. Traffic was snarled the whole length of Paseo Colón, the wide east–west thoroughfare.

Slack sought an opening, then darted left, an illegal turn onto a wrong-way *calle*, cars braking, horns blaring. Alarmed pedestrians cleared the sidewalk for him, and he made it to the next corner. For an exultant several seconds, he was sure he'd got rid of Kitty, but he turned to see her behind him, frozen on his tail, hunched over her handlebars, determined. He waved.

She kept up with him past the Coca-Cola Station, and almost up to the Central Market, but that's where he saw his chance, a light was about to turn red. The traditional practice here was to run the change of lights at every opportunity, but Slack braked, came almost to a halt as it went to red. Then he kicked down and went full throttle.

It was like trying to squeak between jaws about to snap shut, crocodile teeth in the form of three cars, a vegetable truck, a bus, and a red taxi with tassels on its windows whose white-faced driver swerved to miss him, his brakes screaming. Slack, his heart pounding, listened for a mighty crunch of fenders as he accelerated past the crosswalk. None came, and when he glanced behind, he saw traffic was again zooming along the *avenida*. No Kitty Conroy.

After several minutes of zigzagging up and down the irregular checkerboard of the northern barrios, he was satisfied Kitty was history. Stage two of Plan B: Dump the beeper before they had a chance to triangulate. He pulled over for a moment by the old Atlantic railway station, unzipped his fly and reached in, disregarding the offended expressions of two women waiting for a bus. Swinging back into the traffic, he tossed the little bug under the wheels of a passing dump truck. It hadn't been taped securely enough to his dink, he'd explain, must have fallen down a pant leg.

He pulled over to a pay phone, and dialled the number Frank

Sierra had given him, a secure line in Quepos. Slack's main man had maps, he had instructions. All Slack said was, "Plan B."

"*Claro*," Frank said.

The sky was turning a burnished copper as he returned to the road, south to Desamparados, to the old highway to Puriscal, to Quepos, to the Darkside of the Moon.

THE FULL GUACO

— I —

From the window by my hammock, I watch a convoy of egrets, white and silent as angels, in undulating flight through mists golden with the glow of evening. The peace of twilight is broken by Blue-Crowned Parrots settling among the coral blooms of a cassia tree, squabbling for roosts. A Laughing Falcon calls, taunting the prisoner of the Darkside.

Five days have passed since Halcón bowed out of my life with a kiss and a ciao, leaving me feeling emptied, as dry as bleached bones on an alkali lake. He still casts dark shadows; he clouds my view even of these egrets whispering through the sky; beauty is obscured.

I find it hard to conceive that I cracked so completely when the truth came home to me, that I am capable of such frenzied madness. My quest has borne bitter fruit. I have learned that love, too, has a dark side. I have learned too much about love, its wounding truth . . .

Maggie lay her pad down and sagged back into her hammock, feeling lonely, defeated, and anxious. Wait two or three days, Halcón had said, then he would alert rescuers. But five days had passed without contact from them, and she was undergoing episodes of ill forbidding. Had Halcón decided not to tell where he had hidden Maggie and her ever-complaining housemate?

Halcón has no morals, Benito Madrigal would shout; he's a thief; the two of them had been left to rot here. She tried soothing him with reason: they were not about to starve; canned and dried food was in sufficient supply, as was water, gravity-fed from the river. Of course Halcón would make that anonymous phone call; rescue would probably come tonight – tomorrow at the latest. But then she remembered how he had lied to her: his doubtless fanciful sagas of heroism, his unlikely tale of childhood trauma, entertainments for a writer.

She watched Benito prowl about, grumbling. He had been searching for a pry bar, something to wrench the grillwork apart or bend up a corner of the metal roof, but the commando had left them only kitchen tools. He had even tried burning the front door, but it was of a thick, dense wood that resisted flame.

"This is a betrayal of all we have fought for. They are not comrades, but pirates. The swine, they have left us here to die." Now he was trying to pick at the front door lock with the bent twines of a dessert fork.

"No one's going to die. Take one of your pills."

"No, my brain must be sharp. They will come with *asesinos*. That is how we are going to die."

Such talk disturbed Maggie because she almost believed that Benito was, as he put it, cursed with a mystical third eye. With some misgivings, she had agreed to move into Glo's former bedroom; Benito had requested the front-facing room so he could see the invaders coming.

"*Madre de Dios.*" That remark was directed at the fork; one of the twines had broken off and jammed in the keyhole.

Daylight was fading and Maggie's bed beckoning; there seemed no point in staying up and wasting candles, and she was tired. She had been tossing restlessly at night.

Benito was now searching the closet, which had been left unlocked, his hands probing the high shelves where the guns had been stored. "There is only one man who can save us, the big gringo, Jacques. But he has been betrayed, too."

"Why do you say that?"

"They think he is *estúpido*, that they can use him like a pawn."

Did she dare pass on Halcón's message without being satisfied Slack could be trusted? Limón, Sloth Park, nine o'clock, Saturday night: that was tomorrow, and time was running out.

"Caramba!" Benito was shaking with excitement. "They have left this behind!"

He had reached high into the back of the top shelf and pulled out a long weapon wrapped in the burlap sacking of an old rice bag; he peeled the covering away and triumphantly drew out a submachine gun.

"This is a gift from the hand of fate. Before, we were defenceless targets. Now we are an armed force."

"Is that thing loaded? Let me have it."

He held the weapon away from her, retreating toward the stairs, clutching the gun like a baby. That weapon had a clip in it, doubtless with live ammunition; Benito was not of right mind, and the implications were frightful. She could only assume that Gordo, charged with retrieving the guns, had been too lazy to have compiled a checklist of firearms and too short to see to the back of the top shelf.

"Where are you going with that?" She followed him up the stairs.

"I know what I am doing. My life will cost them dearly."

"Benito! No one's trying to hurt you!"

"We are no longer lambs for their slaughter. It will be a famous last stand. Future generations will build a monument here to honour those who held high the banner of freedom."

He slammed the bedroom door and his shouts faded. She tried to open it, but he had turned the deadbolt. She called to him, entreated him, but was answered only with ravings: Senator Walker wants to take over the world from his secret army base; to do so, he must eliminate Benito Madrigal. "Because I am the only one who knows their plan."

"Benito, we can use the gun to shoot out the locks on the door."

"Are you crazy?" he called back. "That would warn them. Also, we must make every bullet count."

In the gloom of falling night, she entered the back bedroom and locked herself in; she would wait out the night and pray that the rescue team would react cautiously. She crawled under the mosquito netting, and wiggled out of her shorts. It was only six o'clock, but she planned to rise early, before Benito, make coffee for him, grind up several of his pills with the beans, and secure that submachine gun.

Clouds had gathered, promising a sticky overcast night. From the wall of forest outside her window came the call of the Laughing Falcon, increasing in cadence, the full *guaco*.

❧

She awoke to the sound of feet crunching on dead leaves, and she held her breath. Then she heard a twig snap and a voice, hoarse and low: "Johnny, you there?"

The glowing dial of her watch read twelve minutes to ten. Benito must have fallen asleep; she prayed he was sufficiently exhausted to remain in that state. She rose quietly and tiptoed to the window.

"Hey, man, *qué pasa*? Where the fuck is everyone?"

She could make out Elmer Jericho now, smell his cigarette; he was shining a flashlight into the house. Why was he expecting Halcón to be in the house? Extending the courtesy of announcing herself seemed fraught with risk.

The only sounds now from Elmer were grunts of displeasure as he continued to circle the house, looking through every downstairs window. She ducked as the flashlight beam curled toward the second floor, and when she next looked out he had vanished.

She hoped he would leave when he was satisfied the house was deserted, and she strained to listen for an engine starting. But she hadn't heard his vehicle arrive; its sounds might not carry well to this side of the house. She could hear only the deep drumming of the river, punctuated by the chirp of crickets. Then came the song of the pootoo: *Woe-woe-woe-woe.*

— 2 —

After descending from the cordillera, Slack held to the back roads of the coastal plain, between the perfect checkerboard rows of African palms, trees like soldiers at attention, nature in fascist uniform. He bypassed the large towns, Parrita and Quepos, though he couldn't avoid smaller communities, townsfolk staring at him, a hulking gringo on a *moto* with two great sacks.

He guessed Ham Bakerfield was going off like a nuclear bomb right about now, the fuckup was at it again. I don't remember you doing a thing right, he'd said. The tradition continues. He had contracted to make his "best efforts" to secure the release of the two aforesaid female persons. These *were* his best efforts. There was even a clause that permitted him, upon request by the party of the first part, to pay to the kidnappers such sums as may be agreed upon.

But they would probably discover he had committed an illegal act, a paper crime hidden in the small print. The agency had its ways, maybe they'd just send Joe Borbón.

Here was the bridge at Paso Indios, a creaky structure formerly used by trains hauling bananas: metal trusses, the Río Naranjo below. Once over the bridge, he turned off the road to a parking area by a low riverbank. That's where he found Frank Sierra's Suzuki, hidden from the road, too close to the bridge to be seen from cars crossing overhead.

Frank was sitting on a rock with a fishing pole, playing out line. Slack checked his bucket, a couple of trout.

"I have had good luck. Let us hope it is contagious."

Frank was a true-blue guy, prepared to share the shit that was going to come down if this turned into Operation Fuckup. Slack wanted to hug him, Frank wasn't the kind of guy you hug, though.

"I'm going to suss out the situation before I bring them the cash. You brought my gun?"

"It is under the seat."

"Keep it handy, just in case."

Slack unbuckled and unclasped the bungee cords that held the duffle bags, then they heaved them into the little four-wheel.

Slack checked his watch – nearly half past eleven. "I'm about fifteen minutes away from the *finca*. I may return in the back seat of Jericho's Jeep with a gun to my head. That's okay, I won't blame them, hell, I'll tell them to shoot me if the dough isn't here. If both women accompany us, we give them the *plata*, we go our way, they go theirs."

He waited for a car to pass over the bridge, then straddled his motorcycle and accelerated up to the main road. One more village, the sleepy burg of Londres – a couple of stores, a couple of bars, a church and a cemetery. Not many people hanging about this late at night. Upriver from the village, the road became narrow and stony, a school, a scattering of homes, now some larger *fincas*. A lot of *extranjeros* like Elmer's pal, Abner Krock, had been moving into the area, they liked the isolation. Now Abner was in stir while Elmer was running free.

When the road took him close to the river, he saw the Naranjo flowing darkly between the trees – nearby was the starting point for his tours, though on a few occasions he'd ventured farther upstream on his own, testing his skills in narrow chutes and jets of raging water. The road switched back, barely a track now.

Somehow, ICE, the power company, had been persuaded to run a line up into this backcountry, and here, around a corner, was the last pole, beyond it a closed iron gate, the miniature Tower of Pisa looming behind it. As Slack cut his engine he smelled the sweet greasy odour of pot. Elmer Jericho ambled toward him from the shadows.

"Hey, man, always a thrill. You bring the scrip?"

"Stashed it, not far away. I want to see the women first."

"Yeah, well, you don't think we'd have them dames right here for you. Like, they're stashed, too, in a different place. Soon as I make a call, they're free as birds."

Slack felt not just dismay but an edge of irritability. "I think I'd better talk to someone who isn't totally lunched." He pushed the gate open and wheeled the bike behind the bodega, then started walking down the trail to the house, Elmer following, talking quickly.

"There's no one there. They split, man. The idea is, me and Johnny, we're letting the broads go as soon as we get on a plane. Like, we got a Piper Comanche waiting near the border. And then we're out of here." He had to hustle to match Slack's long strides. "You take your twenty pieces, give the rest to me, everyone's free, everyone's happy."

"I'm having a little trouble here, Elmer, this isn't the deal."

Elmer grabbed his arm, pulled him to a stop. "Look, man, you gonna show me the money?"

"No, Elmer, why would I do that?"

Elmer backed up a few paces, joint in one hand, a bulky object in the other. "Maybe because I've got a hog leg pointed at your belly button. You don't want your takeout, maybe I'll just grab it all."

Slack willed himself to relax, stay loose, remember your training, don't get your head jammed up. He spoke slowly and carefully. "You're not thinking straight, Elmer. Why would you want to kill me? You figure there's some point in that?"

Elmer didn't seem sure, time stretched as he pondered the logic. Slack thought he heard a noise from behind him, from the road, a vehicle, he thought, but likely just the wind in the trees.

"Where'd you hide the bread, man?"

"Not sure if I remember. I guess you *are* going to have to shoot me, Elmer."

Elmer took a moment to work through the implications. "We'll split it. Hey, man, you can fly out with me. Twin Comanche, man, it'll be there waiting for us, it's all arranged."

"Who's the pilot?"

"An amigo, a Panamanian, I'm connected." A pilot for Cocaine Air, Slack presumed. "Let's forget Johnny. He's a son of a bitch."

Slack was getting the picture now. "He kiss you out?"

A long pause, then Elmer took one last suck off his roach and flicked it. He began softly swearing.

"The slimy fuck. I should of figured, a lawyer, they do it to you every time."

"They're all gone?"

"Yeah, man."

"You check inside for a note?"

"Johnny took the keys."

"Know where they went?"

"Maybe."

Johnny Falcon had said something about backup locations, Elmer knew where they were. But this was more unwelcome news, Slack had slipped the posse only to stumble into a dead end. Halcón hadn't fully trusted his partner, he had reason.

"Let's check out the house. Maybe we can jack those bars apart. Put away the goddamn piece, Elmer. The money's safe, you'll get your share of it, maybe Johnny's, too, okay?"

Elmer lightened up at that suggestion, finally tucked the gun in his belt. He stuck out his hand, his grip a little clammy. "Partners, okay? Jeez, you're my bud, Slack, I'm sorry, I don't know what came over me."

Slack found that wanting in credibility, Elmer saw his main chance was to ally himself with the paymaster.

"It's the acid, man, maybe I shouldn't of done the acid."

"I hope you're joking."

"A little dot, hardly feeling it yet. It's when I get confused, I like to try a little purple passion, straightens out the head, gives a new perspective. Hey, man, I think everything's gonna be all right now. I kind of went off the edge there."

These fraught-filled ramblings continued until they entered the clearing, then Elmer started in on moons and planets and stars, about how everything was "whirling around in circles up there, man, expanding, collapsing. All that shit up there, it's from the big bang." Slack told him to shut up.

The big bang was bright tonight, a full canopy, and the light of a rising three-quarter moon had begun to slide through the trees, he could make out the darkened second storey of the house. Elmer's Jeep was parked under a lemon tree. Slack remembered he'd seen tools under the back seat, so he borrowed the flashlight, rummaged about, retrieved a sturdy jack and tire iron.

"You have some interest in this piece of land, Elmer? It's a nice spot."

"Tell you the truth, I scored it cheap off my buddy a few months ago, but it's like being held by him in trust so my name ain't attached.

I got his power of attorney. Eighty hectares, man, the whole mountain across the road."

Slack shone the light through the front window, no sign of life, no note. Dishes were stacked on shelves, the tile floor swept, everything organized and tidy. There was something charming about the building's general state of wonkiness, a neurotic could be comfortable here.

From somewhere, from the trees, maybe the house, came a sound like a cough or a clearing of throat. Maybe you hear things when you're on edge, or maybe someone was in the house.

"Give a shout upstairs, Elmer, I think I heard a sound."

Slack set out for the back of the house, where the ground was higher, easier to access the windows. Elmer banged on the front door. "*Upe.* Hey, man, anyone here?"

To Slack's amazement, that was greeted with a shout from above: "Yankee swine, go home!" Benito Madrigal was upstairs. Slack nearly fled his skin as Benito let off a deafening roar of automatic gunfire.

Now he was astonished to hear a different voice, not Elmer's: "Hit the dirt, men!" The yell came from out front, the area of the orchard.

Slack didn't wait to sort out what was happening, he dashed to safety, behind the back wall of the house, the jungle close by in case he had to bolt.

Benito was now singing the national anthem at the top of his lungs. He was armed with a chopper, that's what it sounded like. There came a loud voice over a bullhorn, English-accented Spanish: "Put your guns down. Everyone come out with their hands on their heads, and no one gets hurt."

That was the unmistakable no-nonsense voice of Colonel Chuck Walker. Through the wide, facing windows, he saw lights in the distance, from the area of the bodega and the road, one of them was a blue strobe. God knows how, but Walker and his Rangers had followed Slack here – but without telling Ham Bakerfield, who'd so confidently announced he was running this show.

Now he saw a figure speeding toward the trees to his right, a panicky mind-blown Elmer making a run for it, yelling, "I'm a friendly! I'm a friendly!"

The advisers were no doubt armed and antsy, Slack figured it wouldn't be a dazzling idea to lope across the clearing to talk to them. They were still a long way from the house, not taking any chances of exposing themselves. The situation augured disaster, someone was going to get killed, Benito the prime candidate.

He whirled the tire iron, and the jack caught tight between two vertical bars, they were half-inch steel, he had to use all his strength to twist. Sweating and grunting, he finally heard the ping of a broken weld.

"Johnny Diego," came Walker's amplified voice, "are you prepared to negotiate?"

Another burst of automatic fire from the second floor. "We will never surrender!" Benito began singing again: "Hail, oh gentle land, hail, oh mother of love."

The bars began to bend apart. Another weld gave. He rested, panting with the exertion. This was going to take a dangerously long time.

He held his breath – he wasn't sure, but he thought he saw something move within the house. He gripped the bars, peering in, trying to make out shapes in the darkness.

"Jacques?"

There, on the stairs, Maggie Schneider, brandishing a broomstick like a baseball bat. Long thin legs, wide eyes behind her lenses.

"Yeah, it's me, don't be scared," he said in a low, deliberate voice. "Get on the floor, I'm making an opening for you, it's going to take a minute."

She kneeled close to the window ledge, she wasn't wearing much, just a long T-shirt, flip-flops on her feet. She smelled of the soft essences of sleep. He stank, sweaty with his exertions.

"They're all gone. They left a gun behind, Benito found it."

The bullhorn again: "Let the women go free, we will not hurt you."

Slack massaged his aching arm, then started twisting at the jack again, telling himself to stay collected and vigilant, praying Madrigal's macabre standoff would buy him time.

"They took Glo. What's going *on*?"

"Some kind of shitstorm, everything has got gummixed up. Those guys are vigilantes, Walker's gone off half-cocked, I think he's trying to be a hero, and it's blowing up in his face, and when he figures that out, he may not want the story told by witnesses. I'm not taking chances with these characters, they used to run assassination schools."

Another ping, another burst of fire from above. "Send your tanks, send your airplanes! Here we will stand, here we will die!"

Slack wouldn't have time to deal with Benito, he had to focus on Maggie, lead her to safety. "Is there a trail out of here?"

"There's a path to the river."

A final twist, another inch wider. "Think you can get your head through that?"

She sat up, positioned her head against the gap. "Yes."

He released the jack. She took her glasses off, handed them to him, then poked her head through.

"All right, arms out next, and try to make your shoulders vertical." He took her under the armpits, began pulling her gently through the opening. "Thank God you're as skinny as a thief." That wasn't what he meant to say. "Slender. I mean you look good."

A spotlight lit the front of the house, but they remained in shadow, in tight embrace at the window. As her hips wedged in the hole, he tugged, and she popped through with a sound of ripping fabric, sprawling on top of him. She was shaking, and he held her for a moment.

"You okay?"

"A little scratched." She lifted her T-shirt and inspected her underpants, they had opened, exposing one reddened cheek. He tore his eyes from that gentle curve of rump and took her hand.

"Lead me to the river, Maggie."

A second spotlight, soon they'd have the whole area lit up like a casino. "Produce Mrs. Walker and Miss Schneider, we want to see them at the window. Repeat, no one will be harmed."

Hand in hand, crouching beneath the windowsills, they crept toward the far corner of the house. Now he could see, shadowed from the light by trees, a row of stone slabs that meandered down the hill.

Benito called out again. "All great history is written with the ink of blood. This, Señor Walker, is my answer to the lies of the ruling cliques." He fired off another round.

This time he was answered by a couple of shots from the fruit trees, they were followed by Walker's frantic bellow: "Who's that asshole? Cease firing! Clear the area, I want all the civilians back on the road."

Civilians? Who else was out there?

— 3 —

Though she was frantic, Maggie managed not to stumble upon the unevenly spaced steps as she led her protector to the river, finding her way in the patchy moonlight. He was holding her hand, firmly but not roughly, all the while muttering.

"How the hell did they follow me? This smells like fresh shit, not overripe cheese. Benito better run out of ammo before those clowns waste him. They find that *moto*, Walker's going to think I stole all the loot and I'm in cahoots with the guerrillas. He's into new warfare options – shoot first, questions later. We have to find a way out of here. What's with Benito – he didn't take his medicine?"

"He says it clouds his mind." His reasoning powers had been acute enough. *They will come with* asesinos.

They jumped off the last step and scrambled to the river's edge, then stood catching their breath. He retained her hand in his, which felt strong and callused.

"Have you been here before?"

"Yes, a couple of times. With Halcón."

"Is that right?" He seemed displeased, as if he had tuned into her feelings. When Slack sent a beam from his flashlight on an arc across the river, it settled on an inflated air mattress wedged between rocks. "What's that doing here?"

"I'm not sure." She assumed, however, that Halcón and Glo had fetched it from the house for their trysts here, on the soft sand, where he had spurned Maggie's clumsy advances. The memory seared.

Slack pulled the mattress out. "Hello. Reinforced vinyl – and we have rope." A length of it was looped through two holes at the corners. "You swim?"

"Perfectly well, but if you're thinking we're going to ride down that river on that . . ."

"It's what I'm thinking." He pulled a knife from his belt, prowled around the riverbank, slashed at low branches of a palm, and returned with two thick bracts. "Paddles," he said. He made a few knots in the rope, and passed her an end. "You hold that. You'll be on top of me, on my back, and I want you to hold on tight, both arms around my neck. It will be like a water slide – pretend you're in a fun park."

Maggie was hesitant about joining in this enterprise; they would be shooting rapids in the dark, without helmets or life jackets.

"You hold on to the flashlight. Keep your head up. Watch for any stray rocks. The tricky ones make rooster tails in the water." He pulled her gently into the chilly, fast-moving stream and offered his broad, muscled back. "I've been down this stretch a couple of times. It's not much of a river, it's not the Sarapiqui. Fast and narrow, though, class three bordering on four. Twenty minutes of that, then it's a doddle. Class five, I wouldn't risk at night. Six is your basic Niagara Falls."

The prospect of rushing headlong down this raging stream was turning her knees to jelly. But the alternative of staying was more perilous; she had to trust that the kayak man knew what he was doing; he had vast expertise.

"Never shot fast water at night before, though."

She blanched. More gunfire came, followed by Chuck Walker's distant muffled voice through the bullhorn, demanding surrender, and she also thought she heard him call out Slack's name.

"They must have found the Honda; they know I'm around and not going far fast. Let's get a wiggle on." Men were shouting now, closer to the house.

When she lay on top of him, he hooked her ankles with his feet. She extended the flashlight with one arm, wound the other around his neck, gluing her body to his, her face against his thick, sinewy neck. There was a husky smell to him, a scent of recklessness, but she was heartened by his seeming confidence.

"*Viva la revolución*," he said, and pushed off against a rock into deeper water.

And suddenly they were twisting down a swift cataract, turning sideways, glancing off a stone ledge, plummeting downriver again, into a four-foot drop that nearly flipped their flimsy craft. But it did not founder, and Slack, paddling ferociously, manoeuvred them into tamer water where the river was wide and shallow.

"That was not the ultimate experience," Slack said.

The current had slowed, the mattress bumping over submerged stones. Beneath her, Slack was resting, letting the river carry them. She continued to hug him tightly, chest to back, pelvis to buttocks.

"When we drop another few hundred feet, I'm in home waters."

"A few hundred *feet*?"

"Enjoy it while it lasts; this river will be a trickle in a few years after they divert it for hydro. You care about that sort of thing? Damming up the rivers, screwing around with nature?"

"Of course I care."

"You're a birder, that's what your mother told me. In ten years another fifty species will have vanished into avian history. Soon there'll just be crows and pigeons; the Buff-Breasted Blue Warbler will be a dimming memory. I read the draft chapters you left behind at the lodge; I like your style, but I prefer the original concept. I do a bit of writing myself, poetry, mostly."

The man was remarkably verbose, considering their circumstances – but perhaps he was just rambling to ease her tension. They were moving faster now, though the mattress insisted on drifting sideways.

"Let's avoid that crease over there; we want the main channel. Oh, by the way, your parents are in good health, keeping up their spirits. Oops, watch this stopper." They slipped to the side of a rock, then became wedged, but he pushed them free and they accelerated downriver. "They're sharing a hotel room and have been seen holding hands."

Maggie held her breath until they surged into an eddy and slowed. Slack's gladdening information, along with his aimless chatter and indifference to the hazards of the river, began to lessen her fears. "Did you have a talk with them as I asked?"

"I just let the tropical air spin its sultry magic." He squinted at some rapids below them. "It's been ten years since I was last up here, but I remember a vertical just ahead."

"What do you mean by a vertical?"

"A falls. There'll be a hole under it; we may encounter a bit of a reversal this time of year, with the water up."

"A reversal?"

"A backwash at the bottom that wants to suck you around in a circle, up and back. That's why I asked if you could swim. Only the keepers are dangerous."

"*Keepers?*"

"Yes, so grip me tight. Okay, we want to avoid that boil on the left; that's a submerged rock; we've got to hit the chute dead centre . . . Hang on!"

The banks of the river closed in on them, and as they sped through the narrowing channel all thoughts were blanked by the grinding thunder of the falls. Suddenly, they were somersaulting through the air, and she was flung away from him, her legs flailing wildly. She hit the water rear first and plummeted into the deep pool hollowed by the waterfall. She was swept to a sandy bottom, then carried to the surface, but the backwash pulled her under the falls and down again – this *was* the dreaded keeper. She gasped for air as she rose, before being sucked under a second time to begin another cycle.

But this time Slack's arm circled her waist. He tugged her through the powerful grip of the backwash, then kicked and vaulted her to the surface, close to a half-submerged ledge. She was shaking and gasping as he lifted her onto it and boosted himself beside her. "I should have explained – you stay down, go with the outflow. We call it getting Maytagged."

She dared a glance over her shoulder at the waterfall – she had just survived a fifteen-foot drop into a boiling keeper. She was proud that she had not panicked and was grateful for her guide's cool head and bravery. Though she was cold in her sopping T-shirt and ripped panties, her heart was racing with the thrill of her risk-filled ride.

"I lost the flashlight."

"We'll use the moon."

It had risen above the trees and in its light she could see the air mattress being battered by the falls. She could also make out Slack: a tall brawny, greying redhead, weathered skin, rugged features. He was shaven and had recently cut his hair; the rendering was a vast improvement over the televised versions she'd seen.

"That's the worst of it," he said. She was shivering, and moved closer to him. He didn't seem anxious to set off again, but bent on making conversation. "Where did we meet, Maggie?"

"We didn't."

"I'm an unsavoury character in your book, the Quepos town drunk. How did you come up with such a perceptive portrait?"

"From gossip I heard." She was uncertain if she should apologize. He was also reputed to be a rowdy, but he seemed most gentle now; she hoped she had not insulted him.

"I'm not particularly handsome, and I'd like to think I'm not an arrogant snob. Otherwise, you have created a picaresque portrait of the drunken lout."

"You're very defensive."

He grunted. "I have every reason to be. Heads are going to roll over this fiasco, and one of them could be mine. I ought to warn you that I'm almost as paranoid as Benito Madrigal, but in my case it's justified. I have one reliable ally, and he's waiting downstream. If I sound like a jabbering idiot, take it as a compliment; usually I become tongue-tied with women."

"Well, that hardly describes you right now."

"Maybe you're easy to talk to." He said this gruffly, then rose and worked his way over the rocks to the falls and pulled the mattress up the bank.

Maggie felt somewhat assured by this odd, meandering conversation that she could place faith in Slack Cardinal and comfortably pass on Halcón's message. As he was about to step into the river, she held him back.

"I need to settle something with you, Mr. Jacques Cardinal, or whatever your real name is. What's your role in all this? Glo told me you used to be a spy."

He answered with a shrug but no hesitation: "I was shanghaied. It was either that or a long stretch — a political thing, seditious writings. I ran off to Cuba . . . It's a long story, but I've been dragged back in to play stuntman for the free world, and right now I'm not sure who I'm rooting for; I'm having trouble deciding who the good guys are."

"You have to let everyone get away."

"That's the plan. I have the money."

She was surprised by this blunt announcement and heard truth in it. "Halcón gave me a message to be passed on only to you — he doesn't know your history or your role in this, but for some reason he trusts you. Swear to me you will tell no one else."

"Can I tell Frank?"

"Who?"

"My main man."

"Only him. Sloth Park in Limón at nine p.m. tomorrow — that's what he wanted me to tell you; that's where he'll be."

"Halcón *told* you that?"

"He confided in me a great deal."

"That is remarkable."

"We became friends. It's hard to explain; Halcón is . . . well, he's different. Glo kept a greater distance at first, but . . ." Maggie was unable to complete the thought, her ire at Glo welling. "I suppose she tried to put the make on you."

"She came on like a runaway train. You two didn't get along?"

"I took care of her; we had a sensational friendship, but . . . I can't explain it. Glo is a very . . ."

"Lusty woman."

"Yes."

He nodded, seemingly satisfied with that. "All aboard. Couple of small adventures ahead, one we call the bucking bronco, then the loop-de-loop. After that it's child's play."

Though there were no more chutes, holes, or keepers, Maggie endured a frothy whitewater journey for about a mile, clinging anxiously to Slack, two wet bodies in absurd, intimate contact. Twice they spilled as their mattress bounced off boulders, and once they became tangled in the branches of a fallen tree. They found many eddies, however, rest stops where she recounted her seven weeks as a captive: the long treks through the jungle, life at the Darkside. She was too embarrassed to admit her infatuation with Halcón, but told him of her growing attachment to his idealistic soldiers. They shared their concern over Benito Madrigal. "He insists Walker has a secret army and wants to take over the world."

"I'd feel safer if Benito took it over." Electric lights began to show through the trees. "All right, we want to take the left tongue at the top of these next rapids."

They did so without spilling, and Maggie could see an old bridge silhouetted in the moonlight. They were swept down a last cataract, and here, where the river widened and slowed, a portly gentleman was sitting on a rock with a fishing pole, staring intently at Slack Cardinal and his bedraggled rider.

"*Bienvenido*," he said.

— 4 —

Slack thought there might be roadblocks, so he took the wheel, he knew a back road that swung over the hills to the Savegre, and now they were twisting south and east, between hills and rocky pastures, toward the coastal plain. He could see the farms of the lower Savegre valley now, a mile away, moonlight dancing on the river, high *cerros* still on either side.

He was feeling on top of things, a rare burst of optimism, Plan B was still in effect despite a day's delay and tomorrow's detour to Limón.

And one rescue was already well accomplished, Maggie Schneider beside him, dozing, wrapped in a blanket, her short hair wet and flat. She looked like a leggy bird, a graceful, long-necked heron.

The Suzuki rental didn't have a radio, thieves in San José had popped it out, so they couldn't catch the latest bulletins. But reporters had been at the scene, Frank had seen a parade of them pour across the bridge on the road to the Darkside.

"One presumes the first of these vehicles, a Toyota Four Runner, was occupied by Senator Walker and the small force that you have described. Ten minutes later, I counted some six vehicles, among which were two television vans, one with satellite equipment."

These were the civilians Walker had ordered to return to the road. The colonel had brought the world along to witness his dramatic rescue of his glamorous wife, a John Wayne movie, the federal marshal stomping into a saloon for the media event of the century. Pull it off, and Chuck could start thinking about naming his cabinet. He has the right stuff, he stands up to terrorists.

Walker had taken an audacious gamble for glory, but had he thought about the consequences of failure? Frank had the answer. "He succeeds either way. If his best-laid plans go awry – indeed, if mortal tragedy befalls Gloria-May Walker – he then becomes even more the sympathetic hero."

Slack could see that – hearts of America going out to the heroic widower. But he wondered if Chuck Walker was so ambitious and callous as not to care about his wife's safety.

They had maybe thirty minutes yet of driving, it was already close to three a.m. They were exhausted, Maggie still napping, Frank stifling yawns. The trip to Limón would have to be made by daylight, Slack needed at least a few hours' sack time. For this venture he would be armed, Frank had returned his .38.

They were descending into the wide valley carved out by the Savegre, a trail of dust following them. Beyond were the ubiquitous oil palm groves of the *compañía*, then the Costanera, the southern highway. Slack toyed with the idea of finding a phone, he wouldn't mind calling Ham Bakerfield, ask him how it feels when someone's jerking him off, staging a dramatic rescue for the cameras while the president's chosen hostage-saver was looking the other way.

But how had Walker got the jump on Slack? He felt sure he hadn't been followed. The solution was there, staring at him, but still too fuzzy around the edges.

"I'm a friendly," Elmer had yelled, figure that one out. I'm a friendly . . .

The answer seemed to descend from the heavens. "Elmer," he shouted. "Jericho is working for them."

That woke Maggie up, she blinked, slow to catch her bearings.

Frank pounced on the idea. "Yes, of course. The friends in high places."

The smell of overripe cheese was suddenly overwhelming, reeking of circumstantial proof. Walker's cronies were the friends who had saved Elmer from being busted with three hundred pounds of marching powder, the friends who had removed files containing vital dirt on the Special Services veteran. Where had Elmer been hanging his helmet before he showed up in Costa Rica?

"Nicaragua," he said. "Jericho was doing jobs for Colonel Walker's Rangers."

And Maggie chimed in: "Oh, my God, maybe he was." She was looking at him thoughtfully, alert now. "Glo couldn't figure out why his name seemed familiar. She thought Chuck may have mentioned it."

"He's a friendly, all right," Slack said. *I'm connected.* A two-engine Piper Comanche and a Mafia pilot. Elmer had made this link during the Contra war, he'd helped the advisers run the guns-for-coke trade.

He drove in stunned silence, worrying that he'd gone overboard, old man Paranoia creating mischief again, taking over the controls. Then, as the ramifications began to hit home, he cried out, "Jesus *wept!* We've been *jobbed!*"

He sputtered, stumbling over his words, his tongue working faster than his brain. "It's a work of genius – okay, evil genius – no, he's not smart enough – maybe his campaign manager, I don't know. Here it is: Walker knew all along *exactly* where Maggie and Glo were being held. Hell, he knew about the kidnapping in advance. No, strike that – he bloody *planned* it. Putting the snatch on his wife was a set-up from the beginning." He banged his hands on the steering wheel. "Yes!"

"He would never . . ." Maggie shook her head. "That's ridiculous."

"No, this makes sense," said Frank, excited now, too.

"I've got it, here it is, this is how he was going to get elected head of the free world, a staged hostage-taking. Okay, Jericho – he was probably the colonel's bum-boy in Managua – now he's working for Eco-Rico, and Walker thinks, what a perfect spot for that second honeymoon he's been planning. He owns Elmer, he got him off that coke beef. Elmer's been up to the lodge, he knows the lay of the land. But they need a brilliant criminal mind, so they hire Johnny Diego, pay him a big advance, and he minces his way into the People's Popular Vanguard, reinvents them as the Comando Cinco de Mayo, gets them to do the grunt work."

"I don't think Halcón would hire himself out that way," Maggie said.

Slack reconsidered, she was right, Halcón was the classic private entrepreneur, he didn't middle for others, and his distaste for Walker had seemed sincere. "Okay, maybe not, maybe Elmer doesn't tell Halcón it's a set-up, and so he's been duped, too – that fits, Johnny was so leery of Elmer that he skipped out on him."

Frank leaned forward. "Ms. Schneider, what was Senator Walker's demeanour just before the kidnapping?"

"He was distracted, maybe a little agitated."

"He dismissed almost his entire staff," Slack said, "got rid of two of his bodyguards, sent them off to loll about the beach, kept two guys he hoped weren't very heroic."

"I am a believer," Frank said.

Slack was convinced the scheme had been devised in whispers in a darkened backroom, Walker and a few advisers. Everyone, Slack, probably Halcón, even Ham Bakerfield, had been used. He realized grimly there was a reason Walker had pressed him into service with such enthusiasm – the fuckup could be counted on to fall on his face.

From the start, Elmer knew Slack was working undercover, the old snake-eater was a gifted actor, pretending to be dull-witted and gullible. Slack, blinded by naïveté, had believed he'd had this soft drug junkie in his pocket. That galled.

From a hill overlooking the broad coastal plain, Slack could now see the moon-flecked ocean, waves cresting on an endless beach. Soon they were immersed in the vast sea of African palms. Here was a botanical graveyard, a grove of exhausted trees, row on row of ghostly skeletons, tall and grey, forlorn in death.

John Daniels, whom everyone called Jack, came yawning from his house, alerted by the barking of his old dog, Shep, who sniffed at Slack, and, recognizing him, wagged his tail. Slack had known Jack from the early days, a trusted friend who asked few questions. His rustic cabinas, at the seaside village of Matapalo, were buried in trees at the dead end of a sand road, away from inquiring eyes.

"Two units reserved for Harry Wilder," Jack grumbled, "late arrivals." He looked Slack over, his wet clothes stuck to his skin, then at Frank, dozing in the car, at Maggie as she stepped out, the blanket wrapped around her. "I won't ask," Jack said. "Hell, I'm not even curious. You guys want some dry clothes, look in the downstairs closet." He gave Slack the keys to two cabins.

"You must be doing okay, Jack, heard you bought a dish."

"Decided to check out all the weird shit that's going on in the real world, reminds me why I came here. I'll switch it on." Jack yawned again and headed back to bed, leaving his door open.

"Which cabin do you want?" Slack asked Maggie.

"Yours. I don't want to be alone."

They aroused Frank and led him to the nearest unit, where he mumbled his thanks and went directly to bed.

In the house, a tabletop TV offered interminable commercials and business reports. While they waited for the news, Maggie combed through the closet and when she emerged had on shorts and a T-shirt, "Pura Vida, Costa Rica," her nipples making peaks in the fabric. Slack tore his eyes away.

When CNN *Headline News* came on, the story of the hour was, as expected, out of peaceful little Costa Rica. A brief intro, then: "And here, on location, with some *unusual* late-breaking developments, is Latin correspondent Monique Delgado." A brunette with a wide grin that she couldn't seem to suppress.

"Well, Willard, I barely know where to start, but a raid took place in the dead of night upon this isolated house in the rugged hills of southern Costa Rica." A ground-to-satellite transmission showed the area lit up, figures moving about, yellow police tape everywhere, which meant Ham's people had finally showed up.

Monique Delgado talked rapidly, there was much to tell. Late last evening, media had been tipped by an anonymous caller to show up at this location, and arrived to find Senator Chuck Walker and a squad of "anti-terrorist militia" being fired upon while attempting to approach the house, which was later found deserted. "Except for this one man."

Footage was shown of Benito Madrigal walking out past a front door that had been blown off its hinges. Though his hands were on his head, he was singing the national anthem, defiant to the end. Maggie was relieved to see him unharmed, and Slack gave his image a revolutionary salute. "*Qué bruto, maje.*"

"No one has yet been able to explain how Benito Madrigal, supposedly under lock and key in San José, had found his way here, and was then deserted by his small band of supporters. There are many questions being asked, Willard. Allegations have been made that Senator Walker jumped the gun, apparently without the knowledge of the State Department. Some people are describing it as an embarrassing boondoggle."

Walker, the author of that boondoggle and new holder of the title of all-around fuckup, was unavailable for comment. No mention of

Slack Cardinal or Elmer Jericho or any missing four million dollars, no hint that Maggie had escaped.

The only other interesting shot was of Ham Bakerfield pushing a camera away, most of his words bleeped, but something to do with getting these assholes, presumably meaning the press, out of here. The old man was in a rage.

Delgado concluded with a flourish: "Somewhere in this peaceful land, in this so-called Switzerland of the Americas, two brave women continue their horrific ordeal at the hands of a band of fanatics who have boasted they will stop at nothing to realize their demands. Back to you, Willard."

"And we all continue to pray for Gloria-May and Maggie," Willard intoned.

Slack turned off the set and led Maggie to their cabin, it was spartan, a double bed and furniture enough to satisfy the backpack tourists Jack catered to, a curtained alcove with shower and toilet. He placed the duffle bags at the foot of the bed, smoothed them out. "This may be my last and only chance to crash out on four million dollars."

Maggie strolled about, straightening chairs, brushing off the bed, the pillows, tucking corners in.

"I'll be taking the Suzuki tomorrow, so maybe you and Frank can get to Quepos by taxi. Don't talk to anyone but Ham Bakerfield, he's an honest old buzzard, so don't be afraid to pass on our suspicions about Walker. He'll want to pick up Elmer fast; tell him to squeeze him hard. And don't tell him where I'll be tomorrow night."

"I'm not going to Quepos. I'm going with you."

Slack thought she was joking until he saw her set expression. "As much as I'd enjoy your company, I have to say no. I'm not traipsing off to a tea party."

She made a face – that had sounded somehow sexist. "No, you're not dumping me now, Mr. Slack Cardinal. If you're right about Chuck Walker, this is an incredible story and I intend to see it through. As far as I'm concerned you rescued me, so you're stuck with me."

La Brava Schneider. "I'm going to have to think about it. Let's talk in the morning when our heads are clear."

"There's nothing to talk about."

He pulled off his wet shirt. He'd found a baggy sports shirt in Jack's closet, it would do for tomorrow.

"How did you get those scars on your back?"

"You don't want to know."

"They look like whip marks."

"Ancient history." He covered himself with a sheet and lay down on the duffle bags, groaning, all his bones sore.

Maggie took a shower, doused the lights, and stretched out on the bed. There was a long silence, and Slack assumed she had fallen asleep. But she finally said, "You don't have to sleep on those uncomfortable bags. This is a double bed."

"I'm fine here."

"Honestly, there's lots of room."

"I don't think I should."

"Why?"

"Because I wouldn't sleep."

"Why not?"

"You scare me."

A pillow landed on his head, she wasn't going to insist.

— 5 —

Too stimulated by yesterday's dangerous escape, disturbed by concerns over Chuck Walker's intrigues, Maggie had been denied a sound sleep. Her attempts to nap in the Suzuki were thwarted by Slack's continual braking and swerving around potholes. They had been travelling for five hours, since six a.m., climbing up and over the volcanic hump of Costa Rica before descending toward the eastern shore. But now progress was sluggish behind a logging truck, its airbrakes hissing and belching down the bends and twists.

They were in cloud forest, its mists obscuring their route. Occasionally, through gaps, she glimpsed scenes of dream-like beauty, mist tangled in Cortéz trees that were exploding with masses of yellow bloom. But Slack wasn't enjoying the scenery; he was swearing at the truck ahead, convinced bootleg loggers had pillaged its cargo from the forest. His concern for the environment seemed almost obsessive: pesticides from banana plantations were poisoning rivers flowing into the Atlantic, turtles were threatened, reefs endangered.

Her pessimistic tour guide could easily have tiptoed away this morning with the sacks of money and abandoned her to her dreams, but he had awakened her at daybreak. Before leaving, they had aroused Frank Sierra. "I'll check in when you're done explaining to Ham that you don't know where I'm going, and that Maggie insisted on coming along."

That bulge in the buttoned pocket of Slack's shorts was a gun — it made Maggie nervous but did not dim her resolve to help Halcón and his crew escape in safety. She was unsure how she would react to seeing Glo again after the recent fracturing of their friendship.

A roadside cantina emerged from the gloom, and Slack paused there to pick up empanadas, soft drinks, and a few oranges. They continued on, then dropped beneath the fog and pulled off on a dirt driveway from where she could see the aquamarine waters of the Caribbean Sea. She felt self-conscious as they ate because he was staring at her; she often found him doing so, and in a puzzled way. But whenever she directly met his eye, he looked quickly away.

"What's your real name? It's not Jacques Cardinal."

"Jacques Sawchuk. Born in New York, but my mother was French, my father Ukrainian."

"Well, I'm pleased you're still a Jacques — I was worried you'd be a Gaston or an Alphonse."

Unexpectedly — and never before seen — a smile appeared, crinkling the corners of his lips. Usually, he was sternly serious, almost funereal, frightening her with his vast collection of disasters befalling the planet.

"How does a spy become such an eco-freak?"

"One of my last jobs took me inside a group called the Green Commando. Eco-terrorists, that was the standard Interpol line. They opened my eyes; politicians were bickering as the earth was bleeding.

I joined Greenpeace, tried to do my bit; it isn't enough – it's never enough."

He held his bottle of Fanta to the light, as if inspecting it for foreign objects. He took a swallow, then stared glumly at the panorama below, at the clouds massing over the ocean. Mist had gathered in cotton clumps on mountainsides and in the valley below.

"There's still beauty in the world," she said.

As if to prove her point, a gaudy toucan perched nearby and began croaking like a raspy gate. It was soon joined by four companions; all began hopping around a liana bearing clusters of purple berries. "Keelbills," Slack said. "Fruit, nuts, lizards, and other birds' eggs."

The toucans took wing, soaring to a lower tree. "They look like toy airplanes," she said.

"Your mother said you're a nervous flyer. What's that's all about?"

"I can't figure it out."

"It doesn't make sense; you're too spunky." Another smile: she wished he would do that more often. His eyes finally met hers. "I could take you to some of my spots. Maybe we could find the Buff-Breasted Blue Warbler."

"Let's do that. Birding, I'd love to."

"I can show you what is left of beauty."

He said that with soft intensity, and held eye contact. Neither spoke for a few moments, and her garrulous host's sudden incapacity for words made her apprehensive: was she being cautiously wooed? If so, and however warming it felt, she would be acting falsely if she encouraged him. One does not jump out of love as one jumps out of bed.

I'm not ready, she wanted to tell him; my emotions are a shambles. Abruptly she turned from him, not wanting him to see the welling tears.

"Johnny Falcon, right?"

"Yes. I'll get over it."

You scare me, he had said. No wonder.

They were moving at a snail-like pace as they neared the coast; a road crew was paving. "*Perdone, estamos trabajando*," said their sign. Slack translated: "'Sorry, we're working.'" Again, she enjoyed the way his weathered face creased like an old suit when he smiled. She felt embarrassed by her admission she was still Halcón's captive in heart, but Slack had made no attempt to probe further. Indeed, he had abandoned efforts to engage her more closely; perhaps she had been presumptuous, had misread his feelings.

The coastal plain was dotted with ramshackle homes, the climate hot and muggy, the people darker skinned, many of them New World African. From a rise, they glimpsed Limón, a large town laid out in a grid on a finger of land probing the sea. They didn't want to be seen, and, according to Slack, the art of Tico thievery had reached a state of near perfection in this bustling port, so they decided to avoid the town until nightfall. He took them south, along the coastal highway; after several kilometres they found an access road to a stretch of deserted black-sand beach.

The clouds were still building; her skin had become slick with a sheen of sweat. A daytime darkness abruptly set in; the rain announced itself with thick splattering drops, then came with a clamour. As Slack rolled up the windows, Maggie crawled into the back of the car, where she lay down on the sacks of money, hoping to sleep.

She sensed a formality between them now, an altered, more practical relationship – they had important business to transact.

She awoke from an erotic dream feeling disoriented – where was the meadow on which she was lying with her dark-eyed lover? All was a blackness; it was raining, and she was in a vehicle – the sound of its engine had woken her. She climbed into the front seat as Slack pulled onto the road from their beachside rest stop. Her watch read half past eight.

"Sleep well?"

"I'm not sure." Her dream had disturbed her: Halcón's voice, but not his words – *I will be back for you.*

The rain slowed as they entered Limón, a town that looked damp and mildewed, a Somerset Maugham setting. People were strolling about with umbrellas, lining up for buses, gossiping in front of shops. The bars were bustling, the sounds of salsa and reggae spilling onto the streets. Halcón had said he would be waiting in the main square, under the leafy trees with their resident sloths.

Slack circled almost the entire perimeter of the square before nudging the Suzuki into a hole between cargo taxis. Maggie tugged down her cap and looked away from the two older men standing at the curb; but they were laughing and talking animatedly, and ignored her. Afro-Caribbean music came from speakers inside the bar across the street.

Slack handed her the keys. "I'm going to do a walkabout. I won't be far." As he strolled off into the square, she slid into the driver's seat and locked the doors, leery about guarding a millionaire's ransom in this city of thieves. A Guardia Rural officer stopped to talk with the two men standing by her vehicle. When she peeked from under her cap, she observed a bottle being passed to the policeman, who glanced about before drinking from it.

Maggie slid down in her seat, and turned again to the street. In a shadowed doorway near the bar, a man wearing sunglasses was lighting a cigarette. He looked sinister, the only local not partaking in the general gaiety.

Several minutes passed, and she was becoming concerned that Slack had not returned. But he was likely waiting in the darkness with Halcón; they would not want to pique the interest of the Guardia officer.

The policeman continued his stroll, much to Maggie's relief. Then the man across the street flicked his butt into the gutter and walked quickly toward her. She held her breath and suddenly exhaled as she recognized him. She rolled down her window, smiling but anxious.

"How do you come to be here, Maggie?" Halcón bent and kissed her lightly on the lips.

She unlocked the passenger door, then gripped the steering wheel to prevent her hands from shaking. "Get in."

GAMMA RAY BURSTER

— I —

Four persons were lined up behind Slack for the one working pay phone at this corner of Sloth Park, but having waited ten minutes he wasn't going to give up and kept impatiently feeding the machine its diet of twenty-colon coins. For all Slack knew, the receptionist had flown to Baffin Island to fetch Bakerfield to the phone, or maybe the old man was taking the world's longest crap. Or they were stalling, trying to do a trace, but they'd be at least an hour getting here, even by copter.

He couldn't see the Suzuki from behind the bank of phones, Maggie would be fretting. Another coin plunked down the slot, he was fast running out. Get off the pot, Ham.

Finally, a human voice. "He's coming now."

"Where the fuck are you, Slack?" The gruff tones of the spymaster.

"This will be brief. Did you collar Elmer Jericho?"

"For what?"

"For . . . hell, didn't you talk to Frank Sierra? Get ahold of him right away, he's got the whole lowdown."

Ham went off the line for a second. "He's gone off somewhere. He dropped by when I was at the crime scene. What was your motorcycle doing at that joint?"

Frank was not following the amended rules of Plan B — where could he have vanished? Slack hoped Walker's Rangers had not intercepted him.

"Where the blazes did you get to? Will somebody clue me in, god-dammit?" Ham had started to shout, and Slack had to yell over him.

"Where's the junior senator from South Dakota?"

"Listen hard, he's claiming you ran off with his dough and you're in league with the crooks who did the snatch. If you've screwed up again, I'll personally take a scalpel to your hanging decorations –"

Slack cut through again. "*You* listen hard. I've got Maggie Schneider with me, and I'll have Glo in probably a couple of hours. Elmer's been shilling for Walker all along. It's a scam, we've all been shucked by a megalomaniac and his hippie stooge. Don't pull anyone in until you talk to Frank Sierra. *Find* him. Gotta go." He hung up.

They'd probably got their trace, now he had to locate Halcón and boot it out of here to do the transfer. It was well after nine, where the hell was he? Slack had already strolled through the square once, this time he raced through it. No sign of him.

Hurrying back to the street, he was stunned to find the Suzuki Sidekick gone, a rusty Datsun pickup in its place. He made frantic inquiries of the two old-timers at the curb.

"The lady in the Jeep, she drive off, mon. With a man in sun-glasses."

The description they gave fit Halcón. Slack felt crushed by the weight of impending disaster.

"A taxi follow them, mon."

They had been careful observers – the Suzuki had headed not east toward the airport but west, perhaps to the seaport at Moín. Likely, the taxi bore one of Halcón's confederates, maybe Gordo, playing tail-gunner, watching the rear.

Slack felt heavy with defeat. He had a choice, he could walk into the bar and get roaring drunk or he could act on the slimmest of theories: Halcón had a boat at Moín, or maybe a reserved berth on a freighter.

He couldn't bear the thought of calling in again, braving the old man's wrath. This was the final glorious fuckup, the one they'd remember him by.

He strode down the sidewalk to the taxi bank. *"El puerto,"* he told the first driver in line. *"Muy rápido."*

As they sped down streets lined with tin-roofed shacks toward the wasteland east of the waterfront, Slack tried to puzzle through what had happened. Halcón had probably been watching their car from the shadows, he'd seen his chance to grab the dough. Had Maggie gone willingly? What did she think she was doing – tripping off to fairyland to live with her prince? She wasn't thinking clearly, still bonkers over him, she could have stumbled unwittingly into danger.

Slack tried to persuade himself he was overly concerned. Maybe this wasn't such a catastrophe, Halcón's venture had profited him well, he was an honourable man, he would free Glo Walker, and the deal would be signed off, all without Slack's intervention. Maggie would escort Glo to freedom in the Suzuki Sidekick, they could be heading to the nearest phone right now.

That promising alternative boosted his hopes, maybe his ass wouldn't be hung on the line to dry, he would explain the matter had been taken out of his hands, an impetuous act by Maggie Schneider. But how could she have been so rash and irresponsible?

Maybe she'd run off with Halcón with noble intentions, deciding on the fly to do the deal by herself, protecting Slack from the wrath of his handlers. Walker, already squirming, was going to look even more ridiculous with his slanders about Slack being in league with Halcón.

The *taxista*, a handsome greying mestizo, occasionally glanced at Slack in the rear view, frowning but saying nothing, obeying entreaties for speed, breaking minor traffic laws. The rain finally relented as they reached the port, its docks well lit, busy with commerce even at night, the crane working, containers of bananas being lifted aboard a small rusty freighter.

Slack told the driver to wait while he reconnoitred. The freighter didn't have passenger cabins, and he saw no cruise vessels. Smaller launches would be tied up at the entrance to the canals that webbed through the Caribbean lowlands, longboats offering tours to Tortuguero, as far as Barra del Colorado, near the Nicaraguan border.

"To the canal," Slack said.

The driver looked over his shoulder, got a good view of Slack in the light of a lamppost. "I have seen you on television, señor. You are the one who supports the man they call Halcón. I am cheering for your side. Halcón is for the people." A friendly. "Why are you here, señor, if it is not impolite to ask?"

Slack leaned to his ear. "I am helping Halcón escape. We are looking for a rented Suzuki Sidekick."

The canal's dock was in a gated compound, fenced against thieves. A dozen long canopied boats were tied up at the wharf, along with several smaller craft.

His supportive *taxista* honked for the gatekeeper to let them in, then pulled into a parking area. "Maybe this is what you are looking for, señor." Bingo, a stroke of luck, the target vehicle. Slack scrambled from the taxi, looked in the windows of the locked Suzuki, it was empty, no duffle bags.

Slack tried to pay his driver, but his money was refused, Slack was an ally of heroic Halcón. He sprinted to the dock and saw a short fellow busily jotting notes. Gordo, he thought at first, but a closer look revealed him to be, however unlikely, Frank Sierra.

"Excellent, you made the right guess. We have not much time. Do you see — in the distance?"

"Frank, what the hell are you doing here?"

"Look, that is their boat."

A couple of hundred yards north, before the canal curved from sight, he made out a small craft, a light at the bow. Frank flipped through a couple of pages of his notebook. "Five-metre fibreglass cabin cruiser, yellow with green trim, a thirty-horse outboard. It will be slow, we must be faster."

Slack demanded explanations.

"It appeared Mr. Bakerfield would not be available until tonight, so I flew here. I was concerned that you would not have backup." His tone seemed gently chiding, Slack had pulled a boner leaving Maggie alone with the money.

Frank had been sitting in a taxi at the square, watching and waiting, had seen Halcón join Maggie in the Sidekick. No arguments, no coercion, twenty seconds of conversation, and she simply drove off with him. Ten minutes ago, Frank had arrived here to find them throwing the duffle bags into the boat and slipping it from its moorings.

Slack had been down these canals a few times, trips to the mystical beauty of the Tortuguero lagoons. Strung out along the waterways were scattered farms and houses, the occasional bar or soda, then the watery wilderness of Parque Nacional Tortuguero. A labyrinth of side canals and rivers would make the search especially difficult at night.

A twin Comanche, Elmer had said, near the border. Barra del Colorado with its landing strip seemed the likely destination, Nicaragua just a hop over the San Juan River. There were also small strips closer, at Parisimina and Tortuguero, near the Turtle Research Station. Or if Halcón had a safe house on the canal, maybe he wasn't rushing to a plane.

Only a few people were on the dock, a man sitting on the planks with a disassembled outboard, a couple repairing a fishing net by the light of a kerosene lamp, and a stout guy bailing out a fifty-foot taxi launch, "Fast Willie's Reliable All-Day Service." Leaky, though, because Fast Willie was working a pedal-powered bilge pump. But a Merc Eighty-five was clamped onto the stern.

Negotiations proved difficult. Not at night, sorry mon, said Willie, he was stripped to the waist, showing a robust black paunch. Even the prospect of an excessive fare didn't entice him, his wife was in hospital expecting a baby. "I going there right soon."

When they offered to charter his launch, five hundred dollars for the night, it obviously dawned on Willie that these two customers were not only anxious to get underway but possessed of abundant means. He frowned, giving it thought, calculating how much he dared raise the ante.

The yellow-and-green cabin cruiser had disappeared from sight, Slack was irritated. "Name a figure, goddammit."

"Three t'ousan dollar, mon." To allay the shock, he added, "Including extra thirty gallons of gas."

Halcón had half a mile on them already, Slack would pay this thief's ransom. He was reaching for his wad when Halcón's fan, the taxi driver, came between them, pulled Willie aside. They had a low, intense conversation. The man and woman who had been sewing up holes in their nets were now part of the scene, and the small-engine mechanic was on his way. "The gringo, he is a great friend of Johnny Falcon," the *taxista* said. "They are helping him escape."

"It was Halcón we saw," the woman said excitedly to her partner. "He is even more handsome than his pictures. And with a woman. Isn't she the lucky one."

"Was it truly Halcón?" said the mechanic. He crossed himself.

"Damn. Frank, we have to shut down these wild rumours."

"There is an expression I have read in crime novels, paper the joint."

"Four hundred for each day," said Willie. "Plus two hundred deposit." He seemed resentful at having been leaned on, maybe the only local around here who wasn't supporting Halcón for president.

Slack gave Willie a thousand instead, and a hundred to each of the others. "You must say nothing about what you have seen tonight," he urged them.

Sí, señor. Entiendo. We are hurt that you would ask, señor. Slack didn't hold out much hope.

— 2 —

Slack was forced to keep to fifteen knots so he could inspect the vessels tied up by the few rickety homes abutting the shoreline. The engine was running well, the only problem being the leak in the caulking, Frank occasionally having to work the bilge pump. Otherwise he was quietly sitting at the stern watching the fishing bats dip and scoop at the water.

The moon was large, a few days from full, drenching the jungle with a bright light, airbrushing a shimmering path up the centre of the waterway. This was a generous habitat, there were jaguars here, spoonbills, tiger herons, basilisk lizards that walked on water. This was the Costa Rica that Slack loved, right down to the venomous vipers and man-eating crocodiles. Its gentle beauty was marred only by plastic pesticide bags tangled in the branches of shoreline trees, they floated down the lagoons from the plantations. He tried not to think about the murder of turtles in the name of spotless bananas, he had depressed Maggie with his eco-snivelling.

The canal narrowed, a shallow stretch, Slack had to raise the engine as he squeezed past a dredge barge. Finally, they swept into a wide lagoon rimmed with beds of water hyacinth, clumps of which had broken free, garlands strewn across the water. As the time slowly passed, he began to feel a hypnotic effect from the pulling moon, the thrum of the engine, the splash of water against the bow.

A boat motored by, a lantern shining from its cabin. Here was the Pacuare River, he'd kayaked it, and an opening to the sea, the surf drumming from behind palm-lined dunes. He came to a fork, another river or maybe the lagoon dividing, creating an island. He slowed, deliberated, chose the right branch, the main canal, parallel to the shore. But Halcón could have gone up the Pacuare, even chanced heading out to sea.

They passed a couple of houses on stilts, a crowing rooster out of synch with dawn, a barking dog. After several minutes, the channels merged, and a village of sorts came into view on the right bank, a few houses, an old man on a porch enjoying the night, a tiny *pulpería* with its smokes, Cokes, canned tuna, and stale bread.

A few small dugouts were tied up here, but no yellow-and-green cabin cruiser. Slack idled the engine, conferred with Frank.

"I'm thinking we should go back up the other fork." Halcón and his crew would want to be near the *pulpería*, a ready supply of food, propane, toiletries. Frank was looking at the store, too, he nodded his agreement.

Around a bend, a wooden shack, then nothing for a hundred metres. On the right, on the narrow island between the parallel waterways, the moon illuminated a shanty, a couple of pigs sleeping on the porch. Finally, they approached a two-level clapboard house on stilts, a big place for the area, at least five rooms.

There was a dock of sorts, two floating logs chained to a tree, two boats tied to it, an overpowered Zodiac . . . and a five-metre yellow-and-green cabin cruiser.

Slack wasn't going to risk the women's safety with a sudden approach, he would reconnoitre first. He putted slowly past, found a channel through the hyacinth, idled the engine by a tangle of swamp palms.

He motioned to Frank to take over as pilot. "I'm going in by land."

"Take care."

The house couldn't be far, but Slack saw he faced a daunting task penetrating the thick growth near the shore. He'd found a machete in the boat, but no flashlight, he'd have to work by the light of the moon – and quickly, because the pale goddess was now drifting among thickening veils of clouds.

He stepped off the boat onto a root, but felt his footing give way. Almost too late, he realized he was standing on a very large animate object – a crocodile, and suddenly it was submerging, thrashing its tail. Fuelled by the adrenaline of primal fear, he somersaulted over the skein of roots of a tall tree, just out of reach of a pair of snapping jaws.

The boat was drifting away, Frank calling anxiously to him, and in a cracked voice Slack managed some phrases of reassurance, told him to wait thirty minutes, then come in.

All his senses were on alarm as a result of this near-death experience. No more missteps. He calculated his distance from Halcón's house at about a hundred metres. There'd been yucca and *plátanos* behind the house, and a clearing beyond this thicket that likely extended to a trail.

He chopped at a tangle of branches, disturbing a pair of snowy egrets, which flew off with squawks. He finally emerged upon a narrow path – he'd lost the moon, clouds were beginning to fill the sky. A brighter, briefer light, a spiderweb of lightning, a guttural rumble.

The path ascended gently to the clearing, yucca in several scraggy rows, plantains and papayas, the two-storey house rising above them. From this different vantage, he could see a flickering light from an upstairs window, probably a candle. No sign of anyone serving as yard dog, Halcón must have jettisoned his crew, Gordo and Zorro and the rest.

A few fat drops of rain, a flash and another bark of thunder, closer now, a sudden gust of wind, a squall on its way. He thought he heard voices from the house but wasn't sure.

He slipped from tree to tree with elaborate care, scrutinizing everything. Bakerfield had force-fed him the manual back in the seventies, clock all terrain surrounding the target facility, observe the scene both generally and in detail, seek the unusual, locate escape routes.

But need he be so slow and vigilant? He had no enemy here, and only one task – to ensure the transaction was duly completed, the ransom paid, Glo freed. Then he'd shake Halcón's hand and wish him *buen viaje*. Following which he would have a few carefully chosen words with Maggie Schneider.

The clouds had begun to let go their burden, the night went black with drenching rain as he crept down to the dock. A pair of Evinrude 90s on the fifteen-foot Zodiac, a line tied with a slipknot to a ring in the log.

The Zodiac had to be Halcón's getaway vehicle. Johnny could easily make one or other of the airstrips in an hour or two – then maybe Nicaragua, but more likely over the Caribbean to Panama, or Colombia, the corrupt security of San Andres Island.

And what of his partner, the friendly, the consumer of drug salads? Had he been collared or was he hiding? Slack would tell Johnny Diego not to feel guilty about kissing Elmer out, the fellow was a quisling, a shill for Walker. Take your money and run, Halcón.

He ventured farther out on the log, it was wide enough to walk on but slippery in the pelting rain. He knelt and reached around inside the Zodiac, finding nothing of interest, a few marine tools, an anchor. But when he reached into a Velcro side pouch, he fetched out a plastic baggie containing several buds of marijuana, a lump of what was probably hash, and several pills.

Slack's alarms rang, this was not Halcón's boat, he had a visitor, a pissed-off former partner-in-crime. Elmer Jericho had known about this hideout, guessed Halcón would head to it. While Slack had been lollygagging, waiting for the night, Elmer had sped here. Senator Walker had let his friendly slip past the lines . . . and maybe even whisked him to Limón, outfitted him with the fast boat . . . with instructions to do what? Somehow finish the job.

Ed Creeley's words came back: "He's even better off if they snuff her." Could Walker have planned Glo's death, thinking to cast blame on the terrorists? Elmer might have his own bloody agenda, too, revenge against Halcón. *A lawyer, they do it to you every time.*

If Elmer was here, could Walker's Rangers be far behind? Slack moved quickly toward the shelter of the house, working his way among the plantain trees before skipping under the veranda. The house was raised on sturdy posts, a ramshackle staircase the only access.

The squall was abating, but rain made so much din on the roof that he could hear nothing from inside the house. Slack pulled his revolver, cracked it open, spun the chamber, six live bullets. He made his way slowly up the stairs to the porch, hugged the wall, peered through a screened window, almost totally dark, indistinct outlines of clothing or bedding.

The entire house was screened, including the flimsy front door, locked with an eyehook. He looked around a corner, saw the candlelight still glowing from the window. The porch extended far enough to allow an angle view into the room, and his body stiffened as he took in Maggie's profile. She was gagged and trussed with duct tape, her arms tied behind her, still wearing her cap and T-shirt, "Pura Vida, Costa Rica." Her eyes were wide with fear.

He craned over the porch railing as far as he could without toppling and got a partial view of Gloria-May's head, her mouth also taped. Both women were sitting against a post, their wrists tied to it.

Elmer was orating, one of his astral-travelling monologues. Slack could hear more clearly when he put his ear to a crack between the planks.

"There's a vacuum out there, man, our whole universe could tumble into it, it's caused by, okay, what you got is black holes merging with neutron stars. When a supernova explodes, a red supergiant, all life is toast anyway, get what I mean?" He sounded speedy, still on acid, his purple passion pills. "This lump of pig shit we call Earth, it's . . . it's *irrevalent* compared to what's going on up there."

Slack returned to the door and quickly slashed an opening with two swipes of his knife, and released the hook, using his left hand, keeping his revolver in his right. Inside, he felt around – thin mattresses on the floor, some rumpled sheets, a pair of shorts, a man's shirt, a brassiere. More clothing in the corner, washed and neatly stacked. Books, magazines, a carton of Derbys.

An interior door was standing open, and he edged past it into a small kitchen. His hands found the duffle bags, sitting on the floor, open and still full, bundles of hundreds spilling from one of them. Also open were two large, empty suitcases. Candlelight was coming from behind a curtained doorway and from between shelves beside it, stocked with tinned goods. Through a gap with a wide-angle view, he was able to see not only the two women, but Halcón, also gagged, bundled in duct tape. Elmer had somehow thought this through, or been well briefed.

A mosquito coil was burning. The thick stub of a burning candle on the floor beside Halcón illuminated his face with dancing flecks of light. His handsome features had been marred, a puffed-up lower lip, a thin crack of dried blood, an ugly abrasion on one cheek. His eyes stared dark and cold at Elmer, who was standing, facing away from Slack, gripping a handgun.

"Betelgeuse, that's at the shoulder of Orion, you can see it easy, only four hundred light-years away and it's ready to pop. It's what we call a gamma ray burster, in just seconds you got more energy than the entire galaxy produces the whole year. Means finito, man, for the whole solar system. Hoovered right into the old black hole. Seems a waste, don't it, after all the work we put into this fucking joint."

It would be risky to make any hasty moves, he was tripping, he could fire that gun at someone. "The way I look at it, we're like insects in the eternal scheme of things. Less than insects, microbes, specks of dust."

Elmer shambled behind the retaining post, and Slack got a good look at him, sweating, his pupils dilated from the LSD. Slack saw that he was not into some ordinary bad trip, there was something terrible in his eyes. The handgun was a .45, U.S. army issue.

Elmer prodded Halcón hard with his knee. "We used to round up the village heads, teach them respect, we called it pacification. Hey, listen, they used to send me out to do different towns, and if I get nothing or I don't like what I see, I call in the napalm, man. Don't think it didn't bother me, I'm human. But a single other life don't matter in comparison. In the grand scheme, all our fucking lives don't fucking matter."

Slack started as Elmer put his gun to the nape of Halcón's neck. "We're less than insects," he repeated sadly. "Germs, man. Cancer cells."

Slack moved some tinned meat and took a bead on the centre of Elmer's chest. He kept his voice steady. "We're a long way from Vietnam, Elmer. Put the gun down."

Elmer looked around with a wide startled expression. "Who's that? Anyone hear that?"

"I thought we agreed to be partners, Elmer. That was the deal we made."

Elmer cocked his head to the left, then to the right, trying to locate him in the darkness behind the shelves. His barrel was still at Halcón's head. "Hey, man, where'd you come from? Is that you, Slack?"

"I thought we were together in this thing, we weren't going to hurt anybody, we were going to grab the filthy and scram. So put the gun away, we have a plane to catch."

"Let's talk about it, man. Come out where I can see you."

"I'm in the kitchen, Elmer. I'm pointing a .38 snub special at your nose. That's just in case you don't think we're partners any more. I suggest you put your pistol in your pants while we ponder this situation."

A few moments passed while Elmer worked through these new complications. His three prisoners were immobile. Slack saw the distress in Maggie's eyes, rawness. Cool and easy, he told himself.

"Hey, man, we're more than partners. We're like brothers." Elmer kept peering at the shelves, trying to make Slack out. Drugged or not, the man was no fool, a good actor, better at playing dumb than being dumb, he'd pulled one off on Slack, fleeced him like a yokel at a carnival. "Hey, buddy, you alone?"

"I'm in the kitchen with four million friends. I have the money, you have the plane. We've scored, it's fifty–fifty, so let's go. But you have to put the gun down, Elmer. If anyone gets hurt the deal is off."

He was trying to keep this simple, but Elmer again took some time to absorb the information, still threatening Halcón with the .45, though it had drifted from his skull.

"Johnny looks a little roughed up, Elmer, why's that?"

"Aw, he pissed me off. Resistance is futile, I said, but he wouldn't listen."

"Okay, let's leave it at that and let's split. We're partners. We shook on it, remember?"

"I hear you. I'm almost ready to pull out. But I got some business here first. I gotta do what I gotta do."

Slack spoke harshly. "Then I guess the deal's off, and I'm going to have to blow you away."

"That don't sound too awful friendly, Slack. Remember when I told you we should do some jobs together? I meant it. We got chemistry, our minds think alike."

"We could be a dynamic team, Elmer."

"Yeah, we're Butch Cassidy and the Sundance Kid, the gruesome twosome. I really dig you, man, do you know that? But the thing is . . . listen, Slack, what about leaving these here witnesses?"

The .45 was moving, sliding toward Glo's head. Slack thought of taking his chances and plugging him, but it would be chancy, the automatic's safety was off, Elmer was knuckle-tight on the trigger.

"I don't know what you're talking about, amigo. How much dope have you been doing?"

"I'm over the rush. I've levelled, I'm skating, it's cool."

That seemed likely, he seemed capable of reasoning. "Okay, try to think straight. There's no need for anyone to get hurt here."

"Yeah, but they can ID us."

"The cops are going to know anyway, Elmer."

"Not me. Nobody knows nothing about me."

This standoff was exasperating, Slack decided to lay some cards face up, let Elmer know that murdering the innocent would subject him to a worldwide manhunt. Thailand wouldn't be safe, Antarctica wouldn't be safe.

"Sure they do, they know you're Chuck Walker's right arm, they know what the scam is. It's been all over the news tonight, they're looking for you on a murder conspiracy."

Elmer slapped at a mosquito.

"Ease up on that shooter, pal."

"Murder conspiracy, what are you talking?"

"They're putting out a bunch of stuff about how you were hired to chill Walker's wife. Where is the plane, Elmer – Tortuguero, Barra?"

"Hold on – murder, that's horseshit. Where did that come from?"

"The horse's mouth. Walker confessed."

Glo's eye widened, she made muffled angry sounds as she looked up at Elmer, who suddenly didn't seem to know what to do with his gun, staring at it, turning it in his hand. Above him, a big scorpion scuttled along the rafters, a luckless fluttering moth clutched in its pincers.

"Man, he wouldn't do that. Confess? The colonel? No way."

"They broke him, Elmer. I'm in shit, too, I double-crossed the U.S. government." Maybe he was falling for it, Slack would try a little candour. "I used to work for those guys. Did you know that?"

"I heard that somewhere, some kind of secret agent shit. Yeah, I knew the counterfeit beef was a con, they made it up."

"What else did the colonel tell you? That I was just short of retarded, that I was supposed to be the patsy? They figured I'd bugger it up, isn't that right? They thought they could use me, just like they thought they could use you. Hey, Elmer, we're going to get the last laugh on those pricks, you and me, Butch and Sundance."

"You're being straight with me, Slack, I appreciate that. Real tight pals like us, we should've been more open with each other. I wasn't being square with you, either, it's not Thailand, I got a place closer —"

Slack cut him off. "Elmer, we don't want to say where we're going."

"Yeah, right, the witnesses. See, man, that's the trouble."

Slack was starting to worry that Frank Sierra would soon be putting into the dock, the noise of an engine could unhinge these negotiations, the scales were precariously balanced. Elmer was starting to wave his gun around, he was sweating like a racehorse. Slack had to resolve this Mexican standoff.

"Tell you what, I'm going to come out from behind the curtain and we're going to get face to face. We're both going to put our guns away, we're going to watch each other do it, and we're both going to grab a duffle bag and we're going to get the sweet fuck out of here."

Elmer was slow to respond. For some reason he was now staring at the candle, which was melting into a pool of wax. He was still gripping the gun tightly, but pointing it down now, at an angle to the floor.

Maggie was shaking her head, a message: don't show yourself. In a way, doing so was foolish, but Elmer had lost his alertness, had travelled off somewhere. Confident voices whispered to Slack he was winning this game of mental hide-and-seek, wearing Elmer out.

Slack picked up one of the heavy bags of money, hefting it over a shoulder. Then he slid through the part in the curtains.

"*Vámonos*, Elmer, grab the other bag."

Elmer couldn't tear his eyes off the candle, his eyes seemed filled with visions of ancient ghosts. "Man, that's the whole world there, ain't it, in a single dying flame. When it's gone, that's it, darkness."

He appeared to have lapsed into a state of funereal melancholy. Slack had seen other men who'd been damaged in Vietnam, emotionally disabled.

"Let's go."

Elmer sighed, looked at his .45 again, then began to tuck it into his belt.

"The catch."

"Yeah, right."

Elmer slid the safety on, jammed the gun in his belt, watching Slack, who was pocketing his own piece. Elmer found the belt too tight, loosened it a notch, then extended his right hand to Slack. "Partners to the end, man."

Elmer's hand was slippery with perspiration. Slack thought of taking him here and now, using that wrist twist Joe Borbón had taught him, but the better idea was to get him outside first.

He stood aside as Elmer went past into the kitchen and picked up the other sack. Slack gave the captives a reassuring nod. Glo nodded back, Halcón winked. Slack couldn't read anything in Maggie's eyes, she was looking up at the ceiling.

He dashed outside, joining Elmer by the staircase, he was casually fishing through a shirt pocket, calmer, maybe coming down now. He'd brought the empty suitcases, too, but had set them down. The moon was struggling to emerge from the squall's fleeting clouds, the crackles of lightning more distant now.

"Found them two naked on the bed when I got here, middle of the afternoon, man, she's giving him head. I paddled into shore so they wouldn't hear me, if an armada had landed they wouldn't've noticed."

It was coming together for Slack, Elmer had pistol-whipped Halcón, made death threats, sent him on the mission to Limón to pick up the cash. Getting Maggie as an unwanted bonus might have confused him, put a crimp in his plans, maybe the colonel had told him not to attrit too many innocent civilians.

Elmer found what he was looking for in his pocket, another tab of lysergic acid.

"Stow that, for Christ's sake."

But Elmer popped it into his mouth. "Aw, this is tame shit. Keep-awakes. I had maybe two minutes of sack all last night."

The guy was on a chemical binge, Slack would have to truss him up after he pulled on him, immobilize him with the duct tape. He took one of the suitcases, he wanted him well away from the house. "Let's get our butts in gear, Elmer. Where's the plane?"

"Tortuguero town. Panama City, that's where we're going." Elmer shouldered his bag and led Slack down the stairs. "After that, Colombia, I got good protection there, friends in Medellín."

"Who arranged for this plane?"

"One of the friends, also a friend of the colonel." Elmer chuckled. "Johnny, he thought the plane was for him, he bought that all the way. No way, man, it was for me to split out of here in case I got heat. He ain't that smart, Johnny. He ain't got the team spirit you and I got, he's soft, he ain't got the balls to be a musketeer."

"You sure the feds aren't watching the plane?"

"The old man wouldn't rat. You don't know him."

There was a bond between these soldiers, Elmer must have been Chuck's aide-de-camp, his dogsbody. Walker had got his Medal of Honor by rescuing soldiers from behind the lines, it would be no surprise if one of them had been Elmer, someone should have done a trace on those names.

Elmer stepped into the Zodiac and held out his arms for Slack to pass him one of the bags.

Here was a clear opportunity, Slack would toss him the sack, then pull his gun and brace him. This was the moment of truth.

But it was the wrong truth. As Slack started to heave the duffle bag, Elmer wrenched his service pistol from his belt.

"And he wouldn't cop out, not the colonel."

Slack was moving, diving for the water, as the first shot nicked him, causing him to spin, to splash with flailing limbs into the canal. But the second bullet went wayward, beyond his head, when a wooden oar appeared from nowhere, slashing at Elmer's arm.

Though underwater, Slack had a murky moonlit view of Frank Sierra standing in Halcón's yellow launch, wielding the oar again, sending Elmer toppling into the canal as another aimless shot rang out.

Surfacing, he flung his revolver toward Frank. Slack was only ten feet from shore, Elmer five feet farther away, not swimming, just splashing and yelling and making no sense. "King Kong, this is Zebra. Send in the F-11s, asshole!"

Slack was bleeding and his ass hurt like blazes. He swam quickly to shore, then hauled his way up the bank. Frank was now kneeling in the Zodiac, holding the .38.

Slack paused to do damage assessment, he had to contort his body to get an oblique look at his behind. A creaser, ragged horizontal gashes across his buttocks, his pants ripped. It was as if someone had taken a steel-barbed whip to him, an injury painful, unrefined, but not mortal. He removed his shirt and wrapped the wound as best he could, a triangular bandage around his waist and under his crotch.

As he made his way to the dock, he saw a furrow far out in the canal, a wide circle, it had to be the same crocodile he'd stepped on, or its bigger brother. The animal had scented something, maybe Slack's trail of blood, and it was on its way to check.

Elmer was now swimming toward one of the floating logs that composed the dock. Something else was going on, and in his confusion Slack couldn't identify the sound, then realized he was hearing the deep-throated growl of beating props, a helicopter approaching.

Elmer had dropped his automatic during his ungainly swim to the end of the log, and he rested there. "They sent a beater, they're bringing us in." He shouted, "We're over here, man!"

Slack felt disoriented by the confused mélange of pain and noise and images – Elmer's rantings, the growing racket in the sky, the copter's search beam patrolling the shore margins . . . and the crocodile making swift passage toward Elmer.

Slack sprinted for the dock. "Get the hell out of the water!"

Frank Sierra had been watching the copter, but now looked at Slack, the blood running down his thighs, staining his pants.

Voices were drowned by the aircraft, stationary above them, Slack saw the logo of NBC News painted on it. He shouted to Frank above the din of its engine. "Shoot it!"

"The helicopter?" Frank hadn't seen the crocodile.

Elmer tried to boost himself into the Zodiac but fell back, blinded by the copter's searchlight. Slack jumped into the launch and grabbed the revolver from Frank's hand, motioning to him to run to safety.

The croc's eyes were above the waterline for a moment, then it disappeared, diving for Elmer's legs. Slack fired, Elmer cowering below him, his face starkly lit, and whiter yet with fear, he assumed he was the target. Slack emptied the chamber, the tail thrashing now, a darkening of the water, blood. The copter pilot gunned it, sped to safety over the house.

Suddenly, the beast rose from the water, swivelling sideways, a flash of long white belly, its tail and claws fiercely spanking the water, majestic in its appalling death throes. Elmer, gasping, finally made it onto the Zodiac.

Slack retrieved the duffle bags and hurried to the house, calling back to Frank: "Look after Elmer. Where's our boat?"

He pointed down the trail, the path cut by Slack.

The NBC copter was making another wide circle, drowning Elmer's shouts: "Down here, asshole! Take me outta here!" How had a news crew got here so fast? Those Ticos at the dock, probably none of them had been able to keep their mouths shut, the broadcast media had been offering rewards for timely tips.

In the house, the candle stub at Halcón's feet was struggling, barely holding its flame. Glo had gone limp with the release of tension, but Maggie still seemed stressed, her limbs stiff.

He drew his knife, carefully slicing through the tape that bound their wrists, rapidly relating to them the cause of the turbulence outside. "You're going to have to boot it, Johnny, network news is about to descend on us. I cut a trail through the bush, we have a boat waiting for you there, plenty of gas." He separated the last strands of tape and their hands came free.

A roar of engine from the canal brought Slack to the window. He saw a high wake behind the fleeing Zodiac, Elmer was eloping, Frank standing by helplessly, his gun empty. But there'd be nowhere safe for Elmer to hide, Walker's Rangers might want to run him down, too, maybe with a tank.

Halcón and Glo were on their feet now, pulling the tape from their mouths. Glo worked the stiffness from her face, then whooped a rebel yell. Maggie, still seated, was staring up at Slack, hardly moving a muscle.

"You okay?"

She nodded, slowly manoeuvred her hands to her face, began picking at the tape with her fingernails. As Slack bent to help, Glo sprung at him like a cat, took him off his feet as she planted a wet kiss on his lips. Slack winced.

"Oh, shit, sorry, honey, you're hurting."

Halcón's first of act of freedom was to light a cigarette, he was smiling, not rushing off anywhere. "You are bleeding, *maje*. You must seek attention."

"I lost some rear padding, that's all."

"Let me take off that diaper." Glo peeled away his shirt first, it was clinging to him, the blood congealing. Then she tugged at his belt, unzipping his fly.

He clamped his hands to her wrists. "I'm okay."

"Johnny, get the first-aid kit."

The helicopter clattered by again, lower this time, still looking for a spot to set down. "Get going, Johnny, where there's press there'll soon be cops."

Slack grabbed at his undershorts as Glo wrestled his pants off. "Over there, bashful, on the cot, assume the usual position."

He stretched out on it, unresisting now as Glo slipped his briefs down, studying his ass. Halcón handed her gauze and bandages from the emergency kit.

"I don't understand this, Slack, you are letting me escape?" Halcón seemed more confused than pleased. "But I know who you are now, from Gloria-May, you are a police agent. Why are you doing this?"

"Take the money, you earned it."

Halcón's mouth was agape. "But I cannot believe this."

"I'll ask the courts to deduct it from Chester's alimony," said Glo as she finished dressing the wound. She handed Slack some clean clothes, jeans and a shirt.

"Take the money and run, Johnny. That's the deal we made, we're not going to let Chuck welsh on it. You can forget about the plane, though, that's a set-up."

"As I suspected. The good people of Cinco de Mayo are waiting by a river landing with a vehicle."

"You going to look after them?"

"Of course." Halcón picked up just one duffle bag. "The rest of the money is yours, Jacques."

"Give it to Greenpeace. It would only be wasted on Walker's lawyers, he's going to need a few."

"I am not thinking, of course you could not easily hide the money from them. I will find a more discreet way to thank you." Retrieving a pen, Halcón wrote a name and phone number on an empty Derby pack. Mendez, it read, Panama City. "He is a trusted contact, use a safe phone."

The candle had gone out now, but Glo had found a flashlight, and was beaming it at Maggie, still on the floor, slowly and carefully peeling the tape from her mouth. "Honey, get up, don't just sit there, let me help you with that."

Maggie was staring hard at Slack, he thought she was trying to communicate something, but he had to focus all his attention on getting Halcón out of here. He heard a distant thrumming out on the canal, it sounded like boat engines.

Halcón took Glo's hand. "Come, *mi amor*, the night has not many hours left."

"Whoa," Slack said. "She's staying."

Glo shook her head. "It's been right nice knowing y'all, Slack."

"What the hell is going on here?"

Halcón shrugged helplessly. "I am now the prisoner."

Slack saw a softness in his eyes, not quick and darting now, but distant and hazy. Maybe he should have guessed, Halcón had been prepared to give away the entire ransom for Glo, the loot had been in the Suzuki, Johnny could have grabbed the keys, blown Maggie a kiss, and driven off with it.

"You been out in the moonlight too long, Glo?" Slack asked.

"I'm not sure what hit me, maybe a gamma ray burster."

"You are *going* with him?"

"He's a Sagittarius."

Slack found that answer insufficient. "You're out of your mind."

"Hell, I've finally come to my senses, I have a life all of a sudden. Y'all don't suppose I'm going back to Chester and what passes for *his* life? Didn't I hear he was planning my funeral?"

"I will escort them," said Frank. He was outside the door, he'd been watching this interplay, fascinated.

"Two seconds," said Glo. She bent to Maggie's forehead and kissed it, then began whispering in her ear as she peeled the last of the tape from her mouth.

The noises from outside grew louder. Slack looked out, an entire *son et lumière* seemed to be advancing up the lagoon, an invading force of launches. "All aboard, anyone who's going. In ten minutes, it's going to be like Mardi Gras around here."

Glo kissed Maggie on the lips, gave her a fist, said, "Go for it, baby," then took Halcón's hand and followed him out the door.

Halcón paused, took Slack's hand. "Until God brings us together, *maje. Adiós.*"

"*Buena suerte.*"

On the stairs, Halcón received Frank Sierra cordially, with a bow of respect to the man who had so long and doggedly pursued him. As they hurried down the trail, they were laughing, maybe at some old private joke. Glo turned and blew Slack a kiss. "Good luck, lover," she called.

Maggie was still sitting, she hadn't moved an inch.

"You paralyzed? What's wrong?"

"Scorpion." She barely breathed the word.

NO TIME FOR SORROW

— I —

The gruesome little beast had been on the rafters, where Maggie had been watching it sporadically for the last hour, seeking to distract herself, to focus on a lesser horror than her own impending death. Several minutes ago it had dropped, alighting with a soft plopping sound on her shoulder before finding refuge under her T-shirt, between the Pura and the Vida.

"Don't just stand there," she whispered.

He lit a fresh candle, knelt and inspected the bulge made by tail and stinger curled to strike. From outside, she could hear boat horns, shouts.

"The preferred approach is to grab it from beneath the tail while praying." He plucked the trespasser between two fingers, drawing it from her skin by pinching a tent in the T-shirt. "This is nothing. I had one land on me in bed, a damn mother, covered with her babies, about a hundred of them."

"Get rid of that thing."

"We haven't a strong case against the perpetrator; we have to let him go. I'm dealing with guilt enough. I executed a beautiful animal out there, a crocodile. I'm afraid you're going to have to slip out of that shirt."

"I'm beyond modesty."

While he held the pulsing little creature, she raised her arms and slid free of the shirt. As he bore it outside, she took a deep breath, struggled up on rubbery legs, and made her way to the bedroom, selecting a shirt and pants from the pile of clothes.

Slack stayed outside, his back to her while she changed. He was staring out at the flotilla approaching the shore: a dozen boats, a pontoon barge bearing a TV truck that bristled with antennae and transmitters.

Finally came the question she was dreading: "Why didn't you wait for me in Limón?"

He probably thought she had been completely irrational. "I'm sorry, I panicked. Jericho was going to kill Glo if Halcón didn't return with the money in two hours."

"You were thinking with your heart, not your head."

She must find words to thank him for his heroic acts, his kindnesses – though maybe words were not enough. "I think that sweet hunk has the hots for you," Glo had whispered, "so go watch some damn birds with him, take the sunset cruise." Maggie's parting words were briefer: "Sisters in spirit forever, Glo."

She joined Slack at the railing. The barge was nudging its way to shore; the smaller boats were jostling for rights to the two-log dock.

"You know where Halcón is taking her?" he asked.

"He said something about returning to the Andes. They both like to ski. What are we going to tell the press?"

"We stall them, give Bonnie and Clyde enough lead time."

"Slack, you could be in a really bad spot. I'll say I sneaked off with Halcón, okay? I gave him the ransom and you came later."

"Hell, no."

The helicopter had landed not far away; she could hear the engine throttling down. Another now appeared overhead, low and menacing, spearing them in its spotlight. "That'll probably be Bakerfield," Slack said.

She followed him inside, where he lit a few kerosene lamps, then poked among some bottles on a shelf, finding a half-filled quart of *guaro*. He poured a generous ounce in a glass and took a swallow, then suddenly turned to her. "I have something to tell you. I've rehearsed various ways to say this, and I don't know why I'm having so much trouble conveying what I feel, but . . . well, I admire you."

That seemed not the verb he was really seeking. She waited in tense silence for elaboration.

"Maggie, I'm going to say this, and it's not easy – in fact it's damned scary, and maybe for you it's phenomenally awkward news. But I'm developing a thing about you." He drained his glass. "A fairly heavy thing."

"A thing . . . well, that's flattering." She didn't know what else to say.

"I was bowled over when we first met that time outside the Darkside; you were so damn tough and beautiful and caring . . . I read all your books, and I know I'm not your type; you like clean-shaven patricians with tuxedos and Ph.D.s. Or law degrees . . . forget I said that. Anyway, God knows how, but it happened. End of subject. We have visitors."

From behind her came a ruckus: loud voices, feet stomping up the stairs. Her mind was still absorbing Slack's "fairly heavy thing" as she turned, and she collided with a chair, almost falling over it. Before she steadied herself, several flashbulbs blinded her, and she realized – in a moment of crushed vanity – that tomorrow she would be looking ridiculous on the front page of the *Saskatoon Star-Phoenix*.

Within ten minutes, at least thirty media persons had filed inside; the house sagged dangerously with their weight and was loud with gabble and shouted questions. "What happened to the kidnappers?" "Where's Gloria-May?"

Many of the reporters seemed to know him – he had been the source of many caustic sound bites. A grinning Ed Creeley shook their hands. "Bolshevik, eh? You should get the bullshit-artist award, Slack. What the fuck's going on here? We got a whole bunch of eye-witness accounts that Halcón was seen boating up this way with a woman."

"Okay, folks, I'll say this slowly so you can catch every word: the kidnapping was engineered by Senator Chester Walker; he set the whole damn thing up."

That was met with a sudden shocked silence while Slack calmly poured another two fingers of *guaro*. "Chuck also hired a drug dealer by the name of Elmer Jericho to murder his wife. That contract was not completed, Ms. Walker is safe, and Jericho is at this moment on his way to an airfield. That's my opening statement. Maggie?"

She had not expected to be called upon so abruptly. "Well, Mr. Cardinal here was hired by the U.S. government as an undercover agent, and he should get a ton of medals. I'm fine, in excellent shape, obviously; so is Gloria-May. She doesn't want it known where she is. She — how can I put it? — well, obviously she's hiding, her life has been threatened." She added brightly, "She was in cheerful spirits when I last saw her."

She was being looked at with uncomprehending expressions; reporters who had recovered from shock were scribbling furiously as she and Slack recounted Elmer's drug-addled threats and admissions. "I can't get this straight," said CNN's Monique Delgado. "Was Halcón here or not?"

"No immediate comment on that one," Slack said.

Creeley asked, "He get paid off?"

The house shook as six agents burst in, brandishing weapons, searching among the crowd in confusion until they recognized Maggie and Slack. A female agent drew Maggie off to a corner. She tried to fend her off, to return to Slack's side, then was astonished to see a clean-cut young man pointing a pistol at him.

Reporters complained as they were herded toward the door, the photographers still frantically busy with their cameras.

Slack was looking at the gun with a bemused expression, sipping at his *guaro*. "You going to read me my rights, Theodore?"

"That man saved my life at least three times in twenty-four hours." Maggie shouted this, for the ears of the last reporters being pushed out the door. "He saved *all* our lives!"

Now framed in the doorway was the grizzled bulk of Hamilton Bakerfield, looking around, his eyes settling on Maggie. "How are you feeling, Miss Schneider?"

"Damned angry. Tell that man to put his gun away."

"What's with the blood on you, Sawchuk?"

"I took one in the ass for the free world."

"Is what I'm assuming right? You gave Johnny four million dollars and threw in Gloria-May Walker as a tip?"

"Tell Theodore children shouldn't play with guns."

"He's going to escort you out. He's going to put you on a flying machine. When we get where we're going, we're going to talk. If I don't like what I hear I'm going to turn you over to the local civilian authority until I can get an extradition order to haul your sorry ass to Leavenworth."

— 2 —

Blossoms from bedside bouquets filled Maggie's room with sweet competing fragrances. To the grandest was pinned a card with at least a hundred names from her hometown. "You're the pride of Lake Lenore." Her parents had presented it to her last night during a brief, teary reunion while her interrogators took a break. Beverley and Woodrow were in a room down the hall: the Canadian Embassy had arranged their accommodations, a charming San José hostelry.

Shedding her pyjamas, Maggie turned on the spout of the lion's paw tub. The smell of Bakerfield's cigars still clung to her skin: the ordeal had ended at three a.m. While her bath filled, she clicked on the set: on Canal Siete, a panel of experts was debating the events of last night, smiling Ticos who seemed to be taking pleasure from the seduction of a U.S. presidential aspirant's wife by their new national hero. As best she could make out, Glo and Halcón were still on the lam.

She had not had contact with Slack since they were spirited separately to San José. As she had feared, his unabashed generosity and his *je ne sais quoi* attitude to Glo's elopement with the thief had embroiled him in a cauldron of trouble. But given the circumstances – and her unyielding support – Maggie was confident the authorities would soon release him.

As she soaked in the tub, she played back Slack's confession of last night, and excoriated herself – his shy courting ought to have been met by more than stunned silence. No man had ever proclaimed his love to Maggie before – or even a "fairly heavy thing." How could he hold such feelings for her after knowing her so briefly?

As she towelled herself, she tuned to CNN in time to catch footage of last night's bizarre press conference. Here was Slack, calmly tilting his glass of *guaro*, a gun pointed at him. That, said Monique Delgado, was her last image of this "unusual key player, who continues to be held for questioning." Operación Libertad had remained ominously silent all day, and no sightings had been made of "the mysterious Elmer Jericho."

The White House was speaking in cautious tones: many questions were yet to be clarified. Democrats were calling for a senate inquiry and Republicans were in a quandary – some were distancing themselves from the senator, others standing by him, prepared to accept his firm denials of wrongdoing. The FBI was mum: inquiries were being undertaken.

Highlights were shown of a hastily arranged press briefing in Walker's hotel suite. The makeup person had not been able to hide the lines of tension that marred his handsome face, but his voice held firm: "Let me make this abundantly clear, I deeply love my wife. I have absolutely no connection with this character Elmer Jericho. He is a drug addict, a thief, and a fugitive. Why would any sane man believe such a scoundrel?" Glo had been brainwashed and placed in a trance, or possibly even drugged. Ms. Schneider and Mr. Cardinal were victims of a sleaze artist. His lawyers had been instructed to commence proceedings against Jacques Cardinal for slander and the theft of four million dollars.

Maggie turned off the set in disgust and went to her parents' room.

Beverley had had the night to absorb Maggie's tale of her adventures, physical and romantic, and was now ready with words of advice. "It sounds to me like you backed the wrong horse, young lady, falling for a fleece artist instead of that gorgeous big redhead; he's a very gracious man."

"Mom, I didn't plan it that way."

"And him rescuing you life and limb. He cross-examined us about you; he was interested from the start. He may be a bit older than you, but you're no babe in the woodpile, either."

Beverley had almost relinquished hope for Maggie's chances, and here was Galahad riding to the rescue on his painful bottom.

"I suppose he has faults," Beverley said. "To hear him, you'd think all life is doomed on earth – but you're probably just the antidote he needs."

"He sure shoots a mean game of pool," said Woodrow, as if that was enough. Slack had wooed them with gratifying results, buying them dinners, escorting them about Quepos and Manuel Antonio. But she could see the renewed glow of affection in their eyes, and was forced to consider again the irony of feckless love: sometimes the arrows stick to the target; sometimes they simply wound.

Maggie's debriefing resumed that afternoon in the presence of a scowling Hamilton Bakerfield, monitoring a portable recorder, and Paula d'Annunzio, from the U.S. Justice Department, a straight-laced lawyer with a penchant for law enforcement jargon. Had Maggie, she asked, any idea where "the perpetrator" may have taken Mrs. Walker?

"I have answered that question at least five times, Ms. d'Annunzio. They could be in Tuscaloosa as far as I know."

"Do you still take the view that Gloria-May Walker's departure was a voluntary act?"

"She practically danced out."

"She seemed under a spell?"

"There is a deep attraction, and it's real."

"You're not aware if he threatened her."

Maggie rebelled, and spoke with high energy: "It's futile to try to claim that money back. A divorce judge would grant her that much. God, the man conspired to *kill* her."

Bakerfield interrupted: "Yeah, but the money was given to Johnny Diego by Slack Cardinal, no questions asked."

"Mr. Bakerfield, that was an arrangement that you and Senator Walker authorized."

"That's an issue of interpretation," d'Annunzio said. "You told us earlier that Jacques Cardinal and Johnny Diego seemed on friendly terms."

"They weren't in cahoots, if that's what you're implying."

"Your account, Ms. Schneider, suggests that they planned to meet and split the proceeds."

"Halcón offered, Slack declined."

"But on the basis of what you tell us, there is reason to believe they have a private agenda. You are not aware of what ongoing discussions took place between these two men."

Maggie abruptly gained her feet, in a temper at the innuendoes cast by the machine-like Paula D'Annunzio. "Why aren't you arresting Chuck Walker? He reeks of guilt."

"It won't stand up, Ms. Schneider. Without Mr. Jericho, all we have is vague hearsay, inadmissible as evidence."

"Where's Elmer Jericho? Do you have him hidden?"

"I'm not here to lie to you, Ms. Schneider. We haven't found any trace of him."

Maggie turned on Bakerfield. "You let him fly away. He had a plane waiting, and no one bothered to try intercept him. Who gave the order to frame Slack Cardinal?"

"Cool down, Ms. Schneider," Bakerfield said. "We're only trying to get to the nub of this. Okay, let's go to the beginning and fill in some detail."

Maggie sighed and retook her seat.

Got back late to Villas Bongo, now it's the morning after. Some hasty tran-scribing of quotes from Benito Madrigal while my meeting with him is fresh. (I now own a laptop!) Lots of people in the visiting room at the Psiquiatrico hospital. He was lucid (but still insisted Halcón and Glo had conspired to steal the ransom money), seemed to be enjoying his fame, proud he had stood up to Walker's Rangers long enough for Slack and me to escape under his covering fire. "Now the world knows the truth." He wants to run for president again.

"Jacques Cardinal, he is a marked man. Senator Walker's hired assassins are unvanquished yet, despite the blow for liberty that we have rung across the nation." A greater threat comes from influential leaders in San José. "They fear his power. On every street and country lane, the nation is in revolt. The revolution is rumbling at the gates of the palaces of imperialism." Benito is a compelling speaker, and quite a few patients, visitors, even staff, gathered around. Some applauded.

He also believes there'll be an international cover-up: the truth will be twisted. Benito is being proved right on that point, so I'm reaffirming my pledge, I won't leave this country until Slack is freed; I owe him that, and much, much more . . .

Incidentally, though I went on a little charter all the way to San José and back yesterday, I had no fear of flying at all.

Morning sunshine caressed the placid ocean waters by the tropical villa where Maggie had been ensconced for the last ten days. Seduced by thoughts of a swim before the heat of the day, she closed her lap-top – bought yesterday in San José during a shopping spree motivated by visions of the hefty advances promised by a New York agent.

She tried on her new, ultra-revealing bikini. The view in the mir-ror did little damage to the eyes. A few weeks ago, she might not have had the courage to wear it, but a more confident persona had taken up inner residence. "Go for it," Glo had said, and why not?

Gloria-May had done so with typical verve, audaciously throw-ing her former life to the wind. Two weeks had passed since she and

Halcón faded into the night, and though a few Ticos claimed to have seen them (visions akin to sightings of the Virgin Mary), it would appear they had fled the country. Nor was there a sign of Halcón's merry band. And no word from Frank Sierra.

She plucked a towel from a rack, wrapped it around her, and swept out onto the flagstone walk that connected the poolside restaurant to the dozen elegant villas. All but a few were deserted – Costa Rica had not enjoyed favourable press of late. The embassy had offered Maggie a furnished apartment in San José, but her substantial bargaining power (she was a luminary; her sprawl over a chair was splashed across the cover of *Maclean's*) had earned her this hideout: Villas Bongo, nestled into a remote Pacific cove in the Nicoya Peninsula. She couldn't escape the U.S. Justice Department, however – Paula d'Annunzio was coming by today; Maggie had refused to talk to her by phone.

Beverley and Woodrow were also here, in the neighbouring unit. Their relationship had continued to spring new growth in this hothouse climate, and they were preparing to return to Lake Lenore, work the farm, take pressure off the boys and in-laws.

The only other guests in the restaurant were three medical students on spring break who had arrived last night. One of the men offered her yesterday's *Miami Herald*, and after pouring a coffee she studied the front page. Demonstrations were continuing outside the Costa Rican National Assembly; five hundred protesters had marched to the Casa Presidencial. Slack Cardinal had become a martyr for aiding Halcón, who was also growing in myth each day.

Maggie found it unimaginable, except as political farce, that Slack was still in detention; she had raised her own storm of protest when authorities refused to let her visit him in jail. Aiding in the escape of a felon and conspiracy to steal the ransom: those were the charges, the official theory being that Slack had again confused his roles, had crossed over to the enemy. Frank Sierra, surprisingly, had escaped arrest, despite his role as usher for the departing couple. It puzzled her that the detective had not returned her calls to his office in San José.

A third-page feature piece detailed the slippage in electoral support for Chester Walker, who, despite everything, had resumed his campaign. Though his rallies in New Hampshire were large – he was maintaining his hardcore support – most were attending only out of curiosity. He was a fighter, he told his cheering fans; he had never given up in battle. "Wherever you are, Gloria-May, I love you and pray for you." Maggie supposed he had no choice but to continue this burlesque: to retire from the campaign might seem an admission of guilt.

The FBI seemed to be plodding along at the pace of a moose in a slough in making out a case against him, though sources at the Justice Department had hinted that indictments were being drawn up. Essential proof was lacking, which only an account from Elmer Jericho could supply. He could be on Jupiter or Betelgeuse as far as anyone knew.

As she leaned over the table, her towel slipped from around her waist. She looked up to see three pairs of eyes locked upon her.

"You gents studying for your anatomy exams?"

One looked away, flustered. Another nervously fiddled with his camera strap. The third was cockier; he dove into the pool, surfacing near her table. "I felt a sudden need to cool off," he said. "By the way, I'm giving body-surfing lessons at the beach today."

"I might just take you up on that."

As he floated off, grinning at his friends, she turned to an inside page, where she read the welcome news that a stout-hearted judge in San José, critical of the charges against Slack, was proposing to release him on bail of a hundred colones: about thirty cents. This newspaper was a day old, so the judge's offer may already have been acted upon. She had passed on a message through Mr. Carazo, his lawyer, that she was at Villas Bongo, so she expected him to call soon.

She felt a hand touch her, and whirled. "Lady Godiva," said her mother. "I've seen shoelaces wider than that."

Maggie joined her and Woodrow at their table. "This sure beats packing bags of fertilizer from Lenore Feed and Lumber," he said, gazing at the pool, at the smiling crescent beach behind it. "Ten below, that's what the mayor of Saskatoon just told me."

Her parents were running interference for her from press and politicians. Mayor, premier, prime minister, all had been on the phone to Villas Bongo. Among the many reporters who had travelled here to seek and be refused an interview was Ed Creeley. "Chuck's going to walk – you watch," he had told her. "Best way to cover up truth is bury the witness; he's probably snuffed Jericho by now."

Woodrow informed her the mayor had proclaimed this coming Saturday as Maggie Schneider Day: a downtown parade, a civic banquet, a symbolic key to the city.

"Dad, did you tell him I would go along with that? It's too camp, I would only be embarrassed. Tell him I'm staying until Slack is out."

"He got himself sprung," Woodrow said. "Mayor Hrawchuk saw it on the TV this morning; hundreds at the prison gates to greet him."

"Including a flock of young ladies, by the way," said Beverley.

Maggie stayed in the ocean for most of the morning, learning to body surf, enjoying the attentions of three medical students while avoiding Paula d'Annunzio, whom she could see waiting for her at the restaurant. But after Maggie and her friends stretched out in the shade of almond trees, the lawyer made her way down to the sand. There was always a prickly edge to these sessions.

Maggie made introductions. "Paula's a federal prosecutor, so watch out; she specializes in the innocent."

D'Annunzio advised the men to go for a swim and stared them coldly into compliance. "Your other college friend, Buho, has surfaced in Havana. I would guess the rest of the bunch are with him."

"Good for them."

"Have you heard from Cardinal? We thought he might attempt to seek you out."

"He hasn't."

"Well, we have added his name to the missing. He didn't check into a hotel room reserved for him."

"Probably because he didn't want to be kidnapped back to the U.S.A. Or assassinated by Walker's Rangers. Tell me honestly, Paula, who's behind the charges against Slack – Walker's friends in the CIA? The Ticos don't want to proceed; they're totally embarrassed."

"Will you promise to call me at the embassy if he makes contact?"

"I'll promise to think about it."

❧

For the next few days Maggie resisted the temptations of beach and pool, wading instead in paper, entering her ten weeks of notes into her computer. Creativity was blocked only when Slack Cardinal shambled into her thoughts. Again, she phoned his lawyer. Again, Señor Carazo patiently explained that Slack had yet to make contact with his office; he sounded put out at his client.

Maggie Schneider Day was looming, Beverley fielding increasingly urgent calls. From Saskatoon: "Mayor Hrawchuk again, dear, begging, he's prostate at your feet." From the Canadian Embassy: "They've got us three seats in first class. You have to decide."

— 4 —

Maggie stared glumly from her taxi at the frozen landscape. Erratic gusts lifted snow from flat fields, creating white whirlwinds; although the sun was bright in a cloudless sky, the temperature was a glacial fifteen below. She could weather the weather, but would she have the strength tomorrow to survive Maggie Schneider day?

A celebration at CSKN was also on the agenda for this evening. The station manager, J. A. Wilkie, had been among the welcoming party at the airport and had offered three months' leave: "Full pay, no problem."

Her parents had been picked up by Uncle Ralph in his truck; her mother's home would be brimming with relatives: her three brothers, grandparents, cousins from Regina. A visit to Lake Lenore seemed mandatory; the town was also planning a welcome. After that, she would hide from the world, bury herself in work: she was facing a fall delivery deadline for her book.

The downtown lights were switching on and the traffic rush was beginning. She gazed out at the western sky: cold and brittle slants of yellow light from a sun crawling to the horizon; in Costa Rica it dived. She remembered trying to explain snow to Tayra; how could that seem such an elusive concept?

From a bridge spanning the South Saskatchewan River, she could see her apartment. How many winter hours had she spent staring from her window at this curling ice-choked river? For year after tedious year, she had impatiently awaited spring break-up, the joyful sound of gnashing, rushing ice. Was there sunshine in Quepos today? Was it raining in Limón?

Unbidden came the image of Slack Cardinal standing at the railing of the canal house, announcing his fairly heavy thing. She had not acted on her urge to embrace him; it was one of those moments not seized that could haunt one forever.

They were to have gone birding. He had promised to show her what was left of beauty.

Eye on the City was on air but wrapping as she walked into the main studio, where she shook hands and exchanged whispered greetings with co-workers. Behind a huge cake on the set of *The Happy Homemaker Show* was a banner: "Welcome Home, Maggie." Roland Davidson was summing up today's headline stories, the lead item being "our very own Maggie Schneider" returning home "after her two-month ordeal in the untamed jungles of Central America."

He was staring at the prompter, and hadn't noticed her yet. "Shock waves are buffeting Washington following Senator Chuck Walker's surprise second-place showing in the New Hampshire primary. And, finally, a five-billion-dollar wheat deal with China has collapsed – hard times ahead for the prairie grain belt."

Roland turned to Frieda Lisieux. "Well, Frieda, pretty chilly out; we're still in the dog days of winter."

She shivered theatrically. "I'll say. Look for twenty-five below tonight, maybe creeping up to minus ten tomorrow."

Roland looked at the clock and snipped her off. "Lots of sun, though, so get out there, and . . ." Catching sight of Maggie, he stammered, "And, ah, get out to that parade and give Maggie a big Schneider — I mean a welcome. Going to be there, Art?"

"Sure thing, Roland. By the way, I thought the dog days were always in summer."

"Have a good night, everyone."

The lights dimmed, and an air of embarrassment settled in. J. A. Wilkie stared uncomfortably at a Chef Boyardee commercial on the monitors; a control room engineer was stifling laughter.

"Give her a big *Schneider*?" Art Wolsely guffawed as he headed to the drinks table.

The studio doors opened and Maggie's co-workers poured in; Roland hid his chagrin by leading the applause, and then bussed her on the cheek. "I don't know how many times I've said 'our very own Maggie Schneider' on the air."

"Makes me feel like someone's possession."

Wilkie made an effusive welcoming speech, and they all raised their glasses to her. Maggie was surrounded by well-wishers, and began to feel smothered.

"Great tan, you look gorgeous." Frieda Lisieux seized Maggie by the arm. "Let's hit the powder room."

As she made her way there, Maggie was feeling slightly woozy — she had drunk more than she ought to — but, miraculously, did not stumble when she caught her feet in a bundle of power cords.

"I want all the dirt," Frieda said. "Fess up, did you do it with Halcón?"

"It? How do you do an it, Frieda?"

"Come on, you know what I mean. What about the guy who saved your life?"

"I still owe him a big kiss."

"You *owe* him? Jeez, *I'd* have given him something to remember me by."

Maggie's stomach began to heave.

OUR MAN IN PANAMA

— I —

It was mid-afternoon of a stifling day when Slack pulled into Panama City in a taxi held together with baling wire. His flight had been depressing, haze rising from slash-and-burn fires, his malaise exacerbated by a pounding head. But he had declined the offers of smiling flight attendants with their drink trolleys. He was quitting forever again today.

He had earned his thick head the hard way, a three-day blowout, maybe four, not counting time in the joint. The guards had been proud to have him, supportive, sneaking him bottles. Once on freeside, he'd hidden in a burg called Piedades, not far from the airport, a well-stocked rental unit, Frank Sierra had secured it for him. This morning, Frank had spirited him to the airport and to his plane.

The jouncing taxi ride caused a literal pain in the butt. This key part of his anatomy had also been the butt of jokes, Ham Bakerfield barely able to restrain his glee during his visits to the keep. Slack had asked about his fee, his signed contract for three hundred thousand dollars. Ham had shook his head sadly, Walker's cheque hadn't cleared.

Maybe he should've taken his cut at the scene of the crime. But he could stand the hassle, the bounced reward, the Mickey Mouse charges, being served up as the centrepiece of an international charade. What laid him truly low was the silent rebuff he had received from Maggie Schneider. What a look of despair had come over her as he stammered out his inane confession of love.

She had run off and hidden, a ritzy resort on the Nicoya Peninsula. Two days ago, she'd flown back to Canada, he'd seen her on the news, bundled up, waving to greeters, letting everyone see there's still beauty in the world.

There wasn't much of it on this crowded so-called freeway, exhaust fumes fouling the air, the road fenced with billboards to hide the slums. Colonial Panama had been a grand city, cathedrals and palaces, opulent mansions, warehouses of gold, a bustling slave market. Now it looked gutted, greasy repair shops, junkyards, broken pavement.

The squalor and potholes vanished as they entered the banking district. Panama held only two classes, poor thieves and rich thieves, and here was where the latter worked and schemed, Via España, the up-market commercial area with its smart shops and bank towers gleaming in the sun.

He paid off the taxi at the door of one of them, Banco Anglo Colombiano, a shiny new building, glass and brass, an upscale Mafia money laundry. He strode through the wash of cold air, past the armed guards to an information desk, where he was told that Señor Mendez sees no one without an appointment. Halcón's man in Panama threw heavy weight around here.

"I *have* an appointment." He had phoned Mendez this morning, a brief, cautious conversation.

The information officer wrote down his name, hunkered over a telephone, hurriedly returned to him, apologized for having seemed rude, and directed him to an elevator.

On the seventeenth floor, he was led through a maze of busy computer stations into a large office with a massive desk, a gentleman in banker's stripes rising from it with a wide smile and outstretched hand.

"Señor Cardinal, it is with great pleasure I greet you."

"The pleasure is mine, Señor Mendez."

A warm handshake. "We hope you will retain the funds in this institution, you will not find better rates. Safe and discreet, Mr. Cardinal, that is our motto."

Slack puzzled over the bank statement Mendez showed him. In the absence of some clerical mistake, it would appear half a million dollars was sitting in an account in his name.

"Our mutual friend was very generous," Slack said.

Mendez smiled. "My sources tell me the funds were actually wired here by his companion as a small gesture for saving her life."

"I pray they are well."

"They are in fine health, enjoying, I believe, a fresh mountain climate."

"Please pass on my regards to them."

Slack took a long siesta in a comfortable hotel room, getting up as evening approached, in a more buoyant mood after his encounter with the genial Señor Mendez. He had drawn fifty thousand dollars, and before leaving his room he stuffed it in his belt-bag along with his lock-pick kit.

Downstairs, in the lobby, he bought a newspaper before heading out past the ruins of the ancient city, along Panama Bay, through Chinatown. The sky was paling into darkness by the time he arrived at the nipple-shaped peninsula of San Felipe. This tiny fortified butt of land, Casco Viejo, it was called, the old compound, rewarded an evening's stroll, narrow streets, post-colonial architecture, cast-iron balconies, a palette of pastel hues.

He took a bench in Cathedral Plaza and opened his *Herald-Tribune*, reading about Walker's near-win in New Hampshire, then flipping through the pages until he found a story from Saskatoon headed, "5,000 BRAVE FREEZING WEATHER." Here was Margaret Schneider, peeking from between the folds of a heavy parka, an unguarded expression, as if surprised at being captured by a camera. Her immediate plans? "I intend to lock myself in a room with my computer and throw away the key."

She was quoted as being pleased that Mr. Cardinal had been released, wished him well. That sounded sufficiently formal and distant.

A young man sat down beside him, shifty-eyed in the manner of one who plies illegal trades. He tried to strike up a conversation. "Is beautiful evening, señor, you visit first time in Panama?"

"What are you selling?"

The man put a finger to his nose and sniffed, a *cocanero*.

"*Tiene hierba?*"

No, but he had African hash. Slack bought a baby-fist-size chunk for forty bucks and continued his stroll, followed *calle cinco* west from the plaza and its ornate cathedral, the street narrowing as it approached a dead end at the compound walls.

Here was Pensión La Fortuna, a fussy building of French colonial style, iron balconies suspended over the street, tourist stickers on the door, major credit cards honoured.

He introduced himself to the clerk as Harry Wilder and asked if his room was ready. She found his reservation and gave him two keys.

"It is one with a balcony view?"

"Yes, señor. Cuarto 301, it is the room you wanted."

He took the stairs to the third floor, his room was cozy, no cock-roaches. The second key, an old-fashioned skeleton, gave access by a metal-braided door to the balcony. He opened it, gazed out at the narrow, metal-webbed balconies, kids below playing soccer with a rubber ball, a noisy saloon across the street. He stretched out on the bed and tried to work out the rest of his life, he was thinking of hanging up the kayak business, selling his property, too.

After grabbing a few hours of restless sleep, Slack forced himself awake in the small hours, close to three a.m. He lay still for a while, medi-tating in the quiet and the darkness, a peace corrupted only by soft nasal snores from the adjoining room.

Finally, he buckled on his money belt, made his way out to the balcony in his bare feet. A distant glimmer of street lamp cast barred shadows down the narrow way, giving him a hazy light to see by. No life on the street, not many cars, an old Chrysler sedan parked below.

The climb across to the adjoining balcony involved a perilous straddle from railing to railing, Slack making the voyage safely but not soundlessly, the metal creaking under his weight, though not loud enough to wake anyone.

He didn't need his pick-kit for the lock, his skeleton worked, one size fits all. Inside, he stepped around a supply of oranges, tinned ham, corn flakes, and chocolate bars. He crept to the bedside table, where a .38 Smith was sitting. He emptied the chamber, replaced it, then clicked on the light.

The snoring had stopped, and Slack could pick up bodily tension from under the sheets. He twirled a wooden chair, sat on it backwards and leaned forward, resting his chin on his hands. "I'm a friendly," he said.

Elmer took a long time to move. An eye opened, bleary and raw, and finally fixed on Slack. "Hey, man."

"How you doing, sport?"

"Top shelf." The open eye flicked a sideways look at the .38. Gratified to find it still in reaching distance, Elmer assembled a sickly smile.

"You should be feeling like shit, Elmer. You should feel guilty. You never thanked me for saving you from that croc."

"You kidding? You'll always be first in my prayers, man." He seemed straight enough, he must have run out of dope, looked a little edgy without it. There was an ashtray by his bed, rolling papers, but merely the remnants of a few smoked-out doobies.

"I admit I was hoping to split with the bread, but I wasn't trying to blip you away, Slack, just warning you off." Elmer struggled to a sitting position.

"And I know you feel real bad about that, Elmer. Heartsick."

"How'd you get out of Costa Rica? Heard they laid a couple of heavy beefs on you."

"It's just the usual shit and bluster, I got a sharp lawyer."

"I knew you was a crook first time my eyes lighted on you. Johnny give you your split yet?"

Slack didn't feel the need to explain that his new wealth came from Gloria-May in thanks for saving her life from Elmer, or that three hundred thousand of it was owed him by Chuck Walker. He looked around: boxes of cookies on a shelf, a block of cheese. Elmer was in stoned semi-survivalist mode, his former friends could have snuffed him easily if they'd got here first. "Who does your grocery shopping, the maid?"

"Yeah, I haven't been getting out much."

"Good idea, never know when you're going to be hit by a car. You're lucky I found you first, Elmer, before they did."

"I ain't afraid of nobody. How *did* you find me?"

"The guy who knocked you into the canal? Frank Sierra, he's an ace sleuth, he slogged around to every hotel in Panama. We figured your pilot dumped you at the local airport when you couldn't show him any money."

Elmer yawned and stretched, shifting position, a little closer to the gun. Slack would be disappointed if he went for it, he wanted to think better of Elmer, to give him a second chance, there was a side to him he liked.

"The colonel's been telling everybody he never heard of you. Sounds like he's written you off."

That caused Elmer to flinch; devotion dies hard. "After all the shit you told them reporters, he probably wants my balls for his trophy case. I talked too much to you, I trusted you." He reconsidered that, there was an inculpatory ring to it. "Anyway, I was whacked out, man, I was talking a lot of bullshit."

When straight, Elmer was fairly slick and sly, but Slack preferred him stoned, when he was garrulous and incautious. "How's your stash?"

"I'm on empty."

Slack tossed him the small block of hashish. Elmer fondled it, looking at him, musing, calculating, then he seemed to relax. "You just saved my ass again, partner."

He reached over to the bedside table, this was the test. Slack wasn't let down, Elmer went for the rolling papers, not the .38.

"What brings you by, Slack?"

"Couple of things. Some private business. How much do you want for the Darkside?"

Elmer's face showed surprise, then interest, which he quickly masked with a reluctant shake of his head, shifting into salesman mode. "That's my grubstake, man, that's all I got. Two hundred acres, never been logged, comes with the river and three all-year streams up the mountain."

"You said you got it cheap."

Elmer put a match to the hash, softening it. "This some of that African stuff that's around? I owe a hundred and fifty, plus I already paid down thirty. I have to turn a profit."

"I'll give you two hundred and thirty thousand. You've had it for only a few months, you clear fifty grand."

Elmer got out of bed, he was wearing Jockey shorts. He found a squished cigarette in a shirt pocket, mixed the hash with the tobacco, began rolling a spliff.

"Yeah, but look at the house, it's not some Tico piece of shit, it's got design features. Two-eighty."

"Two-fifty, hard cash."

"You got it on you?" Elmer had his eye on Slack's bulging money belt.

"A starter, fifty grand, the rest when the lawyer draws up the papers." He tossed a bundle of bills on the bed.

Elmer couldn't restrain a smile. "You want to sign, like, a deal memo?"

"I'll scribble it out." Slack found a pen and some stationery, and began writing while Elmer got his lungs on the spliff. The guy had done the right thing not going for the gun.

"Wanna hit?" Elmer asked in a clenched voice, Slack shaking his head. Elmer finally let his breath go, smoke seemed to be seeping from him, the room was pungent with its odour. "I feel fucking human again."

Slack handed him the informal deed of sale for the Darkside, his ex-partner was going to need this money.

"What was the colonel going to do, appoint you ambassador to India?"

"I ain't with you."

"If you eliminated Gloria-May so he could get elected."

Elmer took his time, studying the deal memo, signing it, smoking, stalling, maybe wondering how candid he should be.

Slack prompted him. "My impression was your heart wasn't in it."

Elmer accepted that invitation, choosing the path of self-exoneration. "I couldn't've done it. When you caught me there, I'd already decided not to. Hey, that would mean zapping the witnesses, too, real innocent people like that Schneider lady, and what was she doing there?"

Slack wanted something firmer. "Hard to believe you actually intended to kill anyone."

"No way I would've."

"I told the cops I didn't stop you, you stopped yourself."

"I've seen enough blood. I did tough time overseas for Uncle Sam."

A jury of honest Americans might not be offended by that patriotic self-tribute, might even find sympathy for the emotionally wounded war vet who, before testifying against his former hero, won a struggle of conscience.

"Comes down to this, Walker finally gave you an order you couldn't follow."

"I told him the whole thing was nuts, I told him that right off the bat."

"I'm also going to accept that you didn't try to kill me. That'll be on the official record."

"Which side are you working here, Slack, you working for the man or just yourself?"

"I represent some interested parties."

"So those were just more phony raps they laid on you. Try to fool that old freak Elmer, make me think it's safe to talk to an outlaw. I may be dumb, but I'm not stupid. You wired?"

"No, we don't want this recorded, it gets into court, you know what lawyers are like, they misinterpret everything. Anyway, I've got a deal you can live with. Frankly, you can't live without it, the colonel's an old-fashioned soldier, deserters get shot."

Elmer went to the balcony door and stared into the gloom outside. "Yeah, I guess he's written me off. Saved my life over there, in Nam."

"A man can't pay a debt forever."

Elmer nodded and turned to Slack with an expression that testified to a willingness to do business. Slack had tried to persuade Ham that all this subterfuge wasn't necessary, the criminal charges, the two weeks of incarceration. Elmer and Slack had chemistry happening.

"What's the deal? I cooperate?"

"State's evidence against Walker."

"I get a pass?"

"They wanted you to cop to a conspiracy. I said there's no way you'd go for that. I told them you'd want full witness protection."

"No time?"

"You'll be booked, the charges held in abeyance. After it's all over, pick the country of your choice."

"I want to hear it from the man himself."

Slack went to the balcony and called out, "It's a go, Ham."

Bakerfield climbed from the Chrysler sedan.

— 2 —

We search the hours for solitude,
the quiet of herons in their sleep,
a fisher on the wing who falls
into the waves in search of silver
or a woman making her way through mist
in early morning, delicate as water.
We search for this . . .

Slack paused from his labours, stared out his window of welded hearts, musing of herons and kingfishers, of a woman who had flown from him, and whose long silence from a great distance hurt and puzzled him. A Pollyanna and a pessimist, a romance writer and a lamenting poet, it might have been a perfect blend. But once again, Slack had fallen victim to his immeasurable ineptitude with that terrifying other sex. He could hardly bear to recall his donkey act, his stammering attempt to court her.

He had a life without Margaret Schneider, he had some scratch set aside. He'd sold his kayak business, unloaded his old property on a lottery winner from Milwaukee, lauding the native charm of the subdivision across the street, assuring him property values would increase with such burgeoning development. Comfortably endowed, the new squire of the Darkside could go terrestrial, an eco-venture, a *tableau vivant* in the virgin hills, a zip line over the canopy, tours by harness through the treetops. He'd make enough to get by, the main thing would be to educate, make environmental converts, urge them to spread the word.

At the sound of a car engine outside, he ripped his page from the typewriter and placed it in a sheaf with his collection of soon-to-be unpublished poems. Maybe he would find the courage down the road to mail it to Maggie, maybe not. Her loss. He was well rid of her, she didn't deserve poetry. She had not even had the graciousness to write him a note.

From the arched window of the downstairs bedroom, his office-in-home, he could see but a gleaming of blue between the clouds that tumbled past on a run from mountains to sea. The green season had arrived already, in April, it had been raining off and on. A Nissan emerged from the citrus trees and came to a stop by the patio, Ham Bakerfield's driver at the wheel, Theodore. Ham was in the back, it looked like Frank Sierra was with him, too.

These three were the only beings on earth permitted to know Slack was here. He had been two months at the Darkside, sober and lonely. He needed solitude, he was drying out for the last time and forever, no phone, no radio, just an occasional newspaper that Theodore or Ham would bring with the mail.

The latest he knew, from a week-old *Herald-Tribune*, was that Elmer Jericho had been settled into an FBI safe house in Florida and that leaks from interrogation transcripts were fast sinking Walker's ship. The foot soldiers of Cinco de Mayo had not only resurfaced in Havana, but been put on display, a holiday called in their honour, a lavish proletarian wedding planned for the two youngsters Slack had encouraged to head for Cuba.

Jorge Castillo, seizing an opportunity to enhance his presidential bid, had told a crowded press conference he would not be seeking extradition of the misdoers, in fact was urging the president that all be pardoned, including Halcón – a living legend now, a whispered word from him could doom Castillo's chances for the Liberación nomination.

Slack went to the main room to greet Ham, who hadn't bothered to knock. There was no front door, anyway, Slack hadn't yet replaced the one Walker's Rangers rocket-launched off its hinges.

"Wonders never cease, we caught him sober."

Slack was miffed at that, the old man would choke on it before he would ever give him credit. Ham handed him a bundle of newspapers and letters, also a sealed document, a subpoena for Walker's impeachment hearings.

Frank was still standing outside, helping Theodore unload the van. Frank had Tico manners, you don't enter someone's house until asked. Slack didn't usher him in right away, drew him out of earshot of Theodore. Slack was curious about the sudden warming of the climate between Sierra and Minister Castillo, suspected their earlier iciness had been feigned.

"Did you get the job, Frank?"

"Minister Castillo will indeed be seeking a director of criminal investigations. I have been approached."

"He's a smart politician, I take off my hat." Slack had insisted Frank was the true hero of the saga, all Costa Rica loved the polite private eye. "Tell me privately, Frank, as a pal – were you reporting all our little secrets to Castillo?"

"A brilliant deduction, my good friend. I'm afraid so, but I did so with discretion and my own firm advice."

"What kind of advice?"

"For instance, insisting to the minister that I should be at your side in Limón."

All along, the top Ticos knew what was going down, they had been content to stand by and watch the superpower fumble. Doubtless, they also ensured the press turned up at vital occasions. Whether Frank wanted a hug or not, he got one, then Slack led him in with an arm around his shoulders.

Slack wasn't embarrassed by his house, the floors were shining, he had painted all the walls white, a labour of love, the garish colours had made him ill. Ham had found his way into a hammock, he was pulling out a Churchill. "The indictment came down. Conspiracy to kidnap and murder." They'd have to kidnap Slack, or at least video-tape him, he would not go willingly to Washington.

Slack looked through the papers Ham brought. The senator had turned himself in, got bailed in two hours, didn't avoid the press. He was prepared to answer Elmer Jericho's vicious perjuries, he would continue his campaign, he was a soldier.

Ham lit up, but Slack ignored him, another newspaper front page had caught his eye, a London tabloid, the *Mirror*, a front page photo, apparently bought for a considerable sum through an unnamed go-between – Gloria-May and Halcón embracing, she in a sarong, a straw hat set jauntily on Halcón's head. Inside, more copyright photos, the couple dancing, enjoying a glass of wine. Negotiations were under-way, through this same agent, for rights to an interview. Johnny Diego, ever the capitalist, knew fame turns a profit, he was not likely to be easily enticed from his lair by the lure of forgiveness.

"What's the damn bird that's making a racket?" said Theodore, who had just come in, hauling a freezer box, food supplies.

"Laughing Falcon. If you hear the full *guaco* they say it's going to rain." Slack didn't mind the rain, he liked its sadness, it inspired him.

"Don't suppose you've got a beer hanging around here."

"I'm staying on the straight, Ham."

"Good for you." He had to dig down to come up, finally, with a compliment. "You did a damn fine job, Jacques."

❧

His guests stayed too long, there was much to reminisce about, but Frank remembered he had a meeting in Quepos with an important client. It was four o'clock, Slack just had time for his planned trek into the hills to site zip line locations. It had rained hard in the afternoon, the *guaco*'s fulfilled promise, but the sky was clearing to the west. He pulled on boots and laced them, grabbed his machete, he would try to finish the trail he was cutting to the top of his wooded mountain.

Outside, he could hear the river's hiss, the distant grumblings of howlers announcing the coming of evening. No squatter clamour jarred the ears, no *rancheras*, no barking dogs. He had bought peace. Why should he not find, here at the Darkside, at least a close counterfeit of happiness?

He unlatched the fence gate and swung it open, crossed the road, and began to trudge up his narrow switchback trail, under the canopy. An evening breeze blew the mists away and the sun broke free, sending spikes of light through the trees.

An hour and a half of sweaty climbing brought him to a rocky buttress hanging over a scree, an old slide, and almost without warning the view opened up before him. He saw the Río Naranjo slithering through the jungle, saw his little clearing, mist purling around his new home, his forest gleaming green and gold. Beyond, the trees thinned to farmland and town, he could see the hills of Manuel Antonio, the ocean glinting under the lowering sun. A convoy of egrets passed below, stark white against the darkening green forest.

Here was what was left of beauty, a glut of it, an extravagance he longed to share. But that would not be, and he felt empty and forsaken as he watched the sky flame out with a bright emerald spark, the green flash that only lovers see.

376

Dear Rocky,

Now, with these enclosed final pages I complete the terms of our profane contract.

You will note the hero has won the day but not the woman, making for the kind of bittersweet finale that is the hallmark of a Harry Wilder thriller. I can only pray that the discriminating reader will not mock the closing image: Harry sitting alone on the sand of an endless beach, watching a night-heron take wing toward a setting sun that dies with a green spark. We are left contemplating the meaning of love, of life itself.

Who needs blood when you can have bloodless prose? Sorry, Rock, but I told you, I can't kill any more. I'm sorry also if I screwed the project up – I had no choice, a poet retains artistic integrity only through failure, I have my pride. If nothing else, it kept me off booze long enough to complete the cure. It was a catharsis, a dump, a disembowelling.

I leave to the reader to discern Harry's mood as he tries to decipher the ephemeral green message of the dying sun. Is he triumphant? (He foiled Dr. Zork.) Lamenting? (Species are being erased from life's registry faster than anyone can count them.) Or is he enraptured by the slender long-necked *chocuaco*, the night-heron flying into that golden sky? (There's still beauty in the world.) They taunted her in childhood, called her a flamingo. But she is the *chocuaco* who flew away.

Pura vida, anyway.

Jacques.

RETURN TO THE HOUSE
OF HEARTBREAK

— I —

Maggie was begrimed and sweaty from her long drive from San José, and the sun had set by the time she pulled up at the Darkside. She expected Jacques would hear her long before he saw her – the muffler of her rented Lada had loosened on the rocky road from Londres.

She was surprised to see the gate open – Frank Sierra had told her Slack was discouraging visitors. She was to have met Frank today in Quepos – an appointment hastily made long-distance from Saskatoon – but as chance would have it, bumped into him at a gas station, along with Hamilton Bakerfield and his driver. They were on their way back from seeing Jacques. Yes, they confessed, he is staying at the Darkside. Jacques had purchased it!

She had arrived in Costa Rica with no idea how to locate him; Frank Sierra had been reluctant to talk on the phone. Earlier, she had dialled Slack's cell-phone number only to find he had sold his phone.

As she pulled into the grounds, she was welcomed by the rich aroma of angels' trumpets, the flowers that bloom in the night. Memories came like shock waves: picking oranges while astride Halcón's shoulders, Glo dancing on the patio to Buho's sad strumming, the trail to the Naranjo and its scenes of love and tears and of bold flight down its rapids.

An old Land Rover was parked by the *pila*. Not a house light was on, and the door was wide open – then she remembered that Frank had told her Slack had yet to replace it. She was nervous about intruding unannounced: Frank had cautioned that Slack was thriving artistically in isolation. "He said he is repining. It is when he writes the best."

She doubted he could be asleep, not with the throaty growling of engine outside his unshuttered windows. She turned off the ignition and lights and waited in the darkness – there came no sign of stirring from within. Nor was response elicited when she knocked over a chair on her way to the door, or when she called out, "Jacques, it's me. Maggie."

She clicked on the front light. The house was clean but cluttered. The walls were white; *Star Trek* posters had been traded for art, prints by Mamaya, an original oil by the same artist. She strolled about the living room, picking up newspapers, books, straightening papers. On a table were engineering designs, charts with figures, elevations, a sketch of a tower with guy wires.

The bed was gone from the downstairs bedroom, replaced by a wide desk featuring an old upright typewriter. She felt somehow dismayed at seeing the hill of balled-up foolscap overflowing from the wastebasket. She unfolded one, a single line: "Love is the flower that unfurls unseen in the tropical night." She smoothed out another, a draft, words crossed out, pencilled interlinings. The breeze had tossed other, cleaner pages to the floor. She picked one up:

There is in us a need
for silence. Look at the woman
who is heron in her mind.
She has made of life a silence.

There was more than a tinge of loneliness to this, a surrendering to silence. He was repining, Frank said, depressed. She had a horrible, though momentary, vision of him hanging from a ceiling fixture upstairs. That was laughable: he was a round-the-clock worrier, but he was hardly suicidal.

She rushed upstairs anyway. No body in either bedroom. His clothes were in the front-facing one; she wondered if she could persuade him to move – this was *her* room. Now that she was here, he might appreciate the other, with its bigger bed.

In the bathroom, on a stand by the toilet, was an open magazine, a Greenpeace publication: how to raise whole-earth consciousness. That did not fit with the notion of a man in complete despair, nor did the fact he was involved in complex outdoors project. He was probably out in the weather with a flashlight, or he had walked to town, visited a friend.

Maggie lugged in her two suitcases, flight bag, and laptop, then showered, wrapped herself in a robe, and nestled herself into the deep belly of her favourite hammock. She read for a while, the newspaper, a novel. It began to rain, a thrumming increasing in intensity, a powerful pour before it slackened and beat a gentle rhythm on the roof. Maggie's book dropped open on her lap as her eyes closed.

—— 2 ——

It was about midnight when a bellowing voice awakened her: "Am I never to be left in peace?"

Maggie pulled the side of the hammock down, peered over it, saw the six-foot-five frame of Jacques Cardinal filling the doorway, scowling, water dripping from his face. Recognizing his guest, he gaped at her, lost for words.

"Loosen up, I'm a friendly. Where were you, Jacques? You're soaked to the skin."

"Forgot my . . . my flashlight."

He was such a sorry sight that she could not suppress laughter. "Wait, I'll bring some towels."

When she returned with them, he was on the stoop hauling off his boots. "Sorry, Maggie, I had no idea – I saw the rented car; I thought it was a reporter."

"What were you doing out there?"

"Catching a sunset. Thought for a while it was going to be my last – I went the wrong way down the mountain." He was looking at her two suitcases and the laptop. "I thought you were locking yourself in a room and throwing away the key."

"Writer's block. I'll make something hot." Canned soup in a pinch.

They ate at the kitchen counter, sitting side by side on stools. Slack had showered and shaved, too hurriedly from the nick on his chin. She explained how she had tracked him down.

"I get it. You were Frank's important client. He could have warned me."

"I told him I wanted to talk to him first, find out how you were doing."

"And what did he say?"

"Creative, gloomy, and sober."

He seemed to relax; finally there came his face-puckering smile. "As it happens, I'm in the throes of composing something for you."

"I'm honoured." She did not want to tell him she had snooped. *She has made of life a silence.* She was prepared to argue that he was the one who had been silent, cutting himself off this way, not even a postcard.

But now both were silent, attacking their soup and tortillas. Slack finally laid down his spoon, turned to her. "What's going on here, Maggie? Enlighten me."

"You didn't get my letter? It was a long one, some magazine articles and photos."

"Fifty per cent of fat envelopes might make it through the post office."

"Oh, God. That was my speech. You're not prepared for me."

Another smile, and a change of subject: "You didn't happen to see the sunset tonight?"

"I was driving; I could only glance at it. Why?"

A shrug – he seemed disappointed. "Just wondering. Do I dare ask how long you're planning to stay?"

"As long as it takes."

"To do what?"

She wasn't sure. As long as it takes to write, to heal, to love? "I'd like to finish my manuscript here, assuming that's humanly possible. I was coming unravelled with guilt – I never truly thanked you. I didn't respond when you . . . I mean, I . . . I really wish you'd got my letter."

"Where would you like to set up?"

"Any chance of getting my old room back?"

"Hundred per cent chance."

"Dull razor?" She lightly caressed the cut and he jumped slightly at her touch. "How did you get title to this place?"

"Made Elmer Jericho an offer he couldn't refuse."

She took his hand, led him to the living room, began unpacking bulky items: printer, hiking boots, her bird guide. Slack withdrew, stood by a window, watching the rain gurgle down a drainpipe chain. "I'm still trying to come to grips with this," he said.

"Let's just see what . . . you know, what works out. I didn't make a return reservation."

He seemed unable to react to that for several moments, then caught her yawning. "Maybe neither of us are used to being up this late. We can fix up the other bedroom for you for now." Something began to loosen in him, he was starting to talk: she enjoyed his anxious way of jabbering. "Not sure if I'll be able to sleep, though; maybe I'll finish that poem. Dedicated to you; it's about a bird lover, the woman who is a heron in her mind . . . That's how I see you."

"How appropriate – I've lost my fear of flying."

"That never made sense to me. Maybe you just had a fear of flying out of control, of not being grounded." He paused, seemed to be judging his words. "And maybe you took the cure with a heavy dose of Halcón."

A fear of being in love: of not being grounded, a fear of crashing afterwards – Maggie wondered if that was what it all came down to? La Brava Schneider, obsessed with the intricacies of human affection: for all her mature life she had stood petrified at the edge of the cliff. She was finally beginning to realize that the machinery of love was beyond understanding: how it can engulf you at one moment, or sneak upon you across time and distance. *Love is a flower that unfurls unseen in the tropical night.*

"That the first time you were ever in love?"

"Yes. Still recovering." She smiled. "Cold turkey."

"Give it time."

She stood. "Come here, Jacques."

He took a few tentative steps toward her. She put her arms around his neck, studied those deep, sad green eyes. "Jacques – I do like that name." She stroked his hair; he had kept it short, salt-and-red-pepper, slightly curly. As tall as she was, she still had to raise herself on her toes to kiss him; it was a novel experience.

— 3 —

We search the hours for solitude,
the quiet of herons in their sleep,
a fisher on the wing who falls
into the waves in search of silver
or a woman making her way through mist
in early morning, delicate as water.
We search for this, a small stone
in the tide, a broken shell, a crab
so still we think it prays, its claws
raised to our hands as if
what we wait for is return.
What do we do with our hours?
We reach for what comes to us
in quiet. There is in us a need
for silence. Look at the woman
who is heron in her mind.
She has made of life a silence.
See how she holds all her life
in her eyes. She walks among stones.

Far from her in the tidal reach
birds rise into the light.
Who goes to her but herself?
What she has held is hers and hers
alone: to watch the quiet of herons,
a kingfisher falling from all the sky
there is upon this quiet
she gives only to herself, a beach
whose medicine is hers and hers alone.

AUTHOR'S NOTE:

I owe an incalculable debt to Mario Carazo, lawyer, lover of literature, and *buen amigo*, for scanning the manuscript so thoroughly for
linguistic error. My long-time Quepos friends, Roger Connors and
Milo and Tey Bekins, offered advice and inspiration. Modesto and
Fran Watson toured me through the Tortuguero waterways and
refreshed my memory of that beautiful and fragile area of Costa Rica.
Melvin Bejarano served as my kayak guide down the whitewaters of
the Savegre and Naranjo rivers, and guided me as well through common Ticoisms of the lingua franca. The late Donald Melton, a Quepos
archaeologist, was a wealth of historical information.

In a more general sense, I am in debt to all my friends in Costa
Rica, Tico and gringo, for having inspired much of the story and
many of the characters who inhabit these pages. As well, I am obliged
to Brian Brett and Ann Ireland for their comments and to Tekla
Deverell for her tireless in-house editing.

The poem is by Patrick Lane, and will not be found in his many
award-winning collections of verse. As a matter of literary and eco-
logical interest, its inclusion came about this way: several years ago,
Patrick pledged to dedicate a poem to the winner of an auction to
raise funds for a critical marshland area on Pender Island, known as
Medicine Beach. My winning bid was presented to Tekla as a gift.
Patrick (his image of her was as a heron) completed its composition
at our home, on the very keyboard upon which I am, finally, typing
the last period.